## *Wondrous and powerful tales from some of the world's best new writers—*

Djinn are famous for twisting your words so they don't really grant your wish, but two can play that game.

—TURNABOUT

Deacon is a government official, and he's afraid he'll stay that way if he can't break his conditioning.

—A SMOKELESS AND SCORCHING FIRE

It's easy making sales when you can send images of despair into the hearts of your clients.

—THE HOWLER ON THE SALES FLOOR

Alder seeks the secrets of the Windcallers' magic, but his curiosity may destroy the people he loves.

—THE MINARETS OF AN-ZARAT

Jim Bellamy tries to save the life of a girl who died in the wreckage of a train ten years ago.

—THE DEATH FLYER

A tree giant takes in a housekeeper, but she has more secrets than either of them can handle.

—ODD AND UGLY

An ancient myth might provide the key to curing a disease that threatens all of humanity.

—MARA'S SHADOW

A lesson on philosophy in action turns into a deadly encounter.

—THE LESSON

A powerful sorcerer has so disgraced himself, he is afraid of what his family will think should he ever die and meet them on the other side.

—What Lies Beneath

Cara discovers a floating farm parked over her land, blocking the sunlight, and must confront the driver.

—The Face in the Box

In a world controlled by dragons and their henchmen, rock singer Josephine really only wants "death to all collaborators."

—Flee, My Pretty One

Even a court wizard will struggle to fight off armies if his weapons pack no actual punch.

—Illusion

You can put an end to something wondrous, but only at a cost.

—A Bitter Thing

Lily's ability to shift shapes into a bear offers some strange challenges.

—Miss Smokey

On a far world, a nameless man meets a woman of ancient genetic stock, and when trouble follows in his wake, he must choose: her life or his humanity?

—All Light and Darkness

Read on, and let the adventure begin!

*What has been said about the*

# L. RON HUBBARD
*Presents*
# Writers of the Future
*Anthologies*

---

"Not only is the writing excellent . . . it is also extremely varied. There's a lot of hot new talent in it." —*Locus* magazine

"Always a glimpse of tomorrow's stars."
—*Publishers Weekly* starred review

"Where can an aspiring sci-fi artist go to get discovered? . . . Fortunately, there's one opportunity—the Illustrators of the Future Contest—that offers up-and-coming artists an honest-to-goodness shot at science fiction stardom."
—*Sci-Fi* magazine

"I really can't say enough good things about Writers of the Future. . . . It's fair to say that without Writers of the Future, I wouldn't be where I am today."
—Patrick Rothfuss
Writers of the Future Contest winner 2002

"The book you are holding in your hands is our first sight of the next generation of science fiction and fantasy writers."
—Orson Scott Card
Writers of the Future Contest judge

"This is an opportunity of a lifetime." —Larry Elmore
Illustrators of the Future Contest judge

"The road to creating art and getting it published is long, hard and trying. It's amazing to have a group, such as Illustrators of the Future, there to help in this process—creating an outlet where the work can be seen and artists can be heard from all over the globe."

—Rob Prior
Illustrators of the Future Contest judge

"The Writers of the Future experience played a pivotal role during a most impressionable time in my writing career. And afterward, the WotF folks were always around when I had questions or needed help. It was all far more than a mere writing contest."

—Nnedi Okorafor
Writers of the Future Contest published finalist 2002

"If you want a glimpse of the future—the future of science fiction—look at these first publications of tomorrow's masters."

—Kevin J. Anderson
Writers of the Future Contest judge

"Speculative fiction fans will welcome this showcase of new talent. ...Winners of the simultaneous Illustrators of the Future Contest are featured with work as varied and as exciting as the authors."

—*Library Journal* starred review

"The Writers of the Future Contest is a valuable outlet for writers early in their careers. Finalists and winners get a unique spotlight that says 'this is the way to good writing.'"

—Jody Lynn Nye
Writers of the Future Contest judge

"The Contests are amazing competitions. I wish I had something like this when I was getting started—very positive and cool."

—Bob Eggleton
Illustrators of the Future Contest judge

*L. Ron Hubbard* PRESENTS

# *Writers of the Future*

VOLUME 34

*L. Ron Hubbard* PRESENTS

# *Writers of the Future*

VOLUME 34

---

The year's twelve best tales from the
Writers of the Future international writers' program

Illustrated by winners in the Illustrators of the Future
international illustrators' program

Three short stories from authors
L. Ron Hubbard / Brandon Sanderson / Jody Lynn Nye

With essays on writing and illustration by
L. Ron Hubbard / Orson Scott Card / Ciruelo /
Jerry Pournelle

---

Edited by David Farland
Illustrations Art Directed by Echo Chernik

GALAXY PRESS, INC.

Interior Design by Jerry Kelly

This anthology contains works of fiction. Names, characters, places and incidents are either the product of the authors' imaginations or are used fictitiously. Any resemblance to actual events or locales or persons, living or dead, is entirely coincidental. Opinions expressed by nonfiction essayists are their own.

ISBN 978-1-61986-575-4
Printed in the United States of America

# CONTENTS

# *Introduction*

## BY DAVID FARLAND

*David Farland is a* New York Times *bestselling author with more than fifty novels and anthologies to his credit. He has won numerous awards, including the L. Ron Hubbard Gold Award in 1987, and has served as Coordinating Judge of the Writers of the Future for more than a dozen years.*

*He has helped mentor hundreds of new writers, including such #1 bestselling authors as Brandon Sanderson (*The Way of Kings*), Stephenie Meyer (*Twilight*), Brandon Mull (*Fablehaven*), James Dashner (*The Maze Runner*), and others. While writing Star Wars novels in 1998, he was asked to help choose a book to push big for Scholastic, and selected* Harry Potter, *then helped develop a bestseller strategy.*

*In addition to his novels and short stories, Dave has also assisted with video game design and worked as a greenlighting analyst for movies in Hollywood. Dave continues to help mentor writers through the Writers of the Future program, where he acts as first reader, editor of the anthology, and teaches workshops to our winning authors. He also teaches online classes and live workshops.*

*Welcome to* L. Ron Hubbard Presents Writers and Illustrators of the Future, Volume 34.

# *Introduction*

As you may know, the Writers and Illustrators of the Future Contests are the world's largest talent hunt for new authors and illustrators. We receive thousands of submissions of short stories and artwork each quarter from all over the globe, and our judges handpick the very best works which are collected and published in this volume. Every year the Contests continue to grow, and this year they were larger than ever.

You've seen competitions like this in other fields: *The Voice* for singers, or *The World of Dance* for dancers. Both of those shows lend themselves well to television. But this global talent hunt is showcased here in these pages. You can read our winning stories in the anthology or see the gorgeous art for each story on the art plates that follow this article.

As the first reader for the writers Contest, I get to look at thousands of stories each year in search of the best new writers of speculative fiction in the world, and I think we have a tremendous lineup this year.

A lot of authors are curious about the selection process, and I thought I would talk about it just a bit.

When I look for stories, I don't get to see the authors' names. I don't know where the story was sent from, and I have no idea of the gender or age or color of the writer. Frankly, I don't care. I get to judge the stories on quality alone.

So I search for science fiction, fantasy, and speculative horror stories that fit our guidelines. The short stories can't be too long—no more than about seventy pages—nor can they be too short.

It would be difficult to write a story that was very short and still have it be powerful and convincingly brilliant, so most of our stories here fall between 5,000 and 17,000 words long.

As a writer, I've written a lot of science fiction and fantasy, so I don't care which genre of stories you enter, so long as they are speculative fiction. Nor do I care what sex or nationality the characters are.

I do, however, look for commercial fiction—stories that could be sold in an anthology that goes in some cases to elementary schools. For that reason, extreme violence, sexual content, and profanity can be problematic.

I base my judgment of the story on three elements.

First, I look for a fresh and original concept. I want to see ideas in the story that I haven't seen done a thousand times. I love seeing concepts that are new, or that are at least twisted into some new form that I haven't read before.

Second, I study the storytelling skill of the author. I'm looking for intriguing characters that I care about deeply. I ask myself, does the author plot well? Does he or she put in intriguing twists and turns? Are the scenes developed well, and does the climax and the ending of the story work?

Third, I'm looking for stories that show strong writing skills on a verbal level, where the prose is electric and stylistically elegant.

When I find a story that scores high in all three of these categories, I know that I have a potential winner.

But I won't know what my lineup is until I see all of the stories. It's a process of elimination. So I read through the stories and make multiple passes, searching for the best each quarter. Some stories get rejected pretty quickly. Either the idea has been overdone or the content of the story is offensive or perhaps stylistically the writer just doesn't intrigue me.

But if everything looks great, then I put the stories into my "hold" file, for deeper study. This often means that I have to read the whole story to see if the plot holds together and it reaches a great conclusion.

Normally, I will find three or four dozen stories that I like, and then I have to consider each one again, deciding which of those tales will be categorized with finalists, semi-finalists, silver honorable mentions, and honorable mentions.

A lot of authors ask, "What does it take to win an honorable mention?" Here is what it means: Very often I will see a story where the author shows some promise. Sometimes the author has a great style, or an excellent concept, or maybe crafts scenes well. In short, if you win an honorable mention, I see something that I like in your work, and I want you to keep writing. But I have to admit that some of the honorable mentions are exceptionally well done and are just a hair's breadth from being finalists.

A silver honorable mention is usually a very good story that is pretty much publishable, though it might be that the author needs to go through and do a final pass or a bit of rewriting.

With semi-finalist stories, I offer critiques so that the author can find out what needs to be done to be publishable.

And, of course, there are the finalists—the eight stories that go on to our blue-ribbon panel of judges each quarter, so that they can select our first, second, and third place winners.

As I'm judging the stories, our Illustrators of the Future Contest Coordinating Judge, Echo Chernik, looks at the art submissions each quarter and then sends her finalist selections on to the illustrator judges so that they can pick the three winners.

Those art Contest winners are each assigned a prize-winning story to illustrate, so that we get a great artist matched with each writing Contest winner. You can see these commissioned pieces in this book.

Ultimately, as I put the anthology together, I am hoping that I can find diverse types of stories. I want to have strong fantasy pieces, whether they be medieval, contemporary, magical realism, or so on. I also want strong science fiction, whether set on Earth, in space, or on other worlds. I want some creepy horror in the anthology, and I am always searching for top-notch humor.

This year, I'm happy to say that our authors and artists really delivered some exceptional work! So go ahead and dive in. Their artistry will take you to distant worlds in the far future or will explore original fantasy landscapes. You'll find authors who know how to tell a powerful story and write exquisitely. And hopefully we will help you discover one of your new favorite artists of all time!

**CIRUELO**
*Dragon Caller*

**ADAR DARNOV**
*Turnabout*

KYNA TEK

*A Smokeless and Scorching Fire*

**SIDNEY LUGO**
*The Howler on the Sales Floor*

**BRENDA RODRIGUEZ**
*The Minarets of An-Zabat*

**VEN LOCKLEAR**
*The Death Flyer*

REYNA ROCHIN
*Odd and Ugly*

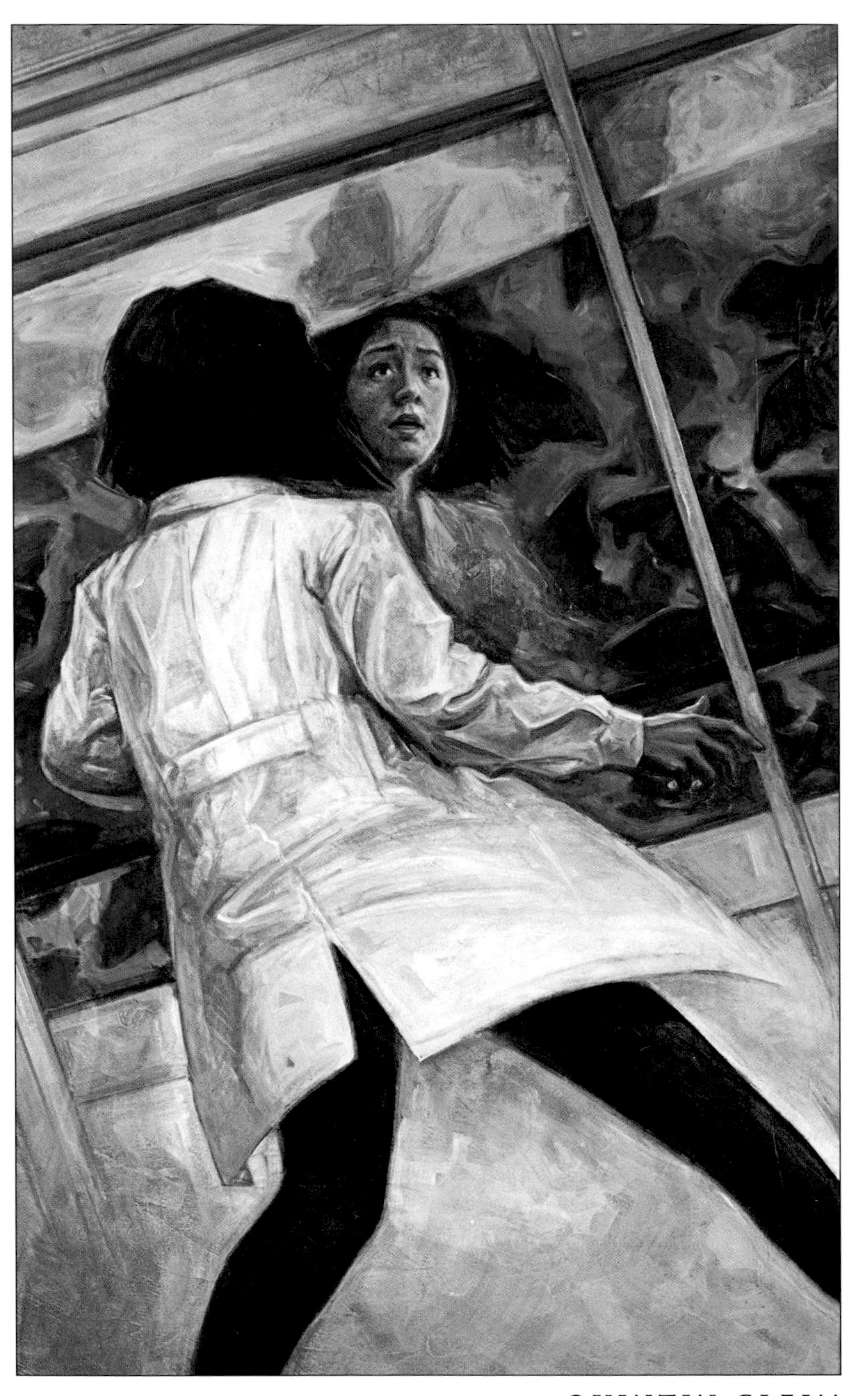

QUINTIN GLEIM

*Mara's Shadow*

BEA JACKSON
*The Lesson*

MAKSYM POLISHCHUK
*What Lies Beneath*

**BRUCE BRENNEISE**
*The Face in the Box*

**ALANA FLETCHER**
*Flee, My Pretty One*

JAZMEN RICHARDSON
*A Bitter Thing*

ANTHONY MORAVIAN

*Miss Smokey*

**DUNCAN HALLECK**
*All Light and Darkness*

# *Illustrators of the Future*

## BY ECHO CHERNIK

*Echo Chernik is a successful advertising and publishing illustrator with twenty years of professional experience and several prestigious publishing awards.*

*Her clients include mainstream companies such as: Miller, Camel, Coors, Celestial Seasonings, Publix Super Markets, Inc., Kmart, Sears, NASCAR, the Sheikh of Dubai, the city of New Orleans, Bellagio resort, the state of Indiana, USPS, Dave Matthews Band, Arlo Guthrie, McDonald's, Procter & Gamble, Trek Bicycle Corporation, Disney, BBC, Mattel, Hasbro and more. She specializes in several styles including decorative, vector, and art nouveau.*

*She is the Coordinating Judge of the Illustrators of the Future Contest. Echo strives to share the important but all-too-often neglected subject of the business aspect of illustration with the winners, as well as preparing them for the reality of a successful career in illustration.*

# *Illustrators of the Future*

There are some people born with the soul of an artist. To these lucky few, the act of creation is like breathing—it is not optional. Artists feel the undeniable need to create and possess an inherent inclination and talent for it, but the recipe for making a living as a successful artist takes more than just talent. It also takes a great amount of desire and ambition, a hefty dash of business sense, and a stubborn streak of will and perseverance to persist in becoming a success regardless of obstacles.

If you dream of a career as a commercial artist, then the Illustrators of the Future Contest is for you. The Contest was created by L. Ron Hubbard to give people with these qualities a step up, a shortcut up the cliff of adversity. It's an amazing opportunity for artists who wish to make a living as illustrators. I only wish that I'd known about the Contest in the early years of my career.

The Contest was founded by Hubbard on the concept that "a culture is as rich and as capable of surviving as it has imaginative artists." I am honored to be the Coordinating Judge for the Illustrators of the Future Contest and to have the very special opportunity—again in the words of Hubbard—to "give tomorrow a new form" by helping young illustrators achieve a strong start. I am extremely pleased to be surrounded by prestigious judges and past winners who dedicate their time and effort because they feel the same.

Participating is easy and free. This Contest was set up to help artists, and it's legitimately one of the best opportunities a young artist can have.

All you have to do is submit three pieces of your best work through www.illustratorsofthefuture.com. You can enter four times a year (quarterly). Finalists are chosen by a panel of industry expert judges. We see entries from all over the world, and you don't even need to speak English to enter or win. Each quarter, three Contest winners are chosen, so at the end of the year, there are a total of twelve winners for the year! Each winner receives a cash award, the opportunity to be published in the renowned annual *L. Ron Hubbard Presents Writers and Illustrators of the Future* anthology, as well as the chance to win the grand prize.

The winners are flown to Hollywood for a huge black-tie celebration and book signing, as well as an entire week learning the ins and outs of being a successful commercial artist in today's world. There are seminars and lectures by famous illustrator judges and guest speakers. It's an invaluable experience centered on providing a head start to the Contest winners with the goal of leaving the young professional artists full of the knowledge and confidence to succeed. Galaxy Press has demonstrated their commitment to past winners by continuing to promote them and point out their accomplishments even after the Contest is over.

Imagine yourself as one of the illustrators. Here's what would happen:

Once you are chosen as a winner, you are assigned a short story written by one of the Writers of the Future winners. You will then work with me (as art director) in the same manner as a working illustrator would work with a publishing house or client. You will submit three thumbnails, which we discuss, and then we will choose one to proceed with. I will help guide you through the process of creating a beautiful illustration for the story. I find that my own best pieces are ones that are not too overly art directed. I use a method of simple suggestion through the process, rather than overly directing—encouraging you to create a portfolio-quality piece that showcases your style, talent, and enthusiasm. I bring to your attention options for symbolism, composition, color scheme, and more that will help make the piece stronger—and then leave it up to you as the artist to interpret how you wish. This will be your published piece in the Writers of the Future anthology, and a strong portfolio piece to win work with.

Artists often struggle with the questions "But am I good enough to win?" "What if I'm not chosen?" "How do I have a better chance of getting chosen?" My best advice is to keep creating and keep entering. We don't judge on style as much as we do on the ability to tell a story. I encourage applicants to try to send in pieces that illustrate a scene as opposed to still lifes.

"Be true to your work and your work will be true to you" is the motto of my alma mater, Pratt Institute. And truer words have never been spoken.

Artists are driven by passion and the desire to express themselves. This is true for not only fine artists, but commercial artists as well. You probably find that you have a favorite style or subject that you really pour yourself into. Other people can see the passion that you put into those particular pieces. Do what you love, and you will find or create a niche for it. Trying to create work in a style that doesn't excite you just to match a trend will never make you as successful as being true to yourself. And if the world doesn't accept your style, keep at it. Keep creating new work, keep submitting to the Contest, and keep showing the world.

What I'm getting at is, if you submit to the Illustrators of the Future Contest and are not chosen, don't give up! You can submit quarterly, and each quarter there is a different batch of entries. Keep believing in yourself and your art, and eventually other people will believe in you too!

# *Turnabout*

*written by*

## *Erik Bundy*

*illustrated by*

ADAR DARNOV

---

### ABOUT THE AUTHOR

*Erik lives in a magical North Carolina forest where mice claiming to be cousins move in for the winter then take the towels when they leave in spring. He suffers from the genetic disorder of being human. Unlike many writers, Erik doesn't keep a cat, partly in deference to his mouse cousins and partly because he couldn't live up to its expectations.*

*His hobbies are hunting dust bunnies with a fork, watching galaxies collide, bounty hunting for runaway socks, and sniffing for truffles while wearing a studded pit-bull collar.*

*Erik is a graduate of the six-week Odyssey Fantasy Writing Workshop. His story, "Turnabout," was inspired by a visit to Morocco with a Spanish tour group.*

### ABOUT THE ILLUSTRATOR

*Adar Darnov was born in New Jersey and mostly grew up there. He was creative as a kid, particularly through drawing. The synagogue where he spent much of his childhood was the breeding ground of his imagination. There he was familiarized with fanciful stories and played imaginative games with friends. As an adolescent, his creativity continued to be supported by family.*

*Throughout middle and high school, he experimented with various artistic identities. He created comic book art, graphic designs and fine art paintings. These corresponded to the different artist mentors he encountered, each imparting on him a unique piece of the artist experience.*

*Adar eventually enrolled for his undergraduate degree in illustration at the School of Visual Arts in New York City. There he learned more about the career of illustration. Then Adar lost sight of the pure joy he derived from art as a child. Fortunately however, one semester he visited long-time friends who were playing popular fantasy board games. This reminded Adar how much he loved imaginative art when he was younger, especially art associated with the games, shows, and books he partook of. This combined with his growing attraction to objective art led him to pursue imaginative realism illustration.*

*After graduating SVA, he experienced many aspects of being an illustrator outside school. Adar continues his education at Academy of Art University in San Francisco, pursuing his master's degree. This is the first time Adar's imaginative realism art has been published.*

# *Turnabout*

After Stephanie left me, I vagabonded alone through the arid Rif Mountains of Morocco—humped under a backpack with dirhams and dollars in one dusty hiking boot and a credit card chafing a callus in the other. Her leaving wasn't going to ruin my rambling.

Near an adobe village famous for being alabaster white in summer and lapis lazuli blue in winter, a sparkle of reflected sunlight snagged my curiosity. It came from under a skeletal bush with a few leathery leaves rattling in the wind. I sidled closer and saw a brass urn the size of my knobby fist. Maybe it had pearls or blood diamonds in it . . . something to lure Steph back to me.

The sun-hot brass stung my fingers, and I dropped it. The urn clinked on the rocky ground, and its little domed lid spilled off.

A snake's head, tongue flickering, eased out of the urn's mouth. I stood there like a doofus, too paralyzed to run, as a sinister blue-black cobra longer than my arm slithered impossibly out of the tiny vessel. The tip of the cobra's tail was a shocking lipstick red.

Strung out beside the urn, it raised its head, hood flared, tongue flittering at me, and kept levitating upward until the cobra balanced on its red-tail point. Then it shimmered into a young Arab woman. Amazed, I was too fascinated to be scared.

She wore red embroidered slippers, leather pants, a vampire's cape, and a dark scarf over her dark hair. Her slitted eyes gleamed like black ice, glassy and deadly.

I whipped a Hand of Fatima charm out of my pocket and shoved it at her face.

Her human tongue darted out between her thin lips. "Do not insult me, Westerner. What is your wish?"

"You're a genie?" I'd thought genies were ponderous eunuchs who wore brocade vests and turbans . . . jinns who vapored out of brass lamps, not urns. "Don't I get three wishes?"

"One wish frees me from my obligation to you, man of clay."

Yeah, and be careful what you wish for. All jinns had a slithery side. What if I asked for fame and got arrested as a serial killer? Or if I asked for riches and my loved ones, or loved one if Steph came back to me, were kidnapped for ransom. If I wanted a long life, would I spend most of it comatose in a hospital bed?

"Is there a downside to my making this wish?"

She stared across the desolate khaki-colored hills and scrub brush with a martyr's expression. Her tongue tasted the dry air. "I must give you a wish, Westerner, but its consequences come to you. I am not your protector. No one is free from fate."

Was it just coincidence that two days after Steph stomped out of my life, a jinni popped into it? As for my wish, well, Steph had abandoned me in noisy Tangier, so I said, "Okay, I wish for you to make a woman I know love me enough to stay with me. For the rest of my life."

The jinni's face drooped into a please-deliver-me expression. "I cannot change your human nature."

"So you're saying you're limited in what you can do for me? First off, I don't get the usual three wishes, then you refuse even to honor my one wish?"

"I can give you gold ingots, a marble palace, things you may touch. I cannot make this woman fall in love with you, man of clay. I cannot make you more agreeable to her."

Inwardly, I flinched. Steph's last words to me, not exactly whispered, more like shouted in the souk, called me a suffocating, selfish prick. I considered myself loyal and helpful, the opposite of selfish. And yeah, sometimes when people pushed me I did come across as a bit contrary.

Now this jinni was pushing me. A free wish without any obligation on my part seemed way too good to be harmless. Everything comes with a price tag tied to it.

"It's odd that I'm the one who found your urn." I waved at the leached-out country around us. "I mean, I'm not following a caravan route or a shepherd's path or anything."

She looked ready to turn me into a donkey turd.

I quickly asked, "What would you wish for?"

Her eyes flickered toward the brass urn then away. "What does it matter, Westerner? You cannot grant it."

Her glance had given me my answer: she wanted freedom. Who wouldn't? "My name's Layton, by the way."

Her lip curled. I was just a talking cockroach to her.

Well, this cockroach didn't take orders from genies, especially limited ones. "Okay, how about if I call you Jenny? Listen, Jenny, since this is a one-time deal, I need to think. I want to get this wish *absolutely* right."

Her womanly form crumpled into a muscular blue-black cobra with a red tail. I stood there, my jaw almost hanging down to my belt buckle, and watched the snake slither away without even a backward hiss.

The jinni had left her brass urn behind, so I stuffed it into my backpack. A genie's prison probably wasn't disposable. I had the promise of a wish and meant to keep that option alive.

Tomorrow was probably going to be an interesting day.

In Morocco, breakfast meant hot sweet tea and two or three crusty pastries filled with almond pudding. Afterward jittering with a sugar rush, I wandered the claustrophobic passages of the clamorous medina, the old quarter. As usual, boys pestered me to buy key chains with Moroccan flags on them, cheap Citizen watches, or bootleg beaded necklaces. Most of them gave up whining and begging alongside of me after ten yards, but one lanky kid leeched onto me. I kept shooing him away, but he harassed me like a blood-starved mosquito. He had the usual short dark hair and peanut-butter skin and wore a faded black T-shirt and jeans. For some reason, his glaring red trainers disturbed me.

He stubbornly pulled junk souvenirs out of a goat-leather bag. He also offered me kif, hashish. As a young guy humping a backpack, I was used to this. Then he held up a silver teardrop pendant dangling on a delicate chain. It was set with blue lapis lazuli.

I shrugged it away, but his huckster eyes saw through my fake disinterest. He was holding the perfect peace offering for Steph. She adored lapis lazuli.

The boy chuckled. "You wish this?"

My brain clicked into revelation. I glanced down at his red trainers, then into his black-hole eyes. The jinni shouldn't have used the word "wish." I consciously relaxed to hide my anger. I had been one word away from losing my wish. "So what happens if I die, Jenny? Would that wipe away your obligation to me?"

A spasm of hatred squirmed across the boy's face. "Yes."

"But you can't be the one who does me in, can you?"

A grimace of regret was her answer.

"Nice to know," I told her. "Tell me, why is my making this wish so important to you?"

A laborer yelled for us to move aside in the narrow passageway and led a donkey loaded with scrap wood between us.

When we came together again, Jenny said, "It is the ritual I must follow."

"Yeah, well, I don't like being tricked. And I shun rituals I don't understand. Tell you what, though. I'll buy that necklace from you." I pulled out a wad of dirhams. "How much do you want for it?"

Jenny threw the pendant and silver chain at me and stalked away with reptilian grace. To a shape-shifting fire demon, money was just paper with the grainy portrait of a king on it.

But maybe I could give this jinni something it did value. Of course, I too was limited in what I could offer. Still, partial freedom, something resembling house arrest, had to be preferable to a cramped brass prison.

I knew better than to expect gratitude. The jinni was a yin and yang creature, sometimes a snake which represented earth, and sometimes earth's elemental opposite, fire. My reward would be in having a travel companion.

I decided to ramble down to the sea and send Steph the peace-offering pendant from feisty Tangier, the seaport where we had parted. So I started to zigzag my way through the crowded medina to the bus station.

A very traditional woman fell into step three paces behind me. She plodded along in an ankle-length, black abaya smelling of myrrh. Her incongruous red slippers let me know trouble stalked my footsteps. My brown skin, brown eyes, and dark hair tended to blend me in with the locals. So having a pretty, young wife in tow didn't raise any eyebrows.

She followed me into the well-worn bus station as if I had her on a leash. At the ticket counter, I asked a young clerk who smelled of rose perfume and wore a flowery silk scarf if I could speak English. She wiggled her shoulders shyly and told me she spoke a little English. She sounded as if she had been born in London and read *The Economist.*

"Did you study English in school?" I asked.

"I was educated in England," she said with bashful pride.

She glanced behind me and lost her smile. I turned to my "wife," who had a bruised cheek and black eye. Jenny cringed when I faced her.

After a moment of open-mouth surprise followed by shame then anger, I pulled out a limp ten-dirham bill and asked the British-educated clerk, "Is this the right amount to give to a beggar woman?"

Jenny bumped past me to the counter and clutched the sympathetic clerk's slim brown hand. She exploded into explanation. My spotty Arabic picked up "marriage" and "not leave me here."

I said, "I'm a Christian. She couldn't marry me."

Jenny said something, and the young woman snarled in my face. "Can you prove this? That you are a Christian?"

I wasn't carrying a Bible or crucifix or anything. Bringing those into a Muslim country, even one as secular as Morocco, was like bringing whiskey to an AA meeting. Instead I had an incriminating Koran tucked in my backpack.

I told the hostile clerk, "Sorry, I left my priest outfit at home."

Sarcasm stoked her righteous anger. "Two tickets then." She gave me a calculating look. "Now I must see your passport."

"No you don't," I said.

I didn't want to whip out my blue American passport. Most of these people considered the United States a terrorist nation. So I usually pretended to be a laid-back Canadian. Nobody hated Canadians or teddy bears.

Two policemen in desert camouflage sauntered over to us, casually carrying lethal M16 rifles, and silently bullied me into handing over my terrorist passport.

The spiteful clerk riffled through it, turned to the information page, frowned, and asked if this really was my passport. I tapped the picture. My hair was longer, and I looked dead, but it was definitely my corpse.

Ms. Spiteful still had her doubts. So the soldiers herded me into a bare room with a concrete floor and single window, its iron bars rusty, its wavy glass smoky from grease. It had no curtain, so I was thankful no one had cleaned the glass when I stripped down to my red briefs. They pawed my clothes, and coins fell out of my cargo pants, dinging on the rough floor. My backpack was ransacked. I got zero points for the Koran.

They were pleased to find the ancient brass urn, a Moroccan cultural artifact. The truth, that I had found it, sounded like a common lie. I didn't tell them a vicious jinni lived in it.

One of the men grinned and pantomimed chopping off my hand for stealing. In the end, though, they decided just to take it away from me. I tried to look angry, to not smile at the prospect of them dealing with the malicious cobra.

Back in the main lobby, I told Ms. Spiteful, "Forget the ticket. I'd rather hitchhike to Tangier than ride in your vermin-infested bus."

She adjusted her flowery scarf over her luxuriant hair, then issued me two tickets. "I do this not for you. For her." She pointed at my cowering "wife," who looked as if she wanted to ask for permission to go to the toilet. Jenny's performance merited an Emmy Award.

"She's not downtrodden," I told the young woman. "You are. Educated in England and happy to be a bus station clerk here." I waved my hand at the marble tiles behind her, brown-stained by water that had leaked from the ceiling. "May you become the third wife of a toothless old man."

Fear flared in her dark Muslim eyes. Could that happen?

I knew I was being the hateful American, but I didn't care. I was stereotyping her and her whole culture, but I didn't care. She deserved my anger. I had walked into this bus station as a simple tourist, wanting to buy a ticket to Tangier, and been strip-searched. What right did she have to punish me? I wasn't some stray mutt anybody could kick.

I left the tickets on the counter, picked up my backpack, and started to walk away. Ms. Spiteful called out that I was to pay for them.

"No," I told her. "I never asked for two tickets."

One of the bored policemen nonchalantly pointed his M16 at my belly button. I spread my arms. "Go ahead, Rambo, shoot me."

He glanced at the clerk, his eyebrows lifted. She compressed her lips and huffed through her nose and picked up the tickets.

Did Jenny know I no longer had the brass urn? Since we were playing roles, I ordered my "wife" to carry my backpack. To my amazement, Jenny picked it up . . . then let it slip off her shoulder and slam down on the tile floor. It was my turn to cringe. Had she just rearranged the guts of my iPad?

Jenny gaped at me in fear, picked it up again, staggered three steps, and dropped it a second time. I rushed forward to grab it away from her. Cowering, she held her hands up to protect her bruised face.

Game, set, and match to the jinni.

Tangier is a rowdy, car-honking seaport where you expect to meet disgruntled prostitutes and old French spies. I haggled with a man wearing an eye patch for a room in a side-street hotel. Cost me a hundred sixty dirhams or sixteen dollars a night, breakfast included.

When I woke the next morning, I was disgusted, but not overly surprised, to find the nomadic urn on the mahogany table beside my bed. It stuck to me like a bad reputation.

I dressed and hurried to a raggedy souk where I dickered for super glue and green duct tape. Back in my room, I glued the domed lid to the urn's mouth and wrapped the entire roll of tape around it.

When I came out of the shower, duct tape covered my backpack like frog skin, and the urn's lid leaned against its brass body with an insolent slant. Jenny had pulled a Houdini on me. I was relieved she hadn't glued my pack's zippers shut.

I wanted to play tourist in gaudy Tangier for a few days but felt like a fugitive. Cobra woman might call in a police raid on my room or do something even worse. So I peeled the tape off my backpack, crammed my stuff into it, locked the urn inside the room, checked out of the hotel, and bought a ferry ticket for Spain. Maybe jinns couldn't harass travelers in El Cid's Europe.

At the seaport, I checked my battered backpack to make sure Jenny hadn't slipped a homemade bomb or packets of heroin inside it. I found the lidded urn in a zippered side pocket. So much for leaving it behind in a cheap hotel room.

I checked my passport to make sure the photo was of me, not some Moroccan criminal or a monkey. I also kept it in my hand so it didn't disappear. I could imagine myself shuttling back and forth between Spain and Morocco because neither country was willing to let me in without a passport.

After we set sail, I stayed outside on a narrow deck to let the breeze cool away my seasickness. My folks were Texas oil people, not sailors. I had to dose myself with Dramamine to go fishing on a lake.

I took the urn out of my backpack and considered tossing it into the heaving sea, but instead shoved it in a pocket of my canvas travel jacket.

An hour later, I leaned against the railing and squinted at the approaching Spanish coastline a few miles away. What adventures waited for me there? I felt movement behind me. Before I could turn, someone grabbed my ankles and hoisted me over the steel railing.

I fell at least two stories, wide-eyed and shrieking the whole way. I hit the water feet first, my legs instinctively together so I didn't drive my testicles into my belly. Clawing the water to stop my descent into liquid darkness, I sank deep. Water burned my sinuses. Finally, I reversed direction and moved upward toward the wavering mirage of light.

As soon as my face broke the surface, I flailed away from the ship so the propellers wouldn't suck me into them. The ferry lumbered away, and I bobbed in its wake. I felt desperate but not panicked . . . not yet. Surely whatever being or force had caused me to find the urn wasn't just going to let me drown.

Wobbling at water level, I couldn't see the Spanish coast, but I knew its direction because the ferry sailed toward it. My backpack lay on its deck. Could I swim to Spain before I drowned? Would some power save me?

Water kept slapping my face . . . irritating as hell. What had gone wrong? The jinni wasn't allowed to kill me. Had she found a loophole in the fossilized laws she followed?

Thinking of a demon calls it to you, I discovered, when a bobbing black sea snake appeared a yard from my dripping nose.

"You can't kill me," I shouted. "You can't." I didn't know a snake could look so amused. "I'm just trying to free you."

Jenny swayed her head in rhythm with the waves as though she wanted to snake-charm me.

"Look," I spluttered, "as long as I don't make a wish, you're free to do whatever you please. Don't you understand? Once I make a wish, you're back in the same relentless cycle. You're just a piston pumping to keep the machine moving. If we can't change the ritual, we can at least delay it while I live." I emphasized the word "live."

The sea snake wriggled closer, turned, and fluttered its red tail at me. It took me half a minute to realize Jenny wasn't mocking me. She had come within my reach so I could grab her, and she could tow me to Spain. I remembered the fable of the trusting frog that agreed to ride a water snake across a river and became lunch.

So instead, I wiggled out of my coat, saw that it floated, and balled it under my chin and chest to buoy me up. I untied my boots, fumbled my credit card and money out of them, and let the sea have my footwear. I didn't need anchors on my feet. Then I began churning the surface toward Spain.

Halfway to the coast, my muscles turned into useless putty, and I had to float in place with my chin on my buoyant coat. Jenny wriggled up beside me and waited for me to grab her muscular body around the middle, which I did. It was like holding a squirming cable. I wasn't exactly waterskiing toward Spain, but my head stayed above water, and we left a wake.

Two fishermen in orange waterproof suits found me, beached and barefoot and mumbling, too far gone to know my own name. Besides money and a credit card, I had my sopping passport and a Moroccan urn in a jacket pocket.

They hauled me to an inn where Spanish women dropped me in a hot bath and force-fed me scalding chicken soup. Everyone seemed pleased to rescue me, as if doing so would bring them good karma.

I figured the opposite was true, that if you saved someone you became responsible for them. It could be gut-busting work. I was "saving" a cantankerous jinni, and that was like trying to stay eight seconds on a Brahma bull. I wasn't a burden anyone should take on lightly, especially now that I kept company with a perverse jinni.

Speaking of which, why had she rescued me? Did she feel responsible for me? I felt surprised she hadn't asked if I "*wished*" to be saved.

Despite the fact that she had thrown me into the sea and despite my not wanting to feel beholden, I felt teary-eyed gratitude to her. It wasn't rational. Anyway, I was now more determined than ever to withhold my wish and give her limited freedom. I would set aside my comfort and grant this genie a wish. How ironic was that?

I supplied the wine and tapas for my goodbye fiesta and rode the 8:15 bus the morning after to Seville. Yenifer, as she called herself now, joined me in a black hoodie, jeans, and sandals that showed off her lurid red toenails. She smelled of cloves, and her slim brown hands were decorated with henna curlicues.

Even though I had her urn, I hadn't seen her for over a month while I recovered from a respiratory illness. She kept her bony elbow on the armrest between us so I couldn't use it.

"You're not allowed to kill me," I whispered. "You were bluffing."

The tip of her tongue flicked out for a microsecond. "I do not intend to be pleasant company for you, man of clay."

"Well, you're a success at that." I jerked a thumb at the sea behind us, which I had thought she might not be able to cross. "So leaving Morocco is no problem for you?"

"You go to Seville. Why?"

"I want to improve my Spanish. What will you do there?"

She shrugged a shoulder sinuously. "We will see what I shall do." She gave me a musing look. "Your girlfriend has moved to Ecuador?"

How did she know that? "Yeah, she teaches English in Quito." Steph had begun politely answering my emails. "She liked your lapis lazuli pendant, by the way."

"So you will learn Spanish to impress her."

"Can't hurt, can it?"

"I think you have an addiction for this woman."

"Do you like hibernating inside the urn?"

"It is the way things must be for me."

"So what's the problem with my not making a wish, with my letting you live outside your cage for a while?"

"You do not do this for me, man of clay. You do this because to oppose the way of things amuses you."

Before the ferry ride, she was right . . . but not anymore. She had kept breath in my body. "Let's not argue."

In Seville, Yenifer slept in her impossible prison every night, walked me to Spanish school every morning, and met me when I came out of class. She expected something to happen and wanted to be in my company when it did. Though Yenifer seemed less hostile now, I avoided walking near curbs so she couldn't shove me in front of a bus.

My Spanish teacher was a white-haired Andalusian with a face rough as basalt and the crusty manner to match. I was scared not to do my homework. The school, a few blocks from the cathedral, had boarded me with a local family in the Triana district, a blue-collar area famous for producing ceramic tiles, matadors, and flamenco dancers.

One Tuesday after Spanish class, Yenifer and I walked onto a bridge, its wrought-iron railings studded with hundreds of padlocks, each engraved with a name or names. Some had hearts painted on them in red nail polish. Halfway across the bridge, Yenifer stopped to chat with a Gypsy woman begging for coins. The woman looked weathered by the ill winds of life, a pitiful puddle of need, her dark, watery eyes pleading for relief.

*"Hola, abuela,"* Yenifer said to her.

I assumed they weren't kin, and Yenifer used the term "grandmother" to show respect. The woman nodded to Yenifer, then straightened out of her cringing crouch and scanned me with the predatory arrogance of a pimp. I frowned down at her.

She kinked one eyebrow and gave me a mocking smile as

she raised an open, gnarled hand toward my thigh. I dropped a couple of euros on her palm. She shook her fist beside her ear, clinking the two coins, then opened her hand to show me the writer Miguel de Cervantes stamped on them.

"You, I think," she said in English, "are like his Don Quixote. You think yourself more important than you are."

"Doesn't everyone?"

She turned her head and spat in disgust. "Like the foolish knight you believe a woman of flesh and sweat is made of lace and rosewater."

Was she talking about Steph? I certainly didn't believe this haughty beggar woman, who smelled of garlic, was made of rosewater. "And you, I think are more than you seem," I told her.

Yenifer hissed laughter. "His Dulcinea lives in Ecuador."

The Gypsy sneered at me. "Like Don Quixote, you fool yourself, man of clay. The Spanish tongue will bring you no comfort." She lifted her chin to indicate Yenifer. "And this one does not ride a donkey behind you. She only serves you one wish."

I hadn't given her the coins to have my fortune told, but I kept quiet. Yenifer treated this Gypsy jinni with respect. I didn't need to rouse a second, more powerful enemy.

She locked eyes with Yenifer then twitched her head toward the Triana side of the river. "Go two blocks and turn left. You will find a shop selling flamenco dresses. I will come clap when you dance."

"Sancho doesn't dance."

Both of them ignored my little joke, and Yenifer walked away after a quick, respectful nod.

Yenifer took the imperious Gypsy's advice. She bought provocative dresses and danced raw, relentless flamenco most nights in a private club, a *peña*. The joy in her dance was contagious. The heartbeats of her aroused audiences fell into step with her Moorish rhythms, with her heel tap-tap-tappings. Every man was a sultan with her in his harem, and every woman saw her own face on the erotic dancer. Yenifer took them from tears to ecstasy and back again, as she willed.

She rented a rose-colored villa with a tile roof. It faced the river. When I visited her, I saw the brass urn on a bookshelf touching a leather-covered copy of *Rihla, The Journey*, a famous if untrue book by medieval traveler Muhammad Ibn Battuta.

My recent adventures would fit his tales. A genie had tried to trick, embarrass, and terrorize me into making a wish . . . not your usual humdrum tourist experiences. I took some satisfaction in the fact that I had slipped some joy into Yenifer's life.

Still, each night I curled up on my cot and slept easier for knowing that now no urn with a fuming jinni inside it haunted my room.

Steph sent me a message in Spanish, the language that would bring me no comfort. My Dulcinea was getting married.

I walked down to the wide Guadalquivir River and sat on a slat bench, the Spanish sunshine like a hot towel slapped across the back of my neck. Palm trees lined the river, just beyond the pedestrian and bike paths. Bitter orange trees formed a row behind me, the ground under them littered with bright rotting fruit orbited by pesky bees.

I drifted through maudlin memories of Steph. Would she wear my lapis lazuli pendant on her honeymoon?

Someone said something and broke into my sorrowing. Yenifer sat beside me, her sinewy presence a warm comfort.

"What will you do?" she repeated.

"Good question. I've lost my zeal for Spanish lessons. But I don't feel like doing much else."

"You wish to travel?"

Movement would distract me, but there would be little joy in it now. "I think I might settle down for awhile. What do you want to do?"

She smiled, a rare act when in my company. "You will grant me a wish, Layton?"

"I live to serve. A Don Quixote can do no less. But I won't force this wish on you." I smiled to show I was teasing her.

ADAR DARNOV

She looked across the wide alga-green river at Triana apartment buildings with cafés and businesses along the street level. "I have danced. Now I wish to create sculpture."

"Stone or clay?"

"I think both. But first I will work with the clay." She smirked at me.

Would she sculpt a man of clay? "Paris, then. Perfect for both of us."

"You know Paris?"

"Enough to like its style."

Something brushed my arm, and the self-satisfied Gypsy jinni sat down on the other side of me. I blinked twice at her (poof!) materialization.

She smelled of sweet tobacco with an under-scent of garlic. Her skirt and blouse were a fiesta of colors, and she had at least two pounds of silver jewelry on her. Grandmother jinni wasn't playing needy beggar woman today.

I said, *"Hola, abuela."*

"Grandmother? We are not alike. I am from the sacred fire, you are from clay."

"I meant it as a title of respect."

"Then it is acceptable."

"So why are you here, grandmother?"

She thrust out her breasts, pushing out the front of her wide-necked Romani blouse. "I come to advise Yenifer, as you call her." She tapped my hand with a forefinger sporting a snake ring, its eye a blue gem. "Why do you not honor the ritual?"

"Why follow a ritual that punishes you?" I asked.

Yenifer sucked in a noisy, despairing breath. "The Time Ruler will punish me for not making his wish."

The Gypsy rubbed her own cheek, frowning in thought. "Yet this has not happened."

"No, it could be said I have been rewarded." This seemed to make Yenifer more anxious than happy.

"Glad you think so," I said, taking full credit for improving her life. "This Time Ruler is your god?"

The Gypsy jinni glared at me. "We have the same God, man of clay, but use a different name. Our Time Ruler is a *wali*, a saint." She pulled a clay pipe from a pocket of her billowy skirt and began loading it with tobacco from a drawstring bag. "Perhaps Time Ruler uses the two of you. But take caution. Time Ruler's attention is not always pleasant."

"Before we reached Spain, Yenifer's attention wasn't exactly a delight for me."

The Gypsy threw her head back and guffawed. Yenifer smiled as if I had praised her.

I asked, "So why did your Time Ruler pick me?"

"Perhaps it is because you do not fear change." She glimmered a catlike smile at me. "Perhaps fire is needed to bake clay."

"Or clay is needed to give fire a purpose."

Yenifer asked, "What will *you* do in Paris, Layton?"

"Improve my French. And maybe I'll learn to sculpt pastries. What woman could resist me then?"

"So you go to Paris for me?"

"In a heartbeat, Dulcinea."

Yenifer peered around me at her Gypsy advisor. "He thinks to change me."

"No," I said. "I cannot change your jinni nature. Paris is a good city for you. There you can learn sculpture. And I'm addicted to *éclairs*."

The old woman lit her little clay pipe. She nodded at the Guadalquivir. "The river always looks the same, but the water is ever-changing. Perhaps you two will renew the ritual."

"Maybe we'll make marmalade from sour fruit."

When Yenifer frowned, not understanding me, I pointed to the riot of oranges rotting under a nearby tree. "No one gathers them because they're too bitter to eat. But you can make marmalade out of them. So let's sweeten your ritual."

The no-nonsense Gypsy jinni nodded. "Rent an apartment in Montparnasse. The cemetery there is home to the *Génie de Sommeil Eternel*." She pointed her pipe stem at Yenifer on the other side of me. "This statue will bring you power."

"We won't live together in Paris," I said. "When we didn't here, the urn stopped stalking me. That's progress. Besides, Yenifer will want to live her own life and have her own studio."

Yenifer sat rigid, staring up into the bottomless blue sky. "Why are you so generous to me, Layton? I grant you a wish only because I must."

"And I've noticed you stopped asking me to make one. Why be kind to you? Because I'm free to do so. Besides, a ritual without generosity in it is a hollow, useless habit." I leaned toward her. "By the way, can you help me find a present for Steph? She's got a wedding coming up."

"Is that your wish?" she asked with a mischievous smile.

"No, just a friendly request for help."

The Gypsy jinni blew out a stream of white pipe smoke. It waggled in the warm air and shaped into a hooded cobra. "And if she decides not give you this help?"

"She has that right. It was a request, not an order." I turned to Yenifer. "If being chained to me bothers you, then just tell me to make a wish, and I'll do it."

Yenifer folded her hennaed hands and stayed silent.

# *A Smokeless and Scorching Fire*

*written by*

## *Erin Cairns*

*illustrated by*

KYNA TEK

---

### ABOUT THE AUTHOR

*Erin Cairns is a gypsy: born in Johannesburg, South Africa, she started school in New Jersey, and finished her formal education in Texas. Her love of stories started at a young age when her father read his favorite books aloud to the family. The tradition is alive and well, although it is now rationed to holidays, when the family gathers together.*

*Erin has been writing stories and receiving rejection letters for years. In an attempt to be rational about her love of writing, she studied at the University of Texas at Dallas in a completely unrelated field. She concurrently ran the UTD writers group, when she decided that if she still had stories of her own to tell, she should start telling them to anyone who would sit still long enough to listen.*

*Between making animations and games, and selling sculptures to local galleries, she enjoys scaring the neighborhood children with horror stories.*

*The journey ahead is much anticipated.*

### ABOUT THE ILLUSTRATOR

*Kyna Tek was born in 1980 at an unnamed refugee camp in Thailand along the Cambodia and Thailand border. Kyna's family eventually immigrated to Tempe, Arizona where he grew up a typical '80s kid playing videogames, watching movies, and reading comics.*

*It wasn't until he attended college that he discovered his passion for drawing and painting. He immersed himself in studies of the arts and his skills grew exponentially.*

*After graduating from college he has continued honing his craft and discovering where he fits in the illustration world. He enjoys pursuing his ever-continuing education through self-study and creating inspired illustrations in the fantasy and science fiction genre.*

# A Smokeless and Scorching Fire

The civilians were dancing on the train again, their feet stomping to the heartbeat of the engine. Forced to sway to the rhythm by the movement of the train, Deacon crushed a sunflower seed between his thumb and index finger. An old woman seated across the aisle fanned herself with a handful of reeds. She glared openly at him.

"Bloody inspections," she muttered to her daughter-in-law, whose head was bowed in respect and submission to her elder. "Isn't enough the factory's going to be shut down, but they sent a *djinn* to do it? Bad manners. Bad luck."

She spoke Usu, a working-class language, and one that Deacon had been punished for learning. It was the one part of him the conditioning couldn't reprogram—language. He betrayed no indication that he understood, but kept himself busy with the sunflower seeds he had bought at the city-station.

He wasn't like these people. He didn't dress in the body-hugging fashions, and if his loose black clothing didn't set him apart, his pale skin and gray eyes certainly did. He hated his eyes, the mark of his inhuman origin. He knew how flat they looked, shallow and artificial.

It had been the first mark of his insanity. Engineered humans didn't have opinions on physical appearance. Deacon wasn't even sure when his madness began. Conditioning should have scrubbed his self-awareness away.

He crushed another seed, rubbing it into a prickly paste.

The passengers stomped their feet down harder. The whole carriage rocked with the frenzy of their excitement. How could something that moved so slowly be so loud? He listened idly to the life around him, pretending to be immersed in the shine of his own black shoes.

The old woman was still complaining about his presence. "It should be on one of the Sand-Beetles. It's not right they put it here, with us."

Ah. She took pleasure in misusing the Usu pronouns, neutering him with language. The cruelty of it stung more than her ill-informed slurs about his job, or his origin. The factory wasn't his destination. His journey would take him to the desert. The factory was just a stop along the way.

He had begged carefully for this assignment. Traded contracts with other Inspectors and negotiated with the Administration. Not once did he let them know he *wanted* this. Wanting wasn't allowed to his kind.

When he closed his eyes, he could see the endless sand, and himself, walking against the wind with his slim, empty briefcase. The sun would beat down on his skin, turning it from pale to bloody, raw, red. But the pain would be nothing. The starvation and dehydration, he would barely notice. It was a walk in the sunshine compared to the re-conditioning he would face if he returned to headquarters and confessed his malfunction. Again, another symptom of his insanity: He did not *want* to be conditioned. The pain. The illness. The *invasion*.

With great effort, he turned his attention away from his madness to the gossip in the cabin. This carriage held a fragment of a wedding party meeting up in the mountains, readying themselves for negotiations and introductions to new family members. What could they offer? What would they accept?

The best stories were shared in families. *Remember when mama washed the floor with papa's best bottle of kashaka? It peeled holes in the linoleum and she was drunk just off the fumes! Remember when Eliza wanted that boy from the—*

KYNA TEK

"Cheap!" a young voice engaged him in the Official language, tearing him from the gossip about people he didn't know and would never meet. Deacon raised his eyes to find a young boy, only eight or nine, holding out a bouquet of wilting flowers. Stubbornness prematurely aged the boy's face. He shook the flowers insistently. "Cheap!" he repeated.

"Come away from him!" the old woman called out in Usu. "Didn't your mother teach you not to speak to ghosts?"

The boy turned to her. "Then will you buy them, grandmother?" he asked in the same language. "If you had the credit, you would spend it on skin-cream."

Her lips ballooned out and her eyebrows descended sharply. From kindly matron to formidable matriarch, the change was fluid, immediate, and well practiced. "You speak to elders like that, you little bastard?"

This theater interfered with the natural rhythm of the train now. People strained their necks and backs to see the scene unfold, deciding on which side they would take. The ecosystem changed, the feet stomping out the dance around their vehicle seemed to rise to a frenzy, though Deacon knew it echoed only in his mind.

He hated confrontation. Another symptom of his madness. *The desert, remember the desert*. It waited. Calm. Empty. Silent.

"How much?" he asked in Official, trusting that the boy knew that much of his language at least.

The boy glanced back, surprised. "Cheap!" he repeated.

"How much?" Deacon waved a blank chip at him, its denomination waiting to be determined.

"Thirty," the boy said.

An outrageous price. But Deacon was rich. Beyond rich. He had the wealth of the Administration at his fingertips, and what else would a *djinn* spend it on? Around him, his traveling company quieted. Intent on the transaction.

He tapped the amount into the chip, and gave it to the boy who promptly pushed it through the scanner hung around his neck while Deacon tried to select a flower. They were all exquisitely ugly, drooping in the heat.

To his surprise the boy shoved the now-blank chip as well as the whole bouquet onto his chest. Deacon barely had time to clasp his hands around the bundle of stems before the boy raced away down the compartment, dodging the frenzied dancers.

The old woman attempted to trip the boy with her cane, but he jumped lithely over this obstacle and the carriage door closed behind him.

Deacon felt rather foolish now, with his bundle of crushed flowers. They smelled like fried food and sickly perfume. He turned this unexpected purchase around in his hands, exploring the strangeness of it. Native plants certainly, by the waxy leaves and spiny petals. Water-efficient traits.

Would there be greenery then, scattered in the sands? He hadn't imagined that.

And the sounds began again. The women muttering about the upcoming celebrations, the wealth sure to be on display. The men grumbling out stories and opinions to anyone who would listen. Deacon felt the thick leaves between his thumb and forefinger. Barely sixteen breaths passed before the door slid open again, slamming against the frame as a burly man burst into their midst. Big and square. Brown. Muscled and scarred from hard labor. His face creased with unkindness.

He scanned the gathering.

"Where's the boy?" he asked the rest of the car in Usu. Nobody answered, just stared at him. Even the old lady's lips tightened. Information was notoriously hard to get out of the working class, but a question required truth from an Inspector. Deacon considered fighting the conditioning to keep silent, but even as resistance strayed through his thoughts, his stomach began to roil, and the phantom daggers of pain began to dig through his scalp.

Lying, even by omission, was not worth the pain. He needed to save his strength. "He went that way," Deacon said, pointing to the door the boy had left through.

But the man caught sight of the flowers in Deacon's hands. He gestured rudely toward them. "Stolen. Take." His Official sounded even worse than the little thief's. Official was a clean language, free from the guttural inflections he clipped into the syllables.

Shrugging, Deacon held out the flowers, but the old woman interfered again. "He's an Inspector, you fool. He's already paid for them."

The stranger scowled, and took a step forward to see Deacon clearly. Behind him, a woman appeared in the cabin's open doorway. She surveyed the crowded carriage with disinterest and distaste.

But she captured everyone else. Even the presence of the loud, aggressive man faded beside her.

Her dark hair was bound in plaits by copper wire, and caught by tiny leaves forged from gold. Each strand glimmered with hints of red henna. She swayed hypnotically to the beat of the train, seeming to slow even its frantic pace.

She wore a bride's veil that hooked over her ears and the bridge of her nose, but the sheer fabric did nothing to hide her face.

It served as only a token attempt at modesty.

"Don't look at her," the old woman muttered to her daughter-in-law, loud enough to warn everyone in the cabin. "That's Mahati's woman."

Mahati's woman stood no taller than Deacon, but she stood with a dignity that gave the impression of height. She wore a dress of intricate chainmail, links of silver wire and drops of metal bead that rippled with a delicate sound when she moved. A light cotton shift kept the metal off her skin and accented the extreme contours of her body.

None of this caught his attention more than her eyes.

Elaborately outlined with kohl, they found him immediately. An expression of understanding, of some deep communication, gleamed in those eyes when she fixed her gaze on him.

She walked forward, past the man who said something to try and stop her progress. She brushed him off like a safari fly and sat beside Deacon.

"What use does a ghost have for flowers?" Mahati's woman asked, her husky voice lending an exotic lilt to her Official.

"What use does anyone have for flowers?" he returned flatly.

She laughed, as if he had said something funny. He tracked the arch of her jaw, calculating the slope of her neck. She was a creature of pure mathematics. To anyone else she might have been beautiful, but he had not yet lost that much of his sanity.

And he remembered the desert. In the sand, his flesh would be stripped away by the winds, ravaged by sand-beasts who wouldn't care that he had been engineered.

"Take them," he said, thrusting the bouquet out to her. "I don't know why I bought them. I didn't know they were stolen."

She hesitated, her eyes traveling to his face.

"Don't you dare, Axeonos," her companion said sharply, but he made no move toward Deacon. He feared the *djinn* as well, it seemed.

She took the bouquet. In these crowded quarters, with the afternoon sun still glaring through the windows, sweat shone on everyone's skin.

But not hers. In the first-class carriages, the heat never made it past the doors. Her cold fingers brushed against his skin as she withdrew the bundle of waxy leaves.

Immediately silence engulfed their fellow travelers. Deacon gazed around at their audience, and followed their attention back in time to see the man's face darken with anger. The woman relaxed against the bench, and through her gently shifting veil Deacon could see a dangerous smile, badly-hidden triumph.

The man started to shout, not in Usu or Official, but some derivation of a mountain language.

"Is something wrong?" Deacon asked the woman.

"Nothing at all, *alma-ami*," she said sweetly, taking his hand in her own.

*My Soul*. The endearment was stressed. He tried to pull his hand away, but she didn't let go. "What is wrong?" he asked the still-silent train.

The grandmother who insulted him answered for the crowd. "Bond-flowers," she said. "Your woman now."

Between her broken Official, the now iridescent anger of the strange man, and the woman's hand still encasing his own, he understood. A local marriage ritual.

The desert was slipping away from his grasp. His masters would learn of this. He would have to report this. There would be an investigation. They would catch him and recondition him.

"I didn't know," he said, trying to shake her hands from his own. "I didn't—"

"It's too late now," Axeonos said triumphantly. "We are bonded now."

"I can't—"

"You have not been registered," her keeper said in Usu. Deacon wasn't a part of this conversation. "You are not married yet."

"He's an Inspector," she answered smugly in the same language. "Registration won't be a problem. We are married in the eye of the God now, and you can tell Mahati to suck his own cock."

"You can't marry a *djinn*," the man sneered. "Mahati will see you stoned for it. I saw you give the flowers to the boy. I *saw* you."

"Excuse me," Deacon broke in weakly. "I did not know. I am sorry, but it isn't legal for me to—"

They were not listening to him.

"He offered the flowers, and I accepted," she said. "You want to fight him for my hand?"

Another moment of stillness fell over them, as if the man actually contemplated violence.

"Don't be a fool," the old woman hissed to the thug. "That's a damned *djinn*. They'll skin us all and starve our villages if you touch him."

The truth. The Administration protected its Inspectors. They had to, when it was so expensive to make them, and they had the tasks that made the Administration so unpopular. If an Inspector was harmed in the execution of his duties, an example would be made of anyone and everyone who had been present.

Silence on the train. Stillness. Two more men entered the carriage, and engaged their leader in hushed, confused dialog in the language Deacon couldn't place. The woman's grip on his hand tightened painfully.

"Please help me," she said quickly, softly, to make sure that no one else could catch the exchange. "Please."

"I have to get off when we reach the desert," he said to her. "I'm sorry—"

"You hear that?" she called shrilly to the man and his entourage, hearing nothing of Deacon's muttered explanations. "We're getting off at the next stop!"

When he stepped off the train, Deacon could see the desert behind the city. The low and level hills swallowed the garish lights of civilization. Tomorrow he would walk into the scorching sand, and in a few days, he would die somewhere out in that untraveled expanse.

"You ever been to Dhulba-Sahuli before?" the woman asked.

"No," Deacon said, and he walked away.

She had only one small suitcase, which trailed behind her like an unwilling pet. It rumbled against the stone behind him, a constant reminder that she followed in his wake.

When they reached the dormitories, Axeonos would not follow him inside. The rumble-shriek of her little suitcase ceased, and for some reason, he stopped as well.

She told him, "I am not spending my wedding night in there."

"It is not your wedding night," Deacon said—a variation on the same thing he had been saying since they had met. "I am not your husband. We are not registered. I will not register you. Tomorrow, your man said he would come for you."

She flicked a hand in the space between them and huffed a dismissal. Still, she didn't move toward the opening gate, and neither did he. "These are my lodgings," he told her. "Why are you not satisfied?"

"Satisfaction has little to do with it, *alma-ami*," she spat the endearment mockingly. "Tonight is my wedding night. Use some of my dowry. Let's go to the Dumaux, or the Shalloota."

"What would the difference be?" he asked. "There are beds here. We will sleep, and then in the morning we will both be gone."

Because she wouldn't follow him, he was forced to wait. Why, though? He should just go in and leave her on the street, but he couldn't seem to move his feet. She watched him, her magnificent eyes narrowed, her hip crooked out, and her hands held on her waist in a colloquial pose of restrained anger. He waited.

"Tonight," she said softly, "is my first night as a free woman. I will not spend it in a *prison*."

"It is not a prison," Deacon said mildly. "It is temporary. We can leave anytime we want, just like the Dumaux or Shalloota, and unlike at the Dumaux or Shalloota, here there are free meals, and bedding, and company."

"Listen to me, you—" she lapsed into Usu, *"blood-sucking, penny-grubbing, pale-face, moronic djinn—"* and back to Official, "I will absolutely *not* spend a single night in that concrete cage. With or without you, I am going to the Shalloota, and I am going to have their most expensive meal, and dance in the most expensive dress I can find."

At Deacon's silence and stillness, she huffed low in her throat. It was a growl, Deacon noted, like a jungle cat. He watched her spin and stalk away down the street, still trailing the tiny suitcase.

He followed her.

They walked down streets and through alleys, Deacon always twenty measured steps behind her. She didn't buy a dress as she threatened. None of those stores would be open at this time, but she went straight to the Shalloota, with its fat columns and sweet-smelling gardens.

She danced in the nightclub attached to the building, under red and blue lights. She danced in the dress of metal rings, alone. She flicked her hands toward the ceiling and curled her fingers as she beckoned to something that couldn't answer, the sway of her hips leading the music.

Not once did her eyes stray to Deacon who stood patiently by the door, by her small pack. She didn't dance with or for anyone. She danced for her own sweat, and when he could see her eyes, they were large and liquid, inebriated.

He should have left. He should never have followed her in the first place. He should never have taken the flowers.

He stood a half-pace behind her when she booked a room. Her limbs were jittery with energy found on the dance floor. Her sweat smelled sweet and foul in the air.

She brushed past him, and he trailed her to the hotel dining room. They were shown to a table by a waiter who inspected them curiously but said nothing. Perhaps he thought Deacon was here to question the woman. Or that she held a position in the Administration, and took advantage of it.

"Don't annul the marriage," she said abruptly, when they were alone again.

"Why?"

She glared at him, but the appearance of their menus stopped her answer. The waiter filled their glasses with water, but before he could move away the woman held out a hand to stall him.

"Every appetizer, and your most expensive meal," she commanded the young man. "And lobster."

"Yes madam," he said politely. "And you sir?"

"Just water," Deacon said.

No questions. The waiter left, and the woman tossed her head aggressively. "I won't agree to an annulment."

"Inspectors cannot get married." And then purely for his own, perverse curiosity, he asked, "Why do you want to be married to me?"

She shrugged, averting her eyes.

"You tricked me," he reminded her gently.

"I was not given a choice," she said. "Why should you? At least now we are even."

The food arrived on a variety of silver platters, carried by a flock of waiters. The dishes covered the table and spilled out onto the makeshift trays set up on rickety stilts. Still, Deacon insisted the place in front of him remain empty. His own makeshift desert, surrounded by plates piled high of exotic food. There was so much. Too much.

At the center, between them, sat the promised lobster. Insectile. Armored. A shade of red that should be impossible to achieve naturally.

"Help yourself," she said airily. "I will not be able to finish it."

The absurd display of food seemed somehow more real and vivid than the room around them. The shapes were smooth, bloated with flavor. Every dish had a distinct scent, but together they coalesced into an exotic perfume that pulled on Deacon's stomach.

Greed was a herald of madness. He could give in and devour everything in sight, eating and eating until even his body broke. He delicately picked up a crystal glass, the liquid inside clear. Tasteless, but quenching.

Tomorrow there would be no water. No food.

She frowned at him. "You don't want to eat?"

His mouth watered, his stomach growling, and his head grew light with the aromas of rich food. "I can't."

"You can't eat? I saw you eating seeds on the train. Or are you really a ghost born of smokeless and scorching fire? Is it mortal souls you hunger for?"

She grinned, trying to excite him into ritualistic play.

"No," he said, and this was painful. The conditioning was a pleasant memory in comparison. Torture could not have been more compelling. "I can't want to eat."

She cocked her head curiously, the smile peeling from her face, discarded in an instant. "You don't look like you can afford to skip this meal."

"We haven't even been introduced," he said, clasping a hand around the glass of water. "I would have thought a marriage ceremony required more . . . words."

"My father is a traditional man." She turned her attention back to the meal. "If it makes you uncomfortable, my name is Axeonos."

“I am called Deacon,” he replied cordially. Politely. As he had been conditioned.

“I didn’t know that Inspectors had names.”

“We don’t have much cause to use them. How did you learn Official?”

“My father.”

Her tone was bitter.

“Was he a good man?” Deacon asked mildly.

“He sold his only daughter to a gangster,” she said. “To me, he is a spider.”

“Why is he a spider?”

“He could have made me and my brothers a home, but he only ever wove traps and he grew fat off the men who tangled in it. His home was his own. He did not share. A spider.”

“I’ve always liked spiders,” Deacon said experimentally, because he did not know what else to say.

“Oh, he was useful,” she agreed, “just as spiders are useful to keep the other insects in check. He taught me how to write and read, how to properly speak Official, and how to balance books. He supplied me with tutors, and anything I wanted, but in the end I was only bait.”

“Not anymore, though,” he said.

“Never again.”

“And what’s to stop him from claiming you again? Or this Mahati?”

She stiffened, the food frozen on its way to her lips. “What do you know of Mahati?” she demanded.

He winced inwardly. A mistake. It was a miracle he hadn’t already been caught. *The desert, the desert.* One more night of pretending at sanity, and he would be free. “I’m an Inspector,” he said. “We know all kinds of things.”

“No, you heard it on the train! You can speak Usu!” she said triumphantly. “I knew it!”

He nodded and she frowned, her victory stolen. “You admit it? I thought Inspectors aren’t allowed. It is a punishable offense, no?”

“It is.”

"Then why tell me?"

"I cannot lie." He took another mouthful of water. *Poison. Bright light. Pictures that moved so fast he felt sick with their movement.* "I have been conditioned."

She sat back. A glass of red wine in her hand shone deep and clear—casting its own kind of light. Her eyes caught on his face, on his own eyes which he hated and his pale, untried skin. "Good to know," she said.

"You sound amused."

She hesitated, her eyes rolling to the ceiling as if considering her own emotions. "Just . . . speculative."

She fell silent for a while as she savored her food and he drank water to keep himself from wanting to taste everything on the table.

The waiter had to fill his glass twice.

"Mahati?" he reminded her.

She shook her mane of dark hair dismissively. "What can he do? I am married to an Inspector, and it would be foolish for him to try anything now. He will go to my father, and that is hardly my problem."

"You said he was a gangster," he said. "Will your father get hurt?"

She hesitated, her eyes dark and veiled. "No," she decided. "My father killed Sasha, the man I loved, to prove that his contract was in good faith. He will also most likely kill my dogs to spite me, but there is too much good history between him and Mahati for this to end badly between them."

"Sasha," he mused, balancing his glass between two fingers.

"Was not a good man either," she said bluntly. "I loved him anyway. But he is dead, and they cannot hurt me anymore, not if I am married to you."

Fabric covered every possible surface of their luxurious room. Carpets, the drapes above the beds, two layers of curtains over the tall windows, thickly upholstered chairs and footstools, it was all too much. Deacon felt like he was sinking.

Extravagance like this wasn't meant for him. Only real people could appreciate the softness and the exquisite colors.

He left his briefcase on the table and stood beside the bed, focusing on the street outside the window. Chairs and tables were set outside under soft neon lights of every color. The glowing canopy zig-zagged between the buildings in every direction, marking the extent of the celebration.

"The bed is big enough for both of us," the woman said. She had already collapsed onto the covers, her hands writhing under the pillows, searching for an edge of the sheets.

"I have work to do," he said absently, staring down into the starkly lit street.

"All night?"

"Yes."

She huffed a disbelieving laugh. "You haven't even visited the factory yet. I think you are skittish. You needn't be. I am too tired to poke fun at my *djinn* tonight."

She wasn't drunk, but obviously exhausted. Deacon said nothing back to her, keeping his gaze fixed on the distant desert, just visible through the buildings. She muttered a curse, then groaned with effort. Deacon didn't have to turn to know she was undressing.

A sigh of release. The sound of metal rain, as she discarded her chainmail beside the bed. "I'm not naked," she said to him, a smile in her voice.

He turned to see her sitting up in the bed, wearing the simple cotton shift that had kept the metal off her skin. She looked better. Less dangerous. "I think under the circumstances, God will forgive us if we do not consummate our marriage tonight."

Under his gaze she removed the metal ornamentation from her hair. There were many pieces.

"I don't believe in God," he said.

She shrugged. "I suppose it is hard for you. You were not made by him, after all."

"No," he said, "but I don't believe he made you either."

"I believe you were made from fire," she said, "like the old books say about the *djinni*." She struggled with a clasp at the back of her head. "I can see it in your eyes."

Again. She was trying to be playful. No one had ever spoken to him the way she did.

"How did you keep your head up, under all of that?" he asked, not sure if he was trying to make a joke. Not likely. He had never had a sense of humor before.

"Practice," she said.

Deacon turned away, back to the desk. He sat down, ignoring the way the pillows encased him, molding to his back. He opened the briefcase only to be staring down at his forbidden treasures.

The evidence of his insanity.

He ran his fingers over the golden watch—an antiquated thing. The smoothness of it had first captivated him. The symmetry of its lines. There were other things, too. Postcards from the cities he had been sent to examine. A stolen painting—the memory of that pain still bit at him as he brushed a hand over its colorful smudges. It was a simple portrait of a man at a desk, the light catching on golden buttons and the folds of his ceremonial dress, mysterious and dark. Deacon did not know why he took it—only that he had to have it. He had to possess it, because it pulled on something in him—an urge stronger than that he had been trained into.

He ran a thumb over the corner of it, feeling the phantom burn that came with guilt—another emotion he supposedly could not feel. Axeonos began to snore, startling him into movement.

He could not linger. He would need all his willpower and strength to complete his final act. He pulled the tablet from underneath his treasures.

The form only had two questions. He was supposed to visit the factory. He was supposed to shut it down. He took the job for that reason. If anybody bothered to see why this desert town leaked money and resources, he would be long gone, and they might guess at his victory.

He shouldn't be able to lie, but he was insane.

And that helped.

*Is the factory profitable?*

No.

*Yes,* he wrote carefully, feeling the betrayal in every nerve of his body. He stared at the word he had written, felt the wrongness of it in his bones. It started as an itch, a burn.

His shoulders stiffened. His brain rebelled. *Untruth!* Pain. He let out a shaking breath. The woman snored behind him. How much time had passed?

*Notes during inspection:*

He readied his stylus and steeled himself. His imagination. How they would wonder at it—how all their conditioning, all their tests had failed.

And his bones in the desert, scraped and bleached white—a monument to this one act of disobedience. He would win.

Dawn peeked under the bathroom door when at last he finished. He had been sick twice, and even now sweat soaked through his clothes. He shook, unable to grip the stylus.

Axeonos had slept through it all. He had retreated to the bathroom to keep the pain to himself. He stood on shaking legs and let the tablet clatter onto the counter. He didn't let his eyes focus on it again. It was bad enough to *know* what he had done without having to face his crime.

His fingers were so numb the buttons on his shirt became almost unmanageable.

The shower thawed his fear and melted through his icy skin. He hugged himself and turned around and around under the torrent, trying his best to soak in every drop of hot water.

Water. There would be none in the desert. Not even enough moisture in the air to keep the sweat on his skin. He closed his eyes and saw himself striding among the dunes.

With his resistance finished, he was released from the compulsion to faint or vomit, though his eyelids felt like sandpaper, and his mouth tasted like blood.

He reveled for a long time before a knock on the door startled him back to his guilt.

"I know it is not possible to use up hot water in the Shalloota, but it seems you are trying."

The woman.

"I'll be out in a moment," he called back, his voice rough from a night of muffled screams.

He switched the water off, scrambled for a towel, and gathered his clothes. As he opened the door, she brushed past him. The sun had risen while he had been in the shower and golden light filtered through the large windows. Outside, vendors were calling out wares, their voices undulating in rhythm with the sounds of foot traffic.

Deacon peered down at the city as it set up for a parade. The streets were full of sound. Instruments warming up, chatter and laughter as the festivities took shape. Barriers rose along the sidewalk, and the beginning of celebratory noise filtered through the air.

His heart began to pick up, a strange sort of excitement rising in his chest, in his head, answering to the noise outside. A madman and a liar, he was. He hissed wordlessly and forced himself away from the window. His only destination today was the desert.

He laid his clothes out on the bed. They were rumpled, and smelled like sweat. It was a uniform of sorts. A blue shirt, black pants, black jacket, black shoes, white collar, all mass-produced for Inspectors.

He ran his hands over the fabrics, smoothing out the wrinkles and spots. Idly he picked at the cuffs, examining the scents of yesterday—the train, the meal, the woman.

The door opened, and he turned.

She was wrapped only in a towel, and for the first time he saw her bare face. Even unadorned by makeup and jewelry she struck him as a fascinating creature.

"What is this?" she held up the tablet, the screen trembling in her hand.

Deacon paused. "Work," he said.

"What were you going to do? Where were you going, if you had already signed off the factory?"

She was afraid. Now he hesitated, but the words were pulled from him. "To the desert," he said.

"Why? There's nothing there but sand for a hundred miles."

"I was going . . . to walk," the words forced themselves from his lips.

She frowned. "Where?"

"I was going to walk until I couldn't."

Her eyes widened. *"Why?"*

"Please," Deacon asked her. "Please don't make me—"

He was too weak to fight the conditioning now.

"Tell me," she commanded.

"I have gone mad," he blurted as the familiar pressure began in his head. The *will* to answer.

She drew back, her brows furrowing in fear and shock.

Of course. He was disgusting, useless. A shadow of his purpose. "I am insane," he confessed again. "And when they find out, I will be reconditioned. They will torture me with poison and light, to force me not to *want*. Not to lie. Not to *think*."

"I do not understand," she said.

Too late now, the desert beckoned in the distance. She would report him, and the Administration would come for him. And then he would be forced back into training.

"How are you mad?" she asked steadily. She stood still and straight, unadorned.

He ran a hand down his face in a claw, scratching at his brow and the bridge of his nose. "See this! This is the face of an Inspector, the body and mind of a *djinn*!"

She retreated, but he went after, reached for her, grasped her wrists, and pulled her close. "Can you see it?" he asked desperately. "The madness? Look at me. You must be able to see it. It *must* be obvious now."

Her chin trembled; she tore free. "You are scaring me."

"No! No! Watch!" He ripped open the briefcase, and showed her his treasures. Those he would take into the desert. He had tried, had been fighting his symptoms, and all the while these things had been corrupting him, turning him inside out with addiction and fear of discovery. He was helpless.

"See?" he said, holding his breath as if afraid to break her concentration. "Do you see it?"

She held her hands over her chest, fingers clasped together as if in prayer. "Oh, my *djinn*," she whispered.

But her expression stilled him. Instead of fright, he read something else. He frowned. Was that delight? Amusement?

No. She had corrected him.

It was speculation.

The day was long, and full of beauty. They ate in the café, amid crowds of people. She bought the most expensive dress she could find, and they wandered in and out of the shops on the main street. Food. Entertainment. They spent money as if it were sand. Time passed quickly, and that night they wandered into the parade, hand in hand, fingers woven together.

The lights spun around them, laughing faces, such a variety of people and costumes. It all blended together. He felt giddy, breathless.

The woman dragged him to an alley, where the stream of people passed by unseeing, like water over rocks, like wind over mountains. This was a pocket where together they were unhurried, protected by darkness and enclosing buildings.

"Would you leave me now?" she asked.

He gazed at the curl of her lips, at the slant of her eyes. "No," he said in her language, intoxicated by the feel of the words on his lips. The first time he had spoken the words he had so long ago learned.

"Then no more talks of the desert," she commanded. "You are *my* djinn now, and I am your woman. Where you go, I go, and I have no wish to walk in the desert."

"I thought you didn't want to be bound," he said, feeling the curl of her ear between his forefinger and thumb, tangling his fingers in the luxury of her hair.

"With you, I am not bound," she smiled. "Together, we will be free."

She curled around him, her breath like the flutter of wings against his skin. "But we must never let them know," she whispered.

"Yes."

He twisted against her, wrapped in her limbs, in her presence. "We must choose when to fight."

He breathed her in, unable to answer, but she understood anyway. Her lips were at his ear. She probably wouldn't hear him anyway. Her voice swelled hypnotically, like the lights in the street, and the echo of the music from the festival. He felt dizzy with the spin of it.

"Shut down the factory."

Of course. It was the only way they could be together. The only way to avoid re-conditioning. He had to play a part, and lying? She was the daughter of a spider. She would teach him how to lie.

# *The Howler on the Sales Floor*

*written by*

## *Jonathan Ficke*

*illustrated by*

SIDNEY LUGO

---

### ABOUT THE AUTHOR

*Jonathan Ficke lives outside of Milwaukee, Wisconsin with his beautiful wife. He graduated from Marquette University with a degree in public relations, which (in a manner of speaking) is another form of speculative storytelling.*

*His older brother introduced him to Tolkien at a young age and, despite his bookshelf's persistent pleas for mercy, he's voraciously consumed the genre ever since. For as long as he can remember, he dreamed of being an author, and the thought of holding a book containing his words in his hands is a dream come true.*

*When he's not reading or writing, he is turning lumber into sawdust and, when all goes according to plan, furniture.*

### ABOUT THE ILLUSTRATOR

*Sidney Lugo was born in 1994 in Guarico, Venezuela. "Sid" to her friends, she grew up most of her life in Caracas, Venezuela and moved to Boston at age nineteen to study Interactive Design.*

*Her childhood memories serve as inspiration for many of her drawings. She developed an interest in fantasy and sci fi from a young age.*

*Sid spent a lot of time looking at French comic books and stories, especially those from the comic anthology* Metal Hurlant. *These kind of surreal sci-fi and fantasy stories stimulated her imagination and inspired her path as an artist.*

*Outside of her studies, she continued to learn and pursue her interest for art. She continues to learn and improve her skills in order to work as a storyboard artist and work on her own comic book.*

*Sid is currently a graphic designer working as a freelancer for private clients.*

# *The Howler on the Sales Floor*

Fluorescent lights embedded in the drop ceiling flickered and pulsed faster than the human eye can perceive, but for eyes formed in the ancient whirling chaos of the Maelstrom, they bathed the conference room in a pleasant light. It was enough to drive a man insane. Luckily, Nya had been born of insanity. The chaotic lights comforted him.

Nya sat at a conference table and sipped his stale coffee. Bill Dudly, his frumpy manager, a balding man with an unkempt neck beard and thick-rimmed glasses, sat across from him. Bill sat next to Julia Andersen, a she-devil from beyond the void. It was Nya's quarterly review, and his cowardly manager had summoned reinforcements in the form of the pencil-skirt-wearing, austere woman with aquiline features and a command of the darkest arts of the known and unknown cosmos: human resources.

"Nya, your sales numbers are exquisite, as always." Bob flipped through a manila folder, each turn of the page jostled his garish tie. Not even in the deepest pits of madness had Nya seen such hideous patterns. His mind, though forged in a crucible of insanity, struggled to comprehend a reality in which such a tie could exist.

Bob asked, "Just as I did last quarter, I need to ask how you do it."

"MY CLIENTS SEE THE EMBODIMENT OF DESPAIR AND MADNESS IN MY EYES, AND THE FUTILITY OF THEIR EXISTENCE IS LAID BARE BEFORE THEM. THEN THEY CANNOT HELP BUT BUY PAPER IN VAST QUANTITIES IN A VAIN

ATTEMPT TO COVER THE DARK REVELATIONS FROM SEEPING INTO THE WORLD," Nya projected the thought deep into Bob's mind and resisted smiling when the man twitched. "TELL ME HOW MUCH MY MORTAL COMPENSATION IS DUE TO BE INCREASED."

Julia fixed her cold green eyes on his. "Do you really think this is an appropriate time to ask for a raise?" Her perfume, aromatic oils suspended in whale vomit, if he didn't miss his mark, both repulsed him and enticed him.

"IS IT NOT MY QUARTERLY REVIEW?"

"Of course it is, Nya. Relax," Bob said.

Julia asked, "How many times has HR needed to remind you about projecting dark realities into the minds of your coworkers?"

"THIS IS HOW MY PEOPLE SPEAK."

She didn't flinch. He met her unyielding eyes and bit back a snarl. He didn't let the sharp lines of her face, her blonde hair, or any other quality that might sway a mortal subject to the whims and desires of the mortal flesh distract him. What a terrible adversary.

"Seven," he said aloud.

"Make it eight," Julia said. "We need to talk about Daryl."

"I am not responsible for Daryl's weak mind." Nya concentrated on forming the words with his tongue and not his consciousness.

"You reduced the poor man to a gibbering husk," Bob countered. "Drive competitors insane, fine. Torment clients into signing purchase orders, and as long as the numbers are good, we can live with it. But your coworkers are your family."

"MY FAMILY EXISTS IN PLANES BEYOND MORTAL COMPREHENSION. THEY WOULD NOT BE UNABLE TO WITHSTAND MY VOICE."

Julia opened her plain black leather portfolio. "After Daryl's manager wrote you up and asked HR to conduct an investigation, you said in your report: 'I am the messenger of the Maelstrom, the Devouring Will made flesh.' You continued to say that you 'opened Daryl's eyes to the coming of the Storm whose dominion is madness and pain beyond comprehension.'" She leaned back and glared. "You can't make threats like that!"

Nya sought to explain. "He was to ensorcell my computer back to functionality. Even in the Maelstrom, we did not have the blue screen of death. Was his job not information technology? Was his task not to fix such issues so I could return to selling paper, as is my task?"

"But, madness and pain beyond comprehension?" Bob did not meet Nya's eyes.

"NOT EVEN THE CHAOS LORDS OF THE MAELSTROM USE MICROSOFT WORD. WHAT FRESH HELL IS THIS PLACE?"

"This place is Howel Percival Lomington, LLC," Bob said, "and we have a very favorable contract with Microsoft for our suite of productivity software."

"Bob, I think he was asking a rhetorical question."

"The HR witch is right."

Julia leaned forward, menacing. "Also, your coworkers have reported you for what is noted in your file as a 'persistent use of archaic disrespectful language.' You can't call me a 'witch!'" Julia slammed her hand on the table. "I'd also like to take this moment to remind you that 'trollop' and 'churl' are also inappropriate. Lastly, none of us can even figure out what 'ebien,' 'eibata,' or 'temum' mean, but your tone suggests they are disrespectful. I'm drawing a line in the sand on those too."

"YOU WOULD STEAL THE WORDS FROM MY TONGUE, HOW IS THAT NOT WITCHCRAFT?" Nya ground his teeth. The mortal coil he wore made violent expressions of impudent rage less dramatic than when he could lash out with tentacles of warped space and time.

"Given your history, this time there will be consequences," Julia said. "You will undergo seven hours of sensitivity training, as well as write a formal apology to Daryl, and the poor man's psychiatrist. For God's sake, we had to offer the psychiatrist a settlement just on account of the things Daryl said during therapy."

Nya met the she-devil's gaze, unwavering and cold in the flickering fluorescent light.

"YOU WOULD MAKE A GOOD SERVANT OF THE STORM. MY FATHER

WOULD WIELD YOU AS A GREAT FELLING BLADE TO REAP THE WHEAT OF THIS WORLD FOR THE FIRE."

"I think you're a valuable member of the team, too," Julia replied. "Don't be late for your first sensitivity session, seven one-hour sessions at five p.m. after the next seven workdays. Your first starts at five today in the Rolling Meadows conference room."

"FIVE? BUT WE HAVE AN OFFICE SOFTBALL GAME TONIGHT!"

"Well, they'll just have to manage without you," Julia said. "And stop with the despair projections. That was the whole point of this meeting."

"The infinite universes bend to a cold, dark, and hopeless end from which none will escape." Nya stood from his chair and towered over his seated adversary. "I have sales calls to make."

A line of white, the cord to his earbud, dangled just on the edge of Nya's vision. The dulcet tones of panpipes danced in his ears, distracting him from the endless rows and columns of sales figures that demanded his attention. He closed his eyes and thought of home, the deep places, the dark places where one could scream with wanton disregard of the clock, never attracting a noise complaint or eviction notices.

When he opened his eyes, the sales figures remained. A calendar with kittens frolicking with yarn hung on the wall of his cubicle. Eight days had passed since he clashed with human resources. He had endured his punishment, seven hours of droning from sensitivity counselors. He was the messenger of Maelstrom. It was his steadfast desire and mission to further the devolution of the mortal plane of existence into darkness, chaos, and entropy, and even he had hated those seven hours.

He took the last sip of too-cool coffee from his mug and frowned. He stood up and stalked away from his desk to the coffeepot, only to find it empty. He suppressed the urge to seek out the culprit who had failed to make a fresh pot to banish the scofflaw's psyche to wander in an unending graveyard of the soul. He began instead to make a fresh pot.

"Good afternoon, Nya," Marty, a short man from accounting

wearing a mustard-yellow short-sleeved dress shirt said as he walked up to the coffee station. "You heart New York, eh?"

"What?" He spun to face the man, coffeepot in hand.

"The—uh—the mug." Marty pointed at the white mug with a tiny red heart on it that Nya carried with him to the coffeepot.

"One day I will go to New York," Nya intoned emotionlessly, returning his attention to the coffee.

"Yeah, it's a cool place to visit."

"I will go there and bring sermons of the beyond to its masses. I will show them the prophecies men dare not speak of."

"Yeah, like a sales call presentation? I didn't know we were expanding into the New York market, but sure. That sounds like a great idea." Marty shifted his weight from foot to foot. "So, softball tonight? We need this game against IT. We're behind them in the standings. We've missed you out there."

"I will use my long arms and superior leverage," Nya promised, "to send that tiny white sphere into dimensions beyond the outfield wall."

"That's—yeah. That's the spirit. Hey, thanks for not, you know, doing that thing where you explode my mind with your voice."

"Sensitivity training." Nya flipped the switch on the coffee maker. "I am told that mortals lose their grip on reality when I speak directly into the depths of their soul. The trainer said your kind finds it 'unnerving.'"

"Something like that," Marty said. "Anyway, see you at the diamond."

Nya stood watching the dark coffee drip down into the pot, slowly filling the carafe with its bitter caffeinated bounty. He could wield nearly infinite power, and yet still he was at the mercy of this gadget taking its time with gurgles and bursts of steam to produce the nectar he needed to get through a long afternoon.

"I can't believe you talk to him," a soft feminine voice said from around a nearby corner. She spoke softly, but Nya's ears were far keener than most humans realized.

"Hey, Angela," Marty said. "He's a little odd, but he's not a bad guy."

"Have you seen Daryl?" Angela said. "He can barely feed himself anymore. I've been waiting for him to fix my email signature for weeks, and all the man does now is mutter about 'vagaries of infinite blackness' and some nonsense about panpipes."

"So maybe Nya went a little overboard. Tell me you're not annoyed by the IT guys every once in a while."

"Annoyed, maybe, but not enough to drive a man insane."

"He's a really good first baseman," Marty said. "And we've still got a chance to catch IT in the standings."

Nya filled his "I Heart NY" mug. Without putting the carafe down, he took a deep drink of the scalding hot coffee. The sensitivity trainer had also told him that drinking coffee that was obviously so hot that it would burn his coworkers was another "unnerving" trait. He frowned and added "wait for coffee to cool" to the list of things with power over him.

He raised the mug to his lips and blew on the surface of the coffee, gently dispersing the delicate tendrils of steam.

"Fine," Angela said. "Just tell me that at least you didn't tell him that we're going to Finnegan's after the game?"

"No, I figured the rest of you would want to ditch him, so I left that out."

Enraged, Nya hurled the carafe into the floor without regard for the scalding coffee or the broken glass. He stormed around the corner of the cubicles that separated him from Angela and Marty.

Angela's face paled and she backed away. A cubicle wall prevented her escape. Marty's face blanched. He looked as if his bladder might fail him—just as Daryl's had.

"MY EARS HEAR ALL THINGS! I AM GOOD ENOUGH FOR THE HITTING OF DINGERS FOR YOUR SOFTBALL TEAM, BUT NOT GOOD ENOUGH FOR THE MUTUAL CONSUMPTION OF ALCOHOL?"

"It's not like that, Nya," Marty said as he backed away. Angela cowered.

SIDNEY LUGO

"ANGELA, PREPARE TO CONFRONT THE DEPTHS OF THE UNSPOKEN PROPHECY."

Her eyes widened as she stared into the visions of dark inevitability he placed in her mind. With each passing second a chorus of unending pain—the majestic howls of souls lost to an eternity of torment—forced the sales floor from her vision. To Angela's fraying consciousness, each moment passed at an agonizing, languid pace. Nya allowed her to wallow in her despair and forced her into the embrace of an entropic universe in which all she had ever held dear withered into the void.

Angela's pupils dilated further, until they consumed her irises with inky blackness. The sweet cadences of her screams filled the office, lending the afternoon a peaceful calm.

Nya smiled and laughed. He cared not who might be unnerved by the earthly expression of his delight.

"Nya," Bob shouted over Angela's wailing as he came upon the scene. "Come on, man. We've talked about this."

The manager knelt by Angela's side, trying to comfort her, but Nya knew that she would never truly recover from the things he'd shown her.

"Perhaps if she underwent sensitivity training," Nya offered, "she'd know not to exclude a family member from recreation."

Marty slipped away around a corner of cubicles. Nya surveyed the office. People stood up, peering over cube walls with hesitant but implacable curiosity. He offered them all a glimpse of the darkness on the other side of the veil, for deep down, all wished for such visions.

"I'm going to have to write this up," Bob threatened.

Nya smiled. Angela's madness sustained him. It was time to test his strength against his most fearsome foe. "I long to join battle once more. Summon me the devil from human resources!"

# *The Minarets of An-Zabat*

*written by*

## *Jeremy TeGrotenhuis*

*illustrated by*

BRENDA RODRIGUEZ

---

### ABOUT THE AUTHOR

*Jeremy TeGrotenhuis is a writer from Eastern Washington State, where he grew up playing make-believe in the same desert that houses the most polluted nuclear waste site in America. He has lived in Beijing, where he studied Mandarin, and in Taipei, where he and his wife Hannah taught English. Currently he lives in Spokane, Washington, where he is pursuing a master's in teaching at Whitworth University, his undergraduate alma mater.*

*The first story Jeremy remembers writing was a mash-up of* Moonraker *and Brian Jacques's* Redwall, *which he wrote when he was too young to be watching* Moonraker, *and he has been writing ever since. His fiction has appeared in two anthologies from TWG Press,* Peak Heat *and* Night Market, *as well as in* Weird Sisters: Lilac City Fairy Tales Volume 3 *from Scablands Books,* Pirates & Ghosts *from Flame Tree Publishing, and in* Beneath Ceaseless Skies *magazine. He is currently revising a fantasy novel set in the same world as "The Minarets of An-Zabat" and finishing the first draft of another, and has half a dozen short stories out on submission at any given time.*

### ABOUT THE ILLUSTRATOR

*Brenda Rodriguez was born in Mexico, but moved to the US before her first birthday and has been here ever since. She started drawing as a child and has never stopped loving it. Brenda attributes her passion for character creation to her interest in video games. Her favorites include* The Legend of Zelda, Kingdom Hearts, *and* Final Fantasy. *She recalls being inspired by them at a young age as a child, and on throughout her life thereafter. To this day, she can thank Nintendo and*

*Square Enix for fueling her aspiration of getting into the entertainment industry as a character artist.*

*Brenda graduated in spring of 2017 with a degree in Computer Graphics Technology from Indiana University–Purdue University Indianapolis. She is now working as a freelance artist and polishing her portfolio to officially break into the industry.*

# *The Minarets of An-Zabat*

## 1

A lattice of silver whirlwinds spiraled up the minarets of An-Zabat. Each minaret was a narrow column holding up the dome of heaven. They numbered in the dozens and jutted from the earth at the heart of the city, rising above the rooftops of its tallest structures. Red banners, emblazoned with the Imperial tetragram, fluttered from the tips of those gilded spires. Each banner served to remind the people of An-Zabat, conquerors of the desert and the sky, that they had been conquered in turn.

I could never have imagined, at my first sight of An-Zabat, how the city would change me. Nor that I would cause those minarets to fall.

Crewmen struck all but the steering sail as the *Naphena's Blessing* coasted on its runner blades and into the elevated harbor. The ship's Windcaller breathed deeply and planted his feet wide apart. The whorled tattoos that covered his arms rippled as he worked his magic. He pushed the wind up and around into the steering sail, guiding the Windship to its moorings.

I tried and failed, not for the first time, to analyze the wake of power left by the Windcaller's magic. Like the sorcery I wielded as Hand of the Emperor, it was elegant and subtle. Yet where Imperial sorcery was filtered and transmitted through the Emperor himself, Windcalling was raw and wild like the Nayeni shamanism that my grandmother had taught. I was arrogant, and fully aware of my arrogance, to imagine myself unraveling the mysteries of Windcalling over the course of a single voyage.

The Windcallers had, after all, shrugged off the Empire's every attempt to steal their secrets.

Perhaps that should have daunted me.

It only piqued my fascination.

A palanquin carried me toward the Imperial Citadel at the heart of An-Zabat. I craned my neck out the window to soak in the sights, smells, and sounds of my new home. The people were bronze-skinned and amber eyed. Their hair had been tinted yellow by the sun, a shade that I had never seen before. Gawkish, hunch-backed dromedaries carried luggage and pulled carts through the crowds. Rich spices and heady perfumes filled the air to mask the smell of so many people and animals crowded beneath the desert sun.

Every few blocks we passed a building blown apart by chemical grenades, or a home scored and blackened by Sienese battle-sorcery. An-Zabat was a vibrant city, but it bore the lingering scars of conquest.

At the center of the city stood a statue of Naphena, the winged goddess of the Great Oasis, carved in sandstone and gilt with silver, rubies, and sapphires. Water that sparkled in the heat of early afternoon cascaded from an urn cradled in her arms. It splashed in the basin of the oasis at her feet, where children played in the clear, cool shallows.

Around the oasis, merchants hawked goods imported from throughout the Empire: shimmering silks and brightly feathered birds, sparkling gems and luxurious wines. Customers haggled with merchants in quick, clipped phrases while tumblers and magicians performed to thunderous applause and a rain of coins. The largest crowd surrounded a woman who spun and leaped in stunning arcs as she sent a pair of scarves fluttering from hand to hand.

I watched her for a dozen heartbeats. As she danced, power rippled from her fingers to pull the wind along the length of her scarves. Their silver embroidery caught the sun as they fluttered through the air.

The Windcallers, it seemed, used their magic for more than war and Windships.

My palanquin left the bazaar and approached the high sandstone walls of the citadel, which were scarred in places by the fractal gouges left by Sienese battle-sorcery. Guards walked the battlements carrying heavy crossbows and wearing bandoleers of grenades.

I had never seen a grenade in use, but my grandmother had told me stories. Trees shattered into splinters that whistled through the air, homes and temples reduced to piles of ash. My father had hired Sienese tutors to provide my education, but my grandmother had taught lessons of her own. She never let me forget how his people came to her country.

All in the past, now. Here I was, successful beyond my father's most fervent wish, transplanted to a foreign country in the service of the Empire. I resolved to focus on the present, and on the future, not on the stories of an old woman who filled my mind with nothing but confusion.

A guard waved my palanquin through the heavy stone gates. The citadel had once been the palace and pleasure garden of An-Zabat's merchant princes. Its new residents had altered it to suit their taste.

Winding canals flowed through the courtyard, feeding shallow ponds. Wooden pavilions in the Sienese style stood throughout a sculpted landscape of grassy hills, bamboo groves, and porous limestone boulders dredged from distant lakes. Pink-plumed herons imported from Southern Sien waded among lilies. The faintest echoes of the bazaar drifted through the air, but deeper into the garden there was silence. After the noisy, dusty, crowded streets of An-Zabat, the pastoral quiet of the garden put me off balance.

A steward led me to the Pavilion of Soaring Verse and announced my arrival. Three men lounged on couches around a narrow, artificial stream that spiraled through the pavilion. An-Zabati servant boys waved fans of peacock feathers while others filled cups with mild plum wine. These they floated on paper rafts down the stream. The lounging officials plucked them from the waters to sip at their leisure.

I knew of these men by reputation, and introductions were swiftly made. Hand Cinder wore dark-blue robes embroidered with gold thread meant to imitate plates of armor. Despite his militant posture and thick jaw, he had an easy smile. Hand Alabaster watched me coldly from behind brass-rimmed spectacles as I lowered myself to a fourth couch. He wore his hair long and unbraided in a style that was fashionable in the Northern Capital, where I had first landed on the mainland after leaving my island home.

Voice Rill wore robes of Imperial Red, undecorated, and his head was shaved. The Imperial tetragram that scarred my left hand and Cinder's and Alabaster's right had been branded above the bridge of his nose. It glimmered like fractured glass. Power rippled from it continuously, maintaining the link between the Emperor and our far corner of his domain.

"Welcome to An-Zabat, Hand Alder," said Voice Rill as I took a seat. "We have been composing poetry in turns. A bit of idleness in the heat of the afternoon, and an opportunity to flex our literary muscles."

"Not that there is much demand for court poetry in An-Zabat," said Hand Cinder. He grinned at Alabaster. "One has to keep the dream of reassignment alive, eh, young Alabaster?"

Hand Alabaster rolled his eyes and adjusted his spectacles.

"I believe it was your turn to recite, was it not?" said Rill.

Alabaster straightened. As he gathered his thoughts, Rill explained the rules of their contest. Each man recited a poem in turn. If the others approved of the poem, they took the next cup to float by on the artificial stream. If they did not, for whatever reason, they let the cup pass.

I began to question the reasonableness of spending the afternoon at a drinking game, but shut my mouth. My career depended upon working with these men. As the first Hand of the Emperor descended from Nayeni blood, the path to success and power would not be made easy for me. I told myself that they were making a minor festival of my arrival, and that I should be flattered.

A paper fan snapped open in Alabaster's fingers. Fashionable poets always performed with their faces obscured. Cued by Alabaster's fan, the servants set about preparing the cups and paper rafts while Alabaster began his recitation:

*The heron leaps from his pool, taking flight,*
*Broad wings flash silver in the sun,*
*My hand skips across the page, smearing ink*
*I dip my brush with thoughts of home.*

He snapped the fan shut. Rill took a cup. I reached for one as well. The poem derived some of its imagery from the classics, but it was evocative.

Alabaster frowned at me as I brought the cup to my lips.

"You use your left hand," he said, narrowing his eyes. "And it is sealed instead of your right. Why?"

Paranoia bubbled up, but I tamped it back down. Instinct—hammered into my skull by my grandmother's constant warnings—told me to keep my scars hidden from anyone who might know anything of magic. But I had learned.

The Sienese had felt the bite of Nayeni shamanism wielded against them, but they had never learned its secrets. Shamans hid their own corpses from prying Sienese sorcerers by self-immolation or by veering into the shape of a beast as they died. If I used shamanism around these men, they would see the rippling patterns of magic and know my secret. But they would not recognize the mark of power my grandmother had carved into my palm.

"It is a disfigurement from my youth," I said. "A teacup shattered in my hand."

Alabaster leaned forward to examine my scars.

"The Left-Handed Easterling," Cinder said. "You're notorious. The first Nayeni to rise to Hand of the Emperor."

"Nayeni on my mother's side," I said, trying to sound flippant, but conscious as I had always been of the reddish tint to my skin, the wave in my hair.

"I fought in the conquest of Nayen," Hand Cinder went on as though I had not spoken. "Voice Rill tells us there are still skirmishes with bandits in the highlands. Ha! Is it really that hard to put down a few gangs of belligerent savages? Voice Golden-Finch and Hand Usher have bungled that province, haven't they?"

"The rebels are resilient, it is true." I struggled to keep my face bright, though shadowed thoughts came unbidden to my mind. Thoughts of Oriole, of our campaign into the highlands, of how I had led him to his death. "Though 'bungled' seems an unkind word."

"Gentlemen, please," Rill said. He inclined his head, as my tutor Koro Ha had often done when chiding me. I became painfully aware of my own anger, the savagery in my voice. My hands curled in my lap. Hands tinted red by savage blood. Easterling blood.

"Hand Cinder," Rill went on, "you did not take a cup."

Cinder frowned at the sudden change of subject. "It was his third composition in a row about homesickness."

"You oppose the theme?" Alabaster peered over the rim of his glasses.

"Yes. And the imagery was overwrought."

Alabaster glared at Cinder, then looked to Rill for support. The Voice bobbed his head thoughtfully from side to side.

"I don't agree, Cinder. I thought it was lovely. What did you think, Hand Alder?"

Alabaster struck me as a self-indulgent ponce, but Cinder was a boor. I had to work with both of them.

"If I had heard two similar poems already, I might share Hand Cinder's opinion." I kept my voice calm and my tone contemplative. I had lost composure for only a moment. It was still possible to save face. "However, I thought this composition stood on its own quite well."

"Pfa!" Hand Cinder waved a hand. "You're only saying that so you won't insult him!"

"Oh, he couldn't possibly think it had real merit!" Alabaster frowned icily at Cinder, then smiled warmly at me. "Thank you for the compliment, Hand Alder. Would you like to recite next?"

"Yes!" Cinder cried. "Let's hear what the Easterling can do!"

I balked, and not only because Cinder had twice used that slur. My tutors and I had passed countless hours composing poetry back and forth, but I had already humiliated myself in front of these important men. Their sudden attention struck all I knew of verse and meter from my mind.

What sort of poetry did they expect from an Easterling?

They were growing impatient. The servants were already preparing the next batch of paper boats. I blurted:

*Sweet plum trickles from the bottle lip . . .*

My mouth hung open. It was childish to derive an image from something happening before my eyes. The servants stared at me as they poured, wondering if I had finished. I groped for the next word, the next phrase.

*Hearth fire warms our frigid bones,*
*New companions on the mountain road,*
*Come and sit, and share my wine.*

To my astonishment they all took cups. Alabaster held his for a moment.

"The rhythm was a little odd," he muttered, then drank.

We passed the rest of the afternoon drinking and chatting and criticizing each other's poetry. By the end I felt comfortable enough to let my cup pass for a meaningless verse about butterflies that Voice Rill had drunkenly stammered.

Servants brought a traditional Sienese meal at nightfall: pork dumplings, fire-pepper beef, five-spice chicken, wheat noodles with wood-ear mushrooms, and young cabbage stir-fried in garlic. I ate, then excused myself. A young man named Khin, who was to be my personal steward in the citadel, showed me to my rooms. They were as spacious as my father's reception hall.

I had long ago abandoned the habit of reciting my grandmother's teachings and practicing the Nayeni Iron Dance, but in the privacy of my quarters I felt the urge that night. Perhaps a reaction to the vertigo of having been thrust into a new place and an unfamiliar role. Or simple homesickness.

Drunk as I was, I fell into the first forms of the Iron Dance before I knew what I was doing. After a dozen steps I let my arms fall slack. Foolishness was all it was. Foolish to cling to traditions that had never really felt my own. Foolish, when they were forbidden by the very Empire I served.

If Cinder caught me at such practice, he would be vindicated. I would be an Easterling in truth.

A creeping fear gripped me. I checked to be sure the seals on my luggage were intact, most importantly the black trunk with its three iron locks. Though nothing seemed to have been opened, my paranoia was not satisfied. I searched through layers of documents and scrolls. Only when I found the small, unassuming brush case in which I kept my grandmother's knife and saw that the wax seal on its latch was still intact could I relax.

I sighed, repacked everything, locked and sealed the black trunk, and flopped onto my bed. I was exhausted from my long journey, and I had drunk a few too many cups of wine. That was all it was. The foolishness of the drunk and the tired. What I needed was rest before I began my work as the Emperor's Hand.

## 2

Though I awoke with a pounding hangover, I wasted no time nursing it. I felt the weight of my responsibilities as the first Hand of the Emperor from Nayen. My actions would reflect not only on me, but on every Nayeni in the civil service. If I distinguished myself, I could disprove the notion that the Nayeni were nothing more than savages, that Nayeni blood was a hindrance and red skin the sign of a slower, more bestial mind.

If I embarrassed myself, those who called me Easterling would shake their heads and smile and say, "You see? Their blood is weak, unfit to serve."

I would serve well, dispel the myth of the savage Easterling, and earn a position as a scholar in the Imperial Academy. There I would be free to sate my curiosity among the brightest and most learned minds in the Empire, and never again would I have to worry about rebel uprisings or administrative minutia. A distant dream, but a motivating one.

After a light breakfast of boiled eggs, dried mango, and ginseng tea, I sought out Voice Rill. I found him in the Gazing Upon Lilies pavilion, which had been built in the center of the largest pond in the citadel. Ripples of power wafted from his forehead and streamed to the East toward the Sienese heartland. I waited on the pavilion's bridge while he made his report and received instructions from the Emperor. The ripples slowed, then faded. A servant came to fetch me.

"You impressed Hand Alabaster last night," Rill said when I joined him.

"Thank you, Voice Rill," I said, and could not help but add, "there is a reason I was selected as Hand of the Emperor. I am eager to begin my work."

Rill stroked his cheeks and nodded, squinting. The silvery tetragram branded upon his forehead rippled and glimmered like the surface of the pond.

"Well, let us be about it, then."

My role, Voice Rill explained, was to serve as Minster of Trade in An-Zabat. This entailed the setting and collection of tariffs and taxes, the monitoring of weights and measures, the management of mineral rights to the Batir Waste, and other basic administrative duties. My most important task, however, was to maintain the tenuous relationship between the Windcallers and the Sienese merchants who relied upon their Windships.

"The Batir Waste devours caravans," Rill said as he led me to the secluded Wind Through Grass pavilion, which would be my office. "Two of every three soldiers who marched from Sien to conquer this city died of thirst. Without the Windcallers, there is no trade in An-Zabat."

I felt a thrill of anticipation. To do my duty well I would have to learn as much as I could about the Windcallers, and of everything I had seen in An-Zabat, they were most fascinating.

One question nagged at me, however. "Voice Rill," I asked, "I do not want to seem insolent, but why are the Windcallers permitted their autonomy? In every other region of the Empire, native magic has either been absorbed into the Canon or eradicated."

Rill paused for a moment before answering. "Without trade, An-Zabat is unsustainable. A few fields grow in the green belt watered by the Great Oasis, but the city has long swelled beyond the ability to feed itself. An-Zabat was once little more than a watering hole for the nomads of the Batir Waste, a place to rest and trade. Now it serves to link the Empire to the distant lands of the West, and there is great wealth to be had in such trade. Yet without the Windcallers and their ships, the waste cannot be crossed.

"We have tried the ordinary methods to induct their magic into the Canon. Capturing and interrogating Windcallers, and so on. No Windships sailed from An-Zabat for a year, and the city nearly starved. Someday we will learn their secrets. For the time being, you will have to negotiate with them, though it is a blight upon the Empire's pride."

"I will not fail the Empire," I said.

Rill smiled at me. "We do not expect you to."

My office was laden with shelves and cabinets that sagged beneath the weight of scrolls, books, and loosely bound documents. A landscape painting depicting the verdant mountains of Southern Sien hung in the only unoccupied stretch of wall. A desk stood beneath the north-facing window. Its few accoutrements included a bell for calling the servants, a small turtle of carved amber, heavy jade paperweights engraved with a pattern of crawling vines, and a slate bowl for grinding ink. The scholarly smell of paper and old incense hung in the air.

My own private Academy. A poor substitute for the real thing, of course.

"Your predecessor was a meticulous records keeper," Voice Rill said with a grandfatherly smile. "You should have no trouble picking up the thread."

As I studied the ledgers, I soon saw that Voice Rill had not exaggerated. Almost all of An-Zabat's wealth came from tariffs and speculation on luxury items traversing the Batir Waste. The Windships brought goods to the city, exchanged them, and set off again. As Minister of Trade, I stood at the center of that financial whirlwind. I had to keep it spinning—had to make it spin faster, and more expansively, if I could—and it only spun by the good grace of the Windcallers.

Voice Rill had not told me the reason for my predecessor's dismissal as Minister of Trade, but in the ledgers I saw the evidence of his ineptitude. Unlike him, I would control the Windcallers. I would ensure the stability and wealth of An-Zabat. I would eliminate this stain on the Empire's pride.

I would do my duty. I would distinguish myself and become known as more than the Left-Handed Easterling.

I was astonishingly naive.

## 3

Weeks passed. Time was becoming distended, my life an endless stream of documents to be deciphered. The sun was setting, and that alone told me that I had been at work too long. That, and my growling stomach. I rang the bell on my desk to call Khin, my steward.

"I would like a meal brought to my office."

"That can be arranged, Your Excellence," said Khin. "However, Hand Alabaster has sent several messages inviting you to dine with him this evening."

"He has?" I looked up from the ledgers. "Why did no one tell me?"

"Voice Rill instructed the staff that you were not to be disturbed, Your Excellence. I can inform Hand Alabaster that you would prefer—"

"No, no. Send a runner to let him know I am on my way," I said, drying and stowing my brushes and returning documents to their shelves.

Standing stones lined the path to the Golden Fortune pavilion, which was nestled beneath a high cliff of basalt columns brought by Windship from Western Sien. The pavilion was built of poplar beams in the classical style, with flanged roofs and whitewashed walls. Incense wafted from one of the windows. Its scent was undercut by the rich, savory smells of the meal Hand Alabaster's servants had prepared.

Alabaster rose to greet me. His office was arranged much as mine was, though the art hanging between his shelves was solemn and melancholy, full of fog and harsh geometry.

"What do you think of your new home?" Hand Alabaster asked as we settled into our seats and the servants filled our cups.

"The little I saw of it on the way to the citadel intrigued me," I said. "Though I must admit the weight and complexity of my responsibilities is daunting."

Alabaster frowned quizzically over the rim of his teacup.

"I meant the garden, Hand Alder," he said. "You strike me as a literary sort—more so than Cinder, certainly. As Minister of Culture, I have put a great deal of effort into the garden."

"Oh, yes, of course," I said, then sipped my tea while I composed my thoughts. "Its design is more classical than the garden in which I sat for my examinations in Nayen. That garden closely adhered to the mountainous landscape of the island, with natural slopes and pools preserved rather than artificial ones constructed."

Alabaster polished his spectacles and stared at me with piercing eyes. "Would you have me make a garden out of sand and rocks?"

"Oh, your method is clearly superior here in An-Zabat," I said, realizing that I had offended him. "You must forgive me. The only garden I knew before my examination was my father's, and he was only a merchant."

"How disappointing," Alabaster muttered, then replaced his spectacles and picked up his ivory eating sticks.

"I want us to be friends, Alder," he said, picking at the food. "Voice Rill is a respectable man, but the gulf of rank between us is too wide for friendship. Cinder is a militant brute. We can work together, but he and I will never be companions."

"Gladly, Alabaster," I said. "Though I fear I will have little time to spend with you. Dealing with the Windcallers seems no easy task."

Alabaster waved dismissively and filled my cup. "No easy task, but not one to occupy much of your time. There is nothing to be done." His voice grew more heated as he spoke. "They are an incorrigible lot."

Alabaster leaned back in his chair. He removed his spectacles and patted his brow with a handkerchief, then gazed out the window as he straightened them on his nose.

"Enough talk of this infernal province," he said, and drained his wine cup. He wiped his mouth, then poured another. "Tell me about yourself, Alder. We should know each other if we are to be friends."

Before long I felt confident in my understanding of An-Zabat's mercantile affairs and began to craft policy. I levied new taxes on grain imports and used that income to refill the Imperial silos. The Windcallers would not be able to starve us into submission, should they oppose any of my reforms.

Alabaster and I continued our companionable meetings. Often he invited me to dine in the Abundant Nectar banquet hall, where a cloud of hummingbirds fluttered among hanging baskets of fluted snapdragons. After a few weeks he began to show me excerpts from the letters he received from his betrothed.

"Do her lines seem perfunctory, to you?" he would ask, handing me a poem she had composed.

I always reassured him, though having never been party to any serious romance, I felt out of my depth.

By the end of my second month in An-Zabat, my work had fallen into a consistent rhythm. Each morning I reviewed Voice Rill's mercantile reports, sent price and value adjustments to the city office of weights and measures, and read correspondences from the minor officials of An-Zabat's bureaucracy. After a light lunch in my office, I wrote a few messages to my subordinates throughout the city, and by late afternoon, I had finished with my duties. This left me with substantially more free time than I had anticipated, and I could only spend so many hours with moony, lovesick Alabaster.

For a Minister of Trade to be so underworked seems absurd, in retrospect. My schedule was too routine, too simple and boring. An-Zabat was a thriving port, yet the business that crossed my desk barely changed from week to week. My insatiable curiosity was given nothing to focus on, left alone to drift toward thoughts of the city beyond the walls of the citadel. The pressure of boredom built and built, like alcohol left to ferment too long, ready to burst at the slightest provocation.

One day, my noon meal was interrupted by the familiar hiss and crack of Imperial battle-sorcery.

"It is only Hand Cinder at drills," Khin assured me as he refilled the cup of tea that I had spilled.

Intrigued by this disruption of my usual routine, I rushed to finish my meal and followed the rhythmic cracks and hisses to an archery range near the southernmost wall of the citadel. The iron scales of Cinder's armor flashed in the sun as he raced back and forth across the archer's line, leaping into the air and lashing out with a whip of crackling yellow lightning that spilled from his hand.

"Hand Alder," he said as I approached. "Have you dug yourself free of today's paperwork?"

"Not yet," I said. "Though what remains is hardly urgent. I

can finish it tonight, but I could not resist my curiosity when I heard sorcery in the garden."

"Part of our duty is to keep sharp," he said, idly flipping the whip that flowed out from the tetragram in his palm. "Rill and Alabaster indulge themselves in literature and the arts. They forget that we are soldiers first." The whip disappeared with a snap as he relaxed his hand. "I spend my free afternoons here, if not in the company of my lovely wife. When did you last practice your sorcery?"

"During my apprenticeship with Hand Usher," I said thinking of Oriole, dead on the blood-soaked ground.

Cinder crossed his arms and cocked a disapproving eyebrow.

"I did not think An-Zabat a warzone," I said, unwilling to tell Cinder that I hoped never to see battle again. "It was conquered a decade ago."

"There is a ceasefire," Cinder said. "But until the Windcallers are brought to heel, An-Zabat is at war. Go on." He gestured toward the target dummies. "Even a neglected blade can still be sharpened. Show me what you can do."

I opened my hand and drew forth the contained, orderly magic of the Empire, filtered through the Imperial Canon, transmitted by the Voices and granted by the will of the Emperor alone. Bright as mercury, given shape by the structures of Sienese power. My every hair stood on end. Magic surged through me, a ripple in my blood and bone. Lightning crackled from the tetragram branded on my left hand and tore through one of the targets.

Cinder was not impressed. I had displayed only the gathering and release of power, without nuance, without thought. I moved on to more complex sorcery.

Rather than a bolt of brute force, I made my sorcery into a liquid blade that hissed as it poured from my hand. Thin slices of a dummy's limbs arced through the air.

After days and weeks of nothing but paperwork and idle, indulgent conversation with Hand Alabaster, the current of physical release pulled me along. I threw darts one at a time—as my grandmother had first taught me to hurl fire—drilling hole after hole through the dummy until it collapsed.

The scent of ozone and charred wool hung over the archery range. My breath came heavily. Sweat soaked my scholar's robes.

"You say you have been Hand for only three years?" Cinder said. He squeezed my shoulder and grinned. "I would have believed a decade. Sorcery comes as naturally to you as poetry, it seems. Are all Easterlings so gifted?"

I did not tell him that I had been practicing magic since my tenth birthday, when my grandmother carved power and a shaman's name into my right hand. I did not tell him that the first spell I ever cast had left me a twisted creature halfway between man and eagle-hawk. I did not tell him that I cultivated skill out of caution against ever suffering such a fate again.

I did not tell him these things. Some of them he already knew.

Instead we said nothing, and drank stream-chilled plum wine and watched the herons jab their beaks among the lilies.

I did not go to the archery range again. Paranoia whispered in the back of my mind. Cinder knew, it said, that I could not possibly have become so adept at sorcery in only three years.

When we'd first met, he'd called me Easterling. He said that he had heard of me. I was notorious simply because of my blood, because no Nayeni had been Hand of the Emperor before me. My scarred hand, my unusual skill, these only stoked suspicions that Cinder carried deep in his heart. There was no trust between us, and there could be no friendship.

Hand Alabaster was no better company. I grew exhausted by his endless melancholy over his distant betrothed. Worse, I began to suspect that he did nothing all day but compose verse for her. As Minister of Culture, he should have been occupied with the creation of An-Zabat's education system. Yet when I visited his office, I saw only small packages of correspondence, less than a tenth of what I dealt with each morning.

"Is this all you do?" I asked him one evening in the Golden

Fortune pavilion while he read and re-read aloud a lovelorn couplet.

"Excuse me?" He peered over the top of his spectacles.

"How is the city's cultural development?" I said, rising from my seat at the table to loom over him. "How many tutors have you brought to An-Zabat? Which promising students are you considering for the first examinations?"

"What does it matter whether there are examinations in this wretched city?" Alabaster said coldly. "These provincial barbarians will never rival the scholars of Sien."

"Nayen was once such a province," I said.

He shrugged and said, "It still is."

Heat rose in my face, and I clenched my jaw shut. I left without a word. He did not call after me, nor did he ever apologize.

My life became lonesome drudgery. Every day I walked from my rooms to my office and back again, a pattern broken only by the occasional solitary wander through the garden. At times the beauty of the garden cheered me, but more often it only deepened my misery. The effort and resources put into maintaining the citadel gardens might have been used to expand the city's agricultural production, to weaken the Windcallers' grip.

An-Zabat would never thrive while ruled from within this poor simulacrum of the Sienese heartland. Alabaster, Cinder, and Rill were fools, willfully ignorant of the city they ruled. Their methods were flawed. I would never distinguish myself by following their example.

"Steward Khin, I wish to go out into the city," I said one afternoon while the servants cleared away the remnant of my noon meal.

Khin's impeccable composure faltered. "Your Excellence, I might arrange a palanquin tour through the Sienese Quarter, if you would like," he said.

"No. I will learn nothing from behind the window of a palanquin."

"A walking tour, then, under guard—"

"I will go out on my own."

Khin stared at me for a moment, stiffening while he tried to find the politest way to express his confusion and concern. "That would be highly unusual, Your Excellence," he said. "And dangerous. There are thieves and beggars, and those who would strike you down simply for being Sienese."

"I am Nayeni as well," I said. "Lend me some old work clothes, and I can disguise myself as one of the servants. The An-Zabati do not know my face."

"There are no Nayeni servants in the citadel."

"Something else the An-Zabati do not know."

"Hand Alder, I truly must advise against—"

"If you will not help me, I will muss one of my older suits or fashion a robe from a bed sheet."

He cringed at the mention of a ruined bed sheet.

"Very well, Your Excellence," he said at last. "Only promise me you will return before nightfall."

I promised, intending only to stretch my legs, indulge my curiosity a bit, and clear my head of the sluggish fog that had filled it these past weeks. While I waited for his return, I painted the palm of my left hand with clay. The An-Zabati would not know me, but they would recognize the Imperial tetragram from the banners that fluttered on their minarets. Khin brought me a pair of loose-fitting trousers and a simple caftan.

"Tell no one where I have gone," I said as he led me to the servants' gate.

"As you command, Your Excellence," Khin said sullenly.

"I'll make it up to you," I said, and slipped out into the city.

Though the An-Zabati would not recognize me, there were Imperial guards who might. Feeling anxious, I ducked into a secluded alleyway to deepen my disguise.

With a breath to steel myself, I wove power with my right hand and passed it over my face. I only thickened my brows and loosened the skin around my mouth and eyes, but it was enough. Not even my own mother would have known me—nor my tutor, who knew me better—and the magic I had worked would leave only the slightest wake.

Though the spell was simple and the changes to my body only slight, I shivered as I fixed them in place. I still had nightmares of the time when I first tried to emulate my grandmother's sorcery. Stunted, brittle-boned limbs saggy with human skin, pinioned with half-formed feathers. Muscles hunched and knotted and unsure of whether to walk or fly, unable to do either. A mouth hard and jutting, and vocal chords that made no sound but a pitiful hiss.

Shaking off these memories, I left the alleyway and headed toward the Great Oasis and its bazaar.

A cascade of sound washed over me. Raised voices haggled over prices, crowds cheered for performers, carts clattered down the street, all mingled with the low roar of the waterfall pouring from Naphena's urn. Smells followed—dry-spiced meats, the tang of oil and salt and sugar, of herds and sweat and excrement. It was chaotic, but after weeks of drudgery, chaos was just the tonic I needed.

My mood brightened at once, and I set about exploring the bazaar. I began my immersion into An-Zabati culture with a survey of its food. First, lamb dry-rubbed with black pepper and fire-roasted till juices dripped down the skewer. Then a cup of brined olives that stung my nose. I was working my way through a bag of honey-candied dates when I saw the dancer.

Her silken scarves glimmered in the sun, even brighter than the coins scattered at her feet. She wore a simple jerkin and the loose-fitting trousers common in An-Zabat, with a few stitches of silver embroidery at the cuffs. Her hair bounced in oiled ringlets as she leaped and spun, but no matter how graceful her movements were, she would never rival her scarves.

Ripples of power—faint, but unmistakable—flowed in the wake of those scarves. As her hands spun, they pulled the scarves to-and-fro on strings of sorcery. The backs of her fingers were marked with the spiral tattoos of a Windcaller.

BRENDA RODRIGUEZ

As once I had studied the ripples of my grandmother's power, now I studied this dancer as she leaped and twirled and coaxed her scarves.

The bazaar began to empty. The sky turned from sapphire blue to deep maroon as the midday heat gave way to the crisp cool of evening, and it slowly dawned on me that I had been watching the dancer for hours. Feeling conspicuous, and remembering Khin's insistence that I be back by nightfall, I retreated toward the citadel. I was nearly to the servants' gate when an iron grip wrapped my upper arms, dragged me into an alleyway, and thrust my face against a wall.

"Please," I stammered. "Take my purse, I'm only a servant!"

I could have fought off my attacker with battle-sorcery, but I would have to explain such an outburst of power to Voice Rill. I doubted he would approve of my sneaking out into the city.

"Do all servants of the Sienese wield magic?"

The voice was feminine, and I realized with a start that no hands touched me, only thick bands of whirling air.

I craned my neck for a glimpse of the dancer. Her hands were splayed wide, no longer coaxing her scarves but sending the wind to grip and hold me.

"I can see the power dripping from you. Some kind of illusion," she said. "You are a spy."

"Only a servant," I insisted. "Please, let me go, I can explain myself."

"Explain first."

"I am Nayeni," I said. I could not tell her that I was Hand of the Emperor. I doubted she had much love for her conquerors. "The Sienese came to my homeland a generation ago. They outlawed our magic, but my grandmother kept it alive and taught me. I rarely use it, but I wanted to see your city. I disguised myself for fear that someone would recognize me. We are not supposed to leave the citadel."

She considered my half-truths. "Show me the mark of your power."

"Here, on my right hand."

She tightened the bands of wind that held me and stepped forward. I opened my hand to show the scars my grandmother had carved.

"How have you kept this secret?" she said.

"The Sienese never learned our magic," I said. "I tell them that I hurt myself as a boy, and they believe me."

"I will not be so easily fooled. Release your spell, Nayeni, and perhaps I will release you."

A shiver passed through me as my face returned to its natural form, leaving behind only an itch around my eyes. The wind holding my wrists faded. I slumped against the wall. The dancer took a step back. Even standing still, the lines of her body were graceful.

"You saw my power, as I saw yours," she said. "It is no secret. The Sienese dogs see our Windshaping in the harbor every day. They tried to steal it, once. They will not try so brazenly again. But they are not above deceit. Forgive me for suspecting you."

"No, you should forgive me," I said. "I understand my own magic incompletely. I thought, perhaps, that by watching your power I might find some insight into my own."

Another half-truth, but she seemed to believe. She folded her arms over her breasts and stepped toward me. My breath caught. It came back perfumed. She smelled of honey, and lavender, and salt.

"Do you hate them?" she asked. My eyes snapped up to meet hers. They were dark, but flecked with amber like specks of desert sand.

"They conquered my homeland," I said, too trapped in her gaze to construct any subtlety. "They destroyed what they could not use."

She stepped away, nodding slowly. "They will do the same here, Nayeni," she said. "I am Winddancing Atar. What are you called?"

"The Sienese call me Alder, but my grandmother named me Foolish Cur."

She stared at me, then grinned, then began to laugh. We were speaking An-Zabati, and I worried for a moment that my Nayeni name did not translate well, or that it held some coarse meaning in her language. I decided it did not matter. My grandmother had meant the name as an insult. And as a reminder.

"I think I will call you Nayeni." She covered her mouth to hide the last few giggles. "You are the first I have met, perhaps the first of your kind in this city, so it is fitting."

She glanced at the setting sun. "Nayeni, there is somewhere I must go. You say you hate Sien?"

I nodded, because I knew she wanted me to, and because I sensed an invitation in her voice and did not want to leave her.

"Come with me," she said and grasped my right wrist. "Maybe you are right. Maybe you can learn something of your magic by learning ours."

As we left the Great Oasis and the bazaar, An-Zabat became a tangled warren of narrow streets and stunted alleyways. My heart raced as Atar led me by the hand. Her skin was cool, and when the breeze tousled her hair it carried her scent. Honey. Lavender. Salt. I fought off intoxication and tried to count the turns.

Atar led me to a heavy door at the end of an alleyway, then down and into catacombs.

I lost all sense of direction in that maze of branching corridors. The light from Atar's dim lantern hardly pierced the deep shadows around us. I forgot entirely the excitement of our sudden courtship which now struck me as far too sudden and hardly a proper courtship. Where was she leading me? Had she ever even said? I had been lured by sex, but even more by the promise of secret knowledge. All I could think of now were knives in the dark.

The sudden, mad impulse to escape nearly overwhelmed me. I could easily strike from behind and break free of Atar, but what then? I could conjure flame for light, but in my rising panic I had lost track of our turnings through the labyrinth.

"How much farther?" I grappled with the fear in my voice. "I cannot be gone too long. One of my masters may call for me."

Without answering she led me to a doorway. I expected a cramped underground room—bedecked, perhaps, in the furniture and instruments of torture, stained with the blood of captured Sienese. Instead the first stars of night and a full moon greeted us. The rhythm of reed-pipe, sitar, and drum echoed up from a sandstone canyon below, where men and women formed a ring around a lone figure who leaped and spun to the music.

"This is the Valley of Rulers." Atar led me down toward the group. "The old kings of An-Zabat dwell here," she said, and I saw that the walls of the canyon were speckled with round, handle-less doors of stone too thick for any man to move.

A continual stream of wind flowed through the canyon. I followed it with my eyes and saw the glow of An-Zabat and its tall, silhouetted spires. We were much farther from the city than I had imagined. The panic that had been put to rest by the sight of the sky rose within me again.

What was I going to do? Flee across the open desert? I could never escape these people, who I suspected were all Windcallers of one fashion or another. One avenue of escape lay open. A magic I had only used once, and nearly left myself a twisted horror.

My grandmother could not save me if I failed.

If I succeeded, Voice Rill and the Hands of the Emperor would feel the rippling wake of my power. It was not a simple feat to change from one thing into another, shedding mass and form. They would feel the ripples, and they would know my secret.

Atar smiled at me. Perhaps our whirlwind romance had not been a ploy, if romance it was. The way her eyes sparkled and her dimples creased when she smiled said it must have been, but I knew so little of women.

A man greeted us. His arms were burly and covered in tattoos. A Windcaller, but gray-haired and past his prime.

"What brings you to the circle?" he raised his voice over the beating drums.

"A cool wind promised water," Atar answered.

He nodded. "All things flow to An-Zabat." His eyes flicked to me with an unspoken question.

"New feet for the dance," Atar said.

"He is foreign."

"He is Nayeni," she countered. "The Empire crushed his people, as it strives to crush ours. And he has magic of his own to share."

The Windcaller regarded me again, seeing for the first time that my skin was dark. Not as dark as his, and my hair was straighter and my eyes lighter than any An-Zabati, but dark, still, unlike the conquerors.

"If he dances, he can stay," the Windcaller said.

"He will dance, Katiz," Atar assured him.

With a last, lingering stare, he returned to his place in the circle. In its center a woman leaped in a flash of bangles. She cast long shadows in the mingled light of moon and torch.

"Katiz puts on a gruff show for newcomers," Atar said as she led me, still holding my hand, to an empty place in the gathering where we could see the dancers clearly. "You can dance, can't you?"

"What if I can't?" I said with a grin. "This seems like something we should have discussed earlier."

Whirlwind romance, however, did not give much time for conversations about cultural difference.

Atar tilted her head and smiled. "Are you telling me you can't?"

In Sien, men did not dance. Dancing was a tool for women, a means by which to seduce a high-ranking husband and secure a stable position. Men drank and composed poetry and painted and sang ballads and argued philosophy and watched women dance.

Fortunately, I was more than Sienese.

I gestured to myself with an acrobat's flourish.

"Do I look like a dancer?"

Atar laughed. My heart leaped, and I grinned like a fool.

"Why yes, Nayeni," she said. "Yes, you do."

The woman in the center made one final leap, then landed with a jangle of bracelets. She returned to her place in the circle. A lean man of martial bearing stepped out from beside her with a curved sword in hand. He began his dance, a whirling, lashing spin around the edge of the ring.

"She was a merchant," Atar said. "He is a Blade-of-the-Wind, a warrior Windshaper."

"They are not all Windshapers?" I said, still wrapping my head around that term. There was only one word for An-Zabati magic in Sienese, for only one use of that magic mattered to the Empire.

Atar shook her head. "Many are. Most are not. Everyone has their dance, Nayeni, for the wind moves us all. Those who can guide the wind lead the dance, but there are as many dances as there are walks of life." There was a proud tilt to her chin. "It is my task to know them all."

The Blade-of-the-Wind leaped high, then landed with a low sweep of his sword. He changed places with the next dancer, a young woman whom Atar identified as a housekeeper. She was followed by a shepherdess, then a farmer—a rare and respected trade in An-Zabat—then a Windcaller from a ship at harbor, and so on. Each dance was unique. Atar told me that each had been passed down for generations, and that once, before the Sienese had come, every person among the An-Zabati knew their dance and knew their place in the world.

"So few come to the dances, now," she said while a young scribe leaped and spun and kicked in rapid, precise arcs. "So many care only for the wealth the Sienese have brought, or the liquors."

"But you are wealthier now, under their rule." The scribe returned to his place in the circle, dangerously near to me. My heart began to pound and my stomach churned. Soon my time would come.

Atar shrugged. "Some say so, and the wealth has moved to different hands, but An-Zabat is an old city. I am sure it has seen richer years." The next dancer dove out onto the sand, then tucked and rolled, then sprung off his toes and dove again like a porpoise leaping from wave to wave.

"Who is he?" I asked.

"A glassblower."

I shook my head, baffled.

"It is said the first glass was made by a great serpent that dwelt in the sun," Atar said. "The glassblowers are rich, now, for the Sienese covet their work. But rulers come and go in An-Zabat."

She gestured toward the tombs built into the walls of the canyon.

"Before you came we were ruled by interlopers from the frigid north. Before them, by merchant princes who paid tribute to the horse tribes of the western grasslands. Before them, there was someone else with spears and soldiers who had claimed the right to rule."

I studied the tombs.

"That is why you meet here," I said. "To remind yourself."

She nodded, pleased that I had understood. "Rulers come and go, but the wind, the Goddess, and her people will remain."

I knew little of An-Zabati history beyond what I had gleaned from Sienese texts, but I knew its economics well. So long as the Windcallers held their monopoly on transport across the desert, they had nothing to fear from new rulers.

The Empire wanted to break that monopoly. I had seen the ledgers. I knew the value of An-Zabat, and how much more wealth could be wrung from it without the Windcallers' heavy fees.

My thoughts were interrupted by the man to my right, who finished his dance, returned to the circle, and clapped me on the shoulder with a wide, eager grin.

I froze.

"It is your turn," Atar urged me. "Show us your dance, Nayeni!"

Despite my earlier jest, I hesitated. She gave me a gentle push. Every eye in the circle fixed on me as I stumbled out into the center of the circle.

Had any foreigner come to the dance before? No Sienese, I was sure. No matter. I had come. I would dance.

It had been years since I had practiced the Iron Dance, but movements trained deep into muscle and bone are not easily forgotten. I shut my eyes and thought back to the abandoned temple, my grandmother watching my steps, correcting the angle of my arms, the arch of my back and knee. My hands curled into fists. They ought to have gripped swords, or at least the rattan dowels I had used for practice.

The first steps came slowly. They were nothing like the whirling and leaping of the An-Zabati, for the Iron Dance had nothing of the wind. It was hard and martial, the remnant of a warrior culture all but snuffed out by Imperial steel, grenade, and sorcery. It was iron tempered by ancient fire. It was a dance in name, but a weapon in truth.

The An-Zabati danced with grace and beauty, and with sorcery. The only grace I understood was the grace of the Sienese: art and poetry, fine clothes and subtle wines. But there can be beauty without grace. And I understood sorcery.

Power rippled from the old scars of my right hand. Arcs of heat and light trailed from my fists as I moved through the Iron Dance. Gasps erupted from the crowd. The drums faltered, but my steps did not. I had never danced to drums.

Too soon I came to the last steps, the final downward blow. I splayed my fingers and threw the fire gathered there. It splashed outward, like burning oil spilled over the sand. The drums rumbled to a stop. The crowd stared in hushed silence as the conjured flames flickered and died. I came to a stop, panting heavily, my caftan soaked with sweat in the lingering desert heat.

"Firecaller . . ."

It began slowly, like the first pulses of high tide lapping at Nayen's shores, and then became a wave crashing over me.

"Firecaller!"

They clapped their hands and cried out for me as I walked to my place in the circle, flushed and astonished at what I had done, and at their reaction.

*"Firecaller!"*

A final cry, and then a receding flurry of applause. Atar smiled and pressed my right hand, her eyes shining, her face as flushed as mine. She leaned to my ear. "You were marvelous. But now it is my turn."

And Atar, who knew every dance of An-Zabat, gave a performance that outshone mine as the sun outshines the stars. No Sienese courtesan could rival her. No lines of poetry could capture her.

Others danced after, but I hardly saw them.

When all who had come had danced, the old Windcaller Katiz stepped into the center of the ring and held aloft a wide bowl decorated with whirlwinds of silver filigree.

"A cool wind promised water!" he cried.

The gathering answered, "All things flow to An-Zabat!"

He knelt and dug a basin. Within it he placed the bowl, so that only its lip could be seen above the sand.

Power rippled from him and into the bowl, and then radiated down into the earth. It was not the pattern of Windshaping, which I knew well by now, but it was similar. A trickle of water seeped into the bottom of the bowl. Soon it was filled.

"Do not look so surprised," Atar said. "There is air in the water, and water in the air, is there not?"

In that moment I felt too ignorant to dispute her.

I turned toward the city. There, beneath it, I saw old magic woven and bound in stone, fixed in place to keep An-Zabat alive. The ripples of power were there when I looked for them, but the waters of An-Zabat were ancient. The pattern of the world had long since embraced them. The greenbelt, the clouds, the layout of the city, all these served to hide the magic that fed the Great Oasis.

This, I realized, was something Voice Rill should have told me. He had not. Either he kept this knowledge from me, or he did not know. If the former, there was no point in sharing what I had learned. If the latter . . .

I looked at Atar. I would not betray her trust more than I already had.

Each dancer dipped cupped hands and drank from the bowl, and then parted ways. Atar led me back through the catacombs. At the door to the city she paused and smiled.

I felt a powerful urge to kiss her, as well as terror that she might never speak to me again if I did.

"You dance well, Firecaller, for an untrained foreigner," she said. "Meet me tomorrow night in the Valley. We will see if you can be taught."

She patted my cheek and left me there, speechless. When she was out of sight, I set off toward the citadel, my mind reeling, my blood racing, my body electrified by the excitement of the night.

New love. New secrets. And, perhaps most importantly, a new name.

## 4

I brought rice gruel and ginseng tea."

The sun shone bright through my window. A tray clattered on my bedside table. Khin never clattered dishes unless he meant to.

"I'm not hung over."

"Oh?" Khin said as he poured my tea. "You were not back until well after nightfall, and you have slept half the morning away."

I stared at him. He went on preparing my meal without meeting my gaze.

"I do not have to defend myself to you," I said sharply.

He stiffened.

"Of course," he said. He bowed and left the room, masking his offense and hurt with practiced grace.

Khin had been a trustworthy steward, if not a friend. I regretted the conflict between us, but I would not give up the Valley of Rulers.

The following months passed in a flurry. By day I tracked tariffs and tax records, adjusted rates of exchange, and monitored the flow of goods in and out of the city. By night I covered my tetragram with clay and slipped away from the citadel to meet Atar. The dance only gathered beneath the full moon, but almost every night she and I would visit the Valley of Rulers and trade stories of our childhoods. I told her everything, up to the day I became Hand of the Emperor.

My grandmother had taught me the myths and history of her people. She had meant for me to keep them alive, to pass them on to future generations of Nayeni. I told them to Atar, who was not Nayeni, but who understood.

She began to teach me dances. Soon I could dance like a scribe, or a merchant. On my second full moon in the Valley of Rulers, I performed the Soldier's Dance to much applause. After, while we walked back to the catacombs under the light of the stars, I asked her to teach me to dance like a Windcaller.

"That secret is not mine to share."

My heart sank.

"Do not despair, Firecaller," she said with a gentle smile. "I will do what I can to help you earn it."

My deepening understanding of the An-Zabati was not only a matter of personal interest. Their attitude of independence and their lack of concern for rulership informed my work as Minister of Trade. I drafted a new policy regarding the Windcallers and brought it to Voice Rill for ratification.

"These are high fees," Voice Rill muttered, leafing through the documents.

"Not fees," I said. "A percentage share. The Windcallers want respect. They see themselves, rightly, as the beating heart of trade in An-Zabat. If we treat them as equal partners, they will work with us."

"And how, Hand Alder, have you become an expert on the wants of the Windcallers?"

"There is a reason I was given this task," I said, avoiding the thrust of his question. I jabbed my finger at the page in his hand. "Look at the numbers, Voice Rill. Yes, the markets will need time to adjust, and some of the silver mines in An-Zabat may close, but we have more than enough silver in Sien. We want foreign goods, valuable goods, to move through this city, into and out of the Empire."

"You are Minister of Trade," Voice Rill said in resignation. "And yes, you were chosen for a reason. Very well." He stamped the pages with the tetragram of his office. "You are very brave, Hand Alder. And very clever. But cleverness can be dangerous unless balanced by wisdom. I hope this does not ruin you."

He had no cause to worry.

As Atar and I grew closer I felt the lies I had told her like a thorn in my heart. Always I had to speak around my deepest doubts and fears, as well as my greatest accomplishments—which, I worried, she would see as my most heinous crimes.

I could not tell her of the years I spent as Hand Usher's apprentice, learning Sienese sorcery and fighting against the very same rebellion that my grandmother had abandoned me to join. Nor could I speak of my friend Oriole who was the son of the Voice of Nayen. Oriole, who had been like a brother to me, who taught me to ride a horse and lead men into battle. Oriole, whose life I could have saved if only I had been willing to cast aside my grandmother's lessons and my Nayeni blood.

When Atar and I were together, I felt torn between the ease of our conversation and the anxiety that any wrong word might betray my lies. I had lived in similar tension most of my life. Secrets and half-truths were my armor, worn since childhood.

But, so armored, I could never fully embrace Atar.

Sitting in my office, staring at the tetragram on my hand, a piece of clay raised and ready, I resolved to hide nothing more from Atar. If she hated me, if she and the other dancers in the valley sought to kill me, so be it. I would be myself with her. I set down the clay.

"I have something to show you," I said beneath the stars while Atar prepared to teach me the next dance. The tombs of An-Zabat's ancient rulers were shrouded in shadow, like dark eyes staring out from beneath heavy brows.

She paused in her stretching, with all the power and beauty of a drawn bow. "What is it?"

What if she hated me? What if she could not accept the truth?

Better to be hated than never truly known.

"I have not been honest with you," I said, and showed the silver lines of the Imperial tetragram on my palm.

She stared at my hand, then at my eyes, her face a hard mask. "You are not a servant."

"No." The world shifted beneath me. My stomach lurched. My heart stuttered, but I said the words. "I am Hand of the Emperor."

She tensed, ready to fight or flee. "Is this some kind of trick?"

I shook my head. "If the Voice or the other Hands learned that I come here, they would have me killed."

She did not run.

She demanded an explanation, which was enough to give me hope.

I told her everything. Her face was like stone but she listened, and her breathing slowed the more she came to understand. When I finished, a long and silent moment passed before she spoke. "You chose the conquerors."

Her voice was cold, her words a condemnation.

"Atar, I hardly feel that I have made a single choice in my life," I said, and was surprised to hear the crack in my voice. I pressed on, the truth flowing freely like ink from a toppled bottle. "Since I was a boy, others have had designs for me, and I knew no better than to follow them. My grandmother meant for me to fight the Sienese. My father wanted me to advance our family's station in the Empire. He set me on the path that led me to the Imperial examination and Hand Usher, who plucked me out of obscurity and made me Hand of the Emperor."

"You could have refused."

"Could I have?" I sounded angry. I felt angry. Not at Atar. I took a deep breath and spoke again, determined to keep my voice calm and measured despite whatever I felt. "By the time I was old enough to understand the danger of my grandmother's lessons, I knew just as well that telling anyone about them would mean both of our deaths. She disappeared one night to join the rebellion without a word to me, let alone an offer to join her. What was I to do? There was a path laid for me by my father and the Empire, and I followed it.

"I have always been two men, Atar. My grandmother and my father. My right hand and my left. Nayeni and Sienese, though I look like neither. There was no room for me to decide what I wanted to be."

Her eyes were bright. As I spoke, her posture had opened. She hesitated in the silence for a heartbeat, then stepped toward me. "Whatever else you are," she said, haltingly at first, gaining confidence as she spoke, "you are a good man, Firecaller. But you are also very confused. What has brought you here, truly?"

"I saw you and your Windshaping," I said. She was very close to me. The wind carried her lavender scent. "Whatever else I am, I have always been curious."

She regarded me, our feet nearly touching. A gust caught her hair. It brushed my arm. She smiled. "And what drew you back, night after night? Curiosity?"

"Of a sort," I managed to say.

"Just to learn Windcalling?" She leaned toward me, her voice a breath of a whisper.

I was feeling extraordinarily honest with her lips only a hand's width from mine.

I answered truthfully, and she kissed me, and I resolved never to lie to her again.

On my fourth full moon in the Valley of Rulers, while Atar commanded the attention of the circle with yet another new dance I had never seen before, the Windcaller Katiz approached me. He had not spoken to me since Atar revealed my true position among the Sienese, but she had vouched for my presence at the dance, and that had been enough for Katiz to let me stay. He crossed his tattooed arms over his chest.

"Winddancing Atar tells me you want to learn my dance, Firecaller."

"Not only the dance," I said, meeting his gaze.

"The dance and the art are the same, Firecaller." He turned toward Atar. Her fingers wove the air. Her scarves twirled over and against each other like serpents of the sea.

"She says you are curious. That this is your only reason. Tell me truthfully: will you steal our secret for your Empire?"

"I could not reveal yours without revealing my own."

Katiz harrumphed.

"A good answer. Self-interest is a far surer guarantee than any promise you could make."

"You will teach me, then?"

"Tomorrow night." His hand closed on my shoulder. "You command fire. Let us see if you can master the wind."

My feet wanted to flatten against the earth. The sweeping movements of my arms felt loose and impotent. Training in the Iron Dance had taught me to plant my feet firmly, but Windcalling required fluid motion. I returned to the citadel disappointed after that first night of training with Windcaller Katiz.

Four weeks later, I earned my tattoos.

"Only thrice before have we given mastery of the wind to an outsider," Katiz said while he ground the ink. "They, like you, came to us already powerful in magic. They, like you, had lost their own people. They, as we hope for you, stayed with us for many years."

Katiz sharpened the radius of a desert hawk into a hollow-tipped needle.

"The first marks go here," Atar said. She touched the underside of my forearm, just below the crook of my elbow. Her finger made three swirls, forming a triangle that pointed toward my hand. A pleasant shiver ran up my arm. She smiled. "One day, if you have your own ship, the whole of both arms will be covered."

I doubted I would ever wear so many marks, and I felt grateful that the tattoos would be so small and high on my arm. The sleeve of a Sienese robe would cover them easily.

"Don't be afraid to wince," Katiz said. "Everyone winces on the first few strikes."

"My grandmother carved my hand with a stone knife," I said. "I doubt this will be much worse."

"We will see, Firecaller," Atar said, and kissed my cheek.

Katiz prodded me with the needle, then rubbed ink into the pinprick wounds. I did wince, and Atar teased me relentlessly for it. The stars were out in full and the moon already descending when Katiz finished.

"Try not to move the arm more than necessary for the next few days," Katiz said. "And for Naphena's sake, don't wash it too vigorously, or the ink will smudge."

I barely heard him. While he had prodded and inked my arm, trickles of new power had flowed into me. Now I seized them and sprang to my feet. It was not so different, after all, from conjuring fire. My arm rose in a slow arc, and a gust billowed up. I pushed forward and down, and it rushed away from me.

"Look, Atar!" I cried, leaping and grinning and giddy. "I can call the wind!"

She ran to me, and together we danced with the zephyrs of the desert and shared a final kiss beneath the setting moon.

I woke late, as I had often done since that first night in the Valley of Rulers, but I smelled no brewing tea, nor any porridge, nor boiled eggs, nor fried dough. No servants scurried about preparing my apartments for the day.

"Khin?" I called.

He did not answer. I dressed and went to the door. My breath came quick and heavy, and my heart had begun to pound. The door was locked. I felt the weight of a wooden beam barring it shut. I shook the handle and heard the rattle of a chain.

"Khin!" I shouted. "What is the meaning of this?"

My tattoo itched beneath its bandage.

No. It had been less than a night. How could they possibly know?

"Khin!" I shouted into the gap of the door frame. Had he kept track of my comings and goings, reported back to Alabaster and Cinder and Rill? I imagined him creeping into my apartments while I slept, leaning over me, drawing down the sheets to reveal my freshly tattooed arm.

"Steward Khin!"

"Good morning, Hand Alder."

Alabaster's voice. He drummed his fingers on the door. I pressed my eye to the gap, hoping for a glimpse of him, but he stood beyond the narrow band of my vision.

"Or should I call you something else?" he purred. "Alder is a Sienese name, after all, and you are so much more, and less, than Sienese."

"What is the meaning of this, Alabaster?"

I sounded desperate. A deep breath to calm myself did little good.

"We have known, Alder. All along we have known. Hand Usher knew in the moment he marked you with the tetragram. His foresight alone kept you from the executioner's grasp. Do you know what the penalty for treason is, Alder?"

"I don't know what you're talking about."

"A teacup? Really? You thought we believed that a shattered teacup made all those little, intricate marks, so carefully arranged around the seams of your palm?" He chuckled. "Do you think we are blind? Hand Usher must have suspected when he made you recompose your examination left-handed. Perhaps even then he foresaw this day."

"This day?" I said, my blood racing. "Hand Alabaster, you are speaking gibberish. Take me to Voice Rill, and we will sort through this misunderstanding."

"The Voices know best of all!" he said, his tone venomous with glee. "It is through them the Canon is transmitted. They are the artery by which power flows from the Emperor to his Hands.

Your foolish use of unrefined, barbarous magic, why, that stood out to them like a clot. This you were never told.

"We paid attention, Alder. Every ripple of your illicit power was studied. We had little use for the provincial, brutal shamanism of Nayen, but deception came naturally to you. That was a skill we could use."

Breath caught in my throat.

"The Windcallers will hold this city hostage no longer," Alabaster went on. "All we needed was the pattern of their magic, the ripple of its use. The art of it will be rebuilt to suit the Canon. Soon Windships will sail under the Imperial tetragram. An-Zabat will be fully ours. So sad that you will not survive to see the product of your labor."

His eye appeared in the gap, staring into mine. I stumbled backward, and he laughed.

"Oh, poor Alder. Did you think you were one of us in truth?" He clicked his tongue. "Come tomorrow's dawn your suffering will end. Cinder is sharpening his sword even as we speak. He is well practiced in administering his blade to Easterling flesh. He has a reputation for keeping his victims alive until that final slice, when their skin comes free."

He left me there, stunned on the floor. Everything I had worked for, the pride I felt as the first Nayeni to become Hand of the Emperor, my hope for a quiet life of study in the Academy, it tore within me, leaving me hollow. I stared at the tetragram branded to my left palm.

The magic that so many Nayeni shamans had destroyed themselves to keep secret. The power to conjure the Wind, key to the survival of the An-Zabati people through countless generations of conquest and reconquest. I had unwittingly given both to the Empire.

I closed my fist, scrambled to my feet, and sought the black chest with three iron locks that I had brought from Nayen. Alabaster and Cinder had made me a prisoner in my own rooms, but they had left me all of my belongings. They knew a great many of my secrets, but not all.

Not all.

The obsidian blade of my grandmother's knife was cool against the tetragram of my palm. I had last felt that blade when she gave me power. Now I used it to take power away.

To fight back I would need magic. Never again would I wield magic while bound to the Canon. Blood spilled from the tetragram as I cut the structures of the Canon away with my branded flesh.

The Canon was gone, a void where I had long felt a well of power. I felt only the free, wild magic of Nayen and An-Zabat. I stared at the ruin of my palm. Everything I had worked for. Everything my father had wanted.

And I realized, now that those things had all been cut away, how badly I had wanted them too.

I wrapped my hand tight in a scrap of linen, thrust the knife through my belt, and began searching for my way out. The door was locked, chained, and barred. There would be guards, and likely Cinder or Alabaster kept watch in case I tried to burn my way out. I went to the windows.

Locked, of course, and bolted from the outside. Where, on the path just a few steps from my house, Khin carried a bundle of laundry.

"Khin!" I shouted, and pounded furiously on the window.

He jerked to a stop and nearly dropped his burden.

"Khin!"

He looked around, frightened, then crept to my window.

"I shouldn't speak to you," he whispered. "Please, Your Excellence, let me be."

"This is a misunderstanding, Khin," I said. "They've locked me in here without a trial. They've denied me food and water, Khin. Please. Just a jug of water. You needn't even bring it to the door. Just pass it through this window."

Again he looked around, searching for prying eyes and ears. "Your Excellence," he said at last, "I . . . shouldn't."

His eyes were sad. He glanced back at me as he walked away.

While I waited, wondering if he would return, I paced my

floor and fought rising nausea. Even if Khin opened the window, it was much too small for me to squeeze through. Not without becoming much, much smaller. Not without magic.

I had twice replaced the bloody linen on my hand and the sun had begun to set by the time Khin returned with a water skin.

"Thank you," I said. "Just open the window and pass it through."

He gave me a last worried look. Second guessing himself, I imagined, wondering whether helping me was worth the risk. I could not blame him. I had been a poor friend, if friend I was. He opened the bolt of the window. I gathered power in my right hand and fought the urge to vomit.

I called the wind to slam the window open. Khin stumbled backward as I launched myself through and into the air. He screamed, but I was past him now, driving myself into the twilight sky on falcon's wings. A ripple of power as vast as the wake of an armada trailed behind me. Alabaster, Cinder, and Rill would know that I had used magic to escape. If I was not careful, they would find me at the end of that wake.

I had one hope. For all they knew of my secrets, they had never learned that I could fly.

## 5

I rode desert thermals out into the Batir Waste, soaring wide around the Valley of Rulers before landing. If the Sienese came looking for me they would be led out into the open desert. I released the spell and stood on wobbly legs. The sun was setting, but heat clung to the sand. I should have taken the water skin from Khin before veering. Cursing my shortsightedness and sucking my cheeks to draw out what little saliva I had, I set off at a flagging jog toward the Valley of Rulers, where Atar would be waiting for me.

If I hurried, I might reach her in time to pass on a warning, to tell her that the Windcallers had been betrayed.

How soon would Cinder begin his cull?

Not tonight, I told myself. So I hoped, and so I believed, and believing gave me the strength to run.

She was waiting for me, sitting on a boulder and watching the doors to the tunnels that flowed to the city. The light of the gibbous moon caught the line of her jaw and her lips, pursed with worry. I was late, and on the night after Katiz had marked me. Did she fear betrayal? No, I told myself. She likely feared that I had been discovered.

Her heart would break when I told her the truth.

I called out to her, and the tension in her body faded. My heart pounded in my chest. She rose and turned toward me, her relief overcome by confusion and concern.

"Why have you come from the desert?" she said as she offered a copper canteen. The water stung my chapped mouth, but it was blessedly wet and cool.

"The Sienese," I said, when I could speak. I opened my left hand to show the bloody bandage. "They stole Windcalling for their Canon."

She stared at my hand, and began to pull away from me.

"You would not have come back if this was your plan!" Her voice rose to a bitter cry. "Or is this another layer of betrayal? Then why say anything!"

"They stole my magic long ago. I thought it my secret all this time, but as soon as they branded me with the Canon they knew. They brought me here knowing that my curiosity would open the door to the Windcallers. Every magic that I worked they saw and studied and stole for their Canon."

"How could you not know! You are schooled in their magic, are you not, Hand of the Emperor?"

"They never told me," I said. "I was never one of them. They gave me power only to ensnare me."

She scoffed. "They made you a fool."

I tried to ignore the wound of her words and pressed on. "Atar, we have to tell the other Windcallers. Once the Empire has the power to drive Windships of their own, they will have no more use for you. What they cannot use, they destroy. You can vanish into the waste. Abandon An-Zabat to the Empire. Run." I thought of my grandmother. "You can strike back later. Gather your power in the desert. Raid their ships and caravans. Flee now to fight tomorrow."

She turned away from me. Her jaw was set, her hands clenched. "No."

"Atar, listen to reason! You cannot fight them. They will kill you to the last!"

"They will not have our city," she said firmly. "Get up, Firecaller. We need to find Katiz."

Black clouds billowed up from the elevated harbor. Gusts of rising wind cut the smoke and swirled it like a spill of ink in water. We stood at the mouth of the alley where Atar had first led me into the tunnels and out to the Valley of Rulers. She curled her hands into fists, and I felt the heat of her anger.

I wanted to make things right, to heal the wounds the truth had dealt.

"Katiz will be at the Guildhall," she said, and stepped out into the city.

"Wait." I caught her wrist. Her forearm went rigid at my touch. "Cinder would attack the Guildhall first. Where would Katiz go to hide?"

She pulled away from me. "There is a place in the tunnels," she said, brushing past me on her way back into the alley.

We took a new route through the tunnels, one that led deeper into the city instead of out into the waste. Our path led down a side corridor that echoed with hushed murmurs. It ended in an open chamber that smelled of the sweat, blood, and fear of many bodies. I recognized most of the gathering from the dances at the Valley of Rulers. Others were strangers to me. Some bore wounds; shallow slashes from Sienese swords, burns and shrapnel cuts from chemical grenades, fractal patterns of ruptured flesh left by a glancing blow from Sienese sorcery. Atar's eyes lingered on those wounds, then glared at me in accusation. While she had been waiting for me in the desert, her people had been fighting.

Katiz stood at the heart of the gathering. He spoke in hushed tones with four other men. One wore Windcaller tattoos. The others carried swords, and I recognized them for Blades-of-the-Wind.

"Atar!" Katiz stood as we approached. "Thank the Goddess. So many have been lost . . ." His voice faded. Though he had seen me behind Atar, for a brief moment he had not recognized me as an outsider. Now, after a moment of reflection, his eyes hardened, and I was again cast out of place.

"Firecaller is with you," he murmured.

"He came to warn us."

"Not soon enough." Katiz stepped toward me, menacing. "You must have known. At the very least you must have overheard something while they planned this." He turned back to his council. "No matter. They have tried to steal Windcalling before. Other rulers have done the same in ages past. Always we survive. Last time we let the city stew in hunger for a year. Let us see how they feel after two!"

A defiant cheer filled the room. I gritted my teeth and glanced at Atar, who watched Katiz grimly.

"It is too late for that," I said as the reverberating voices faded. "They have already stolen your magic."

The room went silent. Whispers began to sound from the corners of the chamber.

"How?" Katiz said. "Did you—"

"He was betrayed," Atar said. "One of the Imperial Hands learned that he was spending time among us and cast a spell on him, to watch us through his eyes." She grabbed my left hand and held it up. The bandage over my palm was stained deep red. "He discovered the spell, cut every scrap of their sorcery from his body, and fled to warn us."

"If what you say is true, the city is lost," Katiz said finally. "We are lost."

"No." Atar stepped forward and set her jaw. "They know how to call the wind, but Firecaller never learned how to draw water. The city is lost to us, but we can deny them their victory."

Katiz's eyes lit up.

"Naphena's urn has poured for thousands of years," he said.

"It can be made dry," said Atar.

He shook his head. "Once we begin, they will realize what we are doing, and they will stop us."

I remembered the bowl in the Valley of Rulers, the silver filigree, so similar to the decoration on the city's minarets. The power beneath An-Zabat. Slow ripples through the centuries that drew every drop of water beneath the waste up into the statue of Naphena, through her urn to the Great Oasis.

"The Sienese have weapons that can destroy a minaret in an instant," Atar said.

"But we have none," said Katiz.

"I can steal grenades for you," I said suddenly. "With my grandmother's magic I can take the appearance of a guard."

"He can," Atar said. "It is why I brought him here."

I reminded myself that she would never forgive me, that when this was done she would hate me, no matter how I helped her, no matter how I struck back against the Sienese.

Katiz frowned at me, then nodded to Atar. "Very well, Winddancer. What is your plan?"

The citadel guard was stretched thin with so many soldiers dedicated to Cinder's cull. I led our small party to the servants' gate: Atar, a Blade-of-the-Wind called Shazir, and two runners who would carry grenades to the minarets furthest from the citadel. They all carried crates stuffed with rags and wore the simple caftans of porters. Atar had hidden her hair beneath a turban and dressed like a man. Not the cleverest of disguises, but we had little time.

I gathered power, hoped that Hand Alabaster and Voice Rill's attentions were elsewhere, and called to mind the face of a minor lieutenant guardsman. The bones of my face stretched and bent, my flesh rippled and shifted as I veered. My robes had earlier become feathers for my wings. They now became the iron scale armor of a Sienese soldier, complete with sash of rank and pointed helm. The two runners looked at me with wide-eyed fear and awe. Shazir gave a begrudging nod of approval. Atar was impatient to be about our work.

A small window set in the door opened to my knock. Khin peered out at me. I panicked, nearly ruining everything, as I remembered how twice I had betrayed him.

"Lieutenant?" he said. "What is the meaning of this? Did Hand Alabaster forget something?" He looked beyond me. "And who are these An-Zabati? Don't you know there is fighting, stupid man?"

His brusque speech took me aback. A steward would be the superior to a lesser officer, I knew, but I was accustomed to a genteel, obsequious Steward Khin. There was a new, foreign harshness in his eyes that reminded me of a whipped dog.

I wondered if my escape were to blame.

More importantly, he had said that Alabaster was out in the city. Cinder would not leave the battle in his hands, which meant they both were away from the citadel. Only Voice Rill remained to see through my disguise and blast us all to bloody, minced chunks.

"Well?" Khin barked.

"Confiscated relics," I said in a voice much deeper than my own. It was a matter of policy to eradicate the backward, barbarous culture of a conquered nation to make way for glorious Sien. A fate An-Zabat had escaped, though not for much longer.

"And who are they?" Khin jabbed a finger at Atar.

"Our fighting men are needed to put down the riots," I said. "These An-Zabati porters were paid well. They have no idea what they're carrying, anyway, and don't speak our language."

Which was true. I had been teaching Atar to speak Sienese, but her command of it was still limited. The men with us knew only numbers and *silver* and *too much!* and the other words that are learned in market stalls.

Khin frowned dubiously, but opened the door.

"Wait here," he said when we had filed inside. "Voice Rill will sort this out. I've had enough of granting unusual requests today."

He turned around, and for the third time I betrayed him. A sharp blow from the heel of my hand left him sprawled and unconscious on the ground. I felt a pang of guilt as we took his heavy key ring and hid him behind a juniper bush.

Most eyes in the citadel were pointed out toward An-Zabat, watching for retaliation. Those that were not had their own tasks and worries to concern them. We were only four servants and a guard among many scurrying about the garden. In the torch-lit dark no one would see that the servants were An-Zabati porters.

A lone guard approached as we neared the armory.

"More grenades are needed at the front," I said before he could speak.

The guard stared at me in shocked confusion.

"Lieutenant Jasper?" he said, horrified. "We carried you back on a stretcher—"

Fluid as the wind, Shazir stepped around me, shifted his crate to one hand, and threw a punch. Power burst from his fist, and behind it, a cylinder of air. The guard's helmet cracked. Blood sprayed from the ruin of his face.

Shazir thrust the crate into my hands and caught the falling guard.

"I will hide him," Shazir said. "Go!"

"Voice Rill could have seen that from the other side of the city!" I snarled. "There is no point in hiding the body. We are likely dead because of you."

He dropped the corpse and glared at me.

"We are here because of *you*, Firecaller."

"Shazir, we have to hurry." Atar pulled us apart, then frowned at me. "You have the keys."

While the others rushed through the door, I looked toward the Gazing Upon Lilies pavilion. Voice Rill surely monitored the battle, attending to every ripple of magic in the city, making continual reports to the Emperor. At any moment he could appear on the hilltop, raise a finger, and strike me down with brilliant rays of power. Without the tetragram on my palm I had only fire and shape-changing. Poor weapons against the vast, nation-toppling Canon.

I returned to my natural form. No sense leaving a beacon burning for Rill to see.

"Firecaller, where are the grenades?" Atar hissed at me.

"This way." I led them to a door marked with the Sienese logograms for *dangerous* and *flammable*. Within was a small, windowless chamber that smelled of sulfur and stale air. Crates of grenades packed in straw stood in careful stacks. Along one wall hung six bandoleers already strung with grenades.

"Take these." I handed two bandoleers to each of Katiz's runners. They nervously strapped them on. This done, they pressed hands with Atar and Shazir and sprinted across the garden to the servants' gate and out toward the minarets they were tasked to destroy.

I held out the remaining bandoleers for Atar.

Her hand lingered as she reached for them.

"Find me," she said at last. "When it is over, come to the dunes above the Valley of Rulers. Katiz and I will be there."

My heart hammered. A thread of life burned in my blood. I wanted to lean over the bandoleer between us and kiss her. But I knew, no matter what either of us wanted, that our paths had never truly converged.

I was not Sienese, but neither was I An-Zabati.

"I will find you," I said.

She smiled, took the bandoleers, and ran, fleet as the forest deer of Nayen.

The crates proved too heavy. I would never be able to run while carrying one. Shazir struggled just as much as I did, I noted with petty satisfaction.

"We need more bandoleers," I said.

While I searched for them he began unloading one of the

crates. I winced at the quiet *clink* as he set each grenade on the stone floor. He hefted the crate and tilted it from side to side to make sure that the remaining grenades would not shift and explode while he ran.

"Hurry, Firecaller," he said from the doorway. "We have little time."

He left me there, but survived only three steps into the main room of the armory.

Power rippled. Sorcery hissed and cracked. Thunder pounded my ears, rattled my ribs, shook the world around me. My nose filled with smoke and plaster dust. My ears rang and my limbs shook. I lay sprawled amid grenades. They clinked together as they rolled across the floor.

My heart stuttered in my chest. My lungs burned. I stifled a gasp, not daring to move. Crates had cracked, but not toppled. Dust poured from my clothes as I carefully stood and fought the urge to call out for Shazir.

Acrid smoke rolled along the ceiling and filled my throat at every breath. I covered my mouth and nose with my sleeve. In the dark I felt my way along the wall and into the main room of the armory, where Hand Cinder waited.

"I should not be surprised," he said, and stepped toward me through the smoke. A hissing whip of sorcery trailed from his hand. "Foolishness is a common trait of the Easterlings. I cannot tell you how many times one of your countrymen could have escaped me, but turned to fight out of some delusional sense of honor instead."

I recovered from the shock of seeing him and groped for a weapon. Swords hung on a rack beside me. I got hold of one and yanked it from its sheath. Cinder's whip lashed out and tore the rack apart. Swords clattered to the ground.

"Ah yes, a sword," Cinder taunted. "You Easterlings are so fond of swords. More honorable than an arrow or a crossbow bolt. Ironic, isn't it, that your sorcery does little more than hide your faces?"

He flourished his whip. It coiled and hissed, a serpent of blazing light. I circled, stepping carefully around the fallen swords. One of the walls had been badly damaged by the blast that killed Shazir. Stars and the orange light of the burning city showed through a jagged gap. It was too small for a man to fit through. Not for a bird.

Cinder's whip cracked in the air between me and the broken wall.

"Shouldn't you be out in the city?" I asked. "Haven't you wanted this battle for years?"

"I've fought enough battles. Alabaster needed this one. That boy is soft. Intelligent and articulate, but soft. Without at least one victory, he will never be taken seriously in the capital."

"You two never seemed like friends."

I took a step toward him. He smiled.

"A charade, as it all was," he said. "You are not the only man capable of deceit."

He riffled his whip along the ground toward my advancing feet. Distance was everything. My sword could still cut him. His whip had more reach, but could not strike instantly.

If he had wanted to, he could have sent a lance of sorcery through my chest from where he stood.

That day I came upon him at the archery range he had been practicing only the whip.

He hated me, and would relish the taunts and the feints and my pitiful attempts to fight back. Our battle was a game. One I could not hope to win.

"Did you know that all the while you thought you served as Minister of Trade, Alabaster did the bulk of the work? He monitored your every decision, and kept most matters of real import away from your desk." Cinder smiled, catlike on the balls of his feet. "None of your accomplishments as Hand of the Emperor were your own. You have only ever been our puppet, Easterling."

I saw flames behind him. A breeze tickled my forearm. I

waited until he cracked the whip again—there!—and retreated backward and to the right, toward the broken wall.

"I may have been your puppet," I said. "But there are still secrets you do not know."

"Oh?" Cinder chuckled, raised the whip, prepared to strike. "Many Easterlings have betrayed their secrets to me. Most screamed and begged for death as their flesh peeled away. Let us see how long you last."

His sorcery flashed, hissed, cracked the air. I dropped my sword. Ripples of power brought fire to my hand. I threw it along the ground, toward the open doorway marked *dangerous* and *flammable*.

I jumped, gathered power, and on falcon's wings rode the blast wave through the broken wall, up and out of the armory and into the smoke-filled skies of An-Zabat.

The armory burst into fire and dust, strips of burning wood and broken weapons. Shouts of alarm rose from the garden as servants and soldiers raced to the scene. In a backward glance I saw no sign of Cinder, alive or dead. He was likely no more than mist and ash.

Power rippled out, a tidal bore surging toward me. A blade of light burned from the wreckage and cut the sky, so bright it dimmed the moon and stars. I dove beneath Cinder's attack. It was poorly aimed. He could not see me, but only lashed out at the wake of power I trailed. He stood in the light of his sorcery. One arm hung limp and charred. His jaw was broken, his face blackened. He was furious.

A flash of light burst from the base of a nearby minaret. Atar, or one of Katiz's runners, had turned the grenades of the Empire against the symbol of their home. A crack like distant thunder sounded. There was the grinding sound of stone separating from stone, the shriek of metal tearing. The minaret began to list to one side, shedding broken pieces that shattered where they fell.

Another burst of light, crack of thunder, cacophony of falling stone and silver.

The ancient power rippling beneath An-Zabat began to fade.

I left the city behind and rode thermals toward the Valley of Rulers. A third minaret fell, and Cinder poured blind rage into the roiling sky.

I never learned how the fighting ended. I know only that, as I stood on the prow of Katiz's Windship, no minarets stood silhouetted by the fires that raged through An-Zabat.

"They will wonder why we destroyed the minarets before we fled," Atar said. She stood beside me. I smelled her sweat, the lavender scent beneath the dust and char that clung to her.

She sidled close and took my hand.

Plumes of sand rose behind the other Windships as they scattered to the four corners of the waste. Katiz drove us east, as I had asked him to.

"When the dust settles in a few days, they will see that Naphena's urn no longer flows. Perhaps the Voice or his Hands will feel the emptiness beneath them, the void where old power once flowed. In six months, perhaps a year, the oasis will be dry. If they have not abandoned the city by then, they will die."

"Not only the Sienese." I turned toward her. "Your people will have to flee as well."

She met my eyes. My heart leaped, then broke for the third time that day. Her smile was sad, but proud.

"We were nomads, once," she said. "There are old men who still know how to bring water from the waste. Old women who still polish the cistern-bowls passed down by their mothers and their grandmothers. They will survive. An-Zabat was only ever a place of rest. A temporary home. Now we will return to our wandering."

She paused. The wind tossed her hair around her face. It streamed out toward the orange glow that hung over her city.

"You destroyed An-Zabat," she said, "but you helped to free its people. There is a place for you among us, if you want it, Firecaller."

I did. My heart ached. My body wanted to gather her to me. To kiss her. To carry her to the cabin. To be An-Zabati.

But I had never been An-Zabati, as I was never truly Sienese, and at the edge of the waste I called a high, easterly wind to carry me on falcon's wings across Sien and the sea.

My grandmother would be waiting, somewhere in the mountains of Nayen.

# *Suspense*

BY L. RON HUBBARD

*L. Ron Hubbard lived a remarkably adventurous and productive life. His versatility and rich, imaginative scope both spanned and ranged far beyond his extensive literary achievements and creative influence. A writer's writer of enormous talent and energy, the breadth and diversity of his writing ultimately embraced more than 560 works and over 63 million words of fiction and nonfiction over his fifty-six-year writing career.*

*Early into Ron's writing career, when he had already established a commanding reputation in many of the genres of popular fiction, he was repeatedly asked to share the secrets of his success with the readers of writers' magazines. He was glad to do so; there is quite a file of his essays published in those days.*

*Here, from the June 1937 issue of* Author and Journalist*—one of the most prominent writers' magazines of the time—is one of those pieces.*

*The question he poses in the article goes to the heart of the creative process: What rivets a reader to the page, "tensely wondering which of two or three momentous things is going to happen first"? The answer L. Ron Hubbard provides, by insightful analysis and example, is both witty and compelling.*

*We use it, along with a number of other essays by Ron, in the annual Writers of the Future workshop. Participants often remark on how relevant it is despite the passage of time. Why shouldn't it be? Fashions in storytelling change, but story remains the same. Here, then, is L. Ron Hubbard's "Suspense," one of the key building blocks to writing a really good story.*

# *Suspense*

Next to checks, the most intangible thing in this business of writing is that quantity "Suspense."

It is quite as elusive as editorial praise, as hard to corner and recognize as a contract writer.

But without any fear of being contradicted, I can state that suspense, or rather, the lack of it, is probably responsible for more rejects than telling an editor he is wrong.

You grab the morning mail, find a long brown envelope. You read a slip which curtly says, "Lacks suspense."

Your wife starts cooking beans, you start swearing at the most enigmatic, unexplanatory, hopeless phrase in all that legion of reject phrases.

If the editor had said, "I don't think your hero had a tough enough time killing Joe Blinker," you could promptly sit down and kill Joe Blinker in a most thorough manner.

But when the editor brands and damns you with that first cousin to infinity, "Suspense," you just sit and swear.

Often the editor, in a hurry and beleaguered by stacks of manuscripts higher than the Empire State, has to tell you something to explain why he doesn't like your wares. So he fastens upon the action, perhaps. You can tell him (and won't, if you're smart) that your action is already so fast that you had to grease your typewriter roller to keep the rubber from getting hot.

Maybe he says your plot isn't any good, but you know doggone well that it is a good plot and has been a good plot for two thousand years.

Maybe, when he gives you those comments, he is, as I say, in a hurry. The editor may hate to tell you you lack suspense because it is something like B.O.—your best friends won't tell you.

But the point is that, whether he says that your Mary Jones reminds him of *The Perils of Pauline*, or that your climax is flat, there's a chance that he means suspense.

Those who have been at this business until their fingernails are worn to stumps are very often overconfident of their technique. I get that way every now and then, until something hauls me back on my haunches and shows me up. You just forget that technique is not a habit, but a constant set of rules to be frequently refreshed in your mind. And so, in the scurry of getting a manuscript in the mail, it is not unusual to overlook some trifling factor which will mean the difference between sale and rejection.

This suspense business is something hard to remember. You know your plot (or should, anyway) before you write it. You forget that the reader doesn't. Out of habit, you think plot is enough to carry you through. Sometimes it won't. You have to fall back on none-too-subtle mechanics.

Take this, for example:

> He slid down between the rocks toward the creek, carrying the canteens clumsily under his arm, silently cursing his sling. A shadow loomed over him.
>
> "Franzawi!" screamed the Arab sentinel.

There we have a standard situation. In the Atlas. The hero has to get to water or his wounded legionnaires will die of thirst. But, obviously, it is very, very flat except for the slight element of surprising the reader.

Surprise doesn't amount to much. That snap-ending tendency doesn't belong in the center of the story. Your reader knew there were Arabs about. He knew the hero was going into danger. But that isn't enough. Not half.

Legionnaire Smith squirmed down between the rocks clutching the canteens, his eyes fixed upon the bright silver spot which was the water hole below. A shadow loomed across the trail before him. Hastily he slipped backward into cover.

An Arab sentinel was standing on the edge of the trail, leaning on his long gun. The man's brown eyes were turned upward, watching a point higher on the cliff, expecting to see some sign of the besieged legionnaires.

Smith started back again, moving as silently as he could, trying to keep the canteens from banging. His sling-supported arm was weak. The canteens were slipping.

He could see the sights on the Arab's rifle and knew they would be lined on him the instant he made a sound.

The silver spot in the ravine was beckoning. He could not return with empty canteens. Maybe the sentinel would not see him if he slipped silently around the other side of this boulder.

He tried it. The man remained staring wolfishly up at the pillbox fort.

Maybe it was possible after all. That bright spot of silver was so near, so maddening to swollen tongues. . . .

Smith's hand came down on a sharp stone. He lifted it with a jerk.

A canteen rattled to the trail.

For seconds nothing stirred or breathed in this scorching world of sun and stone.

Then the sentry moved, stepped a pace up the path, eyes searching the shadows, gnarled hands tight on the rifle stock.

Smith moved closer to the boulder, trying to get out of sight, trying to lure the sentry toward him so that he could be silently killed.

The canteen sparkled in the light.

A resounding shout rocked the blistered hills.

"Franzawi!" cried the sentinel.

The surprise in the first that a sentinel would be there and that Smith was discovered perhaps made the reader blink.

The dragging agony of suspense in the latter made the reader lean tensely forward, devour the page, gulp. . . .

Or at least, I hope it did.

But there's the point. Keep your reader wondering which of two things will happen (i.e., will Smith get through or will he be discovered) and you get his interest. You focus his mind on an intricate succession of events and that is much better than getting him a little groggy with one swift sock to the medulla oblongata.

That is about the only way you can heighten drama out of melodrama.

It is not possible, of course, to list all the ways this method can be used. But it is possible to keep in mind the fact that suspense is better than fight action.

And speaking of fight action, there is one place where Old Man Suspense can be made to work like an Elkton marrying parson.

Fights, at best, are gap fillers. The writer who introduces them for the sake of the fight itself and not for the effects upon the characters is a writer headed for eventual oblivion even in the purely action books.

Confirmed by the prevailing trend, I can state that the old saw about action for the sake of action was right. A story jammed and packed with blow-by-blow accounts of what the hero did to the villain and what the villain did to the hero, with fists, knives, guns, bombs, machine guns, belaying pins, bayonets, poison gas, strychnine, teeth, knees and calks is about as interesting to read as the Congressional Record and about twice as dull. You leave yourself wide open to a reader comment, "Well, what of it?"

But fights accompanied by suspense are another matter.

Witness the situation in which the party of the first part is fighting for possession of a schooner, a girl or a bag of pearls. Unless you have a better example of trite plotting, we proceed. We are on the schooner. The hero sneaks out of the cabin and there is the villain on his way to sink the ship. So we have a fight:

> Jim dived at Bart's legs, but Bart was not easily thrown. They stood apart. Jim led with his left, followed through with his right. Black Bart countered the blows. Bone and sinew cracked in the mighty thunder of conflict. . . . Jim hit with his right. . . . Bart countered with a kick in the shins. . . .

There you have a masterpiece for wastebasket filing. But, believe it, this same old plot and this same old fight look a lot different when you have your suspense added. They might even sell if extracted and toned like this:

> Jim glanced out of the chart room and saw Black Bart. Water dripping from his clothes, his teeth bared, his chest heaving from his long swim, Bart stood in a growing pool which slid down his arms and legs. In his hand he clutched an ax, ready to sever the hawser and release them into the millrace of the sweeping tide. . . .

This is Jim's cue, of course, to knock the stuffing out of Black Bart, but that doesn't make good reading nor very much wordage, for thirty words are enough in which to recount any battle as such, up to and including wars. So we add suspense. For some reason Jim can't leap into the fray right at that moment. Suppose we add that he has these pearls right there and he's afraid Ringo, Black Bart's henchman, will up and swipe them when Jim's back is turned. So first Jim has to stow the pearls.

This gets Bart halfway across the deck toward that straining hawser which he must cut to wreck the schooner and ruin the hero.

Now, you say, we dive into it. Nix. We've got a spot here for some swell suspense. Is Black Bart going to cut that hawser? Is Jim going to get there?

Jim starts. Ringo hasn't been on his way to steal the pearls but to knife Jim, so Jim tangles with Ringo, and Black Bart races toward the hawser some more.

Jim's fight with Ringo is short. About like this:

> Ringo charged, eyes rolling, black face set. Jim glanced toward Bart. He could not turn his back on this charging demon. Yet he had to get that ax.
>
> Jim whirled to meet Ringo. His boot came up and the knife sailed over the rail and into the sea. Ringo reached out with his mighty hands. Jim stepped through and nailed a right on Ringo's button. Skidding, Ringo went down.
>
> Jim sprinted forward toward Bart. The black-bearded Colossus spun about to meet the rush, ax upraised.

Now, if you want to, you can dust off this scrap. But don't give it slug by slug. Hand it out, thus:

> The ax bit down into the planking. Jim tried to recover from his dodge. Bart was upon him, slippery in Jim's grasp. In vain Jim tried to land a solid blow, but Bart was holding him hard.
>
> "Ringo!" roared Bart. "Cut that hawser!"
>
> Ringo, dazed by Jim's blow, struggled up. Held tight in Bart's grasp, Jim saw Ringo lurch forward and yank the ax out of the planking.
>
> "That hawser!" thundered Bart. "I can't hold this fool forever!"

Now, if you wanted that hawser cut in the first place (which you did, because that means more trouble and the suspense of wondering how the schooner will get out of it), cut that hawser right now before the reader suspects that this writing business is just about as mechanical as fixing a Ford.

Action suspense is easy to handle, but you have to know

when to quit and you have to evaluate your drama and ladle it out accordingly.

Even in what the writers call the psychological story you have to rely upon suspense just as mechanical as this.

Give your reader a chance to wonder for a while about the final outcome.

There is one type of suspense, however, so mechanical that it clanks. I mean foreshadowing.

To foreshadow anything is weak. It is like a boxer stalling for the bell. You have to be mighty sure that you've got something outstanding to foreshadow or the reader will nail up your scalp.

It is nice to start ominously like this:

> I knew that night as I sloshed through the driving rain that all was not well. I had a chilly sense of foreboding as though a monster dogged my steps. . . .
>
> If I only had known then what awaited me when the big chimes in the tower should strike midnight, I would have collapsed with terror. . . .

Very good openings. Very, very good. Proven goods, even though the nap is a bit worn. But how many times have writers lived up to those openings? Not very many.

You get off in high, but after you finish you will probably tear out these opening paragraphs—even though Poe was able to get away with this device. Remember the opening of "The Fall of the House of Usher"? You know, the one that goes something like this: "Through the whole of a dark and dismal afternoon."

That is foreshadowing. However, few besides Poe have been able to get away with suspense created by atmosphere alone.

One particular magazine makes a practice of inserting a foreshadow as a first paragraph in every story. I have come to suspect that this is done editorially because the foreshadow is always worse than the story gives you.

It's a far cry from the jungles of Malaysia to New York, and there's a great difference between the yowl of the tiger and the rattle of the L, but in the city that night there stalked the lust of the jungle killers and a man who had one eye. . . .

I have been guilty of using such a mechanism to shoot out in high, but I don't let the paragraph stand until I am pretty doggone sure that I've got everything it takes in the way of plot and menace to back it up.

If you were to take all the suspense out of a story, no matter how many unusual facts and characters you had in it, I don't think it would be read very far.

If you were to take every blow of action out of a story and still leave its suspense (this is possible, because I've done it), you might still have a fine story, probably a better story than before.

There is not, unhappily, any firm from which you can take out a suspense insurance policy. The only way you can do it is to make sure that the reader is sitting there tensely wondering which of two or three momentous things is going to happen first. If you can do that, adroitly, to some of those manuscripts which have come bouncing back, they may be made to stay put.

# *The Death Flyer*

*written by*

## *L. Ron Hubbard*

*illustrated by*

VEN LOCKLEAR

---

### ABOUT THE STORY

*Hubbard's story "The Death Flyer," is his earliest blending of mystery and the supernatural. In this superbly crafted story, a runaway passenger train speeds forever from the past into the future, racing toward an unknowable destiny.*

*And so begins a strange encounter with a young girl in a flame-colored dress.*

*This masterful tale still holds the same unremitting suspense today that it did more than six decades ago, in April 1936, upon its original release. It embodies qualities detailed in the article "Suspense," included in this volume, of which L. Ron Hubbard said "the most intangible thing in this business of writing is that quantity 'Suspense.'"*

### ABOUT THE ILLUSTRATOR

*Ven Locklear is a concept artist and illustrator whose imaginative work involves bizarre creatures, epic fantasy scenes, menacing monsters, and surreal characters. Ven currently creates concept art and illustrations for Liquid Development, where he works on projects for WB Games, Zynga, Disney Interactive, 343 Industries, and Bethesda. Previously, he worked at Triptych Games, where he was lead concept artist on* Borderlands 2: Sir Hammerlock's Big Game Hunt. *He has also taken on projects in the music industry, where he develops creative projects for DJ/Producer Excision.*

*Ven graduated with a BFA in Illustration from Pacific Northwest College of Art. He is a former quarterly winner of the Illustrators of the Future award. His artwork was published in* L. Ron Hubbard Presents Writers of the Future Volume 26.

# *The Death Flyer*

Lost deep in the ebon tangle and echoing against the starless, sullen sky, the owl's dismal chatter came like the rattle in a dying man's throat.

Jim Bellamy paused on the ties, the beat of his heart surging through his throat. The hoot of an owl meant that someone would die.

He forced a smile to his lips at that and shrugged, setting off again through the lonesome tangle which matted the ancient and decayed tracks. He had been a fool to start back this late. He might fall into a hole or through a rotten trestle and break his neck.

But for all his smile, his big shoulders were hunched under his checkered flannel shirt and the scuff of his calks on the gritty cinders fell upon his ears like thunder in the silence.

He had not particularly enjoyed this job of surveying, but in these days, a civil engineer had to take what he could get, even though it meant the tangles and swamps and insects of northern Maine.

He had overstayed himself, checking over his shots. He had sent his crew back to their isolated lumber camp. If anything happened to him that he could not return, they would merely assume that he had chosen to spend the night in the open.

And an inner self or outer self kept telling him that something would happen, that this night was not like other nights. A vibration of unrest was in the air.

He stumbled along the tracks he could not see, and blessed them and cursed them in one breath. This railroad had been deserted for about ten years. Why, he could not exactly remember. Something about their rolling stock going up in smoke. Some wreck or other, he supposed.

Now that his mind was started along that channel, he persisted in digging out fragmentary details of what he had heard. Loggers talk and a civil engineer pretends to listen. Loggers were a superstitious lot, given to tall imaginings.

Yes, he remembered what had happened now. A train had gone through a bridge into a swollen stream and the road had never been able to rebuild for lack of funds and interest on the part of shippers who remembered the incident. It was a shame for all this work to go to waste this way. Rails and ties were still there, all in place. No one in this forgotten forest had had any use for them.

The owl gave his death rattle again. Jim Bellamy quickened his pace. Suddenly he tripped. His stomach felt light. He heard a growing roar reverberate through the trees.

When he tried to get up he was blinded by a yellow eye which grew larger and larger with the noise. He rolled to one side but he could not get off the tracks.

Something was holding his shirt, pinning him down, and the yellow eye stabbed straight through him and held him horror-stricken to the ties.

Good God, it was a train and he was in its path!

He shut his eyes tightly. The roar shook the earth and through it he seemed to hear the call of the owl which had foretold his death.

A shrill screech bit through the roar and then the thunder died to a hiss. Jim Bellamy sat up. Somehow he was no longer on the track but beside it. A mountain of rust-eaten steel reared up before him. Flame licked out and illuminated a cab. A shadowy face peered down.

"Y'all right, stranger?"

VEN LOCKLEAR

"Sure," said Bellamy in a shaky voice. "Sure. I'm all right."

"Well then, why the hell don't you get aboard? You think I've got all night?"

"Sure," said Bellamy, stumbling up to the tender.

"Not here, you fool. What do ya think we got coaches for? Get back there and get aboard. I'm in a hurry tonight. D' you realize it's a quarter past nine?"

Dazedly, Bellamy went back along the line of weather-beaten wooden coaches. Through the dirty windows he could see faces peering curiously at him. The lights which burned in the train, thought Bellamy with a start, threw no reflection on the ground.

He swung himself up into a vestibule which smelled of cinders and soft coal gas and stale cigars and opened the door into a coach. The old-fashioned lamps threw a dismal greenish light along the scarred red plush seats. Half a dozen silent passengers stared moodily ahead, paying him no heed.

Bellamy slid into a seat near the door. The engine panted, the couplings clanked as the engineer took up the slack and then the train went rolling off along the uneven bed.

Bellamy found that he could not think clearly or connectedly. The fall must have given him a nasty crack on the head. Maybe it was worse than he had thought.

He sat motionless for some time. Of his fellow travelers he could see little more than the backs of their heads. There was something unnatural about the way they sat. Tense was the word. Tense and expectant.

A man with dull, corroded brass buttons slouched into the car. His cap was pulled far down over his face and in his gloved hands he held a battered ticket puncher. He came back to where Bellamy sat.

"Ticket, please," and the voice was weary.

Bellamy sat up straight, staring at the face over him. The flesh hung in loose gouts from under the eyes. The teeth were broken behind black lips. A scar on the forehead bled down over the gray flesh but no blood touched the floor. The eyes were unseen, merely black holes in the ashen putty.

Bellamy recovered his voice. "I have no ticket."

The empty voice whined a little. "You're a new one. I never saw you before. We're late now and I can't stop to put you off."

Bellamy fumbled with the breast pocket of his checkered flannel shirt. "I'll give you the money."

"Money? I have no need of money. Not now. All I want is your ticket. Haven't you got a ticket?"

Bellamy detected a motion farther up the car. He saw that the six passengers were getting slowly to their feet and coming back.

They ranged themselves behind the conductor, staring at Bellamy. The air was charged with an evil, decayed smell. Bellamy came halfway to his feet, gripping the edges of the seat, his face blanching.

Not one of those six had visible eyes. Their flesh was the color of dirty lard. Their lips were black and their faces were slashed with many cuts.

A small man, older than the rest, better dressed, pointed a thin, clattering finger at Bellamy. "He is not one of us. He doesn't belong here!"

Bellamy moved closer to the window. The conductor stood to one side. The six, hands loose at their sides, moved slowly ahead, swaying and jolting under the influence of the train.

It was several seconds before Bellamy understood what they were trying to do. Then he realized that their unseen eyes held the threat of death.

He stood up, crouching forward, and though his face was white, his jaw was stubbornly set.

A lanky thing reached him first. Bellamy lashed out with his fist and rocked the tall body back into the others. But they came slowly on as though they hadn't seen. The lanky one was with them again.

Bellamy felt like a trapped animal about to be mangled by a hunter. Big as he was, he was no match for six. Fleshless hands reached out and gripped him. Bodies pressed him back.

He struck as hard as he could, twisting and writhing to get away.

Suddenly, above the clatter of steel wheels on rails, a clear, controlled voice said, "Let him be. He does not know."

The six fell away, backing into the aisle, looking neither to the right nor the left. They were like marionettes on strings, jiggling loosely as the train swayed.

Bellamy braced himself and rubbed at his throat where red marks were beginning to appear. Looking through the six, he was startled to see a young girl in a flame-colored dress poised in the aisle.

Her cheeks were as white as flour, but there was a certain beauty about her which Bellamy could not at once define. She was small, not over five feet four in height. The dress clung to her smooth body and rippled as she moved. Her eyes were dark and sad.

"Go back to your seats," she said.

The six moved woodenly to their places and seated themselves without a backward glance. But the conductor stood his ground.

"He has no ticket," said the conductor.

"I have it," replied the girl with a tired sigh. "I have had it for a long, long while."

She reached into a small red purse she carried and drew out a crumpled green slip which she handed to the man with the corroded brass buttons. He scanned it, and then punched it with a quick snap.

She watched him open the door and disappear and then she came slowly toward Bellamy and, reaching slowly out, took his hands in hers and sank down across from him, searching his face.

"You do not remember," she said gently.

Bellamy shook his head. He was too astonished to answer her immediately. Now that she was near to him he could smell the delicate odor of lilies of the valley. Her fine face was uptilted to him and her hands were shaking.

"I have waited long," she said. "For ten years. And now you have come. I knew that it would be you. The waiting was long but now that you are here, I see that the time was nothing. Please, don't you remember?"

He could make no answer to her even flow of words. He felt somehow that he should know, that he should remember, but his mind was dull.

"Remember how you wired me?" she went on. "How you said, 'Whenever you come, I shall be here on this platform, waiting for you'? And now I see that you have tired of waiting and that you have come to me. You see . . . I could not come to you. I must stay here with these. It is hard sometimes, harder than you know. But now all that is past and you are with me again."

She raised her slim hand to his face and touched his cheeks. "You are not changed . . . and though I cannot see you . . . very well, just to feel you is enough. Please never go away again. I have been so lonely, I have waited so long."

Bellamy felt as though someone had thrust a dagger into his heart and twisted it there. This girl was almost blind. He was afraid to answer her, afraid that his voice would dispel the illusion she cherished.

But speak he must and although the lump was large in his throat, he said, "No. I won't leave you . . . again."

Then somehow he had gathered her close to him and she was vibrant against him and her breath was warm and sweet upon his face. He held her there for a long time.

"Then it is you after all," she murmured. "I waited so long."

The conductor came back, staring at his nickel-plated watch. "He'll make it. He'll make it. But there's only half an hour left."

The girl shivered against Bellamy. "Must it happen again, now that—"

"Must what happen?" Bellamy demanded with a sudden clarity of mind. He felt like a hypnotized person returning to life.

"Why . . . why, the wreck, of course. But then you would not know about that. You were waiting. You were not with me then."

The conductor snapped shut the watch and moved heavily up the car, muttering, "He'll make it."

"The wreck?" said Bellamy.

"Yes. This is August the sixteenth, isn't it? Certainly it must be, otherwise we would not be out. August the sixteenth is the date, don't you see? Ten years ago tonight. I hate it but there is nothing I can do. Wait, dearest. Wait. Perhaps you can stop it. If anyone does, then it will be over."

Bellamy felt his mind grow leaden again. But he stood up, pressing her back into the seat. His eyes were staring and his jaw was set. He knew that somehow this was all wrong, that this couldn't be happening. But it was.

"In ten minutes, *they'll* come aboard. *They'll* hang out a red lantern and we'll stop. If you could make them . . ."

Bellamy stared down at her. His heart was pounding against his ribs and he labored with a problem he could not understand.

A red lantern, eh? And somehow everything would be all right if he could stop this thing. He leaned quickly over her and kissed her soft, moist lips. Then he went up the car past the six passengers. They were still leaning forward staring with their sunken sockets and seeing nothing.

Bellamy swung open the door, walked across the swinging vestibule, pushed open another door and found himself in a baggage car.

The baggage man stared at him and nodded. The baggage man's face was a black shadow and his hands were white and thin.

"What's the use, mister?" said the baggage man. "You can't stop them."

Bellamy swung on by and went through a door. He crawled up over the tender and looked down on the cab. The fireman was throwing coal into the box, sweat standing out and shining in the light. The fireman worked like a machine and the flames belched redly from the open door.

The engineer turned to stare at Bellamy and Bellamy stared back. The engineer's face was nothing but a shadow on which was perched the billed cap of his kind. The engineer's hand was on the throttle, easing it back.

"You can't do anything," said the engineer. "Look out. I gotta stop."

The fireman shoveled with jerky regularity. Bellamy, standing with the firelight hot on his face, said, "Why don't you try? Just this once. Then—"

"It's no use, mister. I've tried it and I can't. That's a red lantern and a flag stop. I got my orders."

Bellamy saw the man haul on the brake. Steam hissed, steel wheels groaned as they slid on the rails. Bellamy saw they were drawing up to a platform overgrown with long weeds. The station house had gradually collapsed into itself until only a few boards were left—a few boards and the drooping roof beam like a gallows against the sullen sky. An ancient sign creaked and banged in the wind. Once again Bellamy heard the call of the owl and shivered.

Suddenly, beside the cab there appeared a shock of black hair. The man reached for the rungs and swung up to the cab, followed by two other men more ragged and dirty than he.

The first one was tall and thick through the body like a carelessly filled bag of rags. His teeth were yellow and his eyes blazed.

"Pull out," said the man. "I'm riding here."

"You can't ride here," cried the engineer.

"Who's to say I can't?"

"I say you can't. Not unless you've got the orders tonight."

"What do I care for orders?" The thick one pulled a heavy, sawed-off shotgun from his coat and pointed it at the engineer.

The fireman jumped forward, shovel raised. The gun roared flame redder than the firebox. A black hole went through the fireman's guts. He fell heavily, clawing at the hot plates, sagging against the boilers. The rank, sickening odor of burning flesh filled the air. One hand was out of sight in the flames.

The engineer jammed the throttle ahead. The train lurched and started. The thick one was laughing and Bellamy smelled whiskey, cheap and strong, upon the fellow's breath. It had happened so fast that he could do nothing.

The engineer was reaching for his hip pocket where a wrench bulged. One of the others yelled a warning. The thick one sent a roaring blast of flame and lead straight into the engineer's face. The man sank across his throttles, throwing them wider.

Bellamy was sick with the cold brutality of it. But the scattergun was empty and he saw no other weapons. He jerked up the fireman's shovel and aimed a blow at the thick one's skull.

The other two, their faces gray blots in the red flame, leaped ahead to snatch at the handle. Bellamy avoided them. The thick one fumbled for shells.

Bellamy yelled with rage and twisted the shovel free. He saw a blackjack come up with a swift, lethal swing. He dodged. The two men he faced laughed and weaved drunkenly. The blackjack landed at the base of Bellamy's neck.

Bellamy stumbled. A fist jarred into his chest. He doubled up, almost out, still trying to fight them back. The big one brought down the muzzle of the scattergun and kicked Bellamy back under the fireman's seat.

Then the three crawled up over the tender and stood for a moment against the sky, shouting at each other to be heard above the roar of the speeding train.

Bellamy, sick and dizzy, crawled out from the corner. He could not think of anything but the girl. These three drunken men were going back toward her. He had heard a snatch of their shouts. That had been enough.

His head was ringing and he could not concentrate. He had the feeling that he was doing wrong to leave the cab but he could not reason why. The engineer was hanging against the throttles, but Bellamy did not understand.

Bellamy crawled up the tender and hitched himself over the coal and down toward the baggage car. He shoved open the door with shaking hands.

The baggage master was sprawled among the shifting trunks.

His hands were outstretched and he did not move. The cashbox was standing open, keys jingling in the padlock.

Bellamy went on back. In the vestibule of the first coach he tripped over a sodden lump. He did not stop to inspect it. He plunged on through the empty coach to the second.

His brain was spinning like a maelstrom when he passed through the second vestibule and then his mind went clear again. He peered through the filthy pane of glass.

How long had he been at this? How much time had passed? Somehow that was important above all else.

The passengers were pressed back against the wall. With his scattergun in hand, the thick one held them at bay while his two companions went through pockets and grips. Their shouts were loud and harsh and their faces laughed but not their eyes.

Inside the coach, Bellamy saw a fire ax in its bracket on the wall. Cautiously, he moved the door inward. The thick one's back was toward him but at any moment one of the passengers might give a sign. One shot at that range from the scattergun . . .

And then Bellamy saw the girl. She was pressed far back against the rearmost seat, her body tense, her hands thrown back in fear. The thick one reached out with a hard hand and jerked her toward him with a bellowed laugh.

He twisted her wrist until she knelt in the aisle and then, holding the scattergun loosely in one hand, he shifted his grip and snatched at her shoulder. Her lips went white with pain. The thick one laughed again.

"Hold her!" he shouted to his aides.

Bellamy was through the door, ax clutched in his two strong hands.

Suddenly the girl whipped free. The thick one's knuckles crashed against her eyes. She screamed and sank back on her knees, sinking down into the aisle.

A mad, mad thought raced through Bellamy's brain. So that's why she was blind.

He raced the length of the car. One of the aides shouted a warning. The thick one whirled, hair streaming down over his bloated gray face. His yellow teeth flashed and the heavy folds of ashy flesh jumped as he moved.

The scattergun was coming up. Bellamy lashed down with the ax. The blade bit cleanly through the matted hair, through the skull, deep into the face. But the big one stood and the wound did not bleed.

The aides screamed and ran, flashing out through the rear door, but the passengers stood with hands still upraised, without expression or movement.

The thick one tottered backward, clawing at the ax, knees buckling. He stumbled out through the door and out of sight.

Bellamy kneeled beside the girl, lifting her gently and holding her against him.

"It's all right," she whispered. "It's all right. You have come at last. I gave them your ticket here. Perhaps . . . perhaps . . . after this there will be . . . but the train! Good God, stop the train!"

Bellamy stared blankly at her without understanding. She clutched at his shirt, raising herself up. "Please, God, please don't let him go again. Please let him stop this. Please!"

She buried her face in his shirt and moaned. Suddenly a brain not Bellamy's took command of him. He started up and faced to the front. He saw the picture of the engineer slouched against the throttles.

Running, he went up the aisle, through the door and down the second coach. He could feel the wheels lifting from the curves under the onslaught of too much speed. The train swayed drunkenly from side to side, threatening to leave the tracks at any moment.

He was aware of someone behind him and he turned back. The girl in red was coming, groping blindly up the aisle, trying to keep up with him.

He swung her into his arms and stepped out into the vestibule. The dead conductor moved restlessly as the train swayed. In the baggage car the baggage master was pinned down under an upset trunk. His arms were still outstretched.

Bellamy pushed the girl up to the tender and followed her.

The rocketing perch was hard to hold. Bellamy slid down into the cab. He heard the girl's scream.

Pulling the engineer away from the throttles, he clutched them and hauled back. He tried to find the brake and could not. Some lever here was the brake. Something on this boiler or in this cab would stop the train. He tripped over the fireman's body and fell heavily, struggling up even before he hit.

The girl cried out again, her hands on his shoulders, trying to drag him to his feet.

"The trestle!" she cried.

He gripped her arms and looked into her drawn face. It was too late for brakes. Too late for anything.

The front trucks left the rails. The roar of water was under them, far under them. The train went off slowly, slowly, disjointed and lashing.

Space was greedy, sucking the cars down.

Holding the girl close to him, Bellamy braced himself against the crash. He could feel her quiver against him, he could hear the moan of agony which came from her tight throat.

The thunder and crushed steel, the roar of escaping steam, the splinter of rended wood, was suddenly swallowed by the cry of swirling water.

"Don't . . . don't go away from me!"

The voice receded, growing fainter and fainter until it was gone. In its place was the whisper of water against the sand.

Rough hands brought Bellamy to his feet. Daylight blinded him and he was aware of an ache which sent quick lightning flashes through his head when he moved.

Through the swirl of faces about him he could see a crumpled ruin against the bank from which protruded a rust-eaten set of trucks. Farther along he could see the hulk of an old locomotive, bent and twisted and brown under the clear sun.

His eyes focused on the faces and a single thought shot a question from him. "What . . . have they . . . where is she?"

"He's balmy," remarked a rodman Bellamy suddenly recognized as his own.

"You'd be balmy too, I guess," retorted a recorder in great heat.

Bellamy's camp cook was feeling Bellamy's head. "It's all right. He ain't hurt none to speak about."

"But the wreck!" pleaded Bellamy.

"What wreck?" said the recorder. "You mean this old train here. That fell off the trestle about ten years ago, I reckon. That's what made 'em shut this line down. About ten years ago it was, and, I think, about this time of the year. But you ain't been in no wreck, Bel. You stumbled off that trestle in the dark and lit in the soft sand. Some drop, ain't it? We been looking for you all morning, but you ain't hurt none."

"You went a hell of a ways past the lumber camp," said the cook. "What was the matter? Soused? Don't tell us you got lost."

"I . . . guess I did," said Bellamy, feeling very weak and dizzy and somehow very sad.

"C'mon," said the rodman, "we'll tote you back to camp. Hell, unless you get well right quick, we'll lose two days or more."

"We . . . won't lose anything," said Bellamy. "I guess we better be getting back to the job."

"Okay with us," said the recorder and helped Bellamy walk up the steep bank. "But I think you'd better lay up for a while. You must have been out for a long time and that ain't so good."

Bellamy stopped at the top and looked back at the old wreck half buried in the sand and water. It was rusty and broken and forgotten, somehow forlorn.

A voice seemed to whisper in his ear, "I will be waiting . . . on the other side. The next time we'll get through."

He looked about him, startled, but his survey crew was silent, waiting for him to go on.

He stepped off down the uneven trail and vanished in the twilight of the woods.

# *Odd and Ugly*

*written by*

## *Vida Cruz*

*illustrated by*

REYNA ROCHIN

---

## ABOUT THE AUTHOR

*Vida Cruz lives in a stunningly woodsy village by a dam in Manila, Philippines with her parents, sister, and six memeable dogs. Formerly a journalist, she now writes children's storybooks that teach Chinese kids English.*

*Due to a combination of a strict upbringing, an all-girls Catholic school, and a weak immune system, Vida decided to liven up her life—and she turned to* Harry Potter, Lord of the Rings, *fairy tales, and romances to do just that. Of course, a steady diet of books and cartoons will eventually compel the dieter to write and draw, which is exactly what happened. But it wasn't enough.*

*Deciding that words were her calling, she worked hard for fellowships to two national workshops and a scholarship to the Clarion Writers Workshop in San Diego. All of these enabled her to travel and discover what a beautiful place the world is.*

*Ironically, traveling also helped her become interested in Philippine history, culture, and mythology. All these inform her fiction, which can be found in* Expanded Horizons, Lontar: The Journal of Southeast Asian Speculative Fiction, *and the* Philippine Speculative Fiction *anthologies.*

*"Odd and Ugly" is the result of all these influences coalescing around the persistent image of a kapre in a tree and a young girl beneath. Sometimes, they were in a graveyard. Sometimes, the girl had a steampunk robot governess with her. Upon asking "Can Beauty and the Beast be retold with this image?" the story finally wrote itself.*

## ABOUT THE ILLUSTRATOR

*Reyna Nicole Rochin was born December 30, 1990 in the suburbs of Los Angeles. Like most artists, she had crayons and paper in her hands since the day she could hold them.*

*As she grew up, there weren't many other artists near her. She spent her childhood playing in the backyard, taking trips to the California beaches, and simply trying to get through life with good grades.*

*Soon after high school, she received a scholarship to play volleyball at San Francisco State University, where life led her next. With her sports background and a degree in Fine Arts (emphasis in drawing and painting), she had no clue what to do—so she took up a career in personal training.*

*A few years later, she found that painting still held her interest in her off hours. So she decided to return to school and was accepted to the Savannah College of Art & Design for an MFA in illustration.*

*Today, she spends her time working hard at school in Atlanta, power lifting, and reading when she gets the chance.*

# *Odd and Ugly*

## I

You come to my tree at high noon in July, sweating, panting, young. So very, very young. I can't help staring at you: it's like watching a walking, talking circular window with square glass stuck through it. I knew you'd come someday, but I'm still so stunned to see you that I disbelieve my own eyes. The small sack in one hand and the clay jar at your hip tell me that you mean to stay, too.

"Are you the kapre from the stories? The one with the shell necklace?" you ask, your voice high and clear. You set your jar down and gather your long, sweat-dampened black hair over your shoulder, away from your nape, as you glance up from under your straw salakot. Your eyes are the color of tablea chocolate bubbling in a cup. I'm startled that I remember so human a sensation.

"That depends," I say. I lower myself so you can see me, a thing moving and detached from the canopy of leaves above, although I'm of the same hues. Humanoid, but decidedly not human. I catch your gaze falling on my necklace: several cowrie shells strung together with black beads and woven thread, with a single shell hanging from the middle like a pendant. Your expression becomes momentarily unsettled; maybe you're startled by my ugliness, just like all the other passersby whom I like to scare. Whatever it is, you shake it off, and the action comes from inside you: a slow resolve that hardens your features and makes you cling tighter to your small sack of belongings. Your boldness is commendable, as always.

I ask you two questions that I already know the answers to: "Who is everyone? And who are you?"

"Everyone is the town, and I am Maria," is your simple answer. I thrill to hear your name. "My tatay owes you a debt."

I remember your father as a frightened young man, clutching a mango stolen from my tree, begging for forgiveness and blabbering about the cravings of his pregnant wife. It feels as if that happened only yesterday. "Ah, you're *that* Maria. You've grown."

You ignore that. "What's your name?"

I laugh, long and low. "Oh, no. You haven't earned that yet, 'neng. And you shouldn't wander out here by yourself. The town's tongues will wag about you meeting a lover."

"Let them wag."

"The Guardia Civil will say that you're conspiring with revolutionaries."

"I don't care about that."

"The friars will denounce you as a witch."

It takes a while, but you give me a slow nod. I'm impressed, though I have no proof that you truly understand the implications of your declarations. You say, "I'm not afraid of them, señor. I've come to erase my tatay's debt."

*Señor.* I've been called many things in my long life, and most of them unpleasant—but never that. The irony tickles me.

I drop to the ground and straighten my back. You barely surpass my collarbones. But my height isn't what gets your attention—you realize that I'm wearing nothing but a loincloth. Your gaze snaps back to my face, though your cheeks are pink-tinged. I grin at your discomfort.

"Erase his debt with what? Another mango?" I know I'm being difficult, but what other way is there to be? This was never going to be an easy situation for either of us. "I've no use for money, and I have everything I need in my realm. Are you going to offer me yourself, 'neng?"

You pout. Your bushy eyebrows meet, and your lower lip sticks out, an arresting dash of pink in your sun-browned face. You're making quick mental calculations.

I'm fighting that part of me that has always adored you.

"Yes," you say in an even tone, flooring me once again. You always were so quick to take up a challenge, as on the day your father first asked if you would like to learn to hack stalks of sugarcane with a bolo knife. I just marvel to see it up close.

And then you add: "I'm going to offer you my services, señor. As your housekeeper."

I don't fight the part of me that is also irritated by you.

## II

It doesn't work that way, a human woman un-courted by a kapre shouldering her way into his tree. I'm supposed to chase you first. I'm supposed to leave small gifts around your house, and you must come to me willingly. *I'm* supposed to choose *you*—or so other kapre told me long ago, when I still attempted socializing with them. I've never actually courted human women before. But here *you* are, choosing *me*—or my home, at least—and I can never refuse someone passage when they wish to enter my home.

"I don't have a house to keep!" I huff.

"Then I'll be your tree-keeper. Or your realm-keeper," you shoot airily over your shoulder as you make your way down my halls. "This is a good deal, you know? You don't even have to give me wages or anything more than a place to stay! I only have to work off the debt!"

I grumble, "You'll just mess everything up, 'neng."

You don't know your way around, and I'm not going to give you a tour—I didn't formally agree to you being my housekeeper, after all—yet you seem unconcerned with becoming lost. I guess you're that confident that you'll get to know all the firefly orb-lit tunnels and caverns, all the gardens and groves that I've filled with collected human treasures—and all the various flora in between—the same way you know your own home.

Still, that doesn't stop me from pulling you by the shoulder when my giant Venus flytrap's jaws snap across the path ahead.

"Be careful, 'neng!" I say, and remember too late what I shouldn't have said. On cue, the whispers begin.

*Is that her?*

*Don't be stupid, that* is *her!*

*Who?*

*You know*—her!

*She's not very pretty, is she?*

*I thought she'd be prettier, too.*

"I'm right here, you know!" you call out, and I can't help but laugh from deep in my gut. First, because their discussion about you is honestly amusing and second, because I'm relieved you stopped them from saying anything more.

Nearby, the fire tree—*delonix regia,* who prefers to be called Delonix—whispers to me alone, *That* is *her, isn't it?*

"It is."

If Delonix were a person, she would nod. She is something like my second-in-command here, the queen of all the flora by some unspoken agreement. She is also my eyes and ears around my realm. *How do you plan to go about this?*

"Go?"

*I assume you have a plan or you would've handed her the stone by now—*

"Delonix," I snap. "Not here."

Honestly, you weren't supposed to be here yet. My intention was to let your father know someday in the distant future that I wanted my debt paid. He wasn't supposed to send you here before that day—so what happened? But I put off asking you in order to introduce you to the flowers. I show you to them all—the spinning vine flowers, the luminescent flowers, the rotting corpse flowers, the toothed flowers, the flowers with faces. I rattle off their names like a carpenter hammers a nail in wood, and I'm impressed when you echo them with accuracy and grace.

"What amazing flowers you all are," you say with a smile that comes from your entire being. You stroke the flowers who allow themselves to be stroked and bow to those who demand to be bowed to. "I look forward to working with you all from now on!"

I allow myself to think just for a fraction of a moment that maybe you *can* handle yourself around here, that maybe it will be nice to talk to someone who isn't rooted to the ground or clouded in malodor. Then I push the thought down like a stone in mud.

I'm glad you're here, but that doesn't mean we can be easygoing with each other.

## III

In August, you discover very quickly that being a housekeeper in my tree is more like being a gardener. Those flowers don't all get hungry at the same time, and not all for the same food. Some of them tend to go on and on about their myriad personal woes or else the tedious gossip of the plant kingdom. Day and night do not pass like they do in the world outside my tree, but I can say with certainty that feeding and talking to everyone is two days of work.

Yet you listen to them all as if your very life depends on it—and in some carnivorous cases, it truly does. You pass sufficient judgments on debates and arguments when called for. You don't appear to be tiring out anytime soon; in fact, you move as if you already belong here, as if you've only just returned to your home. The only thing that gives away your humanity is that you decline the flowers' and the trees' offers of fruit and honey. The fact that you still climb out of my realm to gather your own food and water every now and then means that you don't intend to stay forever. No one may eat anything in a kapre's realm and expect to live in the wider world again.

I don't tell you that women who end up in kapre trees are not meant to leave. I don't tell you that it is completely within my power to bar your passage out. I don't tell you that I've made an exception for you. If you already know all this, you're not letting on.

Somehow, you've also found out—likely from Delonix—that

I sleep in the acacia grove. Or maybe the smell was a giveaway, I don't know—I've been told for years by various creatures that the ash from my cigars can be smelled from miles away. Between feeding and talking to the flowers, you've somehow made time to sweep the ash from the grass. While I'm grateful for the cleaner grove, you've also displaced and rearranged my cigar stash. In fact, you've done that for all the objects in the grove: shiny trinkets and love letters and parasols and all manner of *things* that people have lost in the forest outside over the years. When I discover this, I draw myself up to my full height. I bare my teeth as I tower over you. You stand there scowling up at me, defiant like a lit lantern in darkness.

"I knew you'd mess everything up, 'neng!" I growl. "I can't find anything!"

"Señor, if you just let me explain my categorization system, then you'll be able to find *everything,*" is your none-too-gentle answer.

"I don't want anything categorized! I want everything where they were before!"

"Well, I can't put them back in the exact mess I found them in," your tone has grown frosty with logic now. "That's unreasonable."

*"Unreasonable?"* I thunder. I know *I'm* being unreasonable. I've lived the way I liked, alone, for so long now. Someone else coming here and touching my things reminds me of a more distant time, when I couldn't own anything. I know I'm reacting to those times, but it's too late to stop being irritable. "What's unreasonable is this arrangement! I'm going to pay your tatay a visit—"

"No, no, don't!" You are about to reach for me. I know it, you know it. But something holds you back; I'm willing to bet that it is my ugliness and quite possibly my glower. You lower your hands to your sides; they continue to twitch, so you ball them into fists. "Don't do that, señor. I swore to my parents I'd work off tatay's debt."

Something about the way your head is bent, the way your fists uncurl and pluck at your checkered saya, the way your slippered feet dig into the ground where you stand makes me uncomfortable. What aren't you telling me, I wonder? At last, I say, "All right. I won't. But next time, you better let me know before you clean around here."

You chuckle, a small sound. "The cleaning was as much for my benefit as yours."

I feel the irritation rising in me again. "What do you mean?"

"I'm sleeping in the calachuchi grove next to yours," you say. It is astonishing, now that we've moved on from the subject of your father, how unruffled you are—either with this statement of yours or the fact that faint clouds have begun billowing from my nostrils. "And I can smell your revolting cigars from there."

"Then why didn't you *categorize* the stuff there, 'neng?" I spit out "categorize" like a mouthful of santol pits.

"Oh, I already have," you say that as if it's something I already should have known, and I guess I should have. You always did appreciate order. "I just came in here to do something about the stench and accidentally moved some things. So I thought I'd do something nice for you and clean your grove."

That knocks the wind out of me. I know you learned your thoughtfulness from your mother—I've seen you help her help your elderly neighbors carry bayongs brimming with fish and vegetables from the wet market to their houses. You'd make a fine wife for a human husband—and because I let my guard down just a little, the words spill from my mouth before I can censor them. I regret saying this up until the moment you lower your head.

"Anyone who's heard of me already thinks I'm a troublesome woman," your tone is subdued, just as when we discussed your father. It really doesn't suit you. "I'm not afraid of the new high-and-mighty *haciendero* snatching up our lands, or the Guardia Civil, or the friars in their big churches. My neighbors say that makes me odd, even dangerous."

Anger curls in the pit of my stomach. Oh, if that miserable town only knew. "Then no one in that town deserves you. Even a blind man can see that that makes you brave."

You look up at me again. The big brown pools of your eyes are gleaming.

"Thank you, señor," you say, your voice lowered to a breath. I can't help watching your lips form over the words.

I turn away from the desire to kiss you—from *you*—for all the good it will do.

## IV

Why do no other creatures visit you, señor?"

"Because I don't want them to. And most aren't as thick-faced as you, 'neng."

You let go of the yellow-stained blanket you've been washing in the stream running through my realm, stand up, and give me a dainty curtsy. Your hair falls forward; you've taken to wearing calachuchi flowers in it lately. I don't say so, but they and their sweet fragrance become you. "What a lovely compliment! Thank you, señor."

I choke a laugh on my cigar. The embers fall on the branch where I lounge, then to the grass. The flowers nearest me call to each other, *Look out! You'll get burned!* while the rest giggle and titter with—and not *at*—your sense of humor. Some of them say to me, *She's as thick-faced as you!* They've gotten even bolder with your coming.

You return to the washing. "There's something else I've been wondering about."

"Ah, no end to the wondering with you, is there?"

You don't answer back, but I could swear that there is a hint of a smile in the slight profile I can see from my vantage point. "When I was little, my parents and neighbors used to tell me stories of the diwata of the mountain before she disappeared. Where is she now? Surely she visits you?"

*The diwata of the mountain! The diwata of the mountain!* the flowers chant in singsong.

I hush them. I don't know what to say to you, though, and you can tell. You spin around to find me tapping more ash from the cigar.

"No, she does not," I say at last.

You bite your lip.

"The diwata doesn't visit anyone now, 'neng."

"Isn't that worrying?" you ask. You're crumpling your saya in your hands again, as you always do when you're anxious. "The elders say that she hasn't been seen by anyone for hundreds of years! I thought maybe she kept to her kind or so, but if she doesn't visit even you—"

I support my weight with the branch and lean forward, my interest piqued. "Why are you so worried about her, 'neng? She was long before your time."

"I—" You stare at the grass now. You quiet down as you wrestle with some inner turmoil. "I guess I thought that she'd answer the pleas of her supplicants. I thought she'd protect us from the abuses of the Kastila. If not her people, then her lands."

I lean back against the trunk. "'Neng, if you're under the impression that the diwata is all-powerful, then you're mistaken. The friars came to her promising friendship. By the time their corruption came to light, they'd already turned most of the population to their god. She couldn't drive out the Kastila without help, any more than you can."

You sink to your knees. "So she's abandoned us for good?"

"Hah! Never," I take a puff from my cigar. "She can't abandon you any more than she can abandon her mountain."

"So where is she?"

I hesitate. "Diwata will be found when she wants to be found."

"But will she come back?"

I meet your gaze. Worry swims in it. How young you are, how naive, how innocent.

"Someday. I'm sure of it."

## V

As someone who never had anything, I wanted everything. And yet, how I was ever unsatisfied with spending long days and nights counting stars and fireflies and loving the diwata of the mountain the best way I knew how baffles even me. I wanted to be able to change into animal forms like she could. I wanted so badly to know what it was like to be not me, not in my own skin.

We fought about this a lot, but somehow, I won in the end. Slowly, the diwata began to teach me the secrets of how to change into a chicken, a dog, a goat, a boar, and so much more. Despite her reluctance with all this, she'd always laugh whenever I stopped the transformation halfway. I'd be sprouting feathers or four hoofed legs or a beak or tusks or a bushy tail. Sometimes all at once. We liked going to the river and laughing at how ugly I looked every time I did this. Anyone else would've been frightened by my grotesque appearances, but not her. And still, she remembered to warn me that if I favored one form too long, that form becomes mine.

I think my newfound powers gave me a lengthened life span, for I noticed that people entering the forest brought more advanced weaponry and machinery with them and the natives wore more and more Hispanized clothing. Continually turning into different animals and learning how to move like them gave me their strength, as well.

I began some dangerous experiments soon enough. If I could stop the transformation halfway through the process, couldn't I contain the transformation to just one or two parts of me? I made myself grow twice my height and shrink to a child's size. I started hiding in trees and changing my skin to match the leaves and branches, the way I'd seen kapre from other forests do. My gauge for success was being spotted or not by passersby.

But the day came when my skin wouldn't lose its arboreal colors, and I couldn't return to my true height. I couldn't change a thing about myself for a long time, and there was nothing even the diwata of the mountain could do about that. She had to start visiting me in my tree-ish hiding holes. Eventually, the power to transform returned to me, but I could never hold a new form for long. Even when I learned to change back into my human appearance, I could feel my old skin covering me like an ill-fitting suit. It was no longer who I was; I was stuck as an ugly tree giant, and it was all my fault.

The diwata claimed she didn't care how I looked. I wished I could believe her. I truly hated what I'd become, and I allowed that hate to overpower her voice. My only defense, albeit a flimsy one, is how keeping up my human appearance whenever we were together took up the energy that should've gone to listening and understanding her words.

And then one day, I hid myself from the diwata, knowing that her finding me was no easy task, given that I wasn't born on or around the mountain. I took up residence in a mango tree relatively near the town, knowing that she wouldn't dare go near. The town was now the territory of another god, after all.

I heard a rumor many years later that the diwata had taken to wandering the forest as a human woman and calling out a name—mine. I'd missed the diwata ever since, but it was this news that finally tugged my guilt free of the mire of my self-absorption. I left my tree in search of her.

And when I finally found the diwata, it was the moment before the cliff rocks crumbled beneath her feet. Even that moment was too late.

I've been trying to atone for my stupidity ever since.

## VI

It's early in October, and you are sifting through a pile of lacy mantillas in the santol grove when you find a book. You are so engrossed in your reading that you don't notice I've just returned from an afternoon of intimidating humans who wish to sleep, eat, pray, or make love under my tree. I squat so that my shadow doesn't fall over the pages like your hair does.

When the diwata and I first met many years ago, it was me in the grass, exhausted, hungry, bleeding, and her standing over me, fresh as sunshine. That night is now literally lifetimes ago, and seeing the way we are now, I ache for it.

When you finally let out a short laugh, that's when I ask you what's so funny.

You jump. The book falls to the grass. "How long have you been there?"

"Long enough," I say. "So what's so funny?"

You pick up the book and flip to the page you were last reading. There is a drawing at the top of the page of a boy bending over a crab. The rest of the page is a block of squiggly, flourished text. I frown at it, vaguely remembering it from when I first flipped through the pages. This book was left on a boulder down the path from my tree a few years back.

"You think a boy and a crab are funny?"

You giggle. "It's just so stupid! A lazy boy buys a crab from the market and then tells it to go back to his house so that he can take a nap!"

"Huh? That really *is* stupid."

You're growing more and more confused, and I begin to realize my mistake. "Haven't you read this before?"

When I don't answer, you can only say, "Oh."

A week later, I am walking past your grove when you sprint out and nearly collide with my back. I turn around; you wave a book frantically in my face. "Let me teach you how to read, señor!"

My mouth twists to one side. I'm doubtful. "Why would I need to learn to read?"

"How can you not? You've got so many books in here!" You gesture at the calachuchi trees. "I found five in there, alone! Many of them are religious, but not all! It'd be a waste!"

I tell you a half-truth. "I just like looking at the pictures, 'neng."

You whack my arm with the book you're holding. I flinch, but do nothing. You seem to be getting comfortable with me, at least. "Not all books have pictures—definitely not all the books you've collected. Señor, I think you'd enjoy them more if you could read them!"

Your passion amuses me, impresses me, even, but I really don't want to do this. "'Neng, I have better things to do with my time."

Your eyebrows almost disappear into your hairline. "Like what?"

I turn away with a smirk. "Smoke."

That night, you're not in your grove. You're not in any of the tunnels or caverns we frequent. You're not even outside my tree.

My hand creeps up to the pendant of my cowrie shell necklace. The power within the pendant allows me to see anyone I wish no matter when it is or where they are. But when you were born, I swore that I would use it to check in on you only once a year, on your birthday, for the last twenty years.

This is how I know that you have good parents, as they always strive to teach you something new on your birthday—like when your father taught you to plow your fields with the family carabao when you turned three and when your mother taught you to prune and water flowers to sell at the market when you turned four. During the years when there was a little money saved up, they bought you something new, like slippers with embroidered roses when you turned fifteen or perhaps something novel and tasty, like that large jar of ube jam when you turned sixteen. On your last birthday, earlier this year, your parents gave you a new baro and a checkered saya—the same ones you were wearing when you came to me. You embraced them, happier than I've ever seen you. I thought then that if you're that happy, then I should be happy, too.

I have so far kept my promise, but I'm frazzled enough about your disappearance to break it just this once. Luckily, Delonix whacks my shoulder before I do.

*Calm down,* she says. *She fell asleep in the bamboo grove south of here.*

I'm ready to run there the moment I receive the explanation. "What's Maria doing there?"

REYNA ROCHIN

*She's been gathering all the books she can find in the groves.*

"What for?"

*Isn't it obvious? She's building a place just for books. She's determined to teach you to read.*

I find you in the grove Delonix described. You are lying on your side in such a way that I deduce you fell asleep sitting down and then toppled. A book pillows your cheek and a line of drool runs down the same cheek. Your fingers are squeezed in between the pages of another book while two firefly orbs float above you. A third orb reveals that more books are scattered around you in piles half my height. Have I really picked up that many books from the forest? Why are humans forever losing books in there?

I lift you. You're heavier than I expected, but not all that much trouble to carry. In your grove, I cover you in a worn, time-stained blanket and put a thin pillow under your head, its fluff all but gone. How have I let you sleep in such conditions?

The next night, I sneak into town disguised as a stray dog because I don't want to have to expend precious energy fighting people who see me as a monster. In my true form, I steal a whole four-poster bed from some rich young *mestiza* while she's out visiting her lover. I take some of her dresses and shoes for good measure, too, so that you don't wear out the clothes you arrived in. It's not easy, avoiding the Guardia Civil's night patrol with heavy furniture in tow, but I manage it with a few more disguises. I hide the bed and the clothes in the forest and return to the town, long enough to watch the *mestiza* enter her house just a little after dawn and scream for the Guardia Civil from her bedroom window.

I let you think that the bed is just one more abandoned thing I picked up in the forest, partially because I have fun teasing you that rats have made their home in there. I even threw in two weeks' worth of fruits from the trees beyond my tree. You're grateful anyway, though you point out that I could've given you this bed and those clothes when you first began living here.

Over the next few days, you alter the dresses to fit you, and they fit you well, indeed. When the fruits I got you run out, you still go out and gather your food from the outside world. Yet you look more well-fed and well-rested somehow. Funny how much difference a good bed makes.

When you show me the bamboo-turned-book grove and ask me if you could teach me how to read, I don't refuse you.

## VII

You ask me after one of our reading lessons in November why I collect so much junk. I'm taken aback; I've never said my reasons aloud before. The flowers aren't interested—they complain that the junk takes up space meant for themselves—and Delonix doesn't question me about it.

I begin by pointing at a clock here, digging out a handkerchief there. The words come out in a trickle at first, and then like a river released from a rocky spring. I explain that all these things have stories, whether I witnessed them or not: that a mud-caked set of letters were left by a young woman in the hollow of my tree, where they went undiscovered by her lover for years; that a golden funeral mask was part of the loot some thief buried in a clay pot at the roots of my tree; that a noose was left behind when I scared away several Guardia Civil who were going to execute a poor farmer suspected of sedition and insurrection. And that was just a sampling of the objects I found on and around my tree. I've found countless other things in my jaunts around the forest and the mountain it surrounds, things I invent the stories for: pipes, picnic baskets, slippers with broken straps, salakots, rifles, swords, jewelry, coins, bouquets long since dried out, blankets, rosaries, furniture, food. Sometimes I find these bloody, sometimes muddy, sometimes torn, sometimes whole and new.

You hang on to my every word, rapt, hands clasped on your lap. Sooner or later, you'll ask about my necklace, and when you do, I surprise myself with the ease with which I tell the story.

"It was my mother's. It was the only thing she got to bring out of her homeland."

You are sitting on your ankles when you hear this. You redistribute your weight, straighten your back. "You mean, you didn't always live in this tree?"

"No. And I wasn't always a kapre, either," I say. I imagine my smile is bitter. "I wasn't even born in this land."

"Where were you born?"

"*Portuguesa*. España's rival nation. I was lucky to be brought up by my mother, but I was eventually sold from Lusitano to Lusitano, from Portuguesa to Brasil and back—and then finally to a *conquistador de Castile* headed for the Filipinas. Not long after we landed here, he made me help build the walls of Intramuros in Manila. And that's when I ran from him."

"I see."

"Do you, now?" I squat to your level on the grass. "Kapre. Tree giant. Cafre. African slave. Kafir. One who does not believe in Allah. The meaning changes depending on who says it and where it's said. I am all three things, 'neng."

"And how did you end up like this?"

I feel my smile grow wider. "I asked for this."

Your round eyes go rounder. "You . . . ?"

"And I don't regret it. Or at least, I don't regret it now. Before, I owned nothing. Now, I own more than I'll ever need. There is nothing to return to in my former life."

Your gaze doesn't waver from mine. "What do you regret, then, señor?"

I almost topple backward. "What?"

"Everyone has something they regret. You were human once; I don't think you're an exception to that."

Images of a ground abruptly tapering into sky, a wisp of hair, a flash of white hem, and outstretched fingers race through my mind, suddenly free from the prison I'd locked them in. You reach up to touch my cheek. The gesture is so sudden, so very much like the way you used to do in the past.

"I'm sorry," you say. Your eyes brim with pity. "It's just, you looked like you were about to cry."

The breath I take is sharp. Your touch, the memories—it's all too much. I stand up, which knocks your hand out of the way.

I excuse myself to smoke outside my tree. I know the excuse is a poor one and that I've never cared where I smoked before now, and that I just came back from a trip outside. But you looked so confused and so *sorry*, when it's I who should be begging you for forgiveness. I can't stand here a moment longer.

Why are you here? I'm not ready. I don't know if I'll ever be.

## VIII

I avoid you with an astounding single-mindedness for the next few days. I'm always smoking outside now; whenever you climb out to get your food and water, I conceal myself even higher up the branches of my tree.

However, that doesn't mean I don't watch you. To your credit, you don't try to get my attention. You don't even force me to take up reading lessons again. You simply go about your day in mechanical fashion: you wash old clothes and polish the rust off old metal, you water the flowers and listen to their problems, you eat and drink, but you're not really focused on whatever task you have at hand. Twice, tears slide from your eyes. You wipe these away with vehemence. Was this really my doing?

*No, you idiot, not everything is about you,* Delonix snaps when I ask her. *Maria misses her parents.*

Ah. Why hadn't I thought of that before? You must feel deeply alone here, despite the company you keep. I've certainly been no help.

I make a decision then and there. I find you in the calachuchi grove, folding handkerchiefs.

"Maria!" I call.

You lift your head, your mouth slightly open. You rise to

your feet as if you will totter and fall if you don't move with a deliberate slowness. "What did you call me?"

For some reason, I want to run away. I press my toes into the dirt, however, and grit my teeth as if my soul will escape through my mouth. "Your name. Maria."

"That's the first time I've heard you say it." You sound like you're floating.

Abashed, I soldier on and enter the grove. "I want to give you something. Hold out your hand."

Your eyebrows furrow in suspicion, but you do as I say. I unclasp my necklace and drop it on your palm. Your suspicion is gone, replaced by confusion.

"This necklace is magic," I explain. You look at me, blank and yet wondering. "If you think about the person or people you most want to see while wearing it, it will show you exactly where they are and what they're doing."

It's a good thing you don't ask me whom I've been seeing with it.

You go very still. Even your breathing is subtle. Your gaze probes me from head to toe, as if you'll find some dark motives writ on my body. I shift my weight from foot to foot. I'm about to leave when you finally say, "Thank you." The necklace circles your neck, your hands lost in your thick hair while you struggle with the clasps. Soon, you add, "I'm sorry, señor. Will you help me put this on?"

I want to help you and don't at the same time. Yet you've never specifically requested my help before, and the truth is, despite how much I duck and hide and run, I want to give you everything you want. I grunt my assent, and you give me the necklace. I move to stand behind you. You're so small that I have to bend my knees to level my gaze with the clasp. You part your silken hair and smooth the waves over your shoulders, allowing the scent of coconut milk and calachuchi to waft in my direction. You used to smell like that, long ago. It fills me with a longing that accidentally comes out in a sigh.

"Señor, is there any reason you're tickling my neck?" you ask. I almost drop the necklace. I can't read your tone, and I have no idea what expression you're making. I fight the urge to turn you around.

"I'm sorry," I grunt as I slide the necklace around your neck once again. It's confounding, how much easier it is to put this necklace on myself instead of someone else—or maybe it's just you. I'm trying so hard to focus on the clasp instead of the places where I used to kiss you. I'm trying so hard not to touch your skin, but the clasp is ridiculously small and my fingers ridiculously large. Unavoidably, they brush against your smooth nape. Mercifully, you say nothing.

The moment the clasp is fixed in place, you spin around, and I back away half a step. Your eyes are downcast as you pull your hair behind your shoulders.

"Thank you," you say. Then you lift your head, and there is this look you have that I can't read—rather, that I don't *dare* read. If I read it, I feel as if hope will seep into me, and I already know that that will be too painful to bear.

I gesture at the shell pendant. "Go on. Try it."

Your fingers wrap around the cowrie shell. You don't need to close your eyes, but you do. Nothing happens for a moment, and then all of a sudden, you are squinching your closed eyes and grinding your teeth. Your cheeks are wet with tears. If you pull on the shell anymore, you will give yourself burn marks.

"Tatay! Nanay!" you cry. So much anguish is packed in those two words. As your legs buckle beneath you, I grab your shoulders. In my hands, they seem so thin and fragile. As gently as I can, I shake you. "Maria, Maria! What's wrong?"

Your eyes open. More pearlescent tears fall. You grasp my wrists with what feels like all your strength.

"Please, señor. You've been so kind to me—I shouldn't ask you for more, but grant me this one request, and I'll never ask for anything again," you say, and I hate that you feel you have to beg me for anything. "Please let me go to my parents."

I'd planned to tell you everything, actually. I'd planned to tell you that you'd died once, and who you'd been before you died. I planned to tell you that your soul had flown to the nearest vessel—your parents had been making love some ways down the mountain—but that I'd kept a piece of it, safe, for the day when you're ready to hear all this. I'd planned to tell you that some months later, your father stole a mango from my tree and that I'd asked him to send you to me, someday in the distant future, in return. I'd planned to tell you that I couldn't even make plans to tell you any of this since you first arrived, because I am a coward. Because I've been too afraid of what you'd say. Too afraid that you wouldn't forgive me.

Instead, I'm paralyzed by the outpouring of your emotions and the fear that you'll never come back if I let you go. Yet I cannot be selfish any longer—we're here in the first place because of me. I won't stop you while you pack or as you exit the passage leading to the outside world.

I slide my arms down in such a way that your grip on my wrists is dislodged. Your hands all but disappear in mine. Even your calluses are baby-soft compared to mine. Our gazes meet over my fingertips and their cracked nails. Tears give your eyes a glassy sheen; hope lights up your expression despite that. If only I could make it so that you'd never shed a tear again.

I say, "Take all the time you need."

## IX

After you leave, I prepare to follow you. I'd always intended to follow you, to make sure that you reach your destination unharassed by drunken townspeople, lecherous friars, or suspicious Guardia Civil patrolmen. You'd reach your house, embrace your parents, and never know I was there.

As I stride up the passageway leading out of my tree, I walk past one of Delonix's trees and pat the trunk. "Take care of everything while I'm gone."

*Aray! How would you like it if I whacked you square across the behind?*

I scowl, but keep walking. "You seem crankier than usual."

*I'm a little sore. I gave Maria one of my saplings.*

"What for?"

*She said she was going to use them to mark her parents' grave.*

That stops me midstride. *"What?"*

*You didn't know?* Delonix's tone tilts subtly toward pitying. It takes much effort to refrain from kicking her. *Maria was branded a seditionist and a revolutionary for spitting in the face of the* haciendero *who tried to claim her town's farmlands. It's likely that her parents were executed by the Guardia Civil for hiding her, or for failing to tell them where she went.*

I drag my hands through my hair in frustration and admiration. Why didn't you tell me? I voice that question aloud, too.

*She didn't know they were dead until she was shown that vision. And even then, she didn't tell you the truth because she didn't want you following her and getting hurt on her account.*

"*Of course,* I'd follow her!" I bellow. I could punch Delonix, but she'd make me pay for it later. "I—"

*You what?* Delonix's tone is colder than the December chill. *Whatever you feel for her, she certainly doesn't believe it if she knows it! Do you know nothing about women after all this time? They need to hear you say things before they can believe them!*

## X

My earlier fear of your never coming back, stirred by Delonix's words, has me in its grip and lends urgency to every step. I cross the forest in the shape of a monkey swinging through the trees, and then a lone stallion galloping into the farmlands surrounding the town. Once in town, I become a dog and change course for the cemetery on a wooded hill to the north.

There are no guardsmen posted by the cemetery gate, which immediately arouses my sense of foreboding. No one accosts me while I change into my old human form and amble through the gate as though I belong there.

I soon learn why. In the corner of the cemetery reserved for unmarked graves, a dozen or so Guardia Civil, armed with rifles, have you backed against one of the angel-topped columns that break up the cemetery's wrought-iron fence at intervals. You are the lone person dressed in black among a bunch of dark-blue uniforms. Your hands are raised above your head; farther above your head is a single firefly orb, which they will no doubt use against you as evidence of witchcraft. At your feet lie a black lace mantilla and a spade. A fire tree sapling is planted in a mound of freshly turned grave dirt not too far away. Clumps of dirt still lie in the surrounding grass.

I change into a snake and slither to the back of the group.

A tall, blond-bearded man is talking. The orb-light reveals a sharp profile with a nose that could cut and piercing blue eyes. His body shifts a little, showcasing three medals pinned just above where his heart would be. He is likely the Capitan of the Guardia Civil.

"Binibining delos Reyes, long have we been searching for you," he declares in heavily-accented Tagalog.

"You must not have been searching very hard, Capitan," you say with your characteristic boldness. "I've been close by all these months."

"You don't seem to grasp the severity of your situation, binibini." The Capitan's expression is neutral as he speaks, but when his gaze drags over your person, it transforms into disbelief, and then outrage. "That's Señorita Alonsa Chavez's dress! So *you* are the thief! For certain you stole her bed, too!"

"Yes, Capitan, because I am big and strong enough for such a task."

The Capitan wavers for a moment, then clears his throat. "Maria Esperanza Isabella delos Reyes y Dagdag, you are hereby under arrest for sedition against the crown of España—"

"Such a weighty charge for someone who merely spat in the face of a petty *haciendero* stealing a poor town's lands—"

"—theft, resisting arrest—"

The Capitan's speech bores me, so I don't let him finish. I change into a man, grab a rock bigger than my palm, and ram it against the back of a guardsman's helmeted head. It makes a dent in the man's helmet and he crumples like a fallen doll.

The metallic clanking draws the attention—and the rifles—of the rest of the patrol. As the guardsman falls, I snatch his weapon and hit his neighbor in the gut with the rifle butt. He goes down faster than a bag of rice.

*"El cafre!"* the Capitan shouts. "Bring him down, alive!"

I yell, "Maria! *Run!*"

I change into a cricket as I pounce for the nearest guardsman. He pats and pulls his uniform all over, and three of his comrades crowd round to help him. But I have already dived for the ground, changing into a snake as I do. I wrap myself around a pair of booted feet outside the circle of commotion and pull. The guardsman topples, taking everyone with him. His rifle accidentally fires, but the bullet hits the angel statue. I become a monkey and launch myself at another guardsman's neck and use it to swing around and grab his rifle. The moment my simian fingers close over it, I am a man again, rolling on the ground. I swing the rifle at his legs and shoot another in the knee.

And that's when a bullet finally gets me in the shoulder. I drop the rifle and clutch the wound. It's been a while since I smelled my own blood; I'm surprised the scent is still metallic, still human.

"No!" you scream.

I raise my head. A guardsman has your hands behind your back. Meanwhile, the Capitan and the rest of the patrol surrounds me, guns pointed, even most of those I tripped up. Eight men, in all.

The Capitan examines me while the business end of his rifle is pointed between my eyes.

*"El esclavo, el monstruo, el demonio!"* the Capitan spits. To you, he says, "Binibining delos Reyes, you will also be charged with assisting a runaway slave and witchcraft."

"He is a free man! Let him go!" you cry, to my surprise. Of all the things you could've said. It warms me to hear it, and my courage swells.

"I think not," the Capitan smoothly answers. "A *demonio*

such as this is neither free nor a man. Who shall pay the largest sum for this wretched creature, I wonder? The friars? The militia? Perhaps even the Gobernador-General himself? I can only imagine what they would do with such hell spawn as this, however—"

I grin at the Capitan. "If I may dispute something you said earlier, Capitan, given how much Señorita Chavez spends in *your* bed, she needed neither her own bed nor her dresses."

It is a stab in the dark, but it works. He goes red, as do you. Another shot hits its target, this time my thigh. I grunt, which turns into a groan as the Capitan plants his booted foot on the wound and presses down. The night I ran away from my former master is repeating itself.

The Capitan leans forward and looks down his long nose at me. "I won't kill you, but I need not sell you in one piece!" he says.

Someone else groans, and we all turn toward the source. The guardsman holding you is a writhing ball on the ground, one hand on his foot and the other on his groin. As the Capitan turns his rifle on you, to my infinite surprise, you tug the necklace off so hard that it snaps—and smash the pendant against the column behind you.

The cemetery is flooded with light.

When it recedes, some guardsmen are on the ground while the others stagger between graves like drunkards. All are shouting and clutching their faces.

"My eyes, my eyes!"

"I can't see!"

"*Dios mio!* Help! Help!"

And in the midst of it all, you stand there radiant in white, flowers in your hair, power crackling at your fingertips, the orb haloing your head. Awe and pride bloom within me, a natural reaction every time I see you. Some things just don't change.

While they stumble about, you remove the bullets and close the wounds of the men who've been shot because you don't believe in unnecessary death no matter your form. Then you stand up and flex your fingers.

The ground trembles as the sapling grows into a sturdy tree before my very eyes. Branches as wide as a man and pliable as vines, with each movement creaking like ships and cracking like thunder, knock out the remaining guards with solid conks to their heads. They wrap themselves around the limp bodies and pin them to the wrought-iron fence, the Capitan last of all. What I'd give to see their faces once they awaken.

Yet my own vision is swimming, clouding, blackening. The last thing I see is you turning to me, running, kneeling at my side.

As my eyes close, I swear I hear you call out my name.

## XI

I wake with a start in my own grove, no longer bleeding or in pain. I can't be blamed for thinking that everything that happened in the cemetery was a dream, or that I'd died. But neither situation is true. There is a slight pucker of a scar on my shoulder and its twin is on my thigh, both a lighter green than my skin. They twinge slightly when I stretch and when I walk, and I know they will be there no matter what form I take. My mind is on you, however.

Once I step out of the grove, Delonix says, *Finally. I thought another day and night would pass with you unconscious.*

*He's awake! He's awake!* Hundreds of flowers rustle and echo.

"Where is Maria?" I ask at large. Again, hundreds of voices make themselves heard, all with wildly different answers. But one voice speaks above them all.

"I'm here," you say.

Stray giggles and whispers punctuate the sort-of hush that falls over the flora. I spin in the direction of your voice and drop to one knee, my heart pounding in my throat. I want to catch you in my arms and kiss you and dance all at once—but your face is blank, and what's more, it will take three long strides to get to you. Why are you standing so far away? Are you angry with me?

You close the distance between us by two strides. "Why do you kneel? Stand up."

"You are the diwata of the mountain," I say, as if that will explain it.

"Is that all I am to you?" There is something in your question that makes me look up, wondering, hopeful. You hold your hand out as I do; my cowrie shell necklace, undamaged and completely whole, dangles from your fingers as you say, "This is yours."

You're both Maria the diwata of the mountain and Maria the human woman. Everything and nothing has changed. I feel as if magic lingers where your fingers brush mine when I take the necklace from you and put it on. To distract myself, I ask you, "How long have you known that the white stone was in the necklace?"

Your dark eyes bore into mine. I feel a little faint, but hold my ground. "Only when you gave it to me, and I had that vision."

"It seemed like you never really wanted it."

"I admit that I would've wanted to know about my parents sooner. But some part of me also *didn't* want to know. Besides, you're grumpy but kind. You didn't treat me like a servant or a slave. I'd have been an idiot to leave such good conditions."

Is that the only reason you didn't leave, though? I'm disappointed, but I try not to show it. "And how long have you known about what the stone can do?"

"A week or two? Although small, strange things have been happening to me all my life: I could grow crops quicker, soothe the farm animals better, and any injuries healed unusually fast. What Delonix didn't hint, I pieced together."

"*You* told her?" I raise my voice so that Delonix would know I was speaking to her.

*She said* hint. *I only* hinted. *Besides, you weren't going to hint or reveal a thing,* Delonix said.

*Not a thing! Not a thing! So secretive for no reason!* The flowers whisper-scream.

"Good point," I concede.

"My turn to ask questions," you say. "Why didn't you just tell me about any of this?"

For the first time since we started talking, I look away, down at my own huge, gnarled toes. I clench my fists. "I . . . I couldn't. You weren't ready to hear it, at first. And when you were . . . I still wasn't ready to say it. I was afraid you'd never forgive me. I'm a fool and a coward, Maria."

You say nothing for a long while, which makes me think that you *are* angry with me. I won't blame you if you leave and never come back. Instead, your bare feet pad into view; I'm surprised when I feel your soft palms on either side of my face. I lift my gaze, startled by your nearness.

"Hmph. Well, you could've avoided getting shot if you'd just stayed home. I would've smashed the necklace anyway and handled the Guardia Civil by myself." For the first time since we started talking, you smile, and it lights up your eyes. Perhaps you even feel the rapid beating of my heart; every part of my body certainly does.

"I don't doubt that you would have," I say. In spite of myself, my lips spread into a grin.

"Sweet talker." Your hand trails down my face, down my neck, to the scar on my shoulder, causing a shudder to travel down my spine. You're wearing a small frown, however, as you examine the pale scar. "I had every intention of telling you about my parents once I returned from marking their grave," you say as you trace its grooves. "But I didn't plan beyond that. The risk of me getting caught was too great."

A single tear tumbles down your cheek. I think your parents would've been proud—as proud as I am, if not prouder—if they could see you now, and I say so. I catch another tear on the tip of my finger. You wipe the rest with the back of your hand.

"You weren't meant to follow me," you continue, resting your fist over the scar. "I didn't want you getting hurt. It was like the night we met all over again."

"How is it that you still don't understand?" I press my hand over yours, flattening it against my chest. If you hadn't felt my heartbeat before, you most certainly do now. "I would have followed you either way."

It's your turn to gaze down at my feet now. I rest my forehead atop your head and inhale its sweet coconut-and-calachuchi smell. My other hand circles your waist and pulls you closer.

I hear the flowers holding their breath. Some are squealing as quietly as they can. I'm too lost in these moments with you to care.

"Do you prefer me looking like a human?" I ask.

Your gaze meets mine. Our noses, our lips, are suddenly much closer. "Ezequiel, you idiot," you say, your tears streaming, and although your voice is a touch irritated, I am thrilled to hear it saying my name, at last. "I prefer *you*. I've told you that countless times in different ways!"

I laugh, and as I do, I change into my human form and stop the transformation halfway. Greenish hues play against the black skin, and my hands and feet are of differing sizes. You giggle. Nothing's changed, and it's more than I deserve.

As I change back, I blurt, "Maria. I'm sorry—about everything."

Your eyes fall on my lips. Your fingers are already trailing over them. "I already forgave you a long time ago."

I take your chin and kiss you so softly, our lips barely touch at all. This is not the kiss I was hoping for on our first meeting in such a long time, but it is appropriate, given your mix of emotions.

But then you throw your arms around my neck and kiss me harder, longer. My disappointment melts away, as does time. You taste like rain after a long drought and sunshine and salt tears.

I missed you.

I realize that the flowers are cheering when we part.

*Finally, you two!*

*Well, it's about time!*

*I almost wilted from the suspense!*

You take my hand and tug on it, gesturing down the path. Cheerfully, you say, "Come on, Ezequiel, those farmers could use a little nudge."

I know what you're thinking. "Toward the fires of revolution?"

"And then some."

Always jumping in to help others. It's one of the things I love about you. But it's been so long, and just this once I'd like to be the only one on your mind. I tug your hand in the direction of my grove; you let yourself fall back into my arms, giving me the opportunity to plant three slow kisses down your neck. "Couldn't the fires of revolution wait until morning?"

You spin around and take my mouth in yours. "All right," you say in lowered tones after we part. Lightly, you tap the tip of my nose. "But only until morning."

# *Mara's Shadow*

*written by*

*Darci Stone*

*illustrated by*

QUINTIN GLEIM

---

## ABOUT THE AUTHOR

*Darci Stone graduated from Brigham Young University with a degree in Physics Teaching and a minor in Cultural Anthropology. Her story "Mara's Shadow" was strongly influenced by both her love of science and her love of world cultures. Darci lived at a boarding school in Singapore while attending the United World College of Southeast Asia on scholarship. She also taught English in Russia, and has participated in humanitarian aid projects in India and Cambodia. She currently teaches high school physics in American Fork, Utah and is a web developer for online educational software.*

*Darci married into the world of speculative fiction when she said "yes" to Nebula Award-winner Eric James Stone. While dating, she began attending his weekly writing group. After a while she realized, "I could do that," and started working on a story of her own.*

*Darci has always enjoyed the mix of science and adventure found in the works of Michael Crichton. "Mara's Shadow" draws on these elements, as well as her husband's phobia of moths. This award proves once and for all that Eric "married up," because he only took second place in his quarter for* Writers of the Future Volume 21, *while Darci managed to take first.*

## ABOUT THE ILLUSTRATOR

*Growing up in the forests of southern Ohio, Quintin was transfixed by stories of fantasy and science fiction from early childhood. Starting out primarily as a digital artist he made the switch to oil painting after attending Illuxcon in 2016 and has been captivated by traditional mediums ever since.*

*Currently he is hard at work creating images for his illustrated novel set in a post-apocalyptic American West, populated by fantasy creatures, dinosaurs and other prehistoric beasts.*

*Quintin received a BFA from Shawnee State University in 2017 and currently studies at the Columbus College of Art and Design in pursuit of an MFA.*

# *Mara's Shadow*

## PART I

*Viet Nam Nhat Bao (Daily News)*
5 February 2053
Swedish Hiker Dies on Trek

Peder Fridell, of Sweden, died Monday evening while trekking near Sa Pa. His death is attributed to swelling of the brain caused by a fall earlier in the day. Goran Nilsson, a friend with him on the trek, expressed his own shock. "It just won't load, you know? Yesterday he was here, talking and laughing, and today he's gone."

Ngo Lien finished reading the article, looked at the red X on the far left of the screen, and blinked twice to deactivate her iRis. The sunglasses reverted to normal mode, but a bright green icon in the corner of her vision indicated the Li-Fi connection was strong. She stared out the window of the medical chopper at the misty hilltops below. They were about 200 kilometers from Ha Noi, quite close to the border with China. A village of flimsy huts spread out along the hillside. Dozens of locals stopped what they were doing to look up at the approaching helicopter. From this vantage, Lien could see a large satellite dish hidden in a patch of trees, which made her smile. Tourists liked the rustic facade, but she bet there was a computer hidden in every hut.

The helicopter landed. Her partner Tuan climbed out first, then helped Lien. Two medics were approaching the helicopter, one significantly taller than the other. Behind them, she could see a long reed hut propped up on wooden stilts. Police tape wrapped around bamboo poles created a perimeter. The men were wearing full gear: plastic gloves, face shields, bodysuits. Whatever was in that hut had scared them badly.

She nodded toward the approaching medic. "The news made it sound like an epidural hematoma, so why all this?" Lien gestured to the outfits.

"Department of Tourism doesn't want to scare people away," said the taller man, voice muffled by the suit's helmet, "so they're keeping it quiet, but it looks like some kind of parasite was involved. That's why we called you guys."

By "you guys" he meant The National Institute of Malariology, Parasitology, and Entomology (NIMPE) where she and Tuan worked. Lien understood the need for a cover story. The riots in Southern China the year before had really harmed tourism in Viet Nam, and the economy was still reeling from India's Black Friday. Dead tourists were bad for business.

After suiting up, she followed Tuan and the two medics into the hut—a traditional longhouse. The walls were made of woven reeds, and the bamboo floor swayed slightly with each step. Mosquito nets hung from the ceiling, encasing dozens of sleeping mats. At the far end, one mat still held an occupant.

From a distance, obscured by mesh, the body looked like someone napping in the heat. But as Lien got closer, she could see movement on the surface of the corpse. Lien braced herself. Even so, she wasn't prepared for what she saw when Tuan pulled back the mesh. It was hard to believe the object in front of her was human.

Remnants of a bare torso were exposed, but it was pocked with bloody craters of missing skin and flesh. Small white worms contrasted sharply with the dark-red blood. They were everywhere, climbing on the arms, face, and chest, leaving trails of devoured flesh. Below the neck, Lien could see the edge of a titanium rod reinforcing the collarbone.

"What was his age?" she asked. The damage to the body made it impossible to determine.

"Twenty-eight," said the shorter medic.

That meant he was only a few years older than Lien. He should have had a long life to look forward to.

As she watched, a large wriggling mass climbed out a nostril. She shuddered involuntarily, imagining worms creeping across her own face.

*Get control of yourself. You're an entomologist, bugs are what you do.* She took a deep breath and switched to analytic mode, kneeling for a closer look and narrating her observations to Tuan.

"The worms are roughly 1–2 cm in length." It was hard to form a clear image of their bodies because of all the blood. "They appear to have prolegs." *Odd*, that meant they weren't maggots.

"What was his estimated time of death?" Tuan asked the medics.

"It is hard to know for certain, because of all the damage," said the shorter medic. "But we think he died last night between two and four a.m."

Lien glanced at the time displayed on her glasses—the body had been dead for less than eighteen hours, which was hard to believe. Insects were not uncommon on corpses, but larvae usually showed up several days later. First the parents had to lay eggs, then they needed time to hatch.

The blood also unsettled her. It was congealed and sticky after lying in the heat all day, but the way it pooled around the corpse implied he might not have been dead when the insects arrived. She turned to the shorter medic.

"You've been here most of the day?" He nodded. "Do the worms appear to be eating their way *into* the body, or are they eating their way *out*?"

The man didn't need to think about his answer. "They are definitely coming out."

Field Journal Excerpt
Dolpa District, Nepal
5 April 1889

It was agony unlike any I have experienced before. I heard the loud crack of bone; then pain engulfed me like an avalanche. When they shot my injured horse, I felt envy. I also felt a fool. Our Sherpas had warned us that horses were not fit for the rough mountain passages. Oh, how I regretted my choice as they dragged me for hours on a makeshift litter.

But I should not complain. It has been weeks since we last saw signs of human settlement. This tiny village, hovering between earth and sky, is a miracle. The language barrier poses a problem; even our Sherpa guides are unfamiliar with the dialect. Perhaps geographic isolation is to blame? My Austrian Alps are nothing compared to the Himalayan peaks that form a ring of sentinels around this valley.

After fretting over my injury for a week, the others decided to move on without me. I felt an odd mixture of melancholy and relief as they departed. By all accounts, the way to Lhasa is even more treacherous than what we have already encountered. I pray they are more fortunate than I have been.

The villagers are friendly, yet it is obvious they are not accustomed to outsiders. My blue eyes and thick blonde beard are of particular interest. I had hoped to fill the pages of this journal with accounts of forbidden Lhasa, but I will have to content myself with this small valley instead.

*Japanese Online Journal of Entomology*
7 February 2053

Entomologists in Kunming, China have identified a new species of Lepidoptera. The genetic profile reveals major differences from other known species. Officials did not reveal where the insects were found or release any images.

Lien shifted to the side in her office chair, so Tuan could scan the article over her shoulder. It wasn't a surprise their sample had hit no matches in the EtoGenome database. But she felt surprised by the classification. She had known the worms weren't actually *worms*. The samples they had collected from the corpse had legs, which implied insect. But all her previous experience had taught her to expect maggots or grubs on a dead body, not *caterpillars*. Had Peder really been devoured by larval moths?

"I wish we had access to a genome sequencer," Tuan said . . . again. "Now China is going to take all the credit."

"But Tuan, Viet Nam should be grateful we have such a powerful big brother to watch over and protect us."

Tuan's expression clouded. He was probably trying to decide whether or not she was joking. Lien let him wonder. She really didn't care *who* got credit for the discovery, as long as *she* was given access to the data. And Kunming had shared the full DNA profile.

Tuan's gaze shifted to her . . . chest? She glanced down at the Neo Ao-Dai she was wearing. It had a bright pink lotus embroidered on a black silk background. Then she glanced back at him. His eyes snapped up to meet hers, clearly embarrassed.

"I like your top," he said quickly. "I mean, the top of your outfit. It's a lotus, right? Like you." Lien was impressed he had made the connection between her name and the flower. Although, she would be a lot more impressed if Tuan would stop ogling her and get back to work.

"It's a pity," he said, when she didn't reply. "China taking all the credit. I was hoping maybe we could name the new species for you, since you discovered it."

Lien stared at him for a moment, then quirked an eyebrow. "We find a species of carnivorous moths that devour people alive, and you were hoping to name them after me?"

Tuan froze, then grinned. "On second thought, I suppose it was Peder who discovered them first. So maybe we should name them for him. *Peder Fridelicacy.*"

After three hours of poring over lab images, Lien was in a foul mood. Nothing made sense. She adjusted the settings on the 3D reflecting dish until the virtual image was crisp. Then she rotated the floating image to various angles, zooming in and out. The more she dug around, the more she realized the pieces were not fitting together. It was obvious the larva started *inside* the body and chewed their way to the surface. But how had they got inside in the first place? They were found equally in *every* major organ system, indicating no central origin. Parasitic worms usually built up in the intestines and then migrated to other parts of the body in a predictable pattern. These larvae were just . . . everywhere.

Lien pulled up a series of tissue reports. Surely she could establish a basic timeline for system infections if she looked hard enough. As she scrolled down the report she noticed something—or rather, the lack of something. Eggs. The reports gave head counts of larvae per cubic centimeter and the amount of tissue damage, but not a single reference was made to eggs. Thousands of caterpillars wouldn't appear through spontaneous generation. So where were the eggs now? Lien pulled up report after report. No eggs anywhere. That wasn't just strange, it was impossible. Unless the larvae had entered the body *after* hatching.

Lien imagined thousands of microscopic larvae entering a host and swimming through the bloodstream to every body system, then growing and feeding as they made their way back to the surface. But how could thousands of larvae enter a body at once? Maybe by drinking contaminated water? No, stomach acid would destroy them in minutes. The only viable option seemed to be direct injection to the bloodstream. But how could a moth inject that many offspring into a host?

### 10 April 1889
### Nepal

I could not ask for a better recovery environment. If it weren't for the small biting moths which seem to relish the taste of my foreign blood, I would name this place a paradise. Each evening as I watch the sunset, the majestic peaks make me feel small by comparison, yet important by inclusion.

My leg seems to be healing well, although the villagers insist I not walk. The healer's daughter Nyima tends to me. The girl has proved an engaging companion. She is filled with the boldness and curiosity of youth, and delights in teaching me new words. I think she is as eager to learn about Austria as I am to learn about her village.

### 16 April 1889
### Nepal

I continue to be plagued with fevers and chills in this insufferable valley. Nyima's fathers insist I am experiencing a common childhood ailment, but I believe it is altitude sickness. The only treatments they offer are bitter herbs and horrendous butter tea. No doubt it is brimming with medicinal properties, but it has the same texture and appearance as yak shot, and is equally palatable.

Trying to interpret Nyima's incessant questions—half gestures, half words I can only guess at—makes the headaches worse. And why her ugly goat must sleep inside with us, I cannot guess. Keeping animals inside is commonplace here. But the smell of sharing your home with them is horrendous. I miss the clean sheets and gentle scents of home.

### 1 March 2053
### Viet Nam

Together, Tuan and Lien carried twenty rat cages into the room with the moth tank. Most of the caterpillars were still in chrysalis form, but nearly thirty had emerged as adult moths. It was time to determine the infection mechanism.

Lien watched the adult moths climbing on branches. There was nothing special about them. They had a wingspan of only a few centimeters and were gray and boring. It was a bit of a disappointment really. She lifted a rat cage and slid it into a set of grooves which held it firmly against the larger tank. The moths, which had seemed almost lethargic a moment ago, sprang to life. Several flew toward the rat so energetically they collided with the plastic barrier. Others simply collected on the wall.

Lien disengaged a safety lock, then slid a small panel upward, creating a passage. She kept the opening as small as possible. Two moths immediately crawled through the gap. She released the panel quickly, a built-in spring snapping it shut. A third moth was crushed as it locked back in place.

*"Shă guā!"* Lien said, under her breath. "I accidentally got two." A high-pitched squeal from the rat indicated it had already been bitten. *That was fast.*

"And another rat dies in the name of science," Tuan said, turning to reach for the next cage.

"But not without putting up a good fight first," Lien said. Tuan turned to see what she meant. The rat had managed to catch one of the moths between its front paws and was chewing on its body.

"And in a surprising turn of events," Tuan said, "the man-eating moth is eaten by the moth-eating rat. Is no one safe anymore?"

Lien laughed, but she was only half listening. She peered into the cage closely. Based on the antennae and abdomen, both moths appeared male. Grabbing a marker, she scribbled the data on the side of the cage. "Do you think we should sedate the rats?"

Tuan thought for a moment. "For all we know, eating a moth *is* the infection vector."

"So you're saying Fridell ate some moths?" Lien asked.

"Have you seen what they feed tourists on those treks?" he said, with a dramatic shake of his head. "It sure doesn't look like anything I eat at home."

Lien stared into cage twelve. "Are there *any* females?" she asked.

Tuan had his face pressed against the tank, moths collecting around him. Lien felt grateful for the plastic barrier.

"I don't see any," he said.

Lien moved closer to see for herself, enjoying the musky scent of Tuan's shampoo. Her eyes darted from moth to moth. He was right.

"It *is* a new species," Tuan said at last. "Maybe they exhibit different sex traits."

Lien nodded. "Or maybe they're like clownfish. They all start male, but environmental triggers morph some into females as needed."

Tuan turned to Lien. "You know more random facts than anyone I have ever met."

Lien wasn't sure how to respond.

"That was a compliment," he added, reaching out to put his hand on her shoulder. She was surprised by the physical gesture, but made no move to break it. "I'll bet you're awesome at crossword puzzles," he said.

Lien laughed. "Actually, I am pretty good."

### 22 April 1889
### Nepal

I have finally adjusted to the altitude. It is wonderful to be free of the headaches. The language continues to be a frustrating barrier, but Nyima has been quite patient with me, and I can now recognize a variety of common words. I have started to diagram family trees, because this requires very little language. The female inheritance system in this village fascinates me. It is typical for all the brothers in a household to marry the same woman. I would venture this practice is done as a population control mechanism. Land and resources are scarce, yet few people leave the valley. It is near impossible to determine paternity for certain, which explains why property passes through the woman's line. I must admit the thought of sharing a wife with my own brothers seems repugnant to me. It goes against basic Christian decency.

5 March 2053

Lab Report Summary

Rats 3, 9, 17, and 19 show general immune response. Rats 2 and 15 are comatose. All remaining rats unaffected. No sign of eggs or larvae.

Did you know," began Tuan, pulling Lien's attention from the report she was working on, "there's a wasp that can turn caterpillars into zombies?"

Lien went back to the report. "Glyptapanteles," she said. For a time, the silence was punctuated only by the rapid clicks of computer keys.

"It just reminded me of our case," Tuan said at last. "The wasp injects its eggs inside the caterpillar. They hatch, chew their way out, and then use some kind of mind control to get the dying caterpillar to protect their cocoons."

Lien didn't respond. She really had a lot she needed to get done.

"Wouldn't it be awesome if these larvae climbed in people's brains and turned us into zombies that served the moth queen?"

At first Lien was so intent on her report she just murmured assent. But then she replayed the sentence in her mind.

"Tuan, you watch too much anime."

7 March 2053

Lab Report Summary

Rats 3, 9, 17, and 19 have all returned to normal health. Rat 2 woke from coma but suffers from tremors. Rat 15 remained comatose until death (six days after bite). All other rats symptom free. No sign of eggs or larvae.

Lien tightened her surgical mask, set her iRis to data-capture mode, and then slid a scalpel into the dead rat. They had waited two days for larval worms to appear on the corpse. None had. As she peeled away muscles and tissue, she saw no sign of anything unusual. The rat appeared to have died of dehydration.

She was more confused now than she had been a week ago. Over a hundred moths, but no females. Twenty exposed rats, but no larvae. She didn't know whether to be relieved the bites didn't lead directly to voracious offspring, or to be troubled that they could apparently kill you anyway. Nothing made sense.

30 April 1889
Nepal

My leg continues to ache deeply, but the sharp pains are gone. I am able to hobble about with a cane. Today while out walking, I found a group of girls clustered around the goat pen. Nyima was among them. "Dead goat," she said, pointing to an animal rolling from side to side while bleating feebly. Its hide was covered in large sores, which oozed dark blood onto the short white hair. One of the pustules burst and a large maggot climbed out of the still-living animal. Nyima repeated the phrase "Mara's daughters" three times. When I asked her to explain, she said what I interpreted as, "Stupid man did not eat his goat. Now Mara will take it for herself."

Watching a creature fighting to live as it is consumed by parasites is something that will be difficult to forget. Goat is a common food here in the valley. I can only hope I have not eaten the meat of infected animals. I asked Nyima if Mara's daughters ever hurt people. She said it had not happened for a long time. I am nervous that whatever immunities the villagers have developed will not protect me.

10 March 2053
YouTube video pofNR_WkoCE-TrG
ALL COMMENTS (6,148)
Top Comments ∨

kidclub18 (17 min ago)

OMG! You can actually see the worms crawling in her barf! I've heard of cats puking out worms—but people? That's just nasty.

3BWolfish (4 min ago)

Can't believe morons like you actually believe this crap. Dude. No one barfs bugs. Hoax for sure.

You've gotta watch this," Tuan said, beckoning for Lien to follow him out of the lab room.

"I'm kind of in the middle of something," she said, loading another tube into the centrifuge.

"No, seriously, you need to watch this now."

Lien followed Tuan down the hall to their office, feeling both curious and irritated. When they got there, she could see a video had been loaded to his computer screen.

"YouTube?" she asked, a hint of accusation in her voice.

"Trust me. This is one hundred percent work-related." Tuan clicked play.

The sound quality was horrible. Were they speaking English? She saw people drinking at a bar. The camera was focused on one girl with her head down on the table. Around her people were pumping their fists and cheering. The girl lifted her head. She looked terrible. Pale, sweaty face, trembling hands. She raised a shot glass to her lips and drained it. The crowd cheered. Then the girl started to gag. Several people rushed away from the table. The cameraman laughed, then the girl vomited everywhere. Bright-red vomit, the color of fresh blood. The view dropped quickly from the girl's face to the table itself. At first Lien thought the moving surface was just the result of shaky cam, but after the view refocused she saw dozens of familiar caterpillars.

"Where was this filmed?" she asked.

"Toronto, Canada. Two days ago. The video already has over fifty thousand hits. I would say the 'keeping it quiet' game is about to end."

### 2 May 1889
### Nepal

Ever since the incident with the goat, I have been puzzling over the term "Mara's daughters." The name Mara seemed vaguely familiar to me, but I could not remember why. Today, while reading my book on Buddhist philosophies, I encountered an image titled, "Mara Tempts the Buddha." And I remembered. Mara is the queen of demons.

### 12 March 2053
### Viet Nam

Lien followed the sound of angry voices down the corridor. Were they speaking Mandarin? She found Tuan in the moth room watching an argument between the director and a group of suited men.

"What's happening?" Lien whispered in Viet.

"The typical. China wants to take control of our project . . . and probably engineer a bioweapon."

One of the men glanced over, but Lien doubted he spoke Viet. At a command from their leader, the men started picking up cages and walking out of the room.

"Put that down!" their director shouted. He seized a man's arm. Startled, the man lost his grip on the moth tank he was lifting. Lien watched in horror as the cage flipped off the counter. When it landed, the side panel pushed open a few centimeters. A spring forced the door shut again, but it was too late. At least a dozen moths had escaped.

Before she could react, Tuan pushed her roughly through the door and slammed it shut. Turning, she was surprised to be alone. She heard shouts coming from the other room, but didn't dare open the door. Instead she peered through the glass pane.

Tuan had grabbed the emergency fire extinguisher and was spraying anything that moved. As the frigid foam hit the moths they fell to the floor. Eventually the startled men recovered enough to start stomping and smashing. It was all over in under a minute. As soon as the room had calmed, Lien pushed the door open.

"Don't worry," Tuan said, "we got them." But his reassurance didn't calm her. She stared in horror at his arm. There, just above his wrist, was a large red welt and a small trickle of blood.

QUINTIN GLEIM

Tuan stared at the bite, then looked at the Chinese officials. They were carefully turning the fallen cage upright again. Tuan slid his hand deep into the pocket of his lab coat.

### 5 May 1889
### Nepal

Last night Nyima took me to visit her grandmother. The ugly goat accompanied us, as always. Nyima believes the hapless creature brings her luck. The purpose of the visit was to learn more of Mara's daughters. I questioned Nyima directly, but she refused to answer. She told me that because she is still in Mara's shadow, she must not speak of her.

And so, we went to her grandmother, who apparently has left Mara's shadow. From her I learned a legend, which I will do my best to repeat. Keep in mind that my grasp of the language, while improving, is still quite limited.

There was once a young man who tended goats. One evening, a storm scattered his herd. He searched diligently until every goat was found. But now it was late, and the man grew tired. On the way home, he took the shorter path through Mara's gap, although he knew the passage was forbidden.

Approaching him in the guise of a beautiful woman, Mara sought to lure him from his task. "I can offer you all a man desires," she said. "My body and my love are yours if you but ask."

The man fell silent, and Mara thought she had won, until he opened his mouth to speak. "I have a wife at home, beautiful and strong. What more could I desire?"

Mara tried once more. "I can offer you power and dominion over all you meet."

The man looked at the animals gathered around him. "I command many goats, and they follow me with affection. This is all the power I desire."

Now Mara grew angry. "I can offer you wealth and riches, enough to fill many valleys. Do not deny me again."

The man was not intimidated. "I have children at home, obedient and kind. What greater treasure is there in all the world?"

With this, Mara became enraged. Shedding her disguise, she revealed her true form, a demon fierce and powerful, with sharp fangs and the tongue of a snake.

"A curse I place upon them all," she said. "Your wife will not live to see her children grown. Your goats will feed my daughters instead of yours. And your children will live always in death's shadow."

## 15 March 2053
## Viet Nam

Lien stared at the clock in dismay—was it really that late? The lab was kind of creepy in the middle of the night. Sounds echoed sharply in the empty space instead of being absorbed by soft background chatter.

She *had* to figure this out. Tuan would *not* end up like Peder Fridell. If those hungry little devils thought they were going to eat her lab partner they were seriously mistaken.

It had been three days since they'd moved Tuan into quarantine. And three days of his absence had made her realize something. She *liked* having him around, or at least, she *disliked* having him gone, which was the same thing, wasn't it? Not for the first time in her life, Lien wished her amygdala would communicate more directly with her frontal cortex. Why the hell did evolution think it was a good idea to shoot emotional chemicals into the bloodstream without telling the rest of the brain what they were for?

Pulling up a live video feed, she noticed she was not the only person awake. Tuan lay on the floor of his quarantine room, bouncing a tennis ball off the wall. She watched him on her monitor for a while, reached for the mic button, hesitated, then pushed it.

"How's it going?"

Tuan didn't look toward the wall monitor. "Ninety-eight.

Ninety-nine. One hundred." He caught the ball one last time, then sat up. "Well, the good news is my left hand is finally developing some fine motor skills. Poor thing has always felt a little inferior to his counterpart."

Lien felt amazed he could find humor at a time like this. "You seem to be in a good mood. Aren't you worried?"

He shrugged and tossed the ball onto his hospital-style bed. "I'm just lazy. Imagine if I processed all the emotional angst of dying a young and horrible death, and then it didn't happen? Total waste of energy."

Lien felt surprised. Her own approach to life was the complete opposite. Prepare for the worst—just in case. It was the only way she could feel safe.

"Any news?" he asked.

"Still no sign of parasites in your blood or tissue samples. Although, I have noticed some interesting activity around the bite itself."

"Interesting how?"

"There was a high concentration of baculoviruses."

"That's not unusual for insects."

"True, but the moth venom must have been loaded with the stuff, because it was all over your bite zone."

Tuan looked down reflexively at the scab on his arm. "Maybe it's some bizarre form of moth ovum, you know? An egg, without a shell."

"Oh no. A virus doesn't contain nearly enough DNA to code for an insect. And we watched your cells closely for any sign of viral activation, just in case. Everything looked . . . fine." Lien hoped he hadn't noticed the pause.

"There's something you're not telling me."

*Great.* She really hadn't wanted to bring this up until she knew more. "Well, the odd thing was the viruses attached themselves to glycoproteins in your cell membrane. And then self-destructed."

"That's good, right?"

"Yes. Except glycoproteins are very specific, like a lock and key.

So how did these glycoproteins recognize the virus and then successfully deactivate it, unless your cells have encountered the virus before?"

"So a new species of moth appears and bites me. But my body's immune response indicates I may have been bitten before?"

"Or at least that you have encountered the virus before."

Tuan fell silent for a while. "It's too bad China took all our samples. I wonder if the rats showed a similar response."

Lien smiled. "When you say *all* our samples, that's a bit of an overstatement."

Tuan walked toward the wall screen, clearly interested. "What do you mean?"

"Well, I may have accidentally forgotten to tell the friendly visiting officials about the blood samples in the centrifuge."

Now it was Tuan's turn to smile. "Really? I'm impressed. Have you considered a life of crime? It probably pays better." Then he was suddenly serious again. "And what did you find?"

"Remember the two rats that died? The antibody counts were abnormally high. Which indicates their immune system was fighting something. When I ran the samples using a much finer resolution I found our little friend the baculovirus."

### 10 May 1889
### Nepal

Almost overnight, the valley has thawed. Unfortunately, that means it is now a muddy bog from one end to the other. Although my leg is doing well, I am more clumsy than I used to be. Even when walking carefully, I find my clothing is a filthy mess at the end of each day.

This morning I encountered an odd village tradition. A young man had burned his hand, and Nyima was helping treat the injury. It was clear from Nyima's giggles and chatter that she was enamored. Afterward I teased her, saying that if the man's brothers were as handsome as he, then she would be a lucky girl. I expected embarrassment or even irritation from such a jest. But instead she seemed shocked and confused. She told me she could not marry the man and his brothers because they were, "the wrong color."

At first I thought she must be referring to some shade of hair or skin that I had not perceived. She found this idea humorous, saying that the color of a person's body did not matter when choosing husbands. She was surprised to learn that people from my country do not all share my pale hair and blue eyes.

I eventually learned that Nyima was referring to the color of the man's belt. The village is divided into two major clans. In physical features and cultural traditions, they are impossible to distinguish, at least to my foreign eyes. Yet, intermarriage between the two clans is strictly prohibited. One clan weaves strands of blue into their clothing, whereas the other uses yellow. They weave so many colorful patterns with such a wide variety of hues that I did not notice it on my own. But now I cannot stop seeing it in every person I encounter. Stripes of blue. Stripes of yellow. But never both.

I can detect no tension between the groups. They work and live alongside each other in relative peace. But marriage is forbidden by strong taboos. Infidelity within a clan is met with disapproval. But infidelity between clans is a crime punishable by death.

When I asked Nyima why the marriage rule existed, she told me the man in the story, who angered Mara, came from the blue clan. His wife was yellow. In her jealousy, Mara cursed their love. If blue and yellow mix it will bring her daughters.

## March 2053

Colorado State University: "Insect Parasitic Nematodes"
by P.R. Knutson & S. Anderson

By fighting fire with fire, ingested parasites may be able to target Kunming larvae and destroy them before they harm the human host. Insect parasitic nematodes have been used for decades as effective biotic pesticides. They are harmless to birds, mammals, and plants, and offer an intriguing possibility for the prevention of Kunming deaths.

Lien read the article on her office tablet with interest. Fighting one parasite with another seemed like an odd form of cosmic justice. Although convincing people to swallow a pill of living roundworms wouldn't be easy.

Yawning, she stretched her arms toward the ceiling and heard a satisfying pop. It had been nine days since Tuan's bite. The first few days had been pure hell. But after he passed the one-week mark symptom free, she had started to calm.

Lien stood, and walked to the prep room. She needed to prepare another dilution series for her water weevil case. Before entering she donned a pair of safety goggles. She found her mind wandering back to the Kunming moths.

The number of confirmed deaths was up to four. And police in Perth were examining a case from last year that might be related. Not enough deaths to incite global panic, but enough to interest entomologists the world over. So far, the transmission vector was the biggest mystery of all. The victims didn't seem to share any common link. When the moth struck, it struck fast. People were fine one day, and wriggling corpses the next. Was someone testing a new bio weapon? Who? And why out in the open like this?

Lien heard a door open behind her, but she was focused on the micropipette in her hand. If they needed something, they would ask.

"You know," a nervous voice said, "you never did say thank you."

Lien turned in shock. *Tuan?* Without thinking, she dropped the pipette on the counter and raced to her lab partner. "I thought they weren't releasing you until tomorrow," she said, wrapping her arms around him. He stiffened.

"Are you okay?" she asked. He seemed worried about something. It couldn't be bad news about his condition, or they wouldn't have released him. Right?

"Umm . . . actually . . . I spent the last twenty minutes in the hall trying to plan this conversation. It was going to be beautifully profound. Something about life being short, and how facing death changes everything. But now that I'm here I can't quite remember the details."

Lien felt confused. What was he babbling about? Then, suddenly, he leaned forward, dodged her goggles, and went for a kiss.

Lien's first thought was that he shouldn't be in the prep room without his own goggles. Lien's second thought was that she really didn't care.

## PART II

*Kansas City Star*
EDITORIAL, 17 APRIL 2055
TRAVEL RESTRICTIONS ARE NOT THE SOLUTION TO THE KUNMING CRISIS

On Friday the World Health Organization announced the Kunming death count had passed one thousand, intensifying debates over international travel sanctions. Those who believe locking our borders will protect us are ignoring the facts. In the two years since the moth's discovery, it has repeatedly been shown that physical proximity to other victims does not increase one's own chances of infection. This polarizing debate is a waste of resources. Rather than adding more layers to airport security, we should be channeling our funding toward research.

Lien finished reading the editorial, then lifted Bao to her shoulder and waited for a burp. Tuan snored loudly from his side of the bed. Normally she would love an argument that ended with spending more money on research, but this article hit a raw spot. The world had already been pouring money into this black hole, and there was almost nothing to show for it. Wasn't the universe supposed to follow basic laws? So how did this moth manage to defy them all? Except for gravity, as Tuan had pointed out.

She scanned through a variety of other headlines, reading all that was wrong with the world she had brought Bao into. She held her son close, and hoped they would find answers soon.

Lien grabbed a bottle of cola from the stash she kept under her work desk. It hadn't been a bad night, but even so she needed the caffeine.

"Okay, let's start at the beginning," she said to the man on the phone. "You own a snake shop called 'The Garden of Eden,' and your feeder rats are dying."

"Yeah. At first it was just one. So I threw it out. Figured it must have died a few days earlier, and I just didn't notice. Now they're all dying, and worms are everywhere. I think it's that Kunming thing. What should I do?"

Lien considered. A dead rat probably had maggots in it, and now a paranoid shopkeeper was overreacting. As far as she knew there were no cases of the moth infecting nonhumans. "I'll send someone over to collect samples." Almost as an afterthought, she added, "Where did you get the rats from? Have they reported anything strange?"

"That's why I called your office. These are the rats I got from you guys."

Lien had to process this for a second. "You . . . bought rats from us?"

"Yeah, my friend at your office said you had extras you needed to get rid of, so I took them."

Lien would definitely have to look into that. It was a major violation of office protocol.

"I'll be over this afternoon to collect them myself."

### 15 May 1889
### Nepal

Today the villagers prepared their fields for planting. I offered to help, but was told (although commanded might be closer to the truth) that my leg was not ready for work. And so I watched instead. I noticed tasks were split by gender and marriage status. As a single woman, Nyima fetched water and tended young children. I was surprised to see another woman, clearly past her teenage years, carrying water as well. I asked Nyima why the woman had not yet married. She told me the girl was too young to have children.

I asked Nyima how old a woman should be. And, like so many things in this strange valley, the answer came back to Mara. I was told all children are born in Mara's shadow. And they live in Mara's shadow until their thirtieth summer. Only then are they allowed to marry and start families. I'm amazed the valley can sustain its population with such rules in place.

I told Nyima that in my country, most women marry by their twentieth year. She did not believe me, asking repeatedly about the "cursed children." I assured Nyima that Mara's daughters do not bother our children. At last she conceded Austria might be so far away Mara does not know of it.

## 17 April 2055
## Viet Nam

So then the idiot decided he could make a few extra Yuan selling the rats to a snake shop." Lien was back home ranting to Tuan, who was making ridiculous faces as he bounced Bao on his knees.

"Why were we getting rid of rats in the first place?" he asked, then blew a raspberry.

"A few weeks after China shut us down, a lot of rats in the main tank got sick so they 'destroyed' the whole group." Lien had been so deep into the water weevil project by then, she had never known.

"But that means the symptoms we observed in our moth rats had nothing to do with the bites."

Lien shook her head. "Or it means that whatever the moths

did to our rats was contagious. If it was airborne it could easily have gotten back to the main tank. Then those rats were sold to a snake shop, and now they're producing Kunming larvae."

"But that was over a year ago. Why did the larvae not show up until now?"

"What makes it even odder is which rats are dying. The shop owner still has a few breeder rats from the original generation. They're fine. It only seems to be killing offspring five or six generations down."

Bao started wailing. Tuan had become so absorbed in the conversation he had stopped bouncing. Lien held out her arms. The baby reached for her, and she scooped him up.

"But what I can't understand," Lien said, settling Bao on her hip, "is how the parents are transmitting the virus to their offspring. Maybe when the blood mixes at birth?"

"But Lien," Tuan said, "parents pass things down to their offspring all the time." He pointed to Bao. "That kid looks just like you."

Lien didn't like where this was heading. "You think it's in their DNA."

### 10 June 1889
### Nepal

I have continued interviewing villagers regarding marriage traditions. When a girl is born, her marriage is arranged immediately. Nyima has always known who her husbands will be. I asked if she was bothered about having no choice in the matter. She said there was no reason to reject them. I asked who she would marry if she could choose. She blushed and refused to answer.

Nyima was astounded when I told her that in my country marriage is between one woman and one man, and they choose for themselves. She said that Austria must be a very large valley to hold so many farms and so many babies. It is hard for me to remember sometimes that this tiny valley is the only world she has ever known.

*Svenska Dagbladet (Swedish Daily News)*
22 April 2055
Kunming Moth Strikes Sibling of Peder Fridell
Tora Fridell, a younger sister of the first Kunming victim, has fallen to the same disease. Tora is the second case of an infected sibling, leading medical experts to speculate that susceptibility to the parasites may have a genetic link. However, little progress has been made on identifying what that link is.

The death of Tora Fridell hardened Lien's resolve.

"Are you sure about this?" Tuan asked, leaning back in his favorite recliner. "You could lose your job. Or worse."

"Tuan, you were bitten. If there is *any* possibility this thing can be passed down to offspring, then Bao is at risk. You remember what happened last time. Once they learn we have a lead, they'll take everything away from us. We'll be cut out entirely."

Tuan sighed. "But can't you do the research here?"

"We don't have access to a genome sequencer. If the moth virus really is meddling with our DNA, I'm going to need one. I have connections in Singapore. Besides, if we do find something big, I'm not sure I want to hand it over to Big Brother." She still blamed the government for Tuan's bite.

"One week," he said at last.

"Deal," Lien said. "I already packed my bags."

It was strange to see the blue flag of the Southern Union hanging below Singapore's own flag of red and white. Lien had grown accustomed to the Chinese star. Her taxi pulled up in front of the Yong Loo Lin School of Medicine, and the driver helped unload, grumbling about how heavy the cooler was. She wondered how he would react if he knew it was packed with dead rats.

As the taxi drove away, the glass doors to the school slid open, and a professor emerged. Lien recognized her cousin's husband, Naresh Kapoor. Without bothering to say hello, he opened the cooler and pulled a vacuum-sealed rat out of the ice.

"Just keep my name out of reports," Lien said, "and they're all yours."

Naresh bobbed his head sideways in an Indian nod of assent. "We will start analyzing them immediately."

16 June 1889
Nepal

Today I was given my first goat. I offered much thanks, but insisted I did not need one. My protests were in vain. I was told that now I had a hut of my own, I would need a goat to keep me warm this winter. I teased Nyima that my goat was not as ugly as hers, and asked if she wanted to trade. She seemed offended by the jest. She said her goat had seen almost as many summers as she had, as if being unusually old made it more valuable. Perhaps after a long winter together, my goat and I will also be good friends. I hope Mara stays far away.

25 April 2055
Singapore

Lien could feel Naresh hovering over her shoulder as she pulled up the magnified images.

"There," she pointed to the left side of the screen. "All the monkeys from Group A deactivated the virus immediately, but the monkeys in Group B went into viral replication."

Naresh stroked his beard. "It makes sense. Group A were the monkeys I exposed to moths last year, so they have built an immunity."

Lien shook her head. "No. I don't think that is what's happening." She took a deep breath. This next part was just a theory, but the implications were sinister. "I think the virus is shutting down because the cell is already infected."

"You think the cell receptors that deactivate the virus are coded for by foreign DNA? Interesting. We all assumed they were an immune defense."

"Think about it," said Lien. "If this is a retrovirus, then going through the effort to infect a host that already has the viral DNA would be a total waste."

Naresh thought for a moment. "But, we've tested the virus on dozens of human tissue samples. It deactivates every time. We assumed most humans were immune. But this would mean . . ."

He trailed off, so Lien finished for him. "Most humans are already infected."

Ninety-eight percent?" Tuan asked. Lien was in her hotel room video-chatting with her husband.

"Yeah. That's how many of our human samples tested positive."

"So if your theory is correct . . ."

"Then this is a much bigger problem than we realized. We still haven't finished analyzing the data from the genome sequencer. Hopefully we'll learn something useful."

"When I was bitten," Tuan said, "the virus deactivated. That means I have it too."

Lien nodded. "You and 98% of the planet."

"But how did we get it?"

She sighed. "If the rats are any indication, that is a question for our great-great-grandparents."

21 June 1889
Nepal

Yesterday was the summer solstice, which the village calls the "day of light." Two women, who had reached their thirtieth summers, were given crowns of flowers. Nyima said these women will marry before the summer has ended.

It seems the "day of light" marks when a woman leaves Mara's shadow and the curse is lifted. Each time I ask Nyima to explain, she grows quiet. She sincerely believes talking about it will bring Mara's attention to her. I do not wish to make her uncomfortable, but these fears make it difficult to gather solid information. So instead I questioned her grandmother. She told me that Mara's daughters feed on many things. Yaks. Goats. Even people.

When a child is born, Mara plants her seed inside. The seed takes many years to grow. Animals must be eaten before the seed sprouts. But people are different. Their spirit struggles to overcome the evil seed. If their spirit is strong, they will reach their day of light, and the seed will die. But if their spirit is weak, the seed will grow, and when it blooms, Mara's daughters will appear. If a woman has a child before her day of light, the child will carry the seed of both itself and its mother, making it twice as difficult to escape Mara's shadow.

I asked Nyima if she had ever witnessed a human death from Mara's daughters. She said no. I feel great pity for this village. So bound by fear. I keep hinting to Nyima that perhaps Mara is not as powerful as they suppose. Who knows, my seeds of doubt may yet sprout and help lead this village out of the shadow of superstition.

*Singapore Medical Journal*

26 April 2055

Genetic Vector Identified as Possible Transfer Mechanism of Kunming Moth

ABSTRACT

Genetic profiling of Kunming moth venom reveals eight unique retroviral strands. When entering a somatic cell, the virus replicates, then invades neighboring cells. When entering a germ line cell, the virus fragments and enters the nucleus, passing the foreign DNA on to future offspring.

Lien's pen scribbled quickly across the back side of the abstract. The high-speed train would have her home in only a few hours, but she couldn't stop thinking about the new discoveries. *What we know.* She wrote across the top of the page, then made a bulleted list.

*When generation zero is first exposed, the virus replicates and spreads. Airborne.* The baculovirus could only be transmitted through a direct bite. But once bitten, the host body produced an airborne version that was species specific. But when had the human version appeared and spread? A hundred years ago? Two hundred?

*There are eight distinct retroviruses.* It was not unusual for a virus to display minor mutations. But when they ran the second venom sample it had given a completely different profile than the first. After sequencing dozens of venom samples there appeared to be eight unique viruses. Each moth produced only one.

*Infected persons and their offspring cannot be infected again.* Usually a virus was obsessed with replicating no matter what. But these viruses seemed to respect each other's territory. If an animal had already been infected with Strand A, then Strand B refused to activate, even from a direct moth bite. Maybe this mechanism had evolved to prevent the virus from proliferating too quickly? If the host population went extinct then the virus would too.

The train took a fast turn, and Lien's box of Pocky Sticks slid off her seat and onto the floor. She bent to pick it up, then looked out the window. She could see the high-rise profile of Kuala Lumpur in the distance.

*The viral DNA is passed down to all future offspring.* In regular body cells, the virus had pumped out replications as quickly as possible. But when the virus entered reproductive cells it splintered into tiny fragments and entered the nucleus. Viruses that entered the DNA and were passed to children were rare, but not unheard of. But why did the virus splinter? Why not just insert itself as a single piece? Maybe the virus used dispersion to protect itself from extraction.

*Children inherit viral strands from both parents. We suspect larvae cannot form unless all eight strands are present.* This explained the multigenerational lapse. If the father was infected with Strand A and the mother was infected with Strand B, then the child would inherit both. Assuming all eight strands were necessary for larvae to appear, it would take at *least* four generations for the first death to occur. Random mating meant a lot of redundancy would occur, with both parents passing on the same strands. And yet the rats had shown that four or five generations was plenty.

*Currently, there is no way to test individuals for which strands they carry.* Ironically, the rat samples Lien had brought with her had proved useless. Because the virus scattered into segments when it entered the DNA, it was difficult for genetic sequencing to determine with certainty whether a specific viral strand had entered your DNA or not. Lien was sure they would find unique markers eventually, but it would take time. It drove her crazy knowing she carried the virus, but not having any idea how many strands she had accumulated. Six? Eight? Was she already dead? And whenever she thought about Bao she felt sick. He would have the combination of both Tuan and herself, putting him at a significantly higher risk. She hoped they developed genetic tests soon.

### 20 September 1889
### Nepal

The first morning frosts have shifted the valley into harvest mode. I helped with the winnowing of the barley, a task usually reserved for women. The injury to my leg still prevents me from the heavier labors. It provided me a good opportunity to chat with several of the married women. Apparently Nyima has been spreading my tales of Austria to anyone that will listen. They seem incredulous that our women marry so young and bear so many children. One woman kept referring to my accounts as "story lies," their term for a tall tale. This same woman warned Nyima not to fill her head with my strange customs. But Nyima told the woman that one day she hoped to travel to my valley and see for herself if what I said was true.

## 26 April 2055
## Viet Nam

Even so, the genes accumulate faster than models predict," said Lien. "It's like the universe *wants* them to come together." She had only been home for twenty minutes and poor Tuan was trying to digest all the new information.

"But not all of the rats died," Tuan said hopefully. "Only a few that we know of actually developed larvae. My guess is the percentage of fully infected humans is small. Most of us are probably carrying only one or two strands in our genome."

"But there are almost ten billion people on this planet. If even one percent of us have the full package in our DNA, we're looking at a hundred million deaths. And the next generation will be even worse."

Tuan fell quiet for a moment. Lien wondered if he was thinking about Bao. The baby was currently napping on the couch. He looked so peaceful.

"None of this explains how a virus is generating moths in the first place," Lien said, breaking the silence. "*You're* the one that's got a knack for thinking outside the box. Any brilliant ideas?"

"There's a box?" Tuan said, "Why doesn't anyone tell me these things?" His sincere tone was offset by his signature smirk. "Okay, fine. Show me what you've got and watch me single-handedly save the human species." He reached for her tablet and started flipping through the images.

Any new insights?" Lien asked at dinner. It had been over a week since her return from Singapore, and Tuan had spent hours going through the data.

"Actually, yes. But you aren't going to like it."

Lien stopped eating. She hadn't expected a real answer.

"I think the viral DNA doesn't code for moths at all," Tuan said. "It's just tagging our own genes."

"What do you mean?" Lien asked. The assumption that the viral DNA coded for the moths had seemed like a given.

"Well, ninety percent of the genes found in a fruit fly are also found in a human. I would imagine a moth is similar. The viral DNA doesn't need to create a moth from scratch. It just needs to activate our own genes in the right order."

Lien thought about that for a moment. Tuan was right. Theoretically a human cell had the potential to generate all sorts of earlier evolutionary creatures.

"So our own genes are being used against us," she said, stabbing a chopstick into her wonton.

"Exactly," said Tuan. "It's like a good computer virus. You use the system's own code against itself."

### 15 October 1889
### Nepal

The sunlit snow is painfully bright, and Nyima has warned me I must squint when outside, to prevent blindness. Being trapped indoors has left me restless. I pass the long afternoons teaching Nyima to read and write. She loves learning new "sound pictures" and shows keen aptitude. Yesterday I caught her tracing her name in the snow with a stick . . . as well as the name Pratik. She continues to assure me the two are only friends. But I have seen the way they look at each other. It is a pity they are unable to wed.

### 27 June 2056
### NIMPE Kunming Virus Report

Team A: *Genealogy*

Siblings and children of Kunming casualties within Viet Nam have been identified. These individuals are believed to have a 99.8% probability of eventual moth infection. Individuals have been notified and discouraged from having children until more is known.

Team B: *Detection*

There is speculation that infected individuals secrete unique pheromones which increase sexual attraction between individuals carrying different strains of the virus.

If so, these pheromones may provide an alternate method for diagnosing which viral strains an individual carries.

Team C: *Suppression*

The drug Tryptofluorizine has successfully slowed the growth of Kunming larvae in trial runs. More research is needed to identify potential side effects in the host animal.

Team D: *Activation*

All known victims of the virus have been between the ages of 24 and 28. Current hypothesis is the virus activates when natural aging has reduced the telomeres to a specific length.

Even in her sleep, Lien's brain was analyzing the Kunming virus. Frustrated, she sat up, gently moving Bao off her leg. Maybe if she read something it would clear her mind. Tuan rolled over. He had been restless all night. Eventually he climbed out of bed and checked the thermostat.

"Everything okay?" she asked.

He lifted a hand and pinched the bridge of his nose.

"My head feels like an angry puffer fish is trapped inside."

Bao rolled onto his stomach, then pushed to a sitting position. He gazed at his parents through bleary eyes. Then he flopped once again onto Lien's legs and immediately fell back asleep. Tuan grinned and walked into the bathroom. Lien heard him fill a glass of water. She could see his face reflected in the mirror. He spit into the sink.

*"Quỷ nhỏ!"* he said. Something about his tone filled Lien's stomach with ice. After sliding Bao off her legs, she hurried to the bathroom. In the sink, crawling in spittle and blood, was a small worm.

Lien hurried across the NIMPE lab room. She opened a cabinet door, pulled out bottles, and tossed them to the floor. Her shaking hands knocked over some test tubes. Finally, she found the antiparasitic medications. These were the strongest they had.

Tuan was sitting on the floor, with eyes closed. Bao had crawled over to a low cupboard and was trying to open it. The skin on Tuan's arms and face was developing red bumps. It looked like a nasty case of the measles. *This thing moves fast.* His skin had been clear when he woke up an hour ago. She poured a handful of pills into her hand, twice the usual dosage.

"We'll start with Albendazole," she said, handing the pills to Tuan. "And some Tryptofluorizine."

Tuan put the pills in his mouth. Lien filled a glass beaker in the sink and handed it to him. She grabbed a plastic bin and started throwing a variety of medications inside. When she was satisfied she had what she needed, she turned back to Tuan.

"We need to get you to a hospital."

20 December 1889
Nepal

The days are short and cold, and I long for spring. Sometimes winter storms prevent me from leaving my hut for days at a time. When this happens, my dear goat Anna is my only companion. When the weather permits, I walk to the Pokhrel family home. They have been teaching me to weave. My first project is lumpy, and the pattern devoid of even the most basic symmetry. But the blanket will keep me warm regardless of how ugly it is. I made the mistake of trying to include both yellow and blue in my design, which I should have realized would bring Mara's wrath. Unfortunately, the error was not noticed for some time, and I was forced to unpick hours of work.

Yesterday, I passed Nyima's courtyard, and was surprised to see Pratik emerging from the ground floor, where large animals are kept. I tried to speak to him, but he said he was in a hurry. Several times he glanced back, a guilty expression on his face. I worried at first that he had stolen something, and had just decided to find Nyima, when she emerged from the same door as Pratik. She was surprised to see me, and seemed nervous. When I asked if everything was all right, she said she had just been feeding the goats. She is not a very good liar.

### 28 June 2056
### Viet Nam

Lien filled the cup with crushed ice and walked back to Tuan's hospital room.

"Thank you," he said, reaching out clumsily to take it. After dumping some ice chips into his mouth, he laid back against his pillow and closed his eyes. Lien snapped a quick photo and compared it with one she had taken on arrival. She was relieved to see the red pock marks didn't seem to be getting any worse. Maybe the antiparasitics were working. Maybe the trick was just to catch it in time.

Then she noticed a trickle of blood coming from his left ear. She reached for a tissue. As she bent to wipe it away, she saw a small white worm climbing out of his ear canal. Without thinking she reached for it with the tissue, pulled it away from her husband's face, and crushed it between her fingers. *This isn't happening,* she thought, as she sat back in her chair and started to cry.

Lien studied Tuan's medical scans as the doctor briefed her.

"As far as I know, this is the first time anyone has managed to pause the infestation midstream," the doctor said. "Usually there has been so much damage from the larvae . . ." he paused, looking at her awkwardly before continuing, ". . . from the larvae feeding on the host that we know very little about the initial phases."

Lien nodded. "They estimate there are only four hours between initial symptoms and death." She tried to speak calmly, but a slight tremble in her voice gave her away.

"The drugs you are giving your husband seem to have slowed the progression of the parasites considerably," the doctor continued.

Lien waited for the "but."

"But the damage to his body is so widespread I think his chances of survival are small."

As Lien flipped through the MRI scans she understood what the doctor meant. His body looked like it had thousands of tiny tumors spread throughout every organ system. The doctor pointed to one of the white spots.

"These moth embryos are small. But there are so many of them spread inside such important organs that his body won't be able to function for long. His major organs are already shutting down. And in spite of the medications, new embryos are continuing to form."

Lien dropped the images on the desk. She was a leading expert on the Kunming moth. If anyone could save Tuan, it was her. But the doctor was right, her husband was a dead man, and there was nothing she could do about it.

*People's Daily Newspaper* (China)
29 June 2056
National People's Congress Passes
the Protective Lineage Act

The People's Congress responded decisively to the Kunming epidemic last night by passing a bill aimed at preventing the further spread of this disease. The bill includes mandatory abortions for unborn children of High Probability Infected (HPI) citizens and recommends abortions for Moderate Probability Infected (MPI) couples. These categories are based on genetic proximity to known victims.

General Secretary Yang Shangkun has issued a plea for "all the people to unite against this powerful enemy that threatens the purity of our children." A website and hotline have been created for citizens to report suspected cases of the Kunming virus, as well as to report violations of the Protective Lineage Act. "We must put aside our individual dreams," General Yang declared, "in order to protect the future dreams of the human family."

Lien watched as Bao tottered haphazardly toward her across the hospital tile. His grin was terribly out of sync with the dark heaviness she felt inside. He tumbled roughly to the ground, smacked his forehead, and started to cry. She knew she was supposed to walk over and comfort him. But she stayed in her chair near Tuan's bed feeling strangely disconnected from it all.

She had tried everything she could think of for Tuan. And for a brief time she had thought that maybe, just maybe, it had been enough. But it wasn't. She felt powerless. She liked to believe that she lived in a world where knowledge and skill could protect you. If you just knew enough, if you just worked hard enough, you could be safe. But it wasn't true. Not when your own DNA was programmed to destroy you.

Bao's cries finally pulled her from her thoughts. He had rolled onto his back and seemed confused by her indifference. As Lien looked at her son, she was suddenly filled with anger. No. It was more than anger. Hatred. For a moment, she didn't see her child at all, but rather the disease inside every cell of his tiny body. The ravenous parasites that would devour everything she loved. As she stared at him she felt disgust. She wanted to shout at him to be quiet. To flee from the hospital, and everything it represented, and never come back.

But as quickly as the strange emotions had formed, they melted away, replaced by a burning shame. *How could I think that?* She glanced toward the door nervously, afraid some passer-by could somehow hear her terrible thoughts. Then she rushed to Bao and lifted his thrashing body from the floor. She stroked his back, his face, his arms. He wasn't disgusting. He was precious. He was all she had left. After he had calmed, she looked at the clock on the wall. The nurse would be here soon. "Time to say goodbye to daddy," she whispered in Bao's ear, turning them both to face the still form on the bed.

Ten minutes later, Lien watched as the nurse injected Tuan's IV line with a stimulant to cut through the heavy pain meds in his system. As the doctor had predicted, Tuan's major organ systems had continued to shut down. His kidneys and liver were hit the hardest, turning his skin an unnatural shade. Lien knew the stimulant would only buy her a few minutes, and the strain on his heart might even shorten what time he had left. But she had begged the doctors to rouse him. She needed him awake and alert. She needed the closure of an official goodbye.

Bao was sitting on her knees, gripping the rail of the bed. He peered down at the man in the bed. Lien didn't think he recognized his own father. After a moment, she reached down and shook Tuan's shoulder gently. She said his name several times, getting increasingly louder with each repetition. Eventually, his eyes opened.

Now that the time had come, she didn't know what to say. "Hello," she finally said. "I brought Bao to say . . . hello." She knew Tuan would notice the pause.

Tuan looked up at her. "So it's that bad," he said. She nodded. He lifted his hand and stroked Bao's arm with his finger. "I'm sorry."

Lien felt genuinely surprised. "Sorry? For what? None of this is your fault."

Tuan rested his arm back on the bed. "I'm sorry I'm leaving you," he said. "And I'm sorry that Bao is . . . because of me Bao is . . ."

Lien didn't want him to finish that sentence. She was afraid that saying it out loud would make it real. So she finished it for him. "Because of you, Bao is the most adorable baby on Earth."

Tuan smiled. "I think he gets that from his mother." Then his face got serious. "Lien. I don't want to die. Ever, really. But certainly not like this. So do something for me, okay?"

Lien felt her eyes tearing up, but she fought it as best she could. She reached for his hand. "Of course."

"Figure this thing out," he said.

Lien nodded. And she meant it.

# PART III

Webpage: www.oilremediz.etc
UPDATED: 2057/01/12
NEW WHAT DOCTORS DON'T WANT YOU TO KNOW ABOUT THE KUNMING VIRUS!!

Natural oils have long been used to repel insects from homes, gardens, and even our bodies. This new mix is designed especially to target the Kunming moth and cleanse it from your system before it can cause harm. To purchase for you and your family, click the following link.

*Why didn't I think of that?* Lien thought sarcastically as she read the ad. *If Tuan had only drunk more peppermint tea he'd still be alive.* People believed what they wanted to believe. And right now, they wanted to believe the Kunming nightmare could be avoided. She reached for the mango shake on her coffee table without taking her eyes off the screen, lifted the straw to her mouth, and was surprised to find the cup empty. She had no memory of finishing it. Even with the buzz from the powdered betel nut, she was reaching her limit.

In the six months since Tuan's death, Lien had become obsessed with identifying the historic source of the virus. Her hope was that victim genealogies would lead to a common source, a ground zero. But so far, she had found no pattern at all. There were family lines tracing back to every populated continent in every possible direction. Rather than zooming in on an obvious historic source, the genealogies revealed thousands of possible infection vectors to explore. It was time to admit defeat. This approach was a dead end.

Most of the institute's funding was being pushed in other directions, the global race for a cure fueling a variety of clinical trials designed to prevent the virus from triggering, or remove it from the genome through genetic therapy. Lien didn't think they would succeed. Not any time soon. The virus was too complex, spreading and branching throughout the natural DNA like an enormous oak tree. It made HIV look like an acorn by comparison, and that had taken more than 40 years to cure.

If she could just figure out where it had come from, how it all began, maybe it would help. The institute humored her. After all she had done already, after what had happened to her husband, no one dared to tell her no. But she was working solo. That was fine with her. These days she liked to be alone.

The biggest problem she had encountered was the fact that viral carriers display no outward symptoms. Digging through historic records it was impossible to identify which people carried the virus, or which strands they had.

*If only there was an obvious sign, something that could be traced.* She closed her eyes, and let her thoughts drift along the random eddies that precede sleep. Soon she was thinking of Tuan, remembering how they had met, how they had worked together. She saw him in the lab that day, pushing her through the door to protect her, not knowing it was pointless. That he was already a dead man, long before the moth bit him. She remembered the rats being carried away in their cages. The Chinese had been so careful to take every scrap of research with them. But they hadn't known they were leaving the virus behind. It was already airborne, infecting the other rats in the main holding cage.

Lien's eyes snapped open. The rats in the main tank had become sick when exposed to the airborne virus. If the first generation of exposed humans had responded the same way, then maybe she could find evidence of it in historic records.

When a moth bit you, your body would only replicate the virus and become contagious if you didn't carry *any* of the strands yet. This meant that moth bites and the "flu" they generated were only a threat to 2% of the current population. But the first generation would have been virus free. That meant *everyone* would have been susceptible to the disease. And the symptoms displayed by the infected rats had been unique: seizures, comas, a few deaths. Surely an epidemic like that would have left a trail.

## 6 May 1890
### Nepal

It is hard to believe that in three days I will be leaving this valley forever. The village held a feast tonight in my honor, and bestowed a variety of gifts. I accepted each gift with a sincere thank you, having learned long ago that refusing is a strong insult. I had gifts of my own to give, various knickknacks from Austria.

I tried to give Nyima my book on Buddhist customs. It is far beyond her current reading level, but I thought she would enjoy the many illustrations. However, she grew angry and threw it to the ground. She shouted that she hated me. I have never seen Nyima this upset before, and am unsure whether she is angry that I am leaving, or if there is some other factor at work. Hopefully we can make things good again before I depart. Later in the evening I saw her arguing heatedly with Pratik. Perhaps he is the true target of her anger.

While I am curious whether my companions successfully reached Lhasa, I no longer feel the jealousy I once did. I feel I have experienced the otherness in a way I never dreamed possible. This valley has become a part of me. And I hope that in some small way I too have left my footprint.

*National Geographic*

## January 2057
### Survival of the Furthest: Which Gene Pools Have Dodged the Kunming Catastrophe?

An estimated 10,000 babies are born each day with the full Kunming virus, and as many as 50 million individuals may already be infected. Are any populations immune to this crisis? The answer is yes. Descendants of historically isolated groups, such as the Kalahari Saan, the Andaman Sentinelese, and the Amazon Yanomami may have reason to celebrate. . . .

12 January 2057
Viet Nam

Lien took a short break to read through her news feed while boiling water for pho. After slurping down the noodles, she returned to her research on global epidemics of the twentieth century. Some of them surprised her. The bubonic plague had hit San Francisco in 1900 and then jumped to China. *And I always associated the Black Death with the Middle Ages and Europe.* There were less exotic entries on the list. Influenza. Ebola. Zika. But none of these fit the symptom profile she was looking for.

She narrowed her search, putting in the key words "coma and seizures." She was pleased to see this shortened the list of possibilities significantly. Near the top of the page one blurb caught her eye.

Encephalitis lethargica: commonly referred to as the "sleepy sickness." Symptoms include high fever, sore throat, head pain, disturbed vision. In severe instances, the patient may become comatose and experience Parkinson-like tremors. Fatal in one out of three cases. Cause unknown.

*That is almost a perfect description of the original rats that we exposed to the moths.* Lien felt excited now. This was the first major lead she had had in weeks. She clicked the link to read more.

*Encephalitis lethargica is estimated to have killed over five million people worldwide between the years of 1915–1926. It swept the globe rapidly, and then disappeared. The cause was never identified, but it is believed to have started in Austria. Because of its historic proximity to the much more deadly Spanish Influenza (1918), the encephalitis lethargica pandemic is often overlooked by historians.*

Lien felt a surge of triumph. *This is it! This is really it.* She did a few mental calculations. The article stated that five million people had died and the disease had a one-in-three mortality rate. That meant there were fifteen million cases worldwide. Her own experience with infected rats had shown that only a tenth of them developed any symptoms at all. That meant the actual infection value was closer to 150 million. Lien quickly looked up the world population in 1920. If she was right, then this virus had entered the gene pool over 130 years ago by infecting 8% of the world's population. Something had happened in Austria in 1915. And Lien was going to figure out what it was.

### 8 May 1890
### Nepal

I can't stop my hands from shaking. So many emotions are swirling inside. Rage. Fear. Guilt. What have I done? And what can I do to repair it? I need time to think. But my escorts are leaving in the morning, and so I must decide now.

This afternoon I noticed a crowd gathering near the large juniper tree. Their angry voices carried on the wind. As I drew closer, I saw a small figure huddled in front of the well, concealing her face with a shawl. An elderly woman spat on the girl and shouted. "You bring Mara to us all." Several men were holding stones. I scanned the crowd desperately for Nyima, needing someone to explain. But I couldn't see her anywhere. In that moment, I knew.

Ha Noi > Craigslist > Community > Groups

### 3 February 2057:
### Kunming Support Network
### Monthly Dinner / Coffee Group

Have you or someone you loved tested LC-8 for the Kunming virus? Know that you are not alone. Come draw on each other's strengths and counsel with people that know exactly what you are going through. We meet on the first Saturday of each month. All are welcome.

Lien walked slowly down the narrow alleys that snaked between high-rise apartments. Above her head, dozens of long bamboo poles loaded with laundry extended from windowsills. The city was preparing for Tet Nguyen Dan. Bao clung tightly to her pointer finger, toddling alongside. Her other arm was slung with bulging bags in preparation for tomorrow's festivities. Bao eyed the bright-red decorations with fascination, and several strangers smiled and wished them luck for the new year.

When they reached their apartment building she hoisted Bao to her hip and started up the stairs. He was getting so big. She couldn't believe he would be turning two tomorrow. And she would be turning twenty-eight. *Twenty-eight and a widow.*

Shaking herself from the unhappy thoughts, she kissed Bao on the cheek.

"At least you won't be an orphan," she said.

Her own pheromone profile had come back LC-6, meaning she carried only six of the eight Kunming strands. She felt sympathy for the millions worldwide that were getting back LC-8 results. Tuan's death had been hard enough. Lien thought that knowing in advance would have only made it worse.

Lien let Bao push the doorbell. "Only once," she reminded him.

Her mother opened the door and took Bao, who was eager to cuddle with *bà ngoai.* Lien carried her bags into the kitchen and started pulling out fruit.

"How was it?" her mom asked.

"Depressing," Lien answered truthfully. Her mom had insisted she try the group at least once. But she wasn't ready to talk about Tuan with strangers yet. Lien felt glad her mom didn't ask any follow-up questions.

Bao started jabbering something indecipherable. Her mom nodded and gave a vague response. "Oh my! Really?" Bao seemed delighted by the attention. He had been spending a lot of time with his grandma since Tuan died. Sometimes Lien felt jealous of their relationship. Lien was the mean one that made him brush his teeth and eat his vegetables. Grandma, on the other hand, was his best friend.

Lien knew it was partly her own fault. She had become obsessive about her work, ignoring Bao as she sifted through data. The answer always seemed to dangle just out of reach. If she spent five more minutes she would find it. But five minutes often turned into five hours. And she was no closer to a solution than before.

Lien felt torn in two directions. She wanted to be with Bao, to take him to the park and eat mangos. But every time she looked at him she saw *them*. Thousands of tiny, ravenous larvae just waiting to come out. And the clock was ticking. She couldn't stop until she knew he was safe.

Her mother walked into the kitchen. Bao trailed behind, like a baby duckling.

"Let me help you peel the *nhan*," she said.

She placed Bao in his booster seat and handed him some watermelon, then sat and reached for a knife.

"Did you hear about San Francisco?" her mom asked.

Lien nodded. "Cults are crazy."

Her mom sighed. "Forty-seven Kunming carriers? Fifteen of them children? It's one of the biggest mass suicides since Heaven's Gate."

Lien was just about to change the subject when her pocket chimed. She rinsed her sticky hands, then pulled up the text. It was from an old school friend that now worked in Germany.

*You were right. I found something interesting.*

The text came with some attachments. It was a blurry copy of some death certificates from Austria, as well as some rather unusual autopsy reports.

### 8 May 1890 Nepal

Nyima's mother tried to calm me. She said it was for the first father to decide, and he was a very kind man. But I was not comforted. The village elder was clearly upset, as were many others. In spite of her words, Nyima's mother seemed worried as well.

I asked her what Nyima had done. At first she gave a vague answer, saying only that Nyima had angered Mara. But I continued to press, and she told me Nyima had planted a forbidden seed inside of her. She was with child, a cursed child that needed to be destroyed. Nyima's father must decide now whether to kill Nyima and the child together, or wait until birth and kill only the baby.

And so a group of grown men were standing with stones, while a helpless girl cowered in fear and shame. I have tried to withhold judgments during my stay here. I have tried to see the world from inside this culture's eyes and accept it as it is. But seeing Nyima trembling on the ground, surrounded by angry men, something inside me snapped.

FORWARDED 3 FEB 2057 TO NGUYEN_LIEN@NIMPE.ORG
Translation of Death Certificates:

DATE: 12 November 1915
PLACE: Klosterneuburg, Austria
NAME: Nyima Giri
GENDER: Female
AGE: 52
BIRTH PLACE: Nepal
CAUSE OF DEATH: Strangulation
CORONER'S NOTE: Appears to have committed suicide by hanging. The proximity to her daughter's body suggests she may have been involved in her daughter's death or else traumatized by its discovery.

DATE: 12 November 1915
PLACE: Klosterneuburg, Austria
NAME: Kshyama Giri
GENDER: Female
AGE: 25
BIRTH PLACE: Melk, Austria
CAUSE OF DEATH: Unknown.
CORONER'S NOTE: By the time the body was discovered it had been severely damaged by insects. Neighbors claim to have seen Kshyama only two days before her body was discovered. I have never known insects to appear so quickly or consume so completely.

Lien studied the date on the death certificates. November 1915. It was only a few months later that Austrian neurologist Constantin von Economo encountered the first known cases of encephalitis lethargica. This was definitely a piece of the puzzle.

The first victim was a female from Nepal. But what was she doing in Austria? Lien jotted down the names: Nyima and Kshyama Giri. After six months of searching she had finally found Patient Zero.

8 May 1890
Nepal

I pushed my way angrily through the crowd and picked Nyima up. She seemed so small in my arms. I didn't say anything. Just stood there, glaring at the crowd. Nyima grabbed the front of my coat and buried her face against me, sobbing.

"Please. Take me with you," she begged. "Take me far away where Mara cannot find me."

*Catholic Digest*
5 April 2057
"A Virus Changes Nothing"
by Edward Rowley

Last week's riots in Frankfurt show how ethically complex this situation has become. After the "Kunming Report" was released by the W.H.O., many people are wondering what the next step will be. Should DNA profiling be mandatory? Will it be public record? Developments in the Chinese Confederacy fuel fears that the USA may adopt a similar "No Tolerance" policy. China's heavy-handed attempts to "purify the human bloodline" remind many of the tragic mistakes in our own history. And yet, doing nothing seems equally distasteful. Moderates in Washington are currently pushing for a "Full Disclosure Act," which would require all marriage partners to share viral profiles so that parenting choices are fully informed. Extremists clamor that it isn't enough. They believe the government should "actively prevent" infected births. The Catholic Church has already publicly taken a stance against extreme measures, declaring firmly, "All human lives are sacred. A virus changes nothing."

Lien slipped her arm slowly out from under Bao and placed a pillow to prevent him from rolling off the bed. Since Tuan's death he had refused to fall asleep without being held.

She walked into the living room and opened the large manila envelope that had finally arrived. It had taken her eight weeks to track down the contents of this envelope. First she had found Nyima Giri's immigration records to Austria, as well as Kshyama Giri's birth records. Both documents mentioned the same name: Alfons von Waldstein.

More digging had turned up a variety of interesting facts. Apparently he had crossed northern India on a failed excursion to Tibet, and had returned a year later with a pregnant girl. He denied being the father, but financially supported both the mother and child until he was killed in a hunting accident in 1912.

Lien was fairly confident the child, Kshyama Giri, was the first victim of the virus. And so she had been delighted to discover that Waldstein had kept meticulous travel journals that had been donated to a museum near Vienna. The museum had scanned the pages for historic preservation, and they were happy to give her electronic access. Lien had immediately sent the file out for translation into Viet. And now she held paper copies of both the scanned originals and the Viet translations. It was a thick stack.

Flipping first through the originals, she admired the tall looping handwriting. She could tell by the dates that he had written in the journal daily. Lien prayed the answers she sought were somewhere in those entries. She reached for the translation and started to read.

As the story of Alfons, Nyima, and Pratik unfolded it filled her with a growing sense of dread. She knew how this story ended—one hundred and sixty years later people would start dying. Nine-tenths of the world would carry Mara's curse within their DNA. And so Lien watched each inevitable choice building toward catastrophe.

She reached the scene at the well. Nyima clinging to Alfons, begging for the life of her unborn child. Lien knew what Alfons was going to do next, not just because she had seen the immigration records, but because Alfons was a good man. And that irony somehow made it that much worse. The world had been doomed over a hundred years ago, not by hatred or anger, but by compassion.

Lien screamed at Alfons to leave it be, just let the child die. If she could somehow go there, back to where this had all started, she would pick up the first stone herself. And she would throw it. She would hate herself for it, but one death would save them all. Bao. Tuan. Peder. An infected world. Yes. She would throw that stone if she could, and the realization made her sick inside. With an empty sense of despair, she came to the end of an entry.

*"I will take Nyima with me. I will take her child far away from Mara's cursed valley and give it a chance to live free of fear's dark shadow."*

As she finished the passage, Lien felt a dark knot in her heart. Nyima had not left Mara's shadow behind. She had carried it with her to Austria. Carried it safely within her womb. And now the shadow had spread across the entire world.

Lien was pulled from her melancholy by Bao crying in the other room. She stood, surprised to find light coming through the curtains. When she reached him, a sharp wave of hopelessness hit her. She slid to the floor beside the bed, hugging her knees tightly against her chest. There were no tears. She was past that. Now there was only a heavy blackness pushing her down. Alfons's journals had been her last hope. But there was nothing in them that was even remotely helpful. The valley where the disease originated had no magical cure. Their methods of dealing with the infection were comically close to what the world was using now. Selective breeding. There was nothing in that journal that could help Bao.

For a moment she wondered if the cult in California hadn't had the right idea. What child would want to grow up knowing they were a ticking bomb? That one day their body would devour itself? Maybe it would be more merciful to . . .

And that was the thought that snapped her out of it. That was absolutely ridiculous. When your child was diagnosed with leukemia you didn't kill them, you kept fighting and hoping until the end. And that was exactly what she would do.

21 April 2057

Stanford University Delays
End of Semester Finals to Help Grieving Students

Stanford announced yesterday that end of semester finals will be delayed "indefinitely" as students work through the emotional fallout of campuswide pheromone testing. Working in conjunction with the US Health Department, students were encouraged to take advantage of free pheromone screenings and received their results last week. Many are having a hard time processing it. "This age group is especially susceptible," says Waiola Akintola, a psychology professor at Stanford. "Many are in their midtwenties. An LC-8 profile of self or friends feels like a death sentence. Profiles of LC-6 or LC-7 severely limit who a person can safely have children with. Not knowing how far off a potential cure is, these students are being forced to face some very harsh realities."

Lien signed off on the lab report for the young man and handed it back to him. She motioned for him to take a seat. In the two weeks since obtaining Alfons's journal entries, neither she nor anyone else had found any breakthroughs in the text. While it was nice to know the historic source of the virus, it did nothing to provide a solution to the current global catastrophe. She had decided the next best avenue was to join the team studying how the transformation initiated.

A facility in Brazil had isolated the Kunming Transformation Steroid (KTS). It only took *one* cell in the body with shortened telomeres to trigger the transformation. As soon as that cell started pumping out KTS, neighboring cells responded by producing more KTS and soon it flooded the body.

"We still haven't had any success blocking the cascade reaction?" she asked the tech.

"We can slow the cascade," he answered, "but it doesn't help in the long run. Just delays the inevitable. We can keep rats alive for up to ten days now, but the virus wins every time."

*Ten days? That was an improvement.*

"So we know enough to trigger a transformation, but not enough to stop it?"

The tech nodded. "We can inject an LC-8 host with KTS to trigger a transformation early, but after that it spreads exponentially. We can slow the spread by injecting chemicals in the blood that bind to KTS and are flushed out by the kidneys, but it's not enough."

Lien frowned. "Well, keep trying. There *has* to be a way."

The man opened his mouth, probably to voice his doubts, but a glare from Lien silenced him. He nodded, and left the room.

A quiet chime alerted Lien that she had a new message from an *Important* contact. Pulling it up, she saw it was from the museum in Austria.

*Your recent interest in the journals of Alfons von Waldstein led me to reorganize our files from this period. While doing so, I found another journal which mentions him frequently. I am not sure if it is of any interest to you, but I am attaching the data file.*

Curious, Lien opened the file. It was written in German in what appeared to be a child's awkward scrawl. Lien knew almost no German, but the first line was fairly easy to guess: *Mein Name ist Nyima.*

Was she really looking at a copy of Nyima's journal?

*Kyodo News* (Japan)
24 April 2057
Student Suicide Linked to
Escalating Kunming Fears

Endo Moriko, age 21, was found dead in her dormitory last Friday. Autopsy reports confirm suicide by hanging. Her friend, Rie Isobe, reveals a shocking explanation for the unexpected death. "She stayed home from classes Thursday because of a fever. Then she started getting the rash. She called me in hysterics, and I told her to meet me at the hospital. She never came. I went to her dorm, but it was too late."

Autopsy reports indicate Moriko was not suffering from a Kunming incident, but rather an aggressive case of the chicken pox.

Lien changed Bao into his day clothes and started cooking rice porridge for breakfast. Checking her work mail, she saw the new journal translation had uploaded. As Bao ate his porridge Lien read through the entries quickly. Maybe Nyima herself could offer some insight that Alfons had overlooked.

Lien laughed as she read Nyima's first few entries. "Today I ate cake. It was good." Lien scanned the passages quickly, looking for trigger words. When she came to a passage titled, "My Favorite Goat" she almost skipped it. But when she turned the page she noticed the word "Mara." Maybe it was worth her time after all.

*My Favorite Goat*

*My favorite goat was named Alpa because he was so small. He had brown fur and white spots and loved to run in the tall grass. When Alpa was a baby he got very sick. Mama said that Mara had come to take him away. I cried and cried. When I saw Mara's daughters in Alpa's fur I knew that mama was right, and I said goodbye to my friend. But Alpa did not die.*

*Mama said he was lucky. We gave him a new name. Avinash. It means "cannot be destroyed." When he got old I would not let anyone eat him. Mama complained. She said that Mara would take him if we didn't eat him soon. But Mara never came for him.*

Lien read the story over and over, not sure how to interpret it. Alfons had mentioned Avinash in several of his own entries—a scarred goat that followed Nyima everywhere. Lien remembered an entry that mentioned the age of the goat being unusual. At the time, she had thought nothing of it. But now it seemed to imply something incredibly significant. Had Avinash really survived the Kunming virus? It seemed unlikely. Too many pieces of the story didn't add up. First off, the goat had developed symptoms as a baby, which wasn't how the virus worked at all. Second, "Mara's daughters" always appeared in large swarms and devoured the host quickly. And finally, if the goat did carry the viral genes, then it should have manifested the disease eventually. And yet, Nyima seemed confident the goat had been struck by Mara, and equally confident it had survived.

Have you triggered the cascade in any *baby* rats?" Lien asked the lab tech. Her mind had come back to this possibility over and over. What had made Nyima's goat unique was the early transformation. It had been practically a newborn when the Kunming virus manifested. Maybe this was the key to surviving.

The tech looked at her with an odd expression on his face.

"Um. No. I don't think so. We have been trying to recreate the real-world conditions as closely as possible."

Lien smiled at him. This was exactly what she had hoped he would say. "This week I want you to do something for me. Inject KTS in rats with a variety of ages. Start freshly born and work your way up."

30 April 2057
NIMPE Lab Report

SUMMARY: If the KTS cascade is initiated in the extremely young, it is possible for the host rat to survive the Kunming Transformation. Extrapolations for humans estimate 95% success at age 24 months and 80% success at age 36 months. However, it is unknown whether these survivors will trigger a second transformation when they reach adulthood.

Lien popped the protective plastic cover off the needle. This was it, the point of no return. *Am I doing the right thing?* If this really was the cure, then yes. *But what if . . .*

She looked at Bao, asleep on the couch while a cartoon rooster sang a counting song on TV. An empty bowl of mango pudding rested on the couch beside him, pudding that had been laced with Tryptofluorizine.

Her son was almost twenty-seven months old—past the five percent mortality threshold. And each day the percentage of larval cells in his body was increasing. What she was about to do was a medical version of Russian roulette. True, the odds were in his favor, and they would only get worse if she waited. But still, pulling the trigger when you knew there was a bullet somewhere in the cylinder . . .

Lien shook her head. No. She was not going to let doubt get in her way. Both Alfons and Nyima had mentioned the age of Avinash. For some reason, the goat had triggered early. Then it had grown and passed the age of transformation unharmed.

Lien crossed the room and stood in front of her family shrine. Setting down the needle, she lit two candles in front of Tuan's photo and started a fresh stick of incense. Tuan watched the proceedings with that goofy grin he always wore in photos. *Please.* Lien prayed. *Please let this work.* She watched as her prayer wafted up toward heaven. Then she grabbed the needle, crossed the room, and injected Bao's thigh.

## 5 August 2060
## Viet Nam

Lien held a hand to her mouth in disgust. What was Bao doing?

The other five-year-olds were content to simply pet the animals. But Bao insisted on feeding each and every one of them. And he thought it was hilarious when they tried to swallow his hand as well. She hoped that donkey didn't have lung worms. When a goat licked Bao's face, a man laughed loudly. *This is so embarrassing.*

A young mother darted forward and grabbed her daughter. "No, Bihn. Don't touch it. It's dirty." The frazzled woman was also clutching an infant in her arms. Both children bore the now familiar scars of the Kunming vaccine, but they would fade with time.

"Goats aren't bad," said Bao in surprise as the woman pulled her daughter away from the dangerous animal. "A goat saved the world. My mom and dad helped too."

The woman smiled. "Children say such funny things."

"I want a goat, Mom," said Bao, patting the creature on its head. "Can we get a goat?"

Lien paused, trying to think of a way to change the subject.

Bao grinned up at her, "I think Dad would like it if I had a goat."

Her son was one tough negotiator, but two could play at this game. "How about we start with a rat," said Lien. "You know, they helped to save the world too."

# *Theme*

## BY ORSON SCOTT CARD

*Orson Scott Card is the author of the award-winning novels* Ender's Game, Ender's Shadow, *and* Speaker for the Dead, *which are widely read by adults and younger readers, and are increasingly used in schools. His most recent series, the young adult Pathfinder series (*Pathfinder, Ruins, Visitors*) and the fantasy Mither Mages series (*Lost Gate, Gate Thief, Gatefather*) are taking readers in new directions.*

*Besides these and other science fiction novels, Card writes contemporary fantasy (*Magic Street, Enchantment, Lost Boys*), biblical novels (*Stone Tables, Rachel and Leah*), the American frontier fantasy series The Tales of Alvin Maker (beginning with* Seventh Son*), poetry (*An Open Book*), and many plays and scripts, including his "freshened" Shakespeare scripts for* Romeo & Juliet, The Taming of the Shrew, *and* The Merchant of Venice.

*Card has won numerous awards including the Hugo, Nebula, and World Fantasy Awards. He was born in Washington and grew up in California, Arizona, and Utah. He served a mission for the Church of Jesus Christ of Latter-day Saints (LDS) in Brazil in the early 1970s. Besides his writing, he teaches occasional classes and workshops and directs plays. He frequently teaches writing and literature courses at Southern Virginia University.*

*Card currently lives in Greensboro, North Carolina, with his wife, Kristine Allen Card, where his primary activities are writing a review column for the local* Rhinoceros Times *and feeding birds, squirrels, chipmunks, possums, and raccoons on the patio.*

*Orson Scott Card has been a judge of the Writers of the Future Contest since 1994, having earlier served as a guest instructor at the Writers' Workshops, at both Sag Harbor, Long Island and Pepperdine University in Los Angeles. He was also the featured essayist in volumes four and twenty-two of the Writers of the Future anthology.*

# *Theme*

A few years ago, I wrote a book called *Shadows in Flight.* It was designed to be a half-length novel, so I couldn't sprawl in my world creation and character development. The story followed a father with a genetic disorder that made him astonishingly intelligent and creative, but also afflicted him with gigantism that would, unchecked, eventually kill him.

Before the story began, he took off on a near-lightspeed voyage with those of his children who had the same disorder, in hopes that they could stay alive until somebody found a way to treat or cure the gigantism without losing the brainpower.

Along the way, they run across an ancient colony ship from an alien culture, one that had never reached its destination and now continued as an ecosystem without a purpose, since the colonists were all dead.

As with all far-future science fiction, the burden of world creation takes up a huge amount of expository space—a burden that someone who sets a novel in "San Francisco, 1968" or "an American elementary school in 2009" does not face.

Even though such real-world fiction does require research, it does not require anything like the level of invention that a writer must reach in order to offer the readers a believable story milieu.

Ever since Robert Heinlein taught us all how to deliver the far-future setting to the readers in dribs and drabs, we don't have the huge expository lumps that used to mar early sci-fi: "As you know, Bob, because this planet has so much ammonia/helium/nitrogen/flaming plasma, we'll have to wear our spacesuits/fire-retardant gear/Halloween masks during our entire exploration."

But the fact that our invented world can be delivered to the readers more or less painlessly does not change the hardest burden: the need to *invent* that world. Everything that a writer of contemporary fiction can simply draw from memory, the sci-fi writer has to invent. Whatever we change here will have repercussions there, and somehow we must hold it all in our heads while we're writing.

Now that sci-fi readers also expect at least some level of plausible characterization—which requires well-drawn, interesting relationships between people in the story—the writer must also come up with people and communities that ring true, even if there have been significant changes in human beings.

Add to this the peculiar tensions inside a spaceship containing only three hyper-genius children and their dying father, and you can easily imagine that *all* my concentration was on these relationships *and* their work on a self-cure *and* the workings of the alien colony ship.

The questions that mattered to me were: Why do the characters do what they do? How will they respond to each other's decisions and actions? What is the life cycle of the surviving species on the alien ship? How can the genetic disorder in this family be corrected or compensated for? What happens to someone who can't stop growing, even in a weightless environment? Since each of these questions implies hundreds of others, I didn't have any time or concentration to waste on nonsense unconnected with the story.

In other words, the furthest thing from my mind was to come up with an extraneous "theme," even though this is clearly the main thing that schoolteachers and professors require their literature students to detect and explain.

I know this because I have received so many letters from students that ask, sometimes in these exact words, "What is the theme of [insert book title here]?"

My answer usually has two parts:

1. I'm not in school anymore, so I don't have to think or talk about themes. That's *your* burden.
2. I only think about themes when I'm writing essays. When I write stories, I think only about story. So if you find a theme, I'm happy for you, but I can assure you that it is entirely a natural outgrowth of storytelling or the result of your own personal preoccupations, and not at all the author's intention.

At the end of *Shadows in Flight,* I felt that I had dealt with world and character creation reasonably well. And, near the end, as I showed the father's few steps in a gravity environment, I felt that I had brought that character to fruition—after developing him across five previous novels.

Months later, as we neared the novel's publication date, the producer of the audiobook, Stefan Rudnicki of Skyboat Media, brought together a group of brilliant narrators who had participated in the production of *Shadows in Flight.*

I've been fortunate in having my books narrated by some of the most talented readers in the history of audiobooks, and Stefan (a frequent narrator of my books himself) recorded a round table discussion involving me, Stefan, Emily Rankin, Scott Brick, Gabrielle de Cuir, and Kirby Heyborne.

You can see the discussion at Skyboat Media's website: skyboatmedia.com/enders-game/.

During the discussion, Scott Brick and Kirby Heyborne, in particular, commented on how much the story meant to them as fathers. One of them even referred to it as a "fatherhood book."

That was the first moment that it occurred to me that *Shadows in Flight* was, in fact, this old man's meditation on what fatherhood means to a man nearing the end of his life. It blindsided me, emotionally, especially because one of these great narrators was my eldest daughter, Emily Janice Card, now Rankin.

This was not the first time that I discovered the "theme" of a story of mine well after the fact. At no point in the writing of

*Shadows in Flight* did I think, *I'm going to turn this into an exploration of fatherhood.*

This has happened often in my career. I remember a professional-writers workshop at which my story *Lost Boys* was discussed. Only as some participants commented on the story did I realize that the child who haunts his family after his death was in reality my "exploration" of my relationship with my second son, who, because of his severe cerebral palsy, never took a step, never sat up without aid, and never spoke a sentence in his life. In effect, I realized, I was using haunting as a means of expressing Charlie Ben's place in our family: beloved, central to all of us, and yet scarcely able to influence the course of events.

Then there was the time when, at my first WorldCon, a reader saw my name tag and, recognizing my name, said, "You wrote *A Planet Called Treason*, didn't you?" I pled guilty (the novel is now available as *Treason*), and then he startled me by saying, "I bet you're a Mormon." When I asked him why he thought of that, he said, "As I was reading it, I thought, only a Mormon could have written this book."

Now, having written and produced many plays dealing with Mormon culture, history, and scriptural stories, I had resolved, when I first started writing sci-fi, that I would keep my fiction free of all Mormon references, ideas, or doctrine. I knew that science fiction, like science, is resolutely areligious—everything must have natural or mechanical causes, and can never include a transcendent deity.

So I was stunned at the thought that my totally secular story in *A Planet Called Treason* somehow revealed some subset of my personal beliefs to at least one reader. At first I assumed he simply noticed the reference in my bio to my having served an LDS mission in Brazil—but no, the hardcover he read *had* no jacket and therefore no bio.

Only upon rereading the novel with this conversation in mind did I realize that several completely unconscious, story-centered decisions I had made in developing the world and characters tapped into my personal core: Things I believe about how the world works, which happen to reflect aspects of LDS doctrine that I have internalized so completely that I no longer notice them when they crop up in my work.

Through experiences like this, I have come to realize something important: A storyteller does not need to think up a theme. Themes will emerge in the process of natural storytelling, without any conscious effort on the part of the author.

In fact, I'll go further. If you write in order to demonstrate some deliberate theme, your story will inevitably be bent to accommodate it. The reader is therefore quite likely to notice that theme *and be distracted by it.*

You know what I mean: It's that moment in a movie or TV show or novel when you realize, ah, the writer is preaching to me, and here's the moral lesson I'm supposed to receive.

Whatever theme you consciously put into a story will be consciously received by the readers—and, unless they already agree with you, will be immediately rejected, probably along with the whole story.

Therefore, when you write to a theme, you guarantee that in most cases you will be preaching to the choir, unable to change anybody's mind because your theme is standing in front of the story and blocking the view.

However, in the thousands of unconscious decisions every storyteller makes during the process of invention and writing, you will tap into the deepest places in your unconscious. You will include certain events or ideas because they simply feel right or inevitable to you; usually you aren't even aware that you're *making* a decision.

These unconscious choices access your beliefs at the deepest level: The things you believe without knowing you believe them, because it doesn't occur to you that the universe might be otherwise.

Only upon rereading your own work—usually years later, or with someone else's insights to guide you—do you discover these beliefs. Thus your fiction will reveal to you, not what you *think* you believe, but what you *really* believe.

And because these elements were placed in the story unconsciously, most readers will not notice them either. Instead, they will live inside your moral universe and absorb your deepest thoughts without awareness.

If your readers are uncomfortable with living in your fictional world, they will lose interest in the story, finding some superficial reason to abandon it. But, especially with science fiction, where the readers seek out new experiences, readers will rarely repudiate strangeness. Instead, they'll remain in your moral universe for the duration of the story, and will thereby give it a chance to influence their own deepest worldview.

You're not "converting" them, but rather you're giving them the transcendent reward of story hearing—the chance to live other lives, acquire alien memories, and live inside the mind and heart of a stranger. Whether they are aware of how your story has changed them, their world *is* transformed.

Naturally, your story is also edited and revised by their own inward story, so that they may often "receive" things that don't actually come from your story. But communication does happen, and even if your story is a catalyst rather than a director of their inner transformation, it is that interchange that makes stories the DNA of culture.

We pass our culture person to person through the great network of story exchange. But it is most effective where there is the least deliberate control of the "theme" by the author.

Having a theme is like heckling your own story, keeping readers from receiving your best, most personal gifts.

So as you plan your fiction, if you really want to communicate something important with your readers, you will repel any temptation to preach, to organize your story around a central idea, to make sure your story gets this or that particular idea across to the reader.

Often such messages are really a matter of tagging up with

whatever culture group or elite you want to impress: See how I did that? See how I'm getting "our" message across?

If that's what you really want to do, then write an essay and openly attempt to persuade the readers.

Don't pollute your stories with such toxic distractions. Keep your stories as pure as possible, and trust your unconscious mind to deliver the truths that are most important to you. What enters your stories unconsciously will have far more power and influence than anything you can possibly do on purpose.

# *The Lesson*

*written by*

## *Brandon Sanderson*

*illustrated by*

BEA JACKSON

---

ABOUT THE AUTHOR

*Number-one* New York Times *bestselling author Brandon Sanderson was born in 1975 in Lincoln, Nebraska. By junior high he had lost interest in the novels suggested to him, and he never cracked a book if he could help it. Then an eighth grade teacher, Mrs. Reeder, gave him* Dragonsbane *by Barbara Hambly.*

*Brandon was finishing his thirteenth novel when Moshe Feder at Tor Books bought the sixth he had written. In 2005 Brandon held his first published novel,* Elantris, *in his hands. Tor also published six books in Brandon's Mistborn series, along with* Warbreaker *and then* The Way of Kings, Words of Radiance, *and* Oathbringer, *the first three in the planned ten-volume series The Stormlight Archive. Five books in his middle-grade Alcatraz vs. the Evil Librarians series were released by Starscape. Brandon was chosen to complete Robert Jordan's Wheel of Time series; the final book, A* Memory of Light, *was released in 2013. That year also marked the releases of YA novels* The Rithmatist *from Tor and* Steelheart *from Delacorte—the first book of the Reckoners trilogy, which concluded in 2016 with* Calamity.

*Currently living in Utah with his wife and children, Brandon teaches creative writing at Brigham Young University. He also hosts the Hugo Award-winning writing advice podcast Writing Excuses with Mary Robinette Kowal, Howard Tayler, and Dan Wells.*

*Brandon's work has garnered wide critical acclaim and won numerous awards, including the Hugo. The story you are about read was excerpted from his bestselling novel* The Way of Kings.

## ABOUT THE ILLUSTRATOR

*Brittany Jackson, also known as Bea, is an award-winning freelance illustrator born and raised in the "Motor City" of Detroit, Michigan. Taken by a passion for the arts at a young age, Bea embraced her gift of drawing and learned how to bring her vivid imagination to life in a variety of artistic styles she's studied throughout the years prior to majoring in illustration at the College for Creative Studies. Bea loves the challenges that arts bring, the thrill that comes with learning something new and the satisfaction of using her gifts to help others visualize their dreams. With a strong sense for concepts and design, Bea has become well recognized for her ability to paint a picture from words, communicating ideas—hers and others—through beautiful narrative illustration.*

*She is a former grand-prize winner of the Illustrators of the Future Contest. Her artwork was published in* L. Ron Hubbard Presents Writers of the Future Volume 24.

# *The Lesson*

*It was not uncommon for us to meet native peoples while traveling through the Unclaimed Hills,* Shallan read. *These ancient lands were once one of the Silver Kingdoms, after all. One must wonder if the great-shelled beasts lived among them back then, or if the creatures have come to inhabit the wilderness left by humankind's passing.*

She settled back in her chair, the humid air warm around her. To her left, Jasnah Kholin floated quietly in the pool inset in the floor of the bathing chamber. Jasnah liked to soak in the bath, and Shallan couldn't blame her. During most of Shallan's life, bathing had been an ordeal involving dozens of parshmen carting heated buckets of water, followed by a quick scrub in the brass tub before the water cooled.

Kharbranth's palace offered far more luxury. The stone pool in the ground resembled a small personal lake, luxuriously warmed by clever fabrials that produced heat. Shallan didn't know much about fabrials yet, though part of her was very intrigued. This type was becoming increasingly common. Just the other day, the Conclave staff had sent Jasnah one to heat her chambers.

The water didn't have to be carried in but came out of pipes. At the turn of a lever, water flowed in. It was warm when it entered, and was kept heated by the fabrials set into the sides of the pool. Shallan had bathed in the chamber herself, and it was absolutely marvelous.

The practical decor was of rock decorated with small colorful stones set in mortar up the sides of the walls. Shallan sat beside the pool, fully dressed, reading as she waited on Jasnah's needs. The book was Gavilar's account—as spoken to Jasnah herself years ago—after his first meeting with the strange parshmen later known as the Parshendi.

*Occasionally, during our explorations, we'd meet with natives,* she read. *Not parshmen. Natan people, with their pale bluish skin, wide noses, and wool-like white hair. In exchange for gifts of food, they would point us to the hunting grounds of greatshells.*

*Then we met the parshmen. I'd been on a half-dozen expeditions to Natanatan, but never had I seen anything like this! Parshmen, living on their own? All logic, experience, and science declared that to be an impossibility. Parshmen need the hand of civilized peoples to guide them. This has been proven time and time again. Leave one out in the wilderness, and it will just sit there, doing nothing, until someone comes along to give it orders.*

*Yet here was a group who could hunt, make weapons, build buildings, and—indeed—create their own civilization. We soon realized that this single discovery could expand, perhaps overthrow, all we understood about our gentle servants.*

Shallan moved her eyes down to the bottom of the page where—separated by a line—the undertext was written in a small, cramped script. Most books dictated by men had an undertext, notes added by the woman or ardent who scribed the book. By unspoken agreement, the undertext was never shared out loud. Here, a wife would sometimes clarify—or even contradict—the account of her husband. The only way to preserve such honesty for future scholars was to maintain the sanctity and secrecy of the writing.

*It should be noted,* Jasnah had written in the undertext to this passage, *that I have adapted my father's words—by his own instruction—to make them more appropriate for recording.* That meant she made his dictation sound more scholarly and impressive. *In addition, by most accounts, King Gavilar originally ignored these strange, self-sufficient parshmen. It was only after explanation by his scholars and scribes that he understood the import of what he'd discovered. This inclusion is not meant to highlight my father's ignorance; he was, and is, a warrior. His attention was not on the anthropological import of our expedition, but upon the hunt that was to be its culmination.*

Shallan closed the cover, thoughtful. The volume was from Jasnah's own collection—the Palanaeum had several copies, but Shallan wasn't allowed to bring the Palanaeum's books into a bathing chamber.

Jasnah's clothing lay on a bench at the side of the room. Atop the folded garments, a small golden pouch held the Soulcaster. Shallan glanced at Jasnah. The princess floated faceup in the pool, black hair fanning out behind her in the water, her eyes closed. Her daily bath was the one time she seemed to relax completely. She looked much younger now, stripped of both clothing and intensity, floating like a child resting after a day of active swimming.

Thirty-four years old. That seemed ancient in some regards—some women Jasnah's age had children as old as Shallan. And yet it was also young. Young enough that Jasnah was praised for her beauty, young enough that men declared it a shame she wasn't yet married.

Shallan glanced at the pile of clothing. She carried the broken fabrial in her safepouch. She could swap them here and now. It was the opportunity she'd been waiting for. Jasnah now trusted her enough to relax, soaking in the bathing chamber without worrying about her fabrial.

Could Shallan really do it? Could she betray this woman who had taken her in?

*Considering what I've done before,* she thought, *this is nothing.* It wouldn't be the first time she betrayed someone who trusted her.

She stood up. To the side, Jasnah cracked an eye.

*Blast,* Shallan thought, tucking the book under her arm, pacing, trying to look thoughtful. Jasnah watched her. Not suspiciously. Curiously.

"Why did your father want to make a treaty with the Parshendi?" Shallan found herself asking as she walked.

"Why wouldn't he want to?"

"That's not an answer."

"Of course it is. It's just not one that tells you anything."

"It would help, Brightness, if you would give me a *useful* answer."

"Then ask a useful question."

Shallan set her jaw. "What did the Parshendi have that King Gavilar wanted?"

Jasnah smiled, closing her eyes again. "Closer. But you can probably guess the answer to that."

"Shards."

Jasnah nodded, still relaxed in the water.

"The text doesn't mention them," Shallan said.

"My father didn't speak of them," Jasnah said. "But from things he said . . . well, I now suspect that they motivated the treaty."

"Can you be sure he knew, though? Maybe he just wanted the gemhearts."

"Perhaps," Jasnah said. "The Parshendi seemed amused at our interest in the gemstones woven into their beards." She smiled. "You should have seen our shock when we discovered where they'd gotten them. When the lanceryn died off during the scouring of Aimia, we thought we'd seen the last gemhearts of large size. And yet here was another great-shelled beast with them, living in a land not too distant from Kholinar itself.

"Anyway, the Parshendi were willing to share them with us, so long as they could still hunt them too. To them, if you took the trouble to hunt the chasmfiends, their gemhearts were yours. I doubt a treaty would have been needed for that. And yet, just before leaving to return to Alethkar, my father suddenly began talking fervently of the need for an agreement."

"So what happened? What changed?"

"I can't be certain. However, he once described the strange actions of a Parshendi warrior during a chasmfiend hunt. Instead of reaching for his spear when the greatshell appeared, this man held his hand to the side in a very suspicious way. Only my father saw it; I suspected he believed the man planned to summon a Blade. The Parshendi realized what he was doing, and stopped himself. My father didn't speak of it further, and I assume he didn't want the world's eyes on the Shattered Plains any more than they already were."

Shallan tapped her book. "It seems tenuous. If he was sure about the Blades, he must have seen more."

"I suspect so as well. But I studied the treaty carefully, after his death. The clauses for favored trade status and mutual border crossing could very well have been a step toward folding the Parshendi into Alethkar as a nation. It certainly would have prevented the Parshendi from trading their Shards to other kingdoms without coming to us first. Perhaps that was all he wanted to do."

"But why kill him?" Shallan said, arms crossed, strolling in the direction of Jasnah's folded clothing. "Did the Parshendi realize that he intended to have their Shardblades, and so struck at him pre-emptively?"

"Uncertain," Jasnah said. She sounded skeptical. Why did *she* think the Parshendi killed Gavilar? Shallan nearly asked, but she had a feeling she wouldn't get any more out of Jasnah. The woman expected Shallan to think, discover, and draw conclusions on her own.

Shallan stopped beside the bench. The pouch holding the Soulcaster was open, the drawstrings loose. She could see the precious artifact curled up inside. The swap would be easy. She had used a large chunk of her money to buy gemstones that matched Jasnah's, and had put them into the broken Soulcaster. The two were now exactly identical.

She still hadn't learned anything about using the fabrial; she'd tried to find a way to ask, but Jasnah avoided speaking of the Soulcaster. Pushing harder would be suspicious. Shallan would have to get information elsewhere. Perhaps from Kabsal, or maybe from a book in the Palanaeum.

Regardless, the time was upon her. Shallan found her hand going to her safepouch, and she felt inside of it, running her fingers along the chains of her broken fabrial. Her heart beat faster. She glanced at Jasnah, but the woman was just lying there, floating, eyes closed. What if she opened her eyes?

*Don't think of that!* Shallan told herself. *Just do it. Make the swap. It's so close. . . .*

"You are progressing more quickly than I had assumed you would," Jasnah said suddenly.

Shallan spun, but Jasnah's eyes were still closed. "I was wrong to judge you so harshly because of your prior education. I myself have often said that passion outperforms upbringing. You have the determination and the capacity to become a respected scholar, Shallan. I realize that the answers seem slow in coming, but continue your research. You will have them eventually."

Shallan stood for a moment, hand in her pouch, heart thumping uncontrollably. She felt sick. *I can't do it,* she realized. *Stormfather, but I'm a fool. I came all of this way . . . and now I can't do it!*

She pulled her hand from her pouch and stalked back across the bathing chamber to her chair. What was she going to tell her brothers? Had she just doomed her family? She sat down, setting her book aside and sighing, prompting Jasnah to open her eyes. Jasnah watched her, then righted herself in the water and gestured for the hairsoap.

Gritting her teeth, Shallan stood up and fetched the soap tray for Jasnah, bringing it over and squatting down to proffer it. Jasnah took the powdery hairsoap and mashed it in her hand, lathering it before putting it into her sleek black hair with both hands. Even naked, Jasnah Kholin was composed and in control.

"Perhaps we have spent too much time indoors of late," the princess said. "You look penned up, Shallan. Anxious."

"I'm fine," Shallan said brusquely.

"Hum, yes. As evidenced by your perfectly reasonable, relaxed tone. Perhaps we need to shift some of your training from history to something more hands-on, more visceral."

"Like natural science?" Shallan asked, perking up.

Jasnah tilted her head back. Shallan knelt down on a towel

beside the pool, then reached down with her freehand, massaging the soap into her mistress's lush tresses.

"I was thinking philosophy," Jasnah said.

Shallan blinked. "Philosophy? What good is that?" *Isn't it the art of saying nothing with as many words as possible?*

"Philosophy is an important field of study," Jasnah said sternly. "Particularly if you're going to be involved in court politics. The nature of morality must be considered, and preferably before one is exposed to situations where a moral decision is required."

"Yes, Brightness. Though I fail to see how philosophy is more 'hands-on' than history."

"History, by definition, cannot be experienced directly. As it is happening, it is the present, and that is philosophy's realm."

"That's just a matter of definition."

"Yes," Jasnah said, "all words have a tendency to be subject to how they are defined."

"I suppose," Shallan said, leaning back, letting Jasnah dunk her hair to clean off the soap.

The princess began scrubbing her skin with mildly abrasive soap. "That was a particularly bland response, Shallan. What happened to your wit?"

Shallan glanced at the bench and its precious fabrial. After all this time, she had proven too weak to do what needed to be done. "My wit is on temporary hiatus, Brightness," she said. "Pending review by its colleagues, sincerity and temerity."

Jasnah raised an eyebrow at her.

Shallan sat back on her heels, still kneeling on the towel. "How *do* you know what is right, Jasnah? If you don't listen to the devotaries, how do you decide?"

"That depends upon one's philosophy. What is most important to you?"

"I don't know. Can't you tell me?"

"No," Jasnah replied. "If I gave you the answers, I'd be no better than the devotaries, prescribing beliefs."

"They aren't evil, Jasnah."

"Except when they try to rule the world."

Shallan drew her lips into a thin line. The War of Loss had destroyed the Hierocracy, shattering Vorinism into the devotaries. That was the inevitable result of a religion trying to rule. The devotaries were to teach morals, not enforce them. Enforcement was for the lighteyes.

"You say you can't give me answers," Shallan said. "But can't I ask for the advice of someone wise? Someone who's gone before? Why write our philosophies, draw our conclusions, if not to influence others? You yourself told me that information is worthless unless we use it to make judgments."

Jasnah smiled, dunking her arms and washing off the soap. Shallan caught a victorious glimmer in her eye. She wasn't necessarily advocating ideas because she believed them; she just wanted to push Shallan. It was infuriating. How was Shallan to know what Jasnah really thought if she adopted conflicting points of view like this?

"You act as if there were one answer," Jasnah said, gesturing to Shallan to fetch a towel and climbing from the pool. "A single, eternally perfect response."

Shallan hastily complied, bearing a large, fluffy towel. "Isn't that what philosophy is about? Finding the answers? Seeking the truth, the real meaning of things?"

Toweling off, Jasnah raised an eyebrow at her.

"What?" Shallan asked, suddenly self-conscious.

"I believe it is time for a field exercise," Jasnah said. "Outside of the Palanaeum."

"Now?" Shallan asked. "It's so late!"

"I told you philosophy was a hands-on art," Jasnah said, wrapping the towel around herself, then reaching down and taking the Soulcaster out of its pouch. She slipped the chains around her fingers, securing the gemstones to the back of her hand. "I'll prove it to you. Come, help me dress."

As a child, Shallan had relished those evenings when she'd been able to slip away into the gardens. When the blanket of darkness rested atop the grounds, they had seemed a different place entirely. In those shadows, she'd been able to imagine that the rockbuds, shalebark, and trees were some foreign fauna. The scrapings of cremlings climbing out of cracks had become the footsteps of mysterious people from far-off lands. Large-eyed traders from Shinovar, a greatshell rider from Kadrix, or a narrow boat sailor from the Purelake.

She didn't have those same imaginings when walking Kharbranth at night. Imagining dark wanderers in the night had once been an intriguing game—but here, dark wanderers were likely to be real. Instead of becoming a mysterious, intriguing place at night, Kharbranth seemed much the same to her—just more dangerous.

Jasnah ignored the calls of rickshaw pullers and palanquin porters. She walked slowly in a beautiful dress of violet and gold, Shallan following in blue silk. Jasnah hadn't taken time to have her hair done following her bath, and she wore it loose, cascading across her shoulders, almost scandalous in its freedom.

They walked the Ralinsa—the main thoroughfare that led down the hillside in switchbacks, connecting Conclave and port. Despite the late hour, the roadway was crowded, and many of the men who walked here seemed to bear the night inside of them. They were gruffer, more shadowed of face. Shouts still rang through the city, but those carried the night in them too, measured by the roughness of their words and the sharpness of their tones. The steep, slanted hillside that formed the city was no less crowded with buildings than always, yet these too seemed to draw in the night. Blackened, like stones burned by a fire. Hollow remains.

The bells still rang. In the darkness, each ring was a tiny scream. They made the wind more present, a living thing that caused a chiming cacophony each time it passed. A breeze rose, and an avalanche of sound came tumbling across the Ralinsa. Shallan nearly found herself ducking before it.

"Brightness," Shallan said. "Shouldn't we call for a palanquin?"

"A palanquin might inhibit the lesson."

"I'll be all right learning that lesson during the day, if you wouldn't mind."

Jasnah stopped, looking off the Ralinsa and toward a darker side street. "What do you think of that roadway, Shallan?"

"It doesn't look particularly appealing to me."

"And yet," Jasnah said, "it is the most direct route from the Ralinsa to the theater district."

"Is that where we're going?"

"We aren't 'going' anywhere," Jasnah said, taking off down the side street. "We are acting, pondering, and learning."

Shallan followed nervously. The night swallowed them; only the occasional light from late-night taverns and shops offered illumination. Jasnah wore her black, fingerless glove over her Soulcaster, hiding the light of its gemstones.

Shallan found herself creeping. Her slippered feet could feel every change in the ground underfoot, each pebble and crack. She looked about nervously as they passed a group of workers gathered around a tavern doorway. They were darkeyes, of course. In the night, that distinction seemed more profound.

"Brightness?" Shallan asked in a hushed tone.

"When we are young," Jasnah said, "we want simple answers. There is no greater indication of youth, perhaps, than the desire for everything to be *as it should*. As it has ever been."

Shallan frowned, still watching the men by the tavern over her shoulder.

"The older we grow," Jasnah said, "the more we question. We begin to ask why. And yet, we still want the answers to be simple. We assume that the people around us—adults, leaders—will have those answers. Whatever they give often satisfies us."

"I was never satisfied," Shallan said softly. "I wanted more."

"You were mature," Jasnah said. "What you describe happens to most of us, as we age. Indeed, it seems to me that aging, wisdom, and *wondering* are synonymous. The older we grow, the more likely we are to reject the simple answers. Unless someone gets in our way and demands they be accepted regardless." Jasnah's eyes narrowed. "You wonder why I reject the devotaries."

"I do."

"Most of them seek to stop the questions." Jasnah halted. Then she briefly pulled back her glove, using the light beneath to reveal the street around her. The gemstones on her hand—larger than broams—blazed like torches, red, white, and gray.

"Is it wise to be showing your wealth like that, Brightness?" Shallan said, speaking very softly and glancing about her.

"No," Jasnah said. "It is most certainly not. Particularly not here. You see, this street has gained a particular reputation lately. On three separate occasions during the last two months, theatergoers who chose this route to the main road were accosted by footpads. In each case, the people were murdered."

Shallan felt herself grow pale.

"The city watch," Jasnah said, "has done nothing. Taravangian has sent them several pointed reprimands, but the captain of the watch is cousin to a very influential lighteyes in the city, and Taravangian is not a terribly powerful king. Some suspect that there is more going on, that the footpads might be bribing the watch. The politics of it are irrelevant at the moment for, as you can see, no members of the watch are guarding the place, despite its reputation."

Jasnah pulled her glove back on, plunging the roadway back into darkness. Shallan blinked, her eyes adjusting.

"How foolish," Jasnah said, "would you say it is for us to come here, two undefended women wearing costly clothing and bearing riches?"

"*Very* foolish. Jasnah, can we go? Please. Whatever lesson you have in mind isn't worth this."

Jasnah drew her lips into a line, then looked toward a narrow, darker alleyway off the road they were on. It was almost completely black now that Jasnah had replaced her glove.

"You're at an interesting place in your life, Shallan," Jasnah said, flexing her hand. "You are old enough to wonder, to ask, to reject what is presented to you simply *because* it was presented to you. But you also cling to the idealism of youth. You feel there must be some single, all-defining Truth—and you think that once you find it, all that once confused you will suddenly make sense."

"I . . ." Shallan wanted to argue, but Jasnah's words were tellingly accurate. The terrible things Shallan had done, the terrible thing she had planned to do, haunted her. Was it possible to do something horrible in the name of accomplishing something wonderful?

Jasnah walked into the narrow alleyway.

"Jasnah!" Shallan said. "What are you doing?"

"This is philosophy in action, child," Jasnah said. "Come with me."

Shallan hesitated at the mouth of the alleyway, her heart thumping, her thoughts muddled. The wind blew and bells rang, like frozen raindrops shattering against the stones. In a moment of decision, she rushed after Jasnah, preferring company, even in the dark, to being alone. The shrouded glimmer of the Soulcaster was barely enough to light their way, and Shallan followed in Jasnah's shadow.

Noise from behind. Shallan turned with a start to see several dark forms crowding into the alley. "Oh, Stormfather," she whispered. Why? Why was Jasnah doing this?

Shaking, Shallan grabbed at Jasnah's dress with her freehand. Other shadows were moving in front of them, from the far side of the alley. They grew closer, grunting, splashing through foul, stagnant puddles. Chill water soaked Shallan's slippers.

Jasnah stopped moving. The frail light of her cloaked Soulcaster reflected off metal in the hands of their stalkers. Swords or knives.

These men meant murder. You didn't rob women like Shallan and Jasnah, women with powerful connections, then leave them alive as witnesses. Men like these were not the gentlemen bandits of romantic stories. They lived each day knowing that if they were caught, they would be hanged.

Paralyzed by fear, Shallan couldn't even scream.

*Stormfather, Stormfather, Stormfather!*

"And now," Jasnah said, voice hard and grim, "the lesson." She whipped off her glove.

The sudden light was nearly blinding. Shallan raised a hand against it, stumbling back against the alley wall. There were four men around them. Not the men from the tavern entrance, but others. Men she hadn't noticed watching them. She could see the knives now, and she could also see the murder in their eyes.

Her scream finally broke free.

The men grunted at the glare, but shoved their way forward. A thick-chested man with a dark beard came up to Jasnah, weapon raised. She calmly reached her hand out—fingers splayed—and pressed it against his chest as he swung a knife. Shallan's breath caught in her throat.

Jasnah's hand sank into the man's skin, and he froze. A second later he burned.

No, he *became fire*. Transformed into flames in an eyeblink. Rising around Jasnah's hand, they formed the outline of a man with head thrown back and mouth open. For just a moment, the blaze of the man's death outshone Jasnah's gemstones.

Shallan's scream trailed off. The figure of flames was strangely beautiful. It was gone in a moment, the fire dissipating into the night air, leaving an orange afterimage in Shallan's eyes.

The other three men began to curse, scrambling away, tripping over one another in their panic. One fell. Jasnah turned casually, brushing his shoulder with her fingers as he struggled to his knees. He became crystal, a figure of pure, flawless quartz—his clothing transformed along with him. The diamond in Jasnah's Soulcaster faded, but there was still plenty of Stormlight left to send rainbow sparkles through the transformed corpse.

The other two men fled in opposite directions. Jasnah took a deep breath, closing her eyes, lifting her hand above her head. Shallan held her safehand to her breast, stunned, confused. Terrified.

BEA JACKSON

Stormlight shot from Jasnah's hand like twin bolts of lightning, symmetrical. One struck each of the footpads and they popped, puffing into smoke. Their empty clothing dropped to the ground. With a sharp snap, the smokestone crystal on Jasnah's Soulcaster cracked, its light vanishing, leaving her with just the diamond and the ruby.

The remains of the two footpads rose into the air, small billows of greasy vapor. Jasnah opened her eyes, looking eerily calm. She tugged her glove back on—using her safehand to hold it against her stomach and sliding her freehand fingers in. Then she calmly walked back the way they had come. She left the crystal corpse kneeling with hand upraised. Frozen forever.

Shallan pried herself off the wall and hastened after Jasnah, sickened and amazed. Ardents were forbidden to use their Soulcasters on people. They rarely even used them in front of others. And how had Jasnah struck down two men at a distance? From everything Shallan had read—what little there was to find—Soulcasting required physical contact.

Too overwhelmed to demand answers, she stood silent—freehand held to the side of her head, trying to control her trembling and her gasping breaths—as Jasnah called for a palanquin. One came eventually, and the two women climbed in.

The bearers carried them toward the Ralinsa, their steps jostling Shallan and Jasnah, who sat across from one another in the palanquin. Jasnah idly popped the broken smokestone from her Soulcaster, then tucked it into a pocket. It could be sold to a gemsmith, who could cut smaller gemstones from the salvaged pieces.

"That was horrible," Shallan finally said, hand still held to her breast. "It was one of the most awful things I've ever experienced. You *killed* four men."

"Four men who were planning to beat, rob, kill, and possibly rape us."

"You tempted them into coming for us!"

"Did I force them to commit any crimes?"

"You showed off your gemstones."

"Can a woman not walk with her possessions down the street of a city?"

"At night?" Shallan asked. "Through a rough area? Displaying wealth? You all but asked for what happened!"

"Does that make it right?" Jasnah said, leaning forward. "Do you condone what the men were planning to do?"

"Of course not. But that doesn't make what you did right either!"

"And yet, those men are off the street. The people of this city are that much safer. The issue that Taravangian has been so worried about has been solved, and no more theatergoers will fall to those thugs. How many lives did I just save?"

"I know how many you just took," Shallan said. "And through the power of something that should be holy!"

"Philosophy in action. An important lesson for you."

"You did all this just to prove a point," Shallan said softly. "You did this to *prove* to me that you could. Damnation, Jasnah, how could you *do* something like that?"

Jasnah didn't reply. Shallan stared at the woman, searching for emotion in those expressionless eyes. *Stormfather. Did I ever really know this woman? Who is she, really?*

Jasnah leaned back, watching the city pass. "I did *not* do this just to prove a point, child. I have been feeling for some time that I took advantage of His Majesty's hospitality. He doesn't realize how much trouble he could face for allying himself with me. Besides, men like those . . ." There was something in her voice, an edge Shallan had never heard before.

*What was done to you?* Shallan wondered with horror. *And who did it?*

"Regardless," Jasnah continued, "tonight's actions came about because I chose this path, not because of anything I felt you needed to see. However, the opportunity also presented a chance for instruction, for questions. Am I a monster or am I a hero? Did I just slaughter four men, or did I stop four murderers from walking the streets? Does one *deserve* to have evil done to her by consequence of putting herself where evil can reach her?

Did I have a right to defend myself? Or was I just looking for an excuse to end lives?"

"I don't know," Shallan whispered.

"You will spend the next week researching it and thinking on it. If you wish to be a scholar—a *true* scholar who changes the world—then you will need to face questions like this. There will be times when you must make decisions that churn your stomach, Shallan Davar. I'll have you ready to make those decisions."

Jasnah fell silent, looking out the side as the palanquin bearers marched them up to the Conclave. Too troubled to say more, Shallan suffered the rest of the trip in silence. She followed Jasnah through the hushed hallways to their rooms, passing scholars on their way to the Palanaeum for some midnight study.

Inside their rooms, Shallan helped Jasnah undress, though she hated touching the woman. She shouldn't have felt that way. The men Jasnah had killed were terrible creatures, and she had little doubt that they would have killed her. But it wasn't the act itself so much as the cold callousness of it that bothered her.

Still feeling numb, Shallan fetched Jasnah a sleeping robe as the woman removed her jewelry and set it on the dressing table. "You could have let the other three get away," Shallan said, walking back toward Jasnah, who had sat down to brush her hair. "You only needed to kill one of them."

"No, I didn't," Jasnah said.

"Why? They would have been too frightened to do something like that again."

"You don't know that. I sincerely wanted those men *gone*. A careless barmaid walking home the wrong way cannot protect herself, but I can. And I will."

"You have no authority to do so, not in someone else's city."

"True," Jasnah said. "Another point to consider, I suppose." She raised the brush to her hair, pointedly turning away from Shallan. She closed her eyes, as if to shut Shallan out.

The Soulcaster sat on the dressing table beside Jasnah's earrings. Shallan gritted her teeth, holding the soft, silken robe. Jasnah sat in her white underdress, brushing her hair.

*There will be times when you must make decisions that churn your stomach, Shallan Davar. . . .*

*I've faced them already.*

*I'm facing one now.*

How *dare* Jasnah do this? How *dare* she make Shallan a part of it? How *dare* she use something beautiful and holy as a device for destruction?

Jasnah didn't deserve to own the Soulcaster.

With a swift move of her hand, Shallan tucked the folded robe under her safearm, then shoved her hand into her safepouch and popped out the intact smokestone from her father's Soulcaster. She stepped up to the dressing table, and—using the motion of placing the robe onto the table as a cover—made the exchange. She slid the working Soulcaster into her safehand within its sleeve, stepping back as Jasnah opened her eyes and glanced at the robe, which now sat innocently beside the nonfunctional Soulcaster.

Shallan's breath caught in her throat.

Jasnah closed her eyes again, handing the brush toward Shallan. "Fifty strokes tonight, Shallan. It has been a fatiguing day."

Shallan moved by rote, brushing her mistress's hair while clutching the stolen Soulcaster in her hidden safehand, panicked that Jasnah would notice the swap at any moment.

She didn't. Not when she put on her robe. Not when she tucked the broken Soulcaster away in her jewelry case and locked it with a key she wore around her neck as she slept.

Shallan walked from the room stunned, in turmoil. Exhausted, sickened, confused.

But undiscovered.

# *Paying It Forward*

## BY JERRY POURNELLE

*Dr. Jerry Pournelle was born in Louisiana in 1933. His formal education included a bachelor's degree in engineering, a master's degree in statistics and systems engineering, and two PhDs (psychology and political science). He credited his broad spectrum of practical knowledge to working in such fields as the military, aviation, aerospace, higher education, politics and computers. He was the founder of the Citizen's Advisory Council on National Space Policy and an influential voice in the world of computers and digital technology. For example, he wrote the longest-running column in computer journalism with his user's column, called "Computing at Chaos Manor," published in* Byte Magazine. *As a political thinker, he invented the two-axis political spectrum (alias the "Pournelle chart," which you can learn about online at Baen.com.)*

*In science fiction, Pournelle was a titan. Among his bestsellers are the blockbusters* The Mote in God's Eye, Lucifer's Hammer, Footfall *and* Oath of Fealty, *which were in collaboration with fellow WotF judge Larry Niven, though Jerry had many bestsellers in his own right. He edited numerous anthologies and wrote a range of nonfiction pieces for the SF media. He was also a former president of the Science Fiction Writers of America. Dr. Pournelle received the L. Ron Hubbard Lifetime Achievement Award for Outstanding Contributions to the Arts in 2006. Pournelle served as a WotF judge since 1986 and judged Contest entries through the third quarter of 2017. His memory lives on with this Contest.*

*"There's no such thing as instant success in writing, and it's still important to learn the craft, but one of the best ways of doing that is through success in WotF with its no-nonsense workshops and advice from working successful writers (including me). Not every WotF winner becomes a successful writer, but an astonishing number of them have managed that." —Dr. Jerry Pournelle*

## *Paying It Forward*

A very long time ago I wrote a book and nobody had ever read it. I had a good friend named Robert Heinlein. I asked him if he would read the book for me and tell me if he thought it was any good. That is about the biggest favor any writer can ask another writer to do. Because as Robert once said, most writers don't want criticism, they want praise. But he read it, he tore it apart, he showed me places he thought I should rewrite and when I finished it, he sent it to his agent, and it sold. And I've been writing books ever since, and I've also had the same agent ever since.

Some years later I was talking to Robert and I said I don't know how I'm going to repay you for all the help you've given me. He said, "You can't. There isn't any way you're going to, so you pay it forward."

So I'll repeat Mr. Heinlein's advice to writers, because if you pay attention to his dictums, you don't need to know much else. And if you want to be a writer, you've got to do several things.

The first one is you have to write. You have to actually put your tail in a chair and your fingers on a typewriter or keyboard. You have to write.

You have to finish it. You can't just keep writing things and starting them and carrying them around and hauling them out of your briefcase and reading them to your friends in bars. You have to finish what you write.

And having finished it, you have to stop mucking with it. And get it done and send it to somebody who actually has money to buy it with and presses to print it on. It does you no good to have your best friend read your story or the geek down the street or even your high school teacher. They're not going to buy it from you. The only opinion that counts about your story is whether or not somebody will pay you money for it. And the only reason to rewrite it, as Mr. Heinlein said, is if somebody says, "I like that, but it needs this and this, and if you do that, I'll buy it." Then it's worth it. Otherwise write a new story. Your words are not so precious that you can't just set them aside when it didn't work and start over.

I was talking to a young man tonight and he told me about two novels he's trying to sell. I listened to the ideas and they were both on subjects about which he didn't know very much, but he thought would be interesting. And yet he works in a profession in which there are dozens of darn good stories.

He thinks what he does is dull. Fine, but think about what might happen and it might not be dull. There he knows the details, he knows what's going on.

And don't try to keep working with the stuff already done. Don't try to go back and fix it. Just set it aside and go write a new story.

And if you do that, if you write, you finish what you write, you get it out to people who can buy it, and if you don't sit around endlessly rewriting, then at some point you'll learn to write.

Now in my experience, it takes somewhere around half a million to a million words before you get to the point where you are no longer thinking about what you're writing, and the technique of how you're doing it, and where to put your fingers on the keyboard, and all of the other mechanics of writing and grammar and style. After enough practice, you begin thinking about the story and you tell the story without thinking "I'm writing!" You're just writing it. When you get to that point, then you've got a chance. And until you get to that point, maybe you do, but you probably don't. Because you were building it brick by brick. And building brick by brick usually doesn't make for a very good building—especially if you didn't know what it was going to be, when you keep adding bricks hoping that eventually it is going to look like something you want.

The other advice I would give new writers, is advice Mr. Heinlein gave me a long time ago that has served me well: if you're going to choose grammars and styles, choose good standard grammatical English and what we used to call "high grammatical style." Don't experiment. Don't write with experimental spellings. Don't try to write phonetic spellings. Don't, in other words, try to improve the English language. Use it as correctly as possible.

The reason for that is simple: The number of people who will be irritated by your writing with good standard grammar is very low. The number of people who will simply not want to read it because you wrote with some nonstandard experimental grammar is very high. For example, there are people who think that it would be politically a good thing to change the impersonal pronoun in English from *he* to *she*. Sounds like a good idea, but it makes dreadful reading. It's very hard to read stories that use little gimmicks like that. Just regular high style and good grammar.

And if you don't know good grammar, go learn it. Get a good spell-checking program. Get a good grammatical checking program. Try to fool the grammar program. It will tell you things you know are bad advice. Fine, try to fool it into thinking it's good. And when you get to the point where you can write by all the rules and you can follow all the rules, even though they don't lead you to anything you like, now you are permitted to go play around with the rules and break them and do things to make your work more dramatic and more effective. But if you don't know what the rules are in the first place, how do you know whether what you're doing is a good thing or not?

So Mr. Heinlein essentially made that speech to me forty years ago and I'm paying it forward here.

# *What Lies Beneath*

*written by*

## Cole Hehr

*illustrated by*

## MAKSYM POLISHCHUK

---

### ABOUT THE AUTHOR

*Cole Hehr lives in Norman, Oklahoma with his girlfriend Ariana and works as a direct-care counselor for at-risk teenagers and young adults.*

*A lifelong fan of the written word, Cole began writing fiction after earning a bachelor's degree in history in 2013 and belatedly realized that he preferred storytelling to academia.*

*When he isn't reading or writing, Cole enjoys lifting weights and teaching others about fitness and nutrition. "What Lies Beneath" is his first sale.*

### ABOUT THE ILLUSTRATOR

*Maksym "Max" Polishchuk was born in 1999 in Lviv, an ancient Ukrainian city located at the crossroads of Western and Eastern Europe. Lviv, with its diverse culture and rich history, ultimately became one of the primary sources of Maksym's inspiration, who was always fascinated by the history concealed behind each ancient structure.*

*Such fascination with history, coupled with the discovery of texts of Tolkien and J. K. Rowling, is what ultimately ignited Maksym's interest in illustration. Art was the only way of transforming the stories and worlds he saw in his imagination into something more tangible. In order to help him achieve his dreams, his mother sent him to an art studio, which he attended almost daily over the span of six years, and which helped him nurture his talents and skills.*

*Maksym moved to the US just before his freshman year of high school. Even though his world was transformed completely, the one thing that remained constant was art. Today, Maksym studies political science and international relations at Loyola University Chicago in hopes of creating a better world that is not limited solely by the boundaries of the canvas.*

# *What Lies Beneath*

I refused to let the incense waver even when I felt the cool touch of steel against the back of my neck.

"One stroke is all it would take and the world would be free of you."

I leaned forward, still sitting cross-legged, and placed the incense in the bronze cylinders that sat atop each grave plaque. Two for my spouse, two for my son, and two for my daughter. I cocked my head, glancing down at the shining steel that pressed against my neck. The hand that held it was steady; I didn't feel the hint of a shiver or shake in the blade, and it had followed my leaning with practiced ease.

"You aren't the first to think so." I worked to keep my voice even, without inflection. A threat was one thing, invading the sanctity of my family's gravesite was altogether another. "But you would be the first to make your attempt in this sacred place."

I lifted the small jade platter and nudged the excess ash from each stick of incense onto it. The smell of sandalwood filled the night air as tiny threads of gray smoke curled into the air above my family's graves. "What kin of yours did I slay?"

The voice that answered me was as hard and sharp as the blade at my neck. "My father."

"I've killed many fathers," I said. "Many brothers, sisters, wives and mothers. Sons and daughters. Who was he?"

"Etrolus, Polemarch of Nadamia." I recalled the name and the man that bore it. Stolid, well-built. A soldier among soldiers. Etrolus deserved better than the edge of my sword across his throat, but that was what I had given him. Honor and respect aside, he had stood against me. Now he lay beneath a slab of marble in his family's tomb.

I set down the plate full of smoking ash and turned back to regard the man behind me. He stood tall, wearing the black tunic of a soldier. The sword held to my neck a mere moment before now hung at his side. His face was as sharp and grim as the blade he carried. Bands of wrought bronze adorned his wrists and he bore the thin, aged scars on his shins and forearms of horseman's armor. Silver threaded through his curly hair at the temples and peppered his beard.

"I killed your father nearly forty summers ago. You've just now come for revenge, son of Etrolus?" I asked. Faces of foes long past flitted through my mind.

The other man shook his head. He spoke through clenched teeth. "No. I've come to ask your help."

My thoughts ground to a halt at that. People once used to ask for my assistance. A long time ago. When I first became what I am, and they thought there was anything left other than my killing hands. I couldn't recall the last time anyone had asked for my aid while knowing my identity. In the decades since, it has only ever been for vengeance that any one came to me. Many men and women sought me out to avenge their parents; most of them were eighteen or nineteen, at the youngest. Young lives, snuffed out by my ancient hands.

"What could you possibly need from me?"

The man's chest rose and fell with a deep, steadying breath. I couldn't tell if he was trying to keep his anger in check or to keep from breaking down—one seemed as likely as the other. "I need you to help save my son. You were a man, once. You visit these graves every year. If there is some spark of that man left, then I ask for his aid."

My heart had stopped beating two centuries ago, but for the first time since my family's passing, I felt a tightness in my chest. I looked back at the grave stones, each block of marble topped with burning incense. I'd made my bargain for immortality so that I could take vengeance on those who tore my family from me. My foes were gone, their seed burned from the earth. I knew that for a certainty because I had seen to it. I'd killed the last imperial family member just after I slew Etrolus.

I could have let someone kill me decades ago, but I resisted death at every turn. I refused to die, and the reason why ate at my heart like a worm: I couldn't bear the thought of seeing my family in the afterlife, seeing the knowledge of what I had become dawn in their eyes. How many souls, torn from the mortal coil, had passed into the Graylands and told tales of my butchery and destruction?

"Your son," I said. "How old is he?"

"Twelve summers."

I closed my eyes. Maira and Ladirus had been ten and twelve when a soldier put them to the sword alongside their mother. I thrashed against the memory, forcing it back down beneath the calm, cold weight of more than two hundred years.

"Tell me what must be done."

I sat beside Polemarch Magrius while the priests slaughtered the bull. Acolytes gathered the blood in gilt bowls and drizzled drops of gore into the flaming braziers, while the more experienced priests began carving and dismembering the carcass, marking every organ for this god or that goddess. Beneath the smell of roasting meat and burning herbs rose the stench of manure, old blood, and animal fear-sweat. I'd hated temples when I lived, and I liked them even less in undeath.

"You asked me to save your son, yet we sit in a temple watching old men kill beasts," I said. The nearest acolyte spared me a hurried glance before returning to his duties. Was he too young to know my face? That idea would have been a welcome relief.

"I wished to consult the gods about my plan," Magrius said. He watched as the priest raised the smoking heart free from its flaming tripod of bronze and held it overhead. A good sign, from Magrius's expression. I never could tell the difference between a bad piece of animal innards and a good one when it came to omens.

"You have yet to tell me this plan. Or what manner of trouble your son is in. My life is long, my patience is not." Magrius sighed and rubbed his calloused hands together. He wore only the bands of his office for jewelry. "My son was taken by the cult of Setrepais. I believe they have given him to the sea serpent, though I know not why. I only know that he yet lives. The haruspex sees no death in his future."

"A detachment of spearmen could deal with this cult," I pointed out.

Magrius nodded. "True, but my spearmen cannot go to the bottom of the sea, where I believe the cult has sent him. I have heard—stories. . . ."

"About my immortality?" I offered. Magrius nodded and tugged at his beard nervously. Speaking about his son's kidnapping was no easy feat, I was sure, but few men sat in the presence of a monster and spoke to it of its very nature as an abomination.

"Yes," he said, "That you need no air, nor food or water. . . ."

I smiled, mirthless as stone. "I've heard most of the tales. Few of them are true. I cannot fly, nor change my shape. I don't feed on human flesh or blood, nor do I take souls. Let me speak plainly: I am not human any longer, that much is true. I am dead but not dying, and few things will send me from this world. Deep water is not one of them."

"So you could walk the bottom of the sea, then?" Magrius asked.

"With weighting, yes. Whether or not I can kill Setrepais is another matter. Weighted or not, I am still only a swordsman and Setrepais is said to be like a god among the sea serpents."

Magrius leaned toward me, hope overriding his fear. "But you have slain more than mere men. You slew a coatl-serpent that rides the wind, star-demons that haunt the night. You slew the Sorcerer-King Amiyya and his Golem Queen. If anyone can slay Setrepais, it is you."

"And the cult?"

"They know the way to Setrepais's domain. After you deal with them, I shall have matters made ready for you," he said.

Magrius looked me dead in the eyes for the first time since the graveyard. "Save my son, and I will stand an obelisk in that graveyard, in honor of your family. Twice as tall as a man, bearing their names in gold. I swear it by the gods of this very temple."

A length of bright scarlet silk was wrapped around the hand guard and hilt of my sword, keeping it locked in its sheath. I undid the knot with one hand and unraveled it for the first time in decades. I gave the red silk cord to Magrius. "Keep that until I return. I'll be back before nightfall."

I kept my promise and found Magrius waiting for me at the edge of the Latrian Sea that evening, the wind heavy with the smell of brine. The sun sat on the horizon behind him, limning the sea with an edge of gold where the water met the sky. Beside Magrius stood a handful of soldiers, stripped down to their tunics with only daggers or short swords at their waists. Each soldier carried a weighty piece of bronze, shaped to its particular purpose.

"The cult is dead." I climbed off of my horse and scooped up a handful of sand. I ran the grit across my blade, cleaning away the half-dried gore. The cultists had proved my suspicions true: rich, slovenly men and women for the most part, interested only in the forbidden fruit of worshipping a monster like Setrepais. Sacrilege was a fashion for them. They'd scattered like seeds in the wind when I burst into their congregation.

I'd found the handful of true believers to be more fervent in the defense of their hidden temple, but they had only spears and cudgels to ward my sword away. Their leader, a necromancer of some small talent, believed that she could control me. She realized otherwise when I buried bronze in her chest.

I told none of this to Magrius and let the last flashes of violence fade from my mind. "Is everything in order?"

The Polemarch nodded. "I have everything here. Will you take a boat?"

I shook my head. "I'll walk into the sea. Plunging in from a ship won't give me time to find my bearings."

The soldiers brought the weights to me, like young men coming forward to clad a hero in their shining armor. Or to bind a monster in chains, perhaps. Thick bronze clasped around my wrists and ankles. Metal laid across my shoulders like a yoke and girded my waist in a leather belt laden with plates of bronze, each as thick as my thumb. My sandaled feet sank into the wet sand with every added burden. Bands of bronze ran up my forearms and hung from my neck, clinking every time I moved. A thin mask of glass, bulbous like a bell to fit over my features and rimmed with a seal of bronze, framed my face.

Being sheathed in bronze made moving difficult, but not impossible. I rolled my shoulders and did my best to settle the weight as evenly as I could before turning to face the sea's rolling waves.

"Are you ready?" Magrius offered me my sword. I took it and slipped it through a loop on the weighted belt I wore.

"I am." I trudged to the edge of the water and paused, letting its warm waves wash over my feet. "For what it's worth—your father was one of the only men I ever killed worth remembering. I hope your son grows to be like him." Magrius stared at me in silence and I began my descent.

The wine-dark sea rose to welcome me, sloshing across my legs, its water barely touched by autumn's cooling air. Its embrace inched upward from my ankles, then my knees, and finally to my hips before it began to slow my stride. I dug my heels into the sand and pushed onward, allowing the sea to swallow me up.

One glance to the shore showed me a half-dozen hazy figures, standing like sticks stuck in the sand. Would Magrius and his men wait until his son and I returned? If we didn't, how long would the father stand on that windblown beach, waiting for a child that might never return? I turned away and continued on.

Seawater lapped across the glass plate that guarded my face, leaving rivulets in its wake. I watched the line of water rise up the glass mask until it disappeared over my head, and then I was beneath the water's surface and in another world.

The bronze carried me deeper into the water when I hit the long slope that led down to the sea's bottom. The water's surface flew away from me, a shimmering cascade of light above my head that slowly took the place of the dusk sky. The shallows were murky and impossible to see through for all the kicked-up sand and sea-grit; only when solid stone crunched beneath my feet did the water clear.

To a living person, the depths were dark and without substance; a cold, liquid darkness that provided no sense of distance or size. The water pressed in from all sides, making one feel simultaneously buried alive and adrift in some great void. The only hint of light came from above, rippling and wan as the darkness devoured it from beneath. Silhouetted fish flitted above me in the dying light, refusing to delve into the darker waters.

Monsters see things differently, however. I saw as well in darkness as in the light of day, whether that darkness came from night or from the sea's depths, it mattered little. The shambling undead lacked minds while the thanatophagoi—the death-eating vampires—lacked souls. I lacked humanity, and my damnation ran deeper than theirs, for when I finally did die, I would never be able to leave the Graylands.

The bottom of the sea looked much like what I had always imagined the Graylands to be: an open, rugged expanse of stony ground, its features worn flat by the weight of the water. Here and there rose moldering, weathered structures that I knew to be ancient ruins. Broken pillars of marble and limestone towered over me as I walked along the rotted cobblestone path that led me out to sea. A great school of azure and ocher fish whorled around an ancient statue. Seaweed clumped together around rocks, billowing in the sea's invisible currents and tickling my calves.

The watery world around me never made a sound. I reached out and scraped my fingertips across one of the algae-crusted columns. A puff of verdigris green came free but I heard nothing. Above water, sound was a constant: the wind, one's own breathing, the hundreds of subtle shifts in movement. Below, all was stifled and silent. The only constant was the pressure of the sea as it wrapped me in its cold, heavy embrace. I felt, rather than heard, my bronze weights clank with every step.

Without the sun and stars, I had no way to gauge how long I traversed the sea's floor. The farther I went, the more hoary and ancient the ruins I found: the skeletal remains of cities, built one atop the other until the waters swallowed them all. I knew from the cult's leader that Setrepais held court in the ruins of an ancient temple at the edge of this area, right at the precipice where the seafloor sheared off and the true depths began. Immortal or not, those black waters would swallow me whole. Mankind had tried to explore those deep, dark places in centuries past, but only crushed remains had risen to the surface.

A towering pile of black stone rose up in front of me, a silhouette garbed in the darkness that my inhuman vision failed to penetrate. Every step brought the shape into clearer focus, its lines growing hard and distinct. Massive blocks sat atop one another, massive slabs of basalt fitted together into a towering ziggurat. The foundation disappeared into the ground, sunk partway into the murk by its own weight and age, but the remaining tiers stood tall. A line of obelisks marked a forgotten boulevard leading up to the temple, each thrice as tall as a man.

Carmine-shelled crabs, each as large as a horse, skittered across the temple, scraping its surface clean. The multitude shifted and moved as one, threading back and forth across the structure like ants in a line. I must have crossed some threshold in their awareness when I strode past the first pair of marble obelisks: I saw dozens of eye-stalks shift in my direction, black, unblinking eyes fixed on me. The creatures froze in their ministrations. My hand drifted down to the hilt of my sword. I wondered whether or not I could carve through their shells.

The temple's custodians scuttled off of the structure, but instead of rushing toward me in a horde of scarlet claws and darting legs, they buried themselves into the mud at the temple's base until only their eye-stalks remained visible. Their movements threw up a cloud of murk from the sea's floor that hung like a drab, brown mist. Only when a long, sinuous shadow rose up from behind the temple did I realize that the creatures were prostrating themselves before their god.

Setrepais slithered out of the darkness that formed the horizon beyond the temple and coiled itself around the building, an action that shook the ground beneath my feet until I felt it rattling my bones. Beyond the sun's light, the sea serpent's scales were bone-white, layered across one another like plates in an armored corselet. Its enormous head resembled a mixture between a viper's and a shark's with liquid pools of inky darkness for eyes. A wreath of spikes, each longer than I was tall and bright azure, framed its head like a lion's mane.

I have fought all manner of man and beast but I had never, until then, stood before a creature that called itself a god and could rightly claim the title. Whatever Setrepais was, it was beyond my sword and my slaying. I knew that as soon as I laid eyes on it, and for the first time in centuries I felt something like fear.

The sonorous voice that rumbled forth from the temple reminded me of the deep thunder of a sea storm, or the sound of the earth quaking. It made the water ripple around Setrepais, and I couldn't tell whether or not I heard it in my mind or through the cold water.

"You slew my priestess." Setrepais's gaze settled on me. The sensation reminded me of how it felt to look off a cliff, or up a mountain—a sense of sheer, incalculable enormity.

"Your priestess would not answer my questions," I said, "and if she was so easy to kill, then perhaps she did not deserve to be in your service." The glass and bronze mask over my face made my voice resound in my ears and I knew the water swallowed my words well before they reached the temple, but I doubted the sea serpent before me relied on something so simple as hearing.

MAKSYM POLISHCHUK

"Perhaps. Why have you come? To do to me what you did to my priestess?"

I shook my head. "I come only for the boy, Amandros. I could not kill you, and trying would be folly."

The mane of spines around Setrepais's head ruffled. "The boy is mine. He was born under my stars and will serve me in the Above-Waters."

That explained why the diviners had seen no death in Amandros's future: the cultists sent him to serve Setrepais, not to die as a sacrifice. There was no telling how long the sea serpent might keep the boy hidden away, until Amandros was properly groomed to serve.

"A callow youth makes for a poor warlord," I said. "No matter the powers you imbue on him, a sword through the heart will still lay him low."

The ground beneath my feet lurched with Setrepais's laughter. "When the stars come right and the realms align, I will make my champion immortal. When he sets foot Above-Waters once more, he will be more than a man."

Setrepais didn't want a man, it wanted a monster. The same stars that made me into what I was could do the same to Amandros. I'd made that choice. Setrepais intended to make it for the boy, and at so young an age it would be easy to strip away his humanity until something hard, sharp, and cold remained in its wake. The idea of that, of Amandros being turned into what I chose to be, made my stomach churn with anger. He didn't deserve that, and the world had no dearth of monsters. It scarcely needed another.

"Turning a boy into a man takes years," I said, "and there is no certainty that Amandros will be a warrior of any caliber. Release him into his father's care, and I will serve you, Setrepais."

The great serpent writhed and coiled around its ziggurat. Even through the water, I heard its scales sliding across the black basalt. Its inscrutable gaze watched me for a silence that stretched across interminably long seconds.

"What can you offer me?"

I drew my sword from its sheath in a single motion, and held its double-edged blade of bronze up for the serpent's inspection. I had carried the sword since before my transformation, replacing the pieces—blade, hilt, hand guard, and pommel—with exact replicas as time took its toll on the weapon. To my foes, it gave the illusion that my sword was as ageless as its wielder.

"I am already immortal. I have wielded this blade in war for more than two centuries, and I have no ties that bind me to the world beyond your waters. You want to make an immortal champion—one stands before you now."

"You swear to serve, in exchange for the boy-child's freedom?"

I held out my right hand and drew the sword's edge across it. The water's currents carried my blood away in a fading cloud of scarlet. "I so swear to serve Setrepais, god among sea serpents."

The weight of my oath grew hard and heavy in my chest, a second heart of stone beside the dead one. Sorcery more ancient than Setrepais's temple bound me to his service. I leveled my gaze at the serpent.

"Is it done? Is the boy returned?"

"It is so. That was your price."

"Show me."

Just a few strides from where I stood, the water began to whirl into a wild whorl, tightening and shaping itself into a sphere, separated from the rest of the sea by the tenuous surface of a bubble. It shimmered, mirror-like, and grew lambent with sorcerous light. An image began to resolve itself in the sphere of water as Setrepais turned the sea into a scrying pool.

I saw Magrius and his men standing on the beach. It was dark, but not quite night. The first stars had begun to shine as the sun's light faded into the dark. Out from the surf stumbled Amandros, his tunic and hair sopping wet. He lurched and staggered ashore and Magrius ran to meet him, sweeping the boy up in his arms. No sound came from the image, and as quickly as it came, it dissolved back into the water. The sphere slackened, pulled apart by the current until no hint of it remained.

Setrepais might have shown me an illusion, but the serpent-god needed to keep its end of the bargain to seal the pact. With me as its champion, the sea serpent no longer needed Amandros. It and I were bound together by blood and by oath. It could take no other champion and I no other patron.

Explaining years of war, decades of venting my wrath and angst and vengeance—that I could do, perhaps. My family might wring their hands and hide their faces for a time, but what did it mean compared to serving Setrepais? When I eventually passed from the living world into the gray beyond, would they accept me, knowing that I'd lent my sword to the serpent, or would they turn their faces away forever?

"The pact binds us, now?" I asked.

"It does."

"Then you must wait another star cycle for your champion."

Plunging the sword into my chest proved easier than I'd ever thought possible. I guided it with both hands, keeping the blade poised just so, allowing it to slide between my ribs and pierce my heart. I felt no pain in the act, only a dull, distant warmth that grew in my chest.

The bronze burden I carried forced me to my knees beneath its weight. My hands slipped from the sword and when I looked down I saw its hilt jutting from my chest, the bronze blade transfixed through my torso. The mud beneath my knees rippled and shook as Setrepais thrashed in its inhuman fury, raging at me in its own sibilant tongue.

Perhaps the passing of immortality took longer, or I only felt my dying gasp stretch onward, but I found a strange sense of peace within myself. Afraid, I had clung to my eternal mockery of life for centuries. Now, as my unlife ebbed and waned, I wondered in those lingering moments why I had waited so long.

Dying by my own hand had always been my intent: once I paid the vengeance I owed to the empire that slew my family, I would join them. It had taken the better part of two centuries, but I had destroyed that dynasty root and stem. Yet, when the time came, I didn't.

Fear stayed my hand, fear of death and shame at the depths I'd sunk to in order to pursue revenge. When I made the pact with Setrepais, I put those fears to rest: unmaking the serpent's schemes until the next celestial alignment seemed a worthwhile reason to die. Worth enough, perhaps, to outweigh my earlier shames. I passed from the world beneath its waters.

I spent what time I could with my family and ancestors in the Graylands. I left my venom and vitriol at the bottom of the sea and found some measure of the peace and joy that had eluded me for two centuries. My family has passed into the beyond, to live again with new faces and new hearts, but for a time—for a time I was allowed to see Ladirus's and Maira's smiling faces again, to feel Etanna's embrace once more. I remain a shade for my twisting of life's laws, but I have let go of my regret. Here in the Graylands I will remain, until the realms turn in on themselves and birth something new from their ashes. I am content with so small a punishment for sins as great as mine.

Summon me, theurge or sorcerer, and ask your questions. I will tell you of my death, and the truth of all deaths: that they are small things we must all endure, and only as important as we make them. I lived for my family, and I chose to die for a father and his son. I have met both Magrius and Amandros in their own passage through the Graylands and I know that I chose well. Few in this world are given the blessing of choosing when and how they die. Fewer still are allowed to decide.

# *The Face in the Box*

*written by*

## *Janey Bell*

*illustrated by*

## BRUCE BRENNEISE

---

### ABOUT THE AUTHOR

*Janey Bell is a Chicago writer native to Washington State who specializes in speculative fiction and playwriting. She earned her degree in fiction writing and playwriting from Columbia College Chicago in 2016 and is a 2011 California Arts Scholar. She placed third in the Writers of the Future Contest. Her work can be found in the upcoming edition of the literary magazine* Hair Trigger *and her first play* Bobby Pin Girls *opened in the fall of 2017. She has two cats.*

### ABOUT THE ILLUSTRATOR

*Bruce Brenneise grew up in the countryside by Lake Michigan; nature and fantasy were two of his main interests from childhood. He continued to not-so-secretly focus on magic, monsters, and myths while studying scientific illustration at the University of Michigan. Pursuit of diverse environments and experiences led him around the world in search of artistic inspiration: a field sketching trip to Southern Africa, months amid ancient ruins of Anatolia, not to mention six years working and traveling throughout China and other parts of East Asia. The landscapes he has explored and the vistas one can only find in fiction are at the heart of Bruce's current work as an illustrator and independent artist. He currently lives with his wife and carnivorous plants in Seattle.*

# The Face in the Box

## 1

The pieces of Skyturf slowly migrated across the light blue ceiling of atmosphere, avoiding one of the last true Earth farms; a sunflower field. Cara stood watching, eyes watering with dawn. She turned to wipe them, but when she looked up again, there was a lone Skyturf beginning to hover near the edge of her land. She squinted at it, trying to discern if it was going to block her sunflowers, or if it had slightly gone off course and was about to readjust itself.

The Skyturf didn't turn, but chose instead to stop in the middle of her fields. It hung above her farm, high enough to be a nuisance, but low enough to avoid hovering ships and planes.

"Son of a bitch," Cara said. It had taken nearly six years after her first purchase of the farm, but she had all the permits, all the paperwork, and not one of those Skyturfs were allowed to block her flowers, *protected airspace*, that was the deal. Her fields stretched out before her little bungalow, a sea of green and brown and brilliant gold petals, all gently rocking from side to side.

She would have to put in a complaint to the Skyturf monitor. Cara padded back inside, bare feet on smooth hardwood. She flipped on the lights in the kitchen, and they buzzed to life, sucking power from her solar array in the next field over. Her computer whirred to life. She called out to it while dumping out yesterday's coffee into the sink.

"Activate. Request complaint. Skyturf Monitor. Sector 605," Cara said, making the fresh pot.

"Ready when you are," her computer chirped in a soft, girlish voice.

"Start message: Hi, Brent, it's Cara Fischer, and I seem to have a tract of Skyturf blocking my sunnies. Could you see if a maintenance team can come out today and remove it? I think it's malfunctioning. Thanks, Brent. End message." Cara leaned against the counter while the coffee maker gurgled.

The message was sent, and she went to stand at the sink and look out the lace-draped window to the Skyturf above her farm. Its gray underbelly didn't look any different from the other squares, the hundred foot squares of floating farmland that passed over the sky every day. It stayed put, while everything, the clouds, the other Skyturf, the sun, passed it by.

## 2

Cara stood on the edge of the Skyturf tract, waiting for the thrusters on her boots to cool before taking a look around. The field seemed pretty ordinary, long rows of scraggily cornstalks. It was quiet up here, except for the sound of the wind, which seemed to permeate everything it touched with its hollow cry. Cara shook herself a bit and stepped off the metal edge of the tract and into the dirt. She passed between the stalks, their blooms brushing over her head. The sun shone full-force now, and Brent hadn't replied to her message, no matter how many times she'd checked.

The center of the field would have the tract's computer, and perhaps something could be jury-rigged so that Cara could at least land the tract somewhere it wouldn't be a nuisance. She counted off the rows as she went along, keeping her eyes ahead, not looking down to see that the dirt she was walking on was turning to bright green grass, dotted with wildflowers.

It wasn't until a bumblebee lazily buzzed by that she noticed the stalks were farther and farther spaced out and ahead of her the rows were turning into lush, wild gardens. She breathed in the smells of pollen and grass and summer blooms and found herself in a clearing at the center of the field. A box with a screen sat on a raised area of dirt, overgrown with budding leaves and vines. The screen glowed white, even in the strengthening sunlight. The screen flickered.

"Who's there? Who are you?" A distorted voice said. Cara stepped forward. The voice was small, childlike, but tinged with static and errors in the voice modulation. It came from the machine.

"Easy now, I'm just here for maintenance," Cara said. She had never heard a voice like that from a Skyturf computer, let alone seen one completely overgrown. Nobody had inspected this thing for ages.

"Stay back! T-Tell me who you are."

Cara held her hands up, palms forward. "I'm Cara. Who are you?" The screen flickered again, and certain pixels began to darken, forming what seemed to be a face. Eyes, nose, mouth, all relatively humanlike, but as with the voice, distorted and blurry.

"I don't know," the voice said, and the lips on the mouth moved with it.

"What's your serial number?" Cara asked.

The eyes on the screen looked away. "I don't want to tell you."

Cara let out a long breath. "And why's that?"

"You'll send me back to the factory."

"No," Cara shook her head. "I just want you to leave my protected airspace, okay?"

The face suddenly smiled.

"You're not going to report me?"

Cara tried to smile, but felt the shock of guilt hit her. It was too late for that.

"Of course not."

BRUCE BRENNEISE

"Okay!" The screen flickered, and the face faded away. The ground shifted beneath Cara's feet, and her knees wobbled as the tract of Skyturf dropped in altitude, eventually floating to rest above a small marsh just north of Cara's farm. The cornstalks shuddered with the adjustment, and several of them broke off into bent fingers. When the motion stopped, Cara walked up to the screen and touched the edge of it with her fingertips.

"Hello?"

But the face did not reappear.

## 3

The sunflowers had their faces turned west. Each tremble of the breeze sent their golden crowns bobbing. Sunflower seeds, like other once staples, had become scarce with the decimation of farmland, everything natural succumbing to urban development or sealed off for protection. Even the once-majestic national parks were no strangers to bulldozers, with a population that would not stop growing.

It was good money, but harder work than most other things, now that everything and everyone was either automated or medicated. Nothing to produce, nothing to worry about, nothing but progress. *Progress,* Cara would scoff, *that looked an awful lot like stagnation.*

Brent finally replied and promised that a crew would be out that evening to disassemble the Skyturf and return it to the factory. Cara's fingers lingered over her keyboard as she contemplated telling him about the strange computer that seemed to fuse with the plants around it. She'd heard rumors of plants and computers (especially the experimental sort that got tossed around by the military) coming together to create strange mechanical living creatures, but that was all supposed to be rumors. Nothing but ghost stories made up by those who didn't approve of using living tissue in super computers.

But this was something else entirely. This was an average operating system that had the voice of a child and even had the capability to show expressions. It could refuse orders, too. Cara leaned back in her chair, tilting her chin to the ceiling and staring up at the blank, gray tiles.

## 4

Ms. Fischer?" The bald maintenance worker, Brent, stood on her porch, construction hat tucked under his arm. Cara pushed the screen door open.

"Yes, it's about a half-mile north of here, hovering above some marshland," she told him. The bug zapper crackled. The sun was hanging above the horizon. The man pulled out his phone and gave a quick call to the others nearby, alerting them to the Skyturf's location. Far above them, hundreds of panels followed the trail of the sun, speeding to keep up with its glow.

"It's okay, tracts go crazy all the time, s'nothing to worry about," Brent said. Would it have made a difference if she told him about the conversation she had with the Skyturf?

Cara frowned and returned inside, going to the back of her house with a pair of binoculars to peer out the window. She watched as the maintenance truck neared the rogue cornstalks, and she watched as they disappeared into the rows. She stood for a long while but didn't move or avert her gaze in any way. Her back and arms were beginning to ache. The marsh was cool green and growing darker with every passing moment. Finally, the crew came out. They gathered to talk, then began the process.

Using remote access, they forced the tract to lift into the air. Cara put down her binoculars and went outside to walk across the grass and observe. The tract rose up and then began to quiver. In the distance she could hear a voice, high-pitched and wavering, calling out into the still night.

"Liar! Liar, liar! You told them! Liar!" the voice cried, and Cara wrapped her arms around herself. The tract shook as it began to fold over itself, pushing together to crush the plants between layers of soil and metal. The voice screamed bloody murder while the crew looked on, chattering nervously with each other about the voice. Cara ignored them.

With a screech, the folded tract self-destructed, exploding into a blossom of flame. It rained down burning leaves, and the crew scattered as the blackened carcass of the tract hovered for a moment and then went careening left and crashed into the wet bog, cascading fire the whole way. Cara stood still in the tall grasses, her fingers digging into her arms. The crew stomped out the small fires, snuffing their brief glow.

The sun had set and the stars loomed overhead. Cara could hear the men now. They were lucky, they said.

Cara waded through the grass to the wreckage of the Skyturf. Mangled and broken, it had split open a tree. The screen hung from a cord wrapped around a branch. The box swayed, noose-like. Its face was black, empty and voiceless. Cara turned away and began walking home. Her sobs were muffled by the crackle of burning wood.

## 5

In the morning Cara stood on her porch again, scanning the skies. The pieces of turf wove around her designated spot like ducks avoiding a patch of lily pads. Her body felt heavy. She had tossed in her bed for three hours before getting so frustrated that she'd sat working at her terminal until the sun came up. There was a sharp pounding behind her eyes, but she took no medicine, no painkiller for it.

She kept thinking about the face in the box. The guilt was something she felt unaccustomed to. Working alone with robots most of the time didn't generally come with much workplace drama. Between her and the other farmers was a vague friendliness underlined with a stench of jealousy for Cara's rare farm. But nothing tremendous and emotional had happened like this.

Cara stepped back inside and sank into a kitchen chair, resting her forehead on the table. Her eyes closed, opened, closed again, and then her body yanked her upright.

The suicide of the face in the box kept startling Cara out of sleepiness with first a sharp aural memory of the tract's screaming and then the inevitable explosion making Cara's eyes snap open. She tried to focus on messages and accounting and managing her farm but the face in the box was still there.

Sitting in the vines and flowers, surrounded by butterflies and fire. Screaming.

By noon, she couldn't take it anymore. She went out into the field again to where the wreckage of the Skyturf was piled neatly, to be moved sometime in the days to come. The cord on the box had been cut and the box had been tossed on the pile with the rest. Cara's feet lifted off the ground as she hovered before the pile, taking the box—cold, hollow—into her arms. She floated back to her house, to her private garden where she had her vegetables, and she tucked the box up against the creaking fence.

In her garden she planted the box, sinking the cords deep into the soil where she hoped they might find some solace in the surrounding roots. The sun was beating now. She could feel her skin beginning to burn on the back of her neck and shoulders. She continued, watering the box, wiping the slightly cracked screen and doing all that she could to . . . what, exactly? Bring it back to life? Cara understood plants. She knew that with the right steps and proper care, you could nurse a dead plant back into living, but this was biotech.

When she had finished, she brushed her hands off on her pants, her fingers shaking as she looked at the box, now surrounded by green once more.

## 6

It took four weeks for the box to turn on.

It was early at dawn when Cara stood on her porch and heard the small blips and beeps coming from her garden. She walked out, bare feet sinking into the earth with each step toward the faint glowing box. An earthworm wriggled under her toes and dove deeper. She knelt before the box, staring into the static that had appeared.

"Hello?" Cara said. Her eyes searched the salt-and-pepper storm for any signs of the face, an eye, a hint of a smile, anything. The image flickered and went completely white. Cara sighed and rested her forehead against the edge of the box.

A scratchy voice made itself known. "Who's there? Who are you?"

Cara's head snapped up, and she smiled at the face that was slowly piecing itself together across the screen.

"I'm Cara," she said. "It's nice to meet you."

# *Flee, My Pretty One*

*written by*

## *Eneasz Brodski*

*illustrated by*

ALANA FLETCHER

### ABOUT THE AUTHOR

*Eneasz Brodski lives in Denver, Colorado. He is active in the Bayesian Rationalist community, an eclectic collection of misfits who believe humans can do better. Through the powers of science and technology, he hopes all humans currently living can someday celebrate their 5,000th birthday.*

*Eneasz has a number of meaningful relationships, of many varieties. He was raised in an apocalyptic Christian sect, and while he has left that behind, that childhood colors much of his writing to this day. He's been writing since he could hold a pencil, but has only begun professional efforts in the past few years. He just finished his first novel and hopes to see it in print soon.*

*When he's not writing, podcasting, or blogging, he can often be found gothing it up at a local goth club. He's willing to strike up a conversation with anyone in dark clothes and eyeliner.*

### ABOUT THE ILLUSTRATOR

*Alana Fletcher was born in 1996 in Middletown, NY. She was introduced to the arts at a young age while growing up in Michigan. She took figure-drawing classes at the Kalamazoo Institute of Arts, and continued to develop her work within online communities. She began painting with a mouse in Photoshop, but eventually obtained a Wacom tablet to continue to expand her capabilities.*

*Alana is now attending Ferris State University for Game Design and Digital Animation in Grand Rapids. She concurrently works as a freelance illustrator and concept artist.*

# *Flee, My Pretty One*

From up on the stage, half-blinded by the lights, all I saw of him were piercing blue eyes. The crowd churned before me, pounding music whipping them into a froth, but those eyes glittered calmly in the chaos. They shone at me, reflecting the strobe lights like jewel shards, floating over the bass pulses that rose from the floor to rattle my rib cage.

I stepped to the mic, screamed the chorus line. *"Death to all collaborators!"* His eyes never left mine.

Three beats to my guitar solo. I threw myself into it with a quickened pulse. I would never slack at a gig—this is my communion, the guitar sings my blood. And yet, there's an extra charge to it when you're showing off for someone beautiful. The blood burns a little hotter. Look at me—this is who I am inside. Eat of my body.

When the surge of emotion finally ebbed, I could breathe once more. The last notes faded, we said our thank yous, we turned away. Only his eyes remained unchanged, numinous among the vulgar. I imagined briefly that he loved to submit to vulgar, mohawked girls.

He came up to talk with us afterward, which was too bad. Not because the rest of him sunk the fantasy. He was thin, with the delicate features that make it attractive—I like the pretty boys. No, it's because when new fans come up to see me they realize the slouch isn't a stage affectation. They see me without a guitar to hide my stance, catch me pressing my back against a wall for the relief it brings. They realize I'm twisted. Their interest fades and we both wish we'd just left the damned fantasy undisturbed.

Except he wasn't repelled by me, didn't rebound to Zoe or the guys. He smiled for me. Me alone.

"You rail against collaborators way more than the dragons themselves," he commented after introductions. "You never rage against the damn dragons. Always their human agents. You one of those nonsentience wonks?" A flutter in his voice as he said it, as if he feared challenging me, but couldn't stop himself.

From the corner of my eye I saw Liam perk up from the merch table. When his head swiveled over to us, the raised lights of the club glinted off the metal of his piercings like a flesh-and-silver disco ball. He must have been dying to jump in on this. He believed that dragons have personhood and their own motives. I wasn't so sure. There's those who theorize that the dragons are just dumb optimizers. No self-awareness, simply responding to the stimuli of human desires. We'd stayed up countless nights arguing this.

"I'm with Greenwald," I replied. "We'll probably never know, and it doesn't matter anyway. They don't have human values. The longer they stay off-leash, the worse the world gets."

My pretty fanboy nodded. "I hear they're expecting another wave of refugees from Louisiana this month. How do you explain the repatriation collapse, if not intentional malice?" He stepped forward and motioned to the audio cables as I coiled them. "And can I help you with that?"

We continued our political griping. Neither of us screwed up too badly in the conversation, and it'd been a while since I'd gotten any. He came home with me that night.

I woke up smiling, with that warm glow that comes from being well-laid. Restraints and toys lay scattered around the bed. I rolled over awkwardly to admire his sleeping face. I rested an arm on him, one breast pressing against his bare chest, and I realized I couldn't recall his name. I'm sure he gave it, but who knew he was going to stick around? I hadn't paid that much attention. Crap.

A fist banging against my door startled me. My bandmate Tyrell yelled through the flimsy wood.

"Jo! Wake up! You gotta see this!"

The boy beneath me stirred awake, gazed at me with bleary eyes. "Good morning," he said, and gave me a grin.

I kissed his collarbone, then his neck, and then Tyrell banged on the damn door again.

"Seriously Jo, come check this out! This is big!"

"Fine, I'm up!" I yelled back. "Give me a damn minute!"

I let my gaze wander over the boy's body and back up to his face. "Hey, look," I said, "I feel really lame about this, but I don't remember your name. I'm Josephine. And you're . . . ?"

He laughed, and the rising sun caught his eyes, clear as the sky.

"Hi, Josephine. I'm Aiden."

I grinned. "More later," I promised. I rolled off him, and we pulled on our clothes to go eat and see Tyrell's big deal. Tyrell sat by his laptop in the kitchen, a video queued up for us.

On screen, a business-suited man left a government building. The news banner identified him as an emissary for Hirath'bur, an elder oil-and-gas extraction dragon. A gathered crowd of the unshaven and emaciated exploded in jeers as he stepped out. Hirath'bur destroyed the land where it operated—poisoned the groundwater, blighted the soil. It had been corrupting the government for years with bribes and threats, turning our protectors into its accomplices. Whole counties had been despoiled when rich deposits were discovered. The emissary didn't spare a glance at the angry rabble. Cops corralled the protesters behind thin barriers, their hands at the pepper-spray canisters on their belts.

An unusual movement in the air drew my eye. One of those miniature quadcopters that make up any city's backdrop—routing packages or surveilling traffic or whatever they did. It had been passing overhead, and now tipped into a sharp dive, directly at the emissary. Four bursts of gray smoke erupted from its front. Simultaneously, four bursts of red liquid burst from the emissary's chest, and the man staggered. The drone shot up, high into the air, fleeing the scene. The man dropped, blood soaking his suit and spilling onto the cement. The crowd screamed, scattered, and the video cut off. I stared over at Tyrell.

"The hell just happened?" I asked.

"An assassination," Tyrell replied. "One of three, all within a few minutes, all carried out by modified delivery-drones. They targeted emissaries of major dragons."

"Holy crap. Is this what I think it is?"

"Uh huh. Looks like the resistance just got serious."

My eyes flickered to the boy I'd just met, listening to us intently.

"Um . . . Aiden, maybe you should go. I mean, leave me your number, last night was good, but you probably don't want to get mixed up in this."

Aiden gave me a disbelieving look.

"Are you kidding me?" He gestured to his T-shirt, which sported an image of V as Guy Fawkes, holding crossed daggers before him. Aiden grinned wildly, almost floating. "I've been waiting years for this!"

And so our relationship was born the same day as the resistance. I should have known it was a bad sign.

They hadn't always been called dragons. Centuries ago, when those incorporeal inhuman minds were first discovered, they were called some variation of "messenger" or "muse." Those less kindly inclined called them "whisperers." In an effort to remove the mysticism from the language, Adam Smith referred to them as "the Invisible Handlers."

Quickly their nature became apparent. Under their influence, countrysides were stripped to their bones. Cities choked on toxic smoke. Summoners grew gross with wealth, while the commoners withered into skeletons. Karl Marx coined the term "dragons" in reference to the destructive, rapacious creatures of legend.

The first resistance started same as our current one. Small

groups taking local action. Individual acts of sabotage and vandalism. Growing riots. I hadn't been in a riot yet, but that was about to change. We'd entered midsummer. The city park bustled with activity as I helped erect the stage for a protest concert. We'd received permits and cleared everything with the authorities, because we were still playing by the rules. We hadn't yet relearned the lessons of 1917. Not until buildings are burning do governments take you seriously. It takes a revolution to force them into restricting dragons. "From this day forward, you may not dump your poisonous waste into our water. From this day forward, you may not work our children." Not because our rulers care, but because they fear. Not discernment from above, but demands from below.

Hunched over and irritable, I struggled to lock another folding joint of the stage scaffolding. The midday sun beat down on me with spite. Every single stand and brace needed to be pummeled into submission. I was an inch from flinging the whole thing overhead and stomping off when Aiden's arms descended over me from behind.

He wrapped me in an embrace and nuzzled my hair. "Hey, sexy girl."

I exhaled gratefully, and relaxed back into him. He was lean, gentle affection. With maybe a hint of firmness around the crotch right now. I smiled.

"Here to help us?" I asked.

"Anything to get the show going. I still get goose bumps when you scream. But . . ." He gestured at the cops patrolling the perimeter. "It looks like we're gonna get shut down."

"Nah, don't worry about it. Everything's clear. We got a Free Speech Zone designation for the day."

It still makes me sick to think back on how compliant we were. Free Speech Zones? The dragons had learned to fear the power of government over the last century. Now every dragon had phalanxes of well-funded emissaries. "What is good for Genimette is good for the country," they said. They were patient. Slowly they wormed their way into the machinery of politics. Which is how you get BS like "Free Speech Zones." Maybe there'd been a time when cops served and protected the public. Now they're thugs who serve the dragons and protect their profits.

Our band, Against Dragons, wouldn't go onstage until 9:00 p.m., but other locals were playing nonstop from midafternoon. The music burned violent and spectacular. The cops hated it. Which meant they had to piss on anyone they could. Shouting matches erupted. Twice pepper spray hissed and they hauled off some kid in cuffs. People drifted away, not wanting to deal with the pigs. Those who stayed were on edge. Belligerent, pierced, tattooed punks, sticking it out explicitly because it *did* bother the police, and damn proud of it. We were in good company.

When we took the stage, the setting sun igniting the horizon, the air held a buzzing tension. Like the charge that builds inside you when a storm is rolling in, or the last pregnant note before a DJ drops the bass. I fingered my rosary as I scanned the crowd, matching my tempo to their pulse. We could use this. I pocketed the beads at *salva nos ab igne inferiori*, nodded to Liam. Zoe started us off with a bass riff.

The stage lights picked us out in a giant, harsh halo. As the sky grew darker and the heavens tightened around us, that tension worked itself into our instruments. It seeped into Liam's voice. It became a part of the music. The crowd fed it back to us, boiling, pushing us to a frantic thrashing. My hand clutched at the guitar as I choked it with my fingertips. My heart raced, and we were diving straight from one song into the next without pause. Because screw pauses, we have this burning in our throats, and we don't know any way to get it out other than to roar it at an audience and hear them scream with us.

We smashed into our breakout song and all the riotgrrrlz and punk boys below us roared in approval. We moved as one.

There's four words all piggies hate. They glare from spray-painted buildings and overpasses. They bleed from the shadows of hushed conversations. They're the chorus to this song. "Death to All Collaborators."

The chorus approached, and I stepped to the mic. Instead of looking into the crowd, I looked to the cops looming at the perimeter, and showed some teeth. I picked out one huffing like a pent-up bull. I stared him down. I screamed out my line just for him.

*Death to all collaborators!*

You could call that a mistake, maybe. But it had to start somewhere.

Halfway through my solo, a meaty hand clamped onto my shoulder and spun me around. The amps squealed as the notes died on my strings, and I stood eye-to-chest with a man in a dark-blue uniform, snorting fire.

"This show's over," he rumbled. "You're coming with us."

"Piss off, pig," I spat. I shrugged him off, turned back with derision. My stomach clenched in terror, but I wasn't doing this for myself anymore. This was for everyone who'd put up with their sneering abuse tonight. Put up with it for generations.

His hand shoved me from behind, hitting right at the apex of my hump. I yelped and started staggering forward, but I hadn't gone one step before he wrenched my left arm behind me and screaming pain forced me to my knees.

I twisted, shrieking, as he yanked and pinned my other arm. My spine torqued, wedged vertebrae biting into calcified disks. A zip-cuff cinched one wrist, and I knew I'd be trapped like this for hours, blind with agony. Somewhere I heard Tyrell yelling, the sounds of movement, but they were dim outlines under a flood of pain.

Sudden sharp relief. I collapsed to the floor, gasping for breath. The stage rocked beneath me. I rolled over and saw Aiden grappling with the cop. My boy was no match for the hulking man, but as he pretzeled Aiden into submission, more angry punks leaped over me, piled on. The cop was big, but not a-dozen-angry-teens big, and he tipped over under the onslaught. His hands grasped for something at his belt and heavy boots came down to crunch his fingers before he got there.

Lights flashed, strobing blue and red. Whooping sirens drowned out the music of struggle, replaced it with the music of authority. Liam yelled into the microphone, something hot and angry, and the crowd erupted. Two nearby cops jumped onto the stage to free their trapped brother and Zoe, little Zoe, strode up behind them. She held her bass like a two-handed cudgel, back and to the side. She lunged forward, swung her guitar overhead, and brought it down on the bigger pig's head. The violent jangle of the strings breaking sounded through the park, and it was the sweetest music I'd ever heard. Bottles flew. I could barely hear the sirens over the blood-lust roar of the crowd.

Zoe picked up the mic and yelled into it. "Time to fry some pigs. Let's start some fires!"

The crowd surged like an incoming tide, bursting around the stage at the edges, breaking over the top in fury. I knew after this we were going underground. I staggered to my feet, pushed into the nearest knot of bodies, grasped for Aiden's arm. I dug him from the group stripping the pig's weapons, pulled him into the lee of one of the man-height amps. I still shook with aftershocks of pain, and I needed his attention on me. He took one look at my contorted face and wrapped his arms around me, bent his head down to mine. I clutched at him and raged against a stupid urge to cry.

"Thank you," I said. Plastic zip cuffs dangled from my left wrist. And deep inside a longing swelled, a longing I'd been beating back for weeks. It broke over my inner walls before I even knew it was happening.

"I love you," spilled out of my mouth. My heart sank. I hadn't meant to say it. Damn.

His eyes shone. "I love you, too," he replied, his voice soaring.

Six months later found us hunkered down in the blacked-out basement of Liam's squat, having settled into the fugitive life. I sat on the floor, bent over my phone, resting my back against the wall. Aiden knelt beside me, kneading my shoulders and massaging along the top of my hump. He, Zoe, and Liam observed an informal remembrance of Tyrell in low tones as we waited. Tyrell had disappeared three weeks back, his door kicked in and his place ransacked. The dragons had him now.

Liam's brother Marcus arrived last, a half-hour late. Over an inch shorter than Liam, with more hair and less piercings. Chemical burns ringed his eyes in flaming red. He limped in, favoring his right leg, but grinned when he saw us.

"Christ," Zoe said. "What happened to you?"

"I was at yesterday's protest at Union Station. Brought a megaphone and said some true things."

"And what'd that get you?" Liam asked, raising an eyebrow.

Marcus's grin faltered. "Someone tossed a Molly, before the pigs started cracking heads."

Liam snorted. "We should be past flinging cocktails. If this was LA, the whole district would be in flames, and the pigs would be hiding behind barricades."

"Next time will be bigger. Next time we rush City Hall."

"It's been 'next time' for weeks. We're dying out there. For nothing."

"Hey, back off. You just call us here to bitch us out?"

"No." Liam straightened. "I have something to show you. We can still get our shit in order before they eat us alive."

He led us to the next room, also blacked out. He flicked on a single bare bulb hanging from the ceiling, and something glinted on the floor. A thick line of metal lay on the cement. My eyes followed it, bending smoothly, arcing around the whole room. The line of metal grazed each wall, encompassed where we were standing, and returned to touch itself. A very large circle. It looked faintly yellow. Like gold.

We were in the center of a summoning circle.

"Liam, what the hell is this?" I asked.

Zoe gaped. "Where did you get this much gold?"

Aiden inhaled sharply and jabbed an accusing finger at Liam. "You're going to summon a dragon? Are you insane?"

Liam looked Aiden in the eyes and spoke calmly, as if he'd rehearsed this. "Dragons are a tool. They are a goddamned amazing tool which we're leaving lying around out of ideological purity, and it's costing us lives. If you're willing to kill a man to save your species, you should be willing to use the dragons against each other."

"No." Aiden stated flatly. "Too dangerous. They get out of control. Always."

I spoke up now. "We haven't had a single politician who isn't owned by a dragon for . . . hell, longer than I've been alive. You can vote blue or you can vote red, but you can't vote against the interests of Auramagos. You want to add us to that equation, too? Remove even us as an option?"

"In a gunfight, the side without a gun loses," Liam replied. "You can rage about how unfair that is, but if you don't pick up a gun, you just guarantee that the other side wins."

"Bull," Aiden spat.

"Cells on the West Coast have already summoned some," Liam stated.

That shut us all up. He gave it a second to sink in.

"You haven't wondered how they've been doing so well?" he continued. "They've been using these things for a while. They call them Dragon-Eaters. They're advancing the struggle, and we're dragging them down. We're killing the resistance."

His words hung in the room. The circle of gold held us in its grip like a tourniquet. A bronze bowl rested against one wall, the athame inside it lay in wait. Overshadowing them, a tall wooden crucifix held a beautifully carved corpus of Christ, twisted in agony up toward the heavens. His eyes gazed at me from under the barbed crown, asking me how much I was willing to give to make the future better. How much of myself would I sacrifice for the good of others?

Liam's brother spoke up first. "I'm willing to die for the resistance. I don't want that to be for nothing. If this is what it takes . . . I'll do it."

Zoe nodded. "If this is a mistake, it's not permanent. We're the summoners, we can always banish it."

Aiden looked back and forth among us in dawning disbelief. "Oh no . . . you guys aren't buying this. You can't be buying this."

I opened my mouth to agree with him. A mental image of Tyrell being tortured stopped me. "We can't let them keep getting away with it," I said instead. "If we're defeated, it could be generations before people rise up again. Maybe never. I can't live in that world."

Aiden stared at us, a fire in his eyes. His breathing came heavier. His hands clenched into fists.

"You unbelievable idiots. You're damned if you go down this path. You're all damned, and you're doing it to yourselves."

"Aiden, we're losing. We have to try." I extended a hand, not used to his opposition. He jerked away from me.

"No. The hell with this. I'm outta here. Damn yourself by yourself."

He turned and stormed out. The door creaked slowly in his wake, as if buffeted by the fury of his passing.

"He'll come around," I told the group, ignoring the pinch of doubt in my guts. "I'll bring him over."

Zoe and Marcus murmured agreement.

Liam began the summoning. He knew exactly what he was doing; he'd been preparing for weeks. Within minutes the athame sliced over my palm. The blade split the skin neatly, drawing a perfect red line that wept into the bowl. It mingled with Liam's, Zoe's, and Marcus's. I stared at it as Liam worked, a buzzing in my head. Or was it in the room? It shifted, doubled, spawned low hums.

The gold ring thinned, evaporating, and the air grew heavy with an alien presence. Not just the air. Everything grew heavy—my clothes, my body. Breath came hard. The light from the bulb distorted and played over the walls as if filtered through choppy waters. A foreign mental process shoved against my mind, pushing my thoughts in unwelcome directions.

I glanced at Zoe. Under the distorted light her spiked hair looked like tarantula tufts. Strange shadows shifted behind her, giving her the appearance of having extra limbs. I saw a spider whose life consisted of the constant knitting of webs of emotional dependence, until her entire identity was a tangled social net and the upkeep it required. She crept into the lives of others, insinuating herself under the guise of extroverted friendship. Only by manipulating people did she accomplish anything.

This was the first gift of the dragons—the dragon sight. It strips away the facades we monkeys erect to make ourselves feel noble and pure. It reveals that we are simply biological constructs, responding to incentives, executing crude survival strategies. I looked to Marcus. I saw him whither into little more than a fluttering shadow. Unable to make his own way in a confusing world, he leached vitality from his brother's desperation. Dark tendrils slipped from his lethifold form, grasped after Liam, hanging onto another's life since he couldn't direct his own.

Liam had become a shimmering mirage in the wavering light, almost not there at all. His defiance paled into the flailings of a man who couldn't compete with his peers. He was plain, so he mutilated his face with pounds of metal. His voice couldn't soar, so he screamed and growled instead. Everywhere that he couldn't excel, he carved out his own pool of excess. He couldn't even fight the revolution with his natural talents, so he'd do it as a dragon-summoner.

I'd lived in a dream world where people ran on ideals. The dragon sight stripped that away, showed us our true motivations. I refused to look at myself.

As we gazed at each other, the light stabilized, and the droning hums and buzzes shifted. Wove together. They coalesced into a scratchy whisper—the dragon's murmurings, the second gift. The invisible presence hooked its claws into my psyche. From now on, a part of it would be with me, always. My chest swelled with power as the creature spoke. It began—

*If you wish to prevail against dragons, this is what you must do . . .*

We kept our dragon sight suppressed most of the time. Permanently living in a world stripped of its masks would have driven anyone crazy. I did use the dragon sight on Aiden later that week, though, after five days of him refusing to take my calls or respond to my texts. I'd have done it sooner, but I had trouble tracking him down. I saw an insubstantial, hollow-boned thing that lived vicariously through the emotions of others. He rejoiced when I took my pleasure from him. He exulted in my passion when I raged against the dragons. But above all, he was addicted to the concentrated distillation of emotion that made up primal music. Soaring high in that jet stream was the only time he felt alive.

Immediately I found a new drummer for Against Dragons. As we released new music, Aiden spiraled in closer around me, pulled by a gale of desire, until all I had to do was reach out and pluck him back in. I got what I wanted, but it left a sour taste in my mouth. I'd seen him as a biological construct responding to incentives, rather than a person. I didn't use the dragon sight on him again.

Months later, I sat on the remains of a couch in the remains of an apartment, my guitar in my lap. I fingered the strings absently. Sunlight streamed in from glass sliding doors, still intact, that led out to a balcony twelve stories above an alley strewn with trash. From the kitchen came the smells of Aiden frying us eggs. I pondered, examining the dragon problem, again. For their entire existence, dragons lived only as long as they produced wealth for their summoners. Failure to do so meant "banishment." Death. A single unprofitable year could kill a dragon, regardless of how great the rewards for sacrifice would be five years down the line. With incentives like that, no wonder they scorched the earth to achieve the results we demanded. They were only responding to the survival pressures humanity had placed on them.

A pang of regret cut me, knowing that I couldn't discuss this sort of thing with Aiden anymore. He wouldn't even talk about our Dragon-Eater. He couldn't rejoin our cell, not being a summoner. Fortunately he was extremely valuable as the leader of my sub-cell, as our part of the resistance had flourished in the months following the summoning. Recruiting had skyrocketed. It became so much easier when we saw what motivated people, what kept them loyal, what they could be pushed to do. The dragon sight let us estimate what each member could contribute, how much they were worth. It brought us successes—devastating guerrilla strikes with very acceptable losses on our side. Success was the biggest draw of all. I couldn't believe how quickly our ranks swelled.

Even the smattering of recent failures were easily turned into rousing stories of sacrifice. Nothing fired up our people like a strong martyr.

Aiden emerged from the kitchen carrying two plates loaded with greasy eggs and sausage. A niggling irritation scampered in my mind, scratching away at the corners of my brain like a rat. It nipped at my thoughts, but every time I looked for it, there were only tattered worries and rodent droppings.

Aiden's eyes caught the sunlight, sparkling cerulean blue. I smiled. They brought me back into the living, breathing world. He didn't smile back, but I didn't mind.

"Hey, sexy boy," I greeted, and set my guitar aside. He sat down by me mutely and handed me a plate. I finally noticed his distant expression, his troubled brow. A weight of guilt smothered my hunger. How long had he been like this? I'd been ignoring him again, fretting over last week's barely-salvaged disaster.

"Did I keep you up too late last night?" I asked.

"It's not that. I woke up dreaming of Zoe again."

"Oh." I crossed myself. "Crap, sorry."

"I keep trying to picture her last moments." His voice came timid, as if scared to confide in me. That hurt. I pushed down the urge to use my dragon sight. "I wonder if she was terrified when she ran for the explosives. Was she already shot and bleeding out? Or did she detonate them defiantly, triumphantly? I think I like that better. I can see her with a detonator in hand, yelling at the top of her lungs that they'll never take her alive." A slight smile twisted his face. "Took a hell of a lot of pigs with her."

I nodded and ignored the piece of me searching for an answer that would make it better. Instead I forced up the core of dread that had been smoldering inside me for weeks, hot coals of regret. They burned me when I spoke. "It wasn't a fair trade."

A strong knock startled us. The front door swung open and Liam stepped inside, eyes hard. His brother Marcus followed, as well as a man I didn't recognize. The dragon whispered inside me—*he's brought along extra muscle. Something is going down.*

"Liam?" I asked as he closed the door behind them. "Who's this?"

Liam pursed his lips. His eyes moved to Aiden, his face darkened. That pestering rat at the back of my mind started scurrying again.

"Jo, why haven't you been freaking out about our failures over the last month?"

I hesitated, felt the dragon's cunning prodding my thoughts. "Our estimates are off. We're absorbing the data and adjusting our probabilities. It happens. We'll just have to be more conservative for a while."

Scratch, scratch, scratch. Gnaw, gnaw, gnaw.

"They're off in a consistent way," Liam said. "It looks like chaos at first, until you change a simple basic assumption. Then it becomes a predictable flaw."

Aiden's hand came to rest on my hip. "What are you trying to say?" he asked.

Claw, claw, claw. Bite, bite, bite.

Liam pierced me with a stare. "*You* should be able to see it."

The rat in my mind leaped at his words, and rapidly everything tumbled into place.

Don't look at the data in one pool—split it into two populations. The operations I'm not involved in, failing and succeeding roughly at the rate expected.

The operations I do have a hand in still succeeding often enough, but at a lower rate. Those that do succeed get us less supplies, less info, or cost more lives than expected. Enough success to keep us in the game, but costly enough to slowly bleed us dry.

He was right, I should have been the first to see it. The data is explained if I'm a mole, working with the old dragons to rot us away from inside.

*But if they were convinced that I'm a mole, I'd be dead right now,* came the whisper. The fact that they were here, appealing to me, was evidence they'd reached a different conclusion.

A chill spread from where Aiden's hand rested on my hip. Ice crept up my spine and sunk claws into my chest. Suddenly I couldn't breathe. I turned around to look at Aiden.

"What's up?" he asked, confusion in his eyes.

I looked through the dragon sight. Before me sat a man who only ever saw my hunched back as part of what made me who I am. I wasn't ugly to him. That was rare enough, but out of all the men who weren't turned off by me, how many would I be compatible with? How many took sex the way I loved to give it? How many would be caring and sweet, and love my bitchiness and aggression? How many could know all of me, and love me anyway?

No one else. I couldn't lose him.

So when I'd realized what was happening, I'd suppressed that knowledge. I knew, somewhere, what he'd done. The knowledge skittered in my mind like a rat in the walls. Hiding from sight but sometimes heard fleetingly, hatefully.

I didn't see Aiden below me. I saw my own lies. I'd endangered the resistance with my selfishness. Destroyed resources. Lost advantages. Killed Zoe.

"Oh, God, no." The words escaped like smoke rising from my lungs, trickling from my mouth. I stepped back, back, until I stood pressed against the wall.

"Jo, are you okay?" my lies asked me, concern in his voice. He sounded ignorant, innocent. *He lies well.*

I closed my eyes and banished the dragon sight. Around me the sounds of three men stepping forward, laying hands on Aiden. A brief struggle I couldn't watch. My eyes burned.

"Jo, help me! What the hell? Get off me!"

I opened my eyes and gazed at Aiden, bent over, arms wrenched behind him. Confused, pained.

"Why?" I asked. But I already knew. Biological constructs running off simple incentives. Aiden secretly working with the dragons for months? That kind of bitter dedication only came from someone deeply wronged.

He drew a shallow breath. "Like you care," he said quietly. "You declared humans don't matter. Dragons are the true players in the world, humans are just the pieces they play with. Even you admitted it. Even you. I hope you burn."

We studied each other. He looked so fragile, bound up by angry friends. It hurt to see him like that. To see that in the end, he had been driven to the dragons, too. Aiden had realized that you could only seek vengeance upon a summoner by turning to a dragon of your own. When it came to something he truly, desperately wanted, even Aiden had succumbed. And I had set that precedent.

"Get him out of here."

The other three wrestled him out the sliding door, onto the patio. It overlooked a dozen floors of empty space, terminating in concrete far below.

Aiden struggled, thrashing. "No! Jo! Stop them! Please, Jo!"

Slowly I shuffled up to him on the balcony. My hands trembled. The words scraped my throat on their way out:

"Death to all collaborators."

They heaved him over the edge, and for one infinite split-second he hung in the air, surprise still on his face. Then gravity took him.

He fell, screaming, shattering the serenity of the sky. As he plummeted something bulged under his shirt, something large and swelling. The shirt shredded at the shoulders and downy growths burst from his back.

Long graceful wings, thick with snow-white feathers, erupted from the flesh. They snapped open, spanning yards across, and caught the air in a full embrace.

ALANA FLETCHER

I should have been terrified. I should have recoiled in horror at this invasion into our material realm. The dragons had found a way to affect physical reality. The war was escalating, and there was no knowing where it would go now.

Instead I sank to my knees in gratitude, choking on sobs of relief. Tears spilled down my cheeks. I watched Aiden through a liquid blur as he swooped up, up into the endless blue sky, free of me finally and forever.

I haven't seen him since. I am grateful. The war grows bloodier, and our world grows bizarre. Yet I still craft the most volcanic music I can at night. I scream it into the sky, my personal siren songs. Sometimes I think I can see Aiden's figure far above, suspended from outstretched wings. I imagine he can hear my violent hymns, and I wonder how he would answer my rage. My accusations, my inquisitions.

When the dragons are finally ground to dust, I fear I may snare him and find out.

# *Passion and Profession*

## BY CIRUELO

*Ciruelo Cabral was born in Buenos Aires, Argentina. His formal art training was limited to a few courses in drawing and advertising design, after which, at the age of eighteen, he immediately found work in an ad agency as an illustrator.*

*At twenty-one, he became a freelance illustrator and started a career as a fantasy artist.*

*In 1987, Ciruelo traveled to Europe and settled in Sitges near Barcelona, Spain. He then embarked on a search for publishers for his "worlds of fantasy," eventually finding them in Spain, England, the United States and Germany, reaching an international audience.*

*His US clients include George Lucas, for whom he illustrated the book covers of the trilogy* Chronicles of the Shadow War.

*Ciruelo illustrated the cover for the tenth anniversary's edition of the book* Eragon*, by Christopher Paolini and, in 2016, did over forty ink drawings for* The Official Eragon Coloring Book. *He also created a number of album covers including Steve Vai's* The 7th Song *and* The Elusive Light and Sound*, and* Adam & Eve *for the Swedish rock band, The Flower Kings. He collaborated with Alejandro Jodorowsky on a comic story published in France and in the US. Other clients include Wizards of the Coast, TSR, Berkley, Tor, Warner, Ballantine,* Heavy Metal *magazine,* Playboy *magazine, etc.*

*Another branch of Ciruelo's art is* petropictos, *the art of painting on stone. He created this technique in 1995. It consists of painting on stones where he is able to discover three-dimensional images and create something halfway between a painting and a sculpture. The work captures the public's attention in international exhibitions.*

*At the beginning of 2017 he was invited to the judges' panel for the Illustrators of the Future Contest.*

# *Passion and Profession*

When I'm asked the question, "When did you start drawing?" I like to answer with another question that makes more sense to me: "When did everybody stop drawing?"

Everyone draws when they are kids because art is a natural form of self-expression. But most people abandon it at some point because they are prompted to do a "real" job within a society that considers art just a hobby and a leisure activity.

I just continue to do the same thing I've been doing since childhood. After many years with a professional career, I still maintain the same passion for playing around with lines and colors that I had when I was a kid.

Preserving that primal joy is a constant task I try to accomplish every day as well as stimulating my curiosity and my capacity for wonder.

Those are exercises I advise for everybody in general.

That may sound very romantic for someone who wants to start an artistic career in a world where the financial aspects are a priority, but that's the way I approach my work.

Let's establish up front that professional artists are part of those few privileged people who love their job. I'm convinced that doing the job you love is more rewarding than anything. And that ultimately happiness leads to success. So, that's an unbeatable factor when considering the pursuit of a career passion.

For somebody who wants to be a freelance artist, this

profession provides many other satisfactions, like the possibility to manage one's own time, the opportunity to have a studio at home and the advantage of being one's own boss.

However, some prefer to work as an employee for a company because that simplifies many business issues. And on the artistic side, it may provide wonderful opportunities such as working with a team.

At this point, I should explain a bit about my background: I was born in Argentina and lost my father at the age of four. My mother worked all day to raise two children. I reached the age of eighteen well aware of the meaning of "economic deprivation."

Despite that, in my career as a professional illustrator I have always chosen the more artistic and creative projects instead of the more profitable ones. Probably that's because I was used to living a modest life, so money didn't appeal to me more than the satisfaction of being creatively free, especially within the fantasy art field.

I've been a freelance illustrator since the age of twenty-one, which means that I haven't had a set monthly income since then. However, I have always worked with passion to do my best on every piece, no matter the payment. For that reason, I was able to create a personal style with dragons. My work eventually found its path in the international market, and that means it turned out to be lucrative too.

Based on my personal experience, I give the following advice to young artists: Set your priority on the artistic facet instead of the economic side. This approach will always reward you.

Other more pragmatic recommendations I can give are: Be self-disciplined, learn from practice, improve your skills, experiment, search for the appropriate market, work hard, prepare a good portfolio and send it out to as many potential clients as you can.

For some reason, I have a strong tendency to focus on the less material aspects of art. For example, I love to explore my own imagination, playing with images created in my mind's eye, storing them in my memory and exercising visualization. In fact, one of the things I like the most is to study creativity itself, since I think it is the essence of art and one of the biggest mysteries of humankind.

During long hours painting, I have many interesting thoughts and reflections. I write them down in a notebook along with lots of rough sketches. Some of the sketches become paintings and some of the notes eventually get published in a collection that I call *Notebooks*.

I would like to share a few of those notes here, for they reveal my inner thoughts on the artistic process:

> I understand art as the act in which one applies the best of oneself by employing as much creativity as possible. I believe it to be an alliance between beauty and bliss.
>
> But above all, it is an attitude.
>
> I draw in order to remember. I feel that sometimes we forget we inhabit a sphere that travels through space rotating around other spheres.
>
> We usually forget everything is very magical. I believe art to be the proper attitude that we should adopt when we are before so much magic.
>
> •
>
> I first organized my time by drawing on even-numbered days and writing on odd-numbered days. Faced with my inability to remember what day it was, I switched to drawing in the mornings and writing in the evenings. But I finally chose to put aside any type of planning, drawing and writing at the beckoning of inspiration. I learned to be very messy within my strict organization. And I am sometimes uncertain whether the idea that comes to me is to be captured in a drawing or by way of a written text.

Sometimes these texts get a bit more poetic, which is also a good way of explaining all these magical processes of creating fantasy art:

When I draw, something climbs up my spine, coiling itself around me and whistling. Something itches me in my bones and then pours under my tongue.

They could be electrical impulses or some sort of light that simply overcomes me.

But I'm inclined to think that what stirs inside of me when I draw is in fact particles of stars that merely want to return to their galaxy.

•

Imprisoned by a state of daydreaming, a very young girl looked at one of my drawings with special interest. Within the sparkle of her eyes, I suddenly discovered the same tiny stars that I possessed in my eyes while creating that drawing. I then realized that the most valuable purpose of my art is to spread that sparkle in the eyes of people.

•

When nothing comes to mind to draw, I implement a few tricks to fool my anxiety. For example: I pretend I am distracted and start playing with the pencil, making it doodle spirals and stars. With a little luck, the pencil finds its way and I just follow. The first lines look familiar because they come from muscular memory. They are shapes that time has recorded in my mind and that my hand draws automatically. I have to be patient with them and let them out. Once they have gone, I begin to stalk attentively. That means that I try to hunt any shape that seems interesting to me and extend it, enrich it, feed it. So when the time to daydream arrives, I am succumbed to a river of visions and sensations that begin to tell a tale. Finally, when the drawing has taken shape, all that remains is knowing when to stop.

•

I firmly believe that everyone is born with some sort of artistic talent. The problem is that most people don't harvest it. What's more, they don't realize it even exists. And then, given the obligations of society, they end up working at something that is in no way related to that primitive talent and stray further from their mission. I daresay that therein lies the outlying problem of most human beings.

•

I can give some explanation for most of my drawings, but there are others on which I cannot even venture an opinion. They come from mysterious sources inside me that I do not even know about.

•

The artist learns to wait for magic. In the meantime, he lives with frustration and effort.

The artist nurtures beauty, pursues perfection, probes the abstract, and cherishes magic like the farmer cherishes the rain.

The artist has the vision and the daring; he relies on his eyes and hands.

Yet, he waits for the magic.

•

One day I said, "I'll draw no more. Now I want to be a magician." And when I made magic I realized that it was just like drawing.

# *Illusion*

*written by*

## *Jody Lynn Nye*

*inspired by*

CIRUELO'S *DRAGON CALLER*

---

ABOUT THE AUTHOR

*A native Chicagoan, Jody Lynn Nye is a* New York Times *bestselling author of more than fifty books and 165 short stories. As a part of Bill Fawcett & Associates (she is the "& Associates"), she has helped to edit more than two hundred books, including forty anthologies, with a few under her own name. Her work tends toward the humorous side of sci-fi and fantasy.*

*Along with her individual work, Jody has collaborated with several notable professionals in the field, including Anne McCaffrey, Robert Asprin, John Ringo, and Piers Anthony. She collaborated with Robert Asprin on a number of his famous Myth-Adventures series, and has continued both that and his Dragons Wild series since his death in 2008.*

*Jody runs the two-day intensive writers' workshop at DragonCon, and co-writes the fiction review column in* Galaxy's Edge *magazine, edited by fellow WotF judge Mike Resnick.*

*About "Illusion," she told us: "I love having something to inspire me when I write. I was delighted to have the opportunity to write a story based upon the splendid piece of artwork that forms the cover of this anthology, a fantasy painting by Ciruelo. It so happened that the subject matter dovetailed neatly with another fantasy series I have been working on. Instead of treating with the main character of that series, this story hearkens back decades to her employer, a great wizard—or so he seems.*

*"I started publishing professionally too early to participate in the Writers of the Future Contest, but I would probably have offered something like this for the judges' consideration, heavy on world-building, but light and lively, with good characterization and serious matters at stake."*

## ABOUT THE ILLUSTRATOR

*Ciruelo created* Dragon Caller *with his love for portraying human and dragon relationships. It was first published in his 2007 calendar. Unlike all of the other stories in this anthology, where the illustrations were commissioned for each story, here Jody Lynn Nye conceived her story based on Ciruelo's illustration, which graces the cover of this Writers of the Future volume.*

# *Illusion*

Again!" The Regente of Enth clapped her hands with delight, like the little girl she used to be.

Pleased, Angelo smoothed his impressive silver beard and mustachios with a forefinger, and straightened his tall, T-shaped hat.

"You wouldn't want the same spell over again, would you, your serenity?" the court magician asked. "Having a troupe of pixies come to dance for you is all very well, but they have their own duties and responsibilities to attend to." *As do the grandees and grandaas standing about your throne,* he thought.

"Yes! I do love them so." Zoraida squirmed into the enormous throne. Her heavy amber skirts and voluminous red cloak of office made her seem like a child playing dress-up. Only the jeweled circlet on her thick bronze hair seemed a comfortable fit.

Angelo regarded the young woman with affection. He liked to grant her wishes, to help take her mind off the heavy duties of the office that had been thrust upon her so recently. It didn't matter, he supposed, as they were not real pixies anyhow. Very well, once more wouldn't hurt.

He raised the tall silverwood staff in his left hand and brought the golden ferrule down on the stone floor with an impressive BANG! Angelo always made certain he worked his wonders in a corner of the audience chamber where the rugs did not cover the floor. The noise was nowhere near as impressive if it was muffled by yards of woven silk. Once again, he stroked a hand over the whitstone and drew upon his imagination, fed by storybooks and the tales sung by troubadours. He felt the magic rise within him, like water bubbling in a well. He opened his soul to the beauty of creativity, funneling the ideas in his mind through his body, until streamers of color emerged from his eyes, his mouth, and the palms of his hands. Sight, sound and touch, the images formed, lifting his heart as they came into being. What seemed a wonder to others was no less a miracle to him, though he was its source.

From the very ground they stood upon, fluting arpeggios rose, visible as dancing wisps of colors, until they formed a landscape of both sound and sight. At a grand chord, the mists cleared, revealing tiny, perfectly-shaped beings whirling and leaping in a circle. As each faced the regente, they bowed to her, making gestures of respect to her with delicate hands. The music grew more intricate, adding the sound of instruments that Angelo had heard on his visits to the land of fairies and sprites. He had stopped summoning actual fae to the palace for the regente's entertainment, as they had a tendency to help themselves to jewels from the royal treasury and anything else sparkly that caught their eye. If Zoraida realized the difference, she never mentioned it. Illusion could be its own reward.

The regente clapped her hands to the rhythm, or almost. Her talents, of swordswomanship, philosophy, and listening, did not include any for music. The courtiers present never dared to indicate that they noticed anything wrong. Zoraida had a temper, almost certainly one of the reasons why she had not yet chosen her first consort.

At the corners of the fairy dance, the colors began to run into one another, blue melting into orange and making a muddy brown. Angelo stroked his hand over the big oval whitstone at the top of his staff. The colors brightened, and the dancers leaped and twirled more merrily. The microscopic crumb of the mystic mineral that exploded under his palm was enough to sustain the dance for weeks on end, if need be.

Whitstones were rare, especially ones of the size he possessed. It had come from the hoard of a dragon who remained in his debt to that day. He fed the silver orb with his own energy and that summoned from earth and sky whenever he could, but that only rebuilt smaller morsels of it than he actually used. One day, he would almost certainly have to seek out another. A wizard whose talents were of a more active sort depleted the substance of her or his whitstone far more quickly than he did. Angelo was fortunate that Enth had been peaceful since before he had arrived, decades ago. A sinecure like this made his fellow magical practitioners green with envy. He couldn't help but preen when visiting mages sneered over his growing school of noble apprentices, the wealth evident in his quarters, his magical accoutrements and his dress, and the leisurely life he led, making pretty pictures for his employer.

The third tune drew to a coda, and Angelo made the seeming fae turn to take one more bow to the regente as the pipes swirled one last time. Zoraida applauded so hard that her palms turned red. The rest of the court patted their hands softly, waiting for their ruler's pleasure.

"Again!" The regente tapped the ground with the foot of her long scepter of office.

"No, no, your grace," Angelo said, with an avuncular smile. "The pixies are weary. Let them rest." He swept his staff high, and the entire phantasm vanished, leaving the audience room comfortably ordinary. The courtiers heaved a collective sigh of relief. Even the page sitting on the steps of the throne at the regente's feet looked grateful.

"A marvel!" Zoraida crowed, beaming at him. "You are without a doubt the finest wizard in the world!"

Angelo bowed until his beard touched the hem of his ornate purple robe.

"I thank you, my liege."

The young warrior queen twisted in the oversized throne, made for one of her long-ago ancestors who had six or eight times her bulk, and rucked up her full brocade skirts so she could draw a knee up to rest on the gilded and carved armrest.

"Now, I would have you relate one of your grand adventures,"

Zoraida said, not quite willing to return to the business of reigning. "Tell us about the time you bested three giants who had been laying waste to that village in the north. Or your battle with the necromancer of Fillith! Your heroic exploits have always inspired me, my friend."

Angelo cringed inwardly.

"My lady, the Grand Potestad has a number of requisitions for you to sign," he said, gesturing toward that worthy, who had been shifting from foot to foot through the last illusion. "The minister of justice has cases she needs to bring before you. And the other ricohombres and ricahembras have been so patient, although I am certain that they *loved* the entertainment I provided for you."

"Oh, all right," Zoraida said, beckoning the nobles forward. Potestad Miguel de la Hora, Chancellor of the Exchequer, strode into the head of the queue, his pendulous belly leading the way.

Angelo watched the regente reluctantly resume her duties. She was so young! If only her dear father had not been so unlucky as to die before she had had time to gain some small experience ruling a province. She would have more confidence in her role, and her reputation as a diplomat and leader would have equaled that of her abilities in the field. Reputation was everything, far above ability.

"Your serenity," de la Hora began in his sonorous voice. "Trade with Moris has not been as profitable of late. . . ."

"Your serenity!"

Forgoing all dignity, Condestable Inez de Donunza hurtled into the room. The chief minister cast her ceremonial sword belt into the hands of the nearest man-at-arms and pushed past the rest of the nobles to kneel on the steps at Zoraida's feet.

"What is wrong?" the regente asked, reaching for her friend's hand to help her up. The minister sprang to her feet. Her usual neat braids bounded in her agitation.

"What is wrong?" the condestable echoed. "A scout has just returned from the eastern border. Enth is being invaded! The sky to the east is full of flying snakes, each with a warrior on its back! Armies swarm over the mountain passes beneath them."

At her words, the rest of the court burst into a hubbub of alarm.

The East? Angelo recoiled in dismay. The Solognians!

Enth had had many decades of peace, based upon Constantino's skills as a general and negotiator. Zoraida, his eldest, was just of an age to begin to consolidate her power with diplomatic ties when her father had died. She was entitled to take three consorts. None of her suitors to date was, well, suitable. The most likely candidate, Francour of Sologne, the realm to the East, had a temper almost but not quite as terrible as Zoraida's. The few times that their parents had put them together as children, they had fought like angry weasels. Francour had emerged with more bite marks, which the heiress of Enth counted as victory. Marrying for love was never a consideration, but profound dislike and hatred did make diplomatic ties difficult. Francour remained on the list, though not seriously considered. A pity, as Sologne had many advantages that would add to Enth's influence across the world, and the eastern realm could have used the infusion of hard currency that Enth possessed. Mweko, a prince of Moris, the realm across the narrow sea to the south, was only a third son, though the favorite of his queen mother. Moris had a great navy of trading ships that ranged over the world. Mweko was a delightful companion, charming and handsome, and Zoraida liked him enormously, but Angelo had been told in confidence that he did not seek marriage with a woman. The laird of Escotio, the cold northlands, had all but told Constantino that Zoraida's first and principal consort would be his second son, Amish. Amish was nine years old.

Francour looked like the only reasonable local candidate, but Zoraida always sent his emissaries back without answers. It seemed that Francour had stopped waiting for Zoraida to come around to an economic necessity and meant to take Enth's resources by force.

Zoraida sprang to her feet, her dark eyes blazing.

"Call the army! Summon all of my generals!"

"General Rafello is on his way, my liege," de Donunza said. "He only halted to call for the castle to be secured."

"We must protect our people," Zoraida said. She cast about for a moment, then beckoned Angelo close. "My friend, you are needed."

"For what?" Angelo almost squawked.

Zoraida regarded him with puzzlement. "Why, for the defense of the realm," she said. "You can do anything with your powers. You always told me that."

"I . . ." The wizard pulled his spine straight. "Yes! We shall defend. I shall . . . I must go and study the best way to win this battle, your serenity! Please excuse me. I will return . . . I will return anon." He made an elegant bow. The regente's page ran for the prime minister and the rest of her advisors. Angelo backed out of the room.

In the anteroom, servants, who had already heard the rumor, ran about like ants whose nest had been kicked, paying no attention to the court wizard. Angelo put his forehead against the nearest stone wall, resisting the urge to batter his own brains out on it.

*Oh, great Fate, what am I supposed to do?*

Feeling like a salmon swimming upstream through the crowds of servants and soldiers who poured into the great keep, Angelo rushed back to his tower.

On his hasty ascent along the winding stone staircase that circled the tower from broad base to narrow peak, he observed the frenetic activity below, proving that word of the coming invasion had spread to the entire castle and beyond. Carts laden with goods and herds of beasts crowded in through the portcullis and the postern gates. The palace guard mustered in front of the keep itself, with the sergeant-at-arms berating soldiers who ran toward her, tying on pieces of armor and holding armfuls of weapons against their chests. No one was ready for war, least of all him.

Once in a while, a hustling minion or soldier would look

up and see Angelo with his purple robes fluttering in the cold wind, and their shoulders would relax. Angelo offered a grave wave and a somber smile, and continued his ascent. They relied upon him. He felt that weight ponderously upon his shoulders.

The conical spire of ivory stone that stood at the rear of the castle keep had been the court magician's domicile for over eight centuries. At the top it measured only one trimeter across, so that when one emerged from the stairs that spiraled up around the outside, one stepped directly into the magic circle incised upon the tiled floor, a conceit of his predecessor, the mage Cornelio, and a good joke on visitors, who thought they would only be observing a ritual, not participating in it. The main difficulty with it for everyday use was that while a trimeter, one and one half times the height of a man (Regente Ludovido I, to be precise), it made things more than a trifle snug if one's cabal consisted of more than six people. The magic circle lost something of dignity and demeanor when one had to purify people in groups, then send them to wait, shivering in Enth's cold mountain weather, on the narrow stairs, while everyone else was consecrated and blessed. Since he had been saddled with a multitude of apprentices, from every noble family with the merest hint of magical ability in the realm, he was up to three changes of circle attendants, and ritual purification took more than an hour. At least, the parents paid for their offspring's apprenticeships, and very well, too.

The small chamber did, however, provide him with a useful haven. The impenetrable blue haze that rose around it when he was inside (another conceit of its previous occupant) looked suitably forbidding, and kept interlopers, even the regente's servants, from interrupting his thoughts there.

At the top, the mist thickened, concealing the scene below from view. He passed his hand over the crystal glyph inset in the precious morwood door. The portal creaked open, then slammed dramatically behind him. (Was there no end to Cornelio's histrionic touches? He must have begun his career as a showman!)

But, Angelo mused, he was no better. He, too, had a touch of the carnival charlatan about him. He was a terrible fraud. If he was all the realm of Enth had to defend itself against the Solognians and their poisonous krilla steeds, it was doomed.

His appointment to the court as its official wizard by the present regente's father years ago had been based upon the reputation of his illustrious master, the great mage Budestro. *He* had driven off the hordes of Salamar with a lightning storm called down from the very heavens. Budestro, who consorted with demons, swam with leviathans, and banished dragons with a wave of his mighty hand, was a genuine hero. Angelo had come to Budestro's school as a trembling stripling with, as the great master had proclaimed, "the greatest of promise, almost as great as my own!" But for all his potential, Angelo never could come close to his distinguished teacher's prowess. He, Budestro realized at last and to Angelo's dismay, possessed the very seeming of a great wizard, but not its substance.

That said, Budestro put Angelo forward as one of the prospects when a small kingdom sent an inquiry to the master for a court wizard. Over the years, Angelo had done well enough, moving from assignment to minor assignment to merit consideration when Regente Constantino of Enth sent out his requirements for the newest occupant of the tower.

To everyone's surprise and delight, Angelo proved the perfect match for Enth. He reveled in spectacle, filled every feast day with celestial sparkles and the best of weather. Over time, he had acquired confidence in the one great talent he possessed, even become proud of it. His greatest glory was the friendship of Zoraida, the heiress to the regente throne. She adored him, and everything he did. She trusted him, and often asked his advice. He was truthful about everything he told her, except for that one small detail.

With her father's death, Zoraida had taken the throne. She was not yet the seasoned diplomat or soldier. Enth was seen as vulnerable. Her officers and ministers did their best to bring her to maturity, but alas, the krilla were at the gates or, rather, above them.

Now she believed that he, Angelo, would be their bulwark against the foe, to buy peace and resecure the borders.

Angelo sat in the center of the cold tiles, on the heart of the pentagram, and clutched his head with both hands, the skirts of his elegant robes spread around him. How could he defeat an army? He was an illusionist!

All the grand stories that Angelo had claimed for his own had been exploits performed by his master. His own tales could have stirred no one's soul. The three giants he had "bested" had drunk themselves half to death. He had only told the townsfolk that he had put them into a deep sleep, and let them take care of the ugly details. The battle with the necromancer of Filith had been a chess game, and a poor player that lich had been. Even the dragon whose hoard had produced his whitstone and the other treasures had been a wingling he had rescued in the woods, pursued by a farmer for stealing a goose. Oh, Andoria had grown up to be a massive and fearsome beast, though she still felt beholden to him. They shared a picnic now and again on the slopes of her mountain fastness: an entire sheep for her, a pie and a keg of ale for him. He signaled to Andoria by holding high a crystal she had given him, and she would come. They had had many a golden time together. Angelo recalled every day with pleasure.

The dragon! The crystal!

Angelo lifted his head from his hands, his heart filling with hope. That was his solution! No army could withstand the onslaught of a full-grown dragon!

But Andoria was not at his beck. She had business of her own to attend to, flying with other dragons, adding to her hoard (Angelo never asked how), and hunting to fill her belly and that of her occasional offspring. Even when he wanted to see her, she often didn't see his signal for days on end.

*Yet she would see it soon enough,* Angelo thought, standing and brushing chalk dust from his robes. Yes, if they could hold off the onslaught for a while with the realm's armies, his dragon friend would rid Enth of the invaders. Zoraida was counting on him to work miracles. He must prepare to the best of his abilities. Yes! There was much to be done!

He hurried down to the classroom. The door stood ajar, a sign that all was not right. His dozen apprentices in their plain, plum-colored tunics and dark trousers stood huddled together beside their scarred and stained work tables, listening intently as Mistress Drucella, his journeywoman and housekeeper, explained the news. How were they taking it? He cloaked himself in shadow and insinuated himself into the room.

Across the top of the enormous slate that filled the wall at the front of the room were written the laws of magic, which each would-be wizard had to memorize to pass even the first test of apprenticeship, among them the Law of Confusion, the Rule of Three, the Law of Attraction, the Law of Contagion, and the Law of Distraction. Half a sentence had been scrawled under the last one, meaning that a lesson in it had been under way when the word came.

"This is the safest location you may find yourselves in," the tall, narrow-faced woman said, her hands clenched at her sides. "The best defenses in the realm, the stoutest walls and the bravest guards. We had an excellent harvest this year, so there will be no shortage of food, and the wells in each of the courtyards are guarded by pixies, so the water will stay sweet. Are there any questions?" The severe look she sent around to the trembling students suggested that they had better not have any. Nothing was allowed to be out of place in her domain, no matter what the provocation. Even her tight bun looked like black lacquer instead of individual strands.

But, there was always one in every crowd who failed to see the obvious. The honorable Francisco de Monteleone held up one thick-fingered hand.

"Shouldn't we go somewhere else? This is where the enemy is going to come, isn't it?"

Drucella fixed a basilisk stare on the stocky lad and prepared to flay him with sharp words, but Angelo dropped his cloak of shadow, appearing in their midst like a phantasm. The apprentices gasped and gazed in wonder. They always did. One would think they would have learned to expect his dramatic entrances by then.

He shook his head. If they had realized what a fraud he was, they would be so disappointed. They had to believe in him, now, even if one day the truth came out. Angelo held himself erect. He should be the semblance of the prepared, powerful mage, if not the substance.

"I was going to ask for a volunteer," he said. "I am so glad that one of you stepped forward!"

"But I didn't volunteer," the youth said. He resembled his father, Count Vincente, in that both of them looked like particularly dull cowherds, stolid, lantern-jawed, and strong as their own oxen, perfect for endurance and a simple task.

"Ah, I heard you say you wanted to be somewhere else," the wizard said, enjoying the lad's discomfiture. "That is convenient. I have somewhere for you to go." He clapped sharply once, then opened his palms. The clear blue bubble of crystal dropped out of empty air into his cupped hands. The dragonstone felt good to the touch, cool and hot at the same time. The cone of blue power it emitted, visible to anyone with even a touch of the talent, lit his fingers and splayed a pattern of light on the ceiling. He eyed Francisco. It was a foolproof mission, but de Monteleone was capable of increasing the intensity of his foolhardiness to undo even the greatest of safeguards. Thank goodness he had his noble rank to fall back upon. "This task is of the greatest importance to Enth. I need a messenger stout of heart, strong in bone and sinew, enduring in the face of adversity." *And gullible in wit and will,* Angelo thought, watching the boy straighten up on his stool at each increasing compliment. Francisco sprang to his feet.

"I will do it, sir!" he exclaimed.

"Good. Here are your instructions. Listen carefully." Angelo plunked the globe into the boy's palm. "Take this to the highest peak on the Naral Massif. Hold it up in the air. Wait until the dragon comes. Bring her here."

"That's all?" Francisco asked, clutching the stone orb.

"Yes!"

"No incantations? No spells? No potions? No magic passes or dances?"

"Oh, certainly, if you wish," Angelo said, patting him on the head, though the boy stood several hands taller than he did. "You may chant, 'Come, dragon, come,' and perform the tarantella. That won't help, but it might help keep you warmer on the mountaintop. On your way, then. Take a stout cloak, rations and a bedroll." He shooed Francisco toward the open portal. The lad hesitated in the doorway.

"What about a sword?"

"Good idea! She can use it to pick her teeth." Francisco scurried away, in search of supplies. *A sword! Really. To defend against a friendly dragon?* The other apprentices tittered. Angelo rounded upon them. "Don't laugh! He will have the easiest task of all of us. There is much to plan. Now, listen closely."

The Grandee Angelo, Court Wizard of Enth!" announced the herald pursuivant, as the Herald Regente himself was already engaged at the long table full of nobles and ministers of the realm. He repeated it, but his voice was drowned out in the hubbub. Angelo gave the balding, middle-aged man in the blue-and-silver livery a kindly look. None of them were ready for a situation like this.

"But why *aren't* we prepared?" the condestable demanded, probably echoing the thoughts of everyone present.

"Too long at peace," growled General Rafello. The chief of all the armed forces of Enth stood a head taller than anyone else present, and seemed even more massive because of his sapling-straight posture and heavy leather cloak. He flattened both rough palms on the broad planks of the table. Massive relief maps had been assembled from interlocking pieces like a giant jigsaw. Featureless game pawns painted gold for Enth's troops and red to indicate Solognian forces had been deployed on the carved valleys and passes. The red vastly outnumbered the gold.

CIRUELO

"It wasn't for want of me insisting we increase our defenses and soldiers under arms."

"Who could have foreseen that Sologne would invade?" Ricahembra Elisabetta Incypta asked. "Who would know that they were building up their army so much?"

"I did!" said Rafello. "Our late liege allowed the numbers to fall over the years of calm. We could have gone on longer, but our regente, forgive me for saying so, your serenity, rejected the suit of Prince Francour four times. He could not help but take it as an insult, not to mention dashing his kingdom's hopes. The decline of Sologne's economy has been known for some time. It would seem apparent that he wishes to take what he needs by means of force, as a last resort to solve their problems, and to assuage his pride. Now we do not have enough soldiers or siege weaponry to send to the front. Not that we would be able to counter so many krilla! Further reports from my scouts say there are as many as three thousand!"

Angelo slid into his chair on Zoraida's left. She sent him a hopeful glance. He smiled in a reassuring manner.

"Nonsense," said Count Guillerme Salazin, the realm's treasurer, his pointed black beard bobbing with every syllable. "That would be the hatching of two decades, and cost a fortune to feed. If they are so desperate, they do not have those resources. Your scouts panicked and multiplied the invaders by a hundred."

"How dare you suggest my scouts are cowards?" Rafello demanded, pounding both fists on the table. His mustaches seemed to uncurl and curl in his fury.

"What's done is done," Zoraida said, holding up her hands to silence them. "The enemy approaches! We must face this onslaught with what we have, not what we wish we had." It was well said, something that her late father might have uttered. The fretting ministers looked wistful and worried.

"With your permission, your serenity, I would send to Moris for reinforcements," Rafello said. "Their man-sized landsnakes could help hold back the ground forces!"

"Send the message immediately to the queen," the regente

said. The general flicked a finger in the direction of one of his military aides, who dashed out the door.

Angelo cleared his throat, drawing every eye in the room to him.

"It is at least two weeks' march from the south shore even once they sail across the sea, your serenity. They will never arrive in time. Escotio's army is close to our northern border, but still far away. We are on our own. Sologne is on the border closest to the castle. If the invaders are in the mountain pass, we have mere days to prepare a defense."

"What do you know of defending a realm, magician?" Rafello sneered. "You tell stories and make pretty pictures."

"He is a great wizard!" Zoraida said, her eyes flashing.

"If he is such a great wizard," the general said, lowering his enormous eyebrows over his bony nose, "then why doesn't he cause the Solognian army to turn around and go home?"

"That is precisely what I intend to do," Angelo said, confident and grave. The ministers broke out into exclamations of disbelief. From his eyes and hands, he sent colors to form shapes on the features of the raised relief map. In a moment, tiny figures marching two by two under a Solognian flag took the place of the clumsy pawns. "See here: they must come west through here to reach the castle. It is the only access point, so here your forces will meet them." A vast troop in gold, with Enth's dark-blue and silver banners flying, appeared at the mouth of the pass, blocking the red from advancing.

"You don't need to tell me that," Rafello said, his eyebrows lowering still farther. We will throw all our forces at them there. We will fight to the last soldier, to the last arrow and bolt in our quivers! They shall not conquer this citadel."

Angelo caused the two armies to wade into one another, swords arcing and arrows flying. Some fell immediately. Others bled convincingly from wounds in body or limb, but continued to fight. The red forces overwhelmed them and forced them back, back, back to the very gates of the castle and inside, where unarmed men and women in livery dropped to the ground, bleeding their lives out. Suddenly, the winged snakes swooped from the sky to worry the fighters in gold. They harried the cavalry that survived, and surrounded the keep. A tiny figure that resembled Zoraida slashed with a silver-bladed sword at the striking beasts. Her defenders fell one by one. Around him, the ministers gasped.

"And the krilla?" Angelo asked. "Do we have enough to withstand them and their poison? The archers and sword-wielders who ride upon them?"

Every eye turned to the general. His mustachios seemed to wilt.

"No," he said. "I have only forty krilla. My forces are spread to every border. They cannot gather here in time. Can you cause the earth to heave up and swallow Sologne's army? Can you cause lightning to rain down on them and destroy those cursed flying monsters? How can you achieve victory against such odds?"

Angelo couldn't help but smile, the expression lifting the corners of his mustache.

"I can't. But I can help to lessen the loss of life and cause Prince Francour to turn back. Not right away, but very soon after he arrives."

"How?" Zoraida asked, her eyes wide.

The wizard patted her hand. He had just struck on a desperate, but possible solution. "By making him think that he has won, but not the prize that he seeks."

Angelo's apprentices greeted the visiting ministers and other dignitaries with grace, helping them up the narrow stairs to the top of the mystic tower. The spire was under guard by the household cavalry, two dozen picked krilla riders, all that remained in the citadel of the airborne force.

As always, a crowd in the trimeter room was a tight fit, but every minister in the castle who had not taken to horse or to krilla wanted to watch Angelo's plan take shape. They clustered around the enormous crystal sphere, a relic of LaDarnel, the third court magician who had served the royal family of Enth, making a modicum of room for Zoraida, who had changed from her court finery into her field uniform of leather tunic and boots.

He had never been as proud of his apprentices as at that moment. Grandaa Alessandra TalEmbra, a big, strapping girl from the western provinces, her blond braids bound up under a borrowed helmet, stood with the volunteer archers and spear carriers in the very bottom of the pass. At the bottom of the sphere, they saw her gloved palm. All around the perimeter of the globe were the images of men and women in leathern tunics and caps, holding their weapons ready, every face as nervous as if they were facing a tax audit.

"How is it we see what is happening so far away?" Rafello asked, digging in one nostril with the nail of his little finger.

"The Law of Contagion," Angelo explained. "These two magical orbs touched one another during a joining ritual, so everything that happens around the one is visible through the other."

Hastily, the general whipped his finger away from his nose.

"Why do I not have one of these crystals?" Rafello demanded, to cover his embarrassment.

"You do not have the wits to use it," Angelo said, frankly. "If you had any magical talent, you would have learned it in childhood, and you would probably have been one of my students, instead of joining the army."

"I will conscript your apprentices, all of them!"

Angelo sighed.

"You nearly have, general. My students have left their studies to help to defend this realm. May we have this argument later?"

"Very well," Rafello said, the blaze in his eyes assuring Angelo that the discussion would be resumed in the very near future.

Alessandra held the crystal out to the left and right, just in time to see the fifty hunters disappear into the thick woods to either side of the two trimeter-wide gravel-topped road. Two hundred peasants armed with bows and spears, cloaked by wizardry in the semblance of trained fighters, stood more or less in formation, awaiting the signal. One company of real soldiers were split front and back, to keep them from running away. Angelo couldn't say he blamed them. They wanted to defend the realm, but they were scared, as any sensible person would be.

A deathly shriek came out of the very air, the cry of the krilla. Suddenly, the air was full of wings. The gigantic red-and-yellow-banded snakes, each with a human rider, swooped out of the sky toward the first ranks. At the company's head rode Francour, whooping and laughing.

"I hate him," Zoraida said, through gritted teeth. Angelo reached over to pat her hand.

The soldiers loosed quarrels from their crossbows, then dropped them onto their tethers to lift sword against the airborne foes.

"Let fly!" the master bowman bellowed from the woods. Arrows arched from among the trees. The riders had to raise their shields to protect themselves from the onslaught. At least one of the winged serpents fell, to be chopped to pieces by the Enthian defenders. But foot soldiers were no match for flying troops, especially with beasts that wielded a poisonous bite.

*Make it look good*, Angelo murmured. *Steady. Steady. Now!*

The Enth cavalry rose up from the forest. The lieutenant in charge, the finest rider in the realm with the finest steed, made straight for Francour. The prince recoiled, then raised his sword to defend himself. The lieutenant, acting on strict orders, zipped around him in a circle.

"Gnyaaah!" the lead officer shouted, putting his thumb to his nose. Then he lit out at a sharp vector to the south, his reptile almost flat out on the air.

"Gnyaaah!" the squad bellowed, following their commander's lead.

The prince's dark eyebrows shot up his forehead.

"Kill them!" he yelled, spurring his lashing steed.

As predicted, the Solognian force followed them, bellowing, shooting bolts from their crossbows. The Enthians fled, their krilla weaving from side to side to avoid the arrows. Below, suddenly deprived of their air cover, the Solognian army poured from the mountain pass, swords high and teeth bared.

The professional soldiers at the head of the Enth forces met them bravely, fighting with sword and shield, shouting their defiance. The peasants in their midst loosed their spears, fortunately missing all of the defenders. It soon became clear that the numbers of the invading force completely overwhelmed the number of Enth soldiers. At a nod from the captain of the armed forces, the peasants fled.

Alessandra held her position bravely, though the view through the crystal trembled with her fear. As the last spear-wielding peasant soldier passed her, she took to her heels after him. The pursuing Solognian troops looked puzzled, then triumphant. They bellowed their success, and began a chant of victory.

"The enemy comes," Count Guillerme said, glumly. "We must prepare."

"Indeed. Now is the time for you to conceal yourself, your serenity," Angelo told Zoraida.

She raised her head, her chin held proudly.

"I am the regente," she said. "I do not hide from any enemy. I must lead my people, to success or failure!"

"My dear, you are without a doubt the object of this invasion," Angelo said. "If they succeed in capturing you, it doesn't matter if we manage to expel them. Remain here. It is comfortable, and protected by myriad spells as well as the mystic mist. You can watch all through the crystal. It will obey your will."

"She has magic?" Rafello asked, looking from one to the other.

"Oh, yes," Angelo said, regarding her proudly. "She would have been a serviceable enchantress, but her destiny is to lead."

Rafello was accustomed to accepting orders without question, but this took a good deal of swallowing. Eventually, he managed it, and went on to the next concern. "But Francour seeks her. He will not stop until he finds her."

"And he shall find her," Angelo said, removing his tall hat and sending it floating up to the ceiling. "This is all part of the story we are telling the Solognians, the illusion we are performing for them." This transformation didn't even require touching his whitstone. The magic flowed from his eyes, mouth and palms, tickling up and down his body. He knew every plane and curve of her face and bestowed it on himself. His hair darkened and flowed into elegant braids, and his fluttering robes took on the semblance of Zoraida's best court gown. At the last minute, he made his beard and mustachios disappear, revealing smooth cheeks and jaw. He drew the rest of the power back inside himself to settle his nerves, and smiled at the ministers. "How do I look?"

The astonishment on every face proved he had succeeded. He preened and touched his cheek with a delicate forefinger. The ministers looked repulsed and intrigued at the same time.

"My disguise appears to be a success!" Angelo said. "Then, let us go meet my future consort." He hoisted his staff in one hand and headed for the stairs.

"Yes . . . your serenity." Rafello hopped to open the door for him.

Not a few of the castle denizens had wanted to throw Angelo from the walls instead of going along with his humiliating suggestions. Only the order of the condestable to follow his instructions kept him from being murdered. His maroon-clad apprentices had spread out across the vast citadel's environs to make preparations and to find hiding places from which to work their wonders. All the visible signs of wealth that they could remove were pulled down and hidden, in the bottom of middens, the depths of sewers, underneath pig sties, and below washtubs and piles of dirty clothes.

The ministers arrayed themselves in their oldest and most disreputable garments, some borrowed from their own grooms and servants. Scarcely a jewel was to be found among their adornments.

"This is a disgrace," Ricahembra Elisabetta snarled, swiping her hair underneath a tattered veil tied with a ribbon, without her usual tiara to anchor it.

"It is temporary," Angelo promised her. "Rescue is coming, I swear it."

"Hmmph!"

"The enemy comes!" a guard called from the wall above the portcullis.

"Fling open the gates!" Angelo shouted. He arranged himself with dignity, chin high and borrowed crown set straight on his hair.

Sologne's army marched in, but the prince himself flitted in over the walls on his krilla, followed by a score of soldiers and attendants on their own steeds. His cheeks were wind-whipped until his normally pale cheeks bloomed red, and his long black hair lay in tangles. His hissing steed descended to the inlaid stones of the courtyard, folded its wings, and coiled into a loop. Francour bounded from the saddle. His brows were drawn down in fury.

"Regente Zoraida, your insult to me could not be ignored one more day," he said. "I have defeated your incompetent and cowardly troops." Beside Angelo, Rafello growled. Angelo kicked him with the side of his foot. The illusion he had cast on the general to imitate Zoraida's petite, dark-skinned lady-in-waiting wouldn't hold for long if he emitted those baritone rumbles. "I claim your realm and all the riches therein as tribute to me and my family! You are now my chattel. Bow to me!"

Angelo held out his skirts and curtseyed. This was as much playacting as the appearance of dignity he maintained every day. Rafello and the other ministers and servants gasped to see "her" kneel on Francour's demand.

"I yield, Prince Francour," Angelo said, humbly. The Solognian grinned and grasped one of his hands to yank her upright.

"I can be merciful and gracious. We shall be married soon. But I will not be your consort. As your conqueror, you shall be mine, as is all you once ruled. You are regente no longer. And don't you dare bite me again!"

"I won't. In truth, we welcome you to our realm—your realm, your grace," Angelo said, careful to maintain Zoraida's fluting tones. "I did not *want* to insult you, sir, but I could not let you see the truth of our situation. If your messenger didn't tell you of what he could not possibly fail to have seen, it was only postponing the terrible day for a little while. We were too ashamed to admit it."

Francour's brows flew upward.

"Admit what?"

Angelo wrung his hands together. "The depths of our embarrassment! The shame of our destitution. The terrible situation in which my *entire realm* has found itself. The gleam of our former glory has faded away, sire! Thank you, oh, thank you for coming to our rescue!"

Then, Francour saw for the first time the careful desolation of the courtyard. All of Angelo's apprentices, under Mistress Drucella's iron hand, had cast illusions everywhere: broken windows, cracked stonework, missing slates on the roof. Maintaining them would take all of their concentration and not a little of the precious whitstone in Angelo's staff, yet he had to admit how effective the semblance was. Horses and cattle he knew to be well-fed looked skinny and ill-kept, and the people of the castle had rubbed dirt into their clothing and faces.

"I am afraid," Angelo said, "that we are not able to give you the welcome that you deserve."

How long can you maintain this subterfuge?" Drucella asked Angelo. His journeywoman served as his tiring-woman, giving her the excuse to come and go from his quarters. She brushed and braided the wizard's long hair, just in case Francour or any of his soldiers burst into the regente's private chambers, as they had more than once over the previous three days. From the artfully crooked window frame, the magician peered down at the scene in the courtyard. Francour led his troops into one building after another, searching for the riches that he assumed were there. So far, their quest had been in vain.

The Solognian quartermaster, a stout man of four or five decades, peered over the pathetic cattle and fowl presented for his inspection, looking for suitable animals for his master's feasting. The castle's cooks had been given free rein to adulterate any meal as they chose, and their efforts had been magnificently horrible. A few cunningly placed rats' heads and a very spoiled potato had caused one of the cook's boys to be beaten and tossed out of the feast hall the previous night. The servers had quite rightly congratulated themselves.

"As long as I need to," Angelo said. He touched the whitstone in his staff. It showed signs of erosion under the constant drain he had to put on it. His apprentices were too inexperienced to mete out the very minimum of whits needed. Angelo could feel every fragment of stone burst away from it. He worried that the stone would not last until he managed to horrify Francour into leaving. If it failed, all would be revealed, all but the presence of Zoraida in the tower. Thankfully, she was safe, no matter what happened. "The dragon must come soon."

He peered out across the mountains, scanning the skies. To the north, he saw the blue cone of light, the beacon as yet unanswered. Francisco faithfully maintained his vigil, to no avail. Curse it, had Andoria gone off with another one of her lovers? She must come. She must!

Yet, by day ten of the terrible occupation, Andoria had still not appeared. Even Angelo, who had to show the bravest face of all, began to tire of the taste of moldy cheese and stale bread. Not even illusion could disguise the dusty odor and rancid taste. Many of the visitors had gone down sick because of the spoiled food.

Once in a while, the servants tried to make themselves some decent food in the lower chambers of the castle, but if the invaders smelled good cooking, they fell on it like a pack of hungry dogs, kicking and punching others out of the way to find something edible.

The Solognians had raided the town at the bottom of the hill, but the mayor and guildmasters had been forewarned, too. Drucella herself had ridden down in secret to explain the situation and convince them to cooperate. The quartermaster and a hundred troops returned, looking shamefaced at the meager and downright dangerous bounty that they had obtained. Angelo marveled at the number of rotten apples and ill-cured meats that emerged from cellars. Even he began to wonder if Enth was as well-off as it had once seemed.

In desperation, the krilla were sent home again and again to the borders of Sologne to bring victuals. Risking a revolt by his own troops, Francour kept those for himself and his inner circle.

"Ah, my bride!" the Solognian prince chortled, as Angelo made a timid entrance into the feasting hall, clad in demure pink and white. Not one of the nobility of Enth was present, only Francour's cronies and their krilla.

They had not been entirely unsuccessful in their search for valuable goods. In the corners of the room, priceless tapestries and silk carpets lay rolled up. On top of those were scattered silver ewers and bowls, golden platters, jeweled goblets, tiaras, jewelry and chains of office ripped from the necks of the ministers. Angelo smiled to himself. The hoard did not represent a tenth of what had been on display up until the day before the Solognians arrived.

In the giant fireplace, a whole pig and two fat geese imported from Sologne turned on a spit, dripping grease into the hissing flames. The smell of roasting meat made the wizard's mouth water. Francour tore off a hunk of meat from the haunch of rabbit in his hand with his teeth.

"Join us!" He beckoned for Angelo to sit close, but the wizard kept a distance. "No, here! Beside me!" He wrapped an arm around the wizard and hauled him to his side. He held the haunch of coney under his nose. "Here! Have a bite."

Angelo hated to show any signs of weakness, but the meat smelled so good. It had been days since his last decent meal. He leaned forward to take the morsel, but Francour yanked it away at the last second, and shoved his grinning face at him instead.

"Kiss me, Zoraida!" he shouted, as the others laughed.

Angelo was grateful that the regente was hidden away in the

tower. If Francour had tried that on her, she would have bitten right through his lip. Angelo raised his hands in mock horror and pushed the prince back with all his strength. Francour went flying backward. Angelo sprang up, out of the prince's reach.

"Oh, no, my liege! Not until the wedding!"

"By heaven, you're a fierce one." Francour said, scrambling to his feet. He threw the joint of meat into the fireplace. One of the snakes pursued it, then lay on the stones hissing in fury as the flames exploded, depriving it of its prize. "Yes, the wedding! Let's get that over with as soon as we can! At least, I will get some decent wedding presents out of this pathetic country."

Francour ordered Condestable Inez and Count Guillerme to accompany him, Angelo and his minions down to the city at the base of the citadel's peak, Rainbow Gate. When they flew in, Angelo was delighted at the seeming devastation and dire poverty he surveyed from above. Drucella and the apprentices had done well in the city. Rainbow Gate looked as if it was haunted, not a living town. Rats scurried from shadow to shadow, chittering. Angelo recognized the fine hand of Dayeed, his youngest apprentice, who showed marked talent for enchanting vermin. One day he would be able to control even the largest of animals. The boy had to be hidden somewhere close by.

As the Solognian herald had demanded of them, the lord mayor and the head of each of the guilds were present in the town square. They regarded the Solognians and their reptilian mounts with equal dread.

"Why, no, my lord," the mayor said. Ordinarily, he looked plump and prosperous, and his wife dressed in the height of fashion. Instead, his clothes appeared to have been fashioned from scratchy, noisome gunny sacks belted with rope. Angelo applauded their initiative. "We have nothing better than what we send up to the citadel."

"It's the best place in the realm," the master of the millers' guild said. "We're proud of that."

"We send them our very best work," the master goldsmith

added, smiling nervously. He had to wear his chain of office, despite it drawing the greedy eye of their visitor. "It is to honor our lady regente." He bowed to Angelo, who dipped his head slightly in return.

Francour looked as though he wanted to snatch the ornate chain. He balled up his fist instead and held it under the merchant's chin.

"I marry your regente tomorrow. Bring all of your gold and silver to me as gifts for that happy celebration! Go back and bring it all forth, now! I demand it, as your new lord and master!"

The master smith hesitated. He cleared his throat, and nervously stroked the necklace.

"But, your grace," he said, with an oily bow. "By the laws of our land, as my *new* liege I owe you every copper of my taxes, but my merchandise is my *property*. Surely you don't mean to confiscate that which I *own*." He spread out his hands. "There are some who would say the same might happen to your own merchants' representatives, if they cross the border into Enth, to trade with us, should such a thing become known. The practice might even spread to other lands, and anarchy would ensue."

Francour gaped like a fish, his mouth opening and closing.

"That is true, your grace," Angelo said, trying to look demure. "The rule of law is important. To suspend that would prove . . . difficult."

"No, we wouldn't want to set a precedent, would we?" the condestable said, cocking her head at the prince. "What would your esteemed father say, your grace, if you were to suspend the *rule of law*?"

Francour grumbled. He balled up his fists, but his lackeys prevented him from lunging forward to use them on the guildmasters. These days his complexion never seemed to dim from red fury.

"You will show honor to me as your new liege! I expect wedding presents! And send me some decent food for the feast!"

"Of course, your grace. Those will come from our very

hearts, I assure you, your grace!" The guildmasters shot Zoraida sympathetic glances as they departed, with Angelo riding pillion behind Francour on his krilla.

*Ha-ha!* Angelo thought. *Time to make it worse yet.*

As he and Francour landed in the courtyard, he rubbed his hand over the whitstone in his staff. The mystic stone had shrunk by a third already, but he had no choice. Instead of just seeing, they must *feel* this one.

Screaming erupted from the kitchens at the rear of the castle. The frantic noise spread, followed by hissing and clattering. Servants erupted from the door and fled past them.

"What now?" Francour demanded, then gasped. "By all that is sacred!"

Out of the door came a wave of black, shiny-shelled cockroaches the size of hen's eggs. The flood of insects poured out onto the stone paving. A host of them made for Francour's mount. They crested over it, making the winged snake leap about, biting at its own tail. It took off into the sky, followed by the other krilla.

"Come back here!" Francour yelled, then batted at the ones that started to climb his boots. The other Solognians batted at the gigantic insects, shrieking in fear. Even though it ate away at his stone further, he made the roaches nip at their victims. The newcomers fled, batting and stamping on their small attackers. They scrambled over one another to reach higher ground, as if to escape the insects.

Crack! The whitstone in Angelo's staff split with an audible report. Angelo stared, horrified. He had to stop, lest it crumble away entirely. Hastily, he gathered what energy he could, and let it flow out through his hands. The wave of roaches receded and seemed to melt away, down into the cracks between the paving stones of the courtyard.

"Fire and lightning!" Francour swore, as the last insect disappeared. "Does that happen often?"

Angelo stood demurely on the steps, the only one left in the courtyard, letting the waves of roaches bump up against the skirts of his robe as if they were of no moment. "Only once a day, my lord. Usually there are more of them, you know."

"Once a day?" Francour repeated, eyes wide with disbelief. "This place is insane! The wedding will take place tomorrow! Then, I can leave this place under a governor. You will return with me to Sologne."

"As you wish, my liege," Angelo said. "May I return to my quarters to prepare?"

"Anything!" Francour shouted.

Angelo curtseyed, and retreated to the regente's private quarters.

So he was to be carried off to Sologne, he thought as he stumped up the stairs. Well, if nothing else, then Francour still would not have captured Zoraida. He glanced out of the arched window of the regente's chamber toward his tower, to reassure himself that the protective blue cloud was in place. To his horror, it was gone.

"Well, what's been happening?" Zoraida asked.

Angelo spun. The young regente sat in her dressing table chair, one knee up on the arm.

"My lady, you can't be here!" Angelo sputtered.

"I have to know what is happening to my people!" Zoraida said. "I have been watching, but I have to do something! I cannot believe how terrible everything looks, everywhere. What is with all these spider webs?" She kicked at the nearest, a huge, wispy octagon clinging between her bed and the wall. Her foot passed right through. "Oh! They're not real."

"My lady, I must protest," Angelo said, lowering his voice. "The tower was the safest place in the realm for you. You must return there immediately." He took her arm and urged her toward the door.

Zoraida shook loose from his grasp. "I am not afraid of that donkey. You will save me and all of my people. You have the power to defeat this monstrous brat! Call up a windstorm! Flood the castle and wash them away! Strike him dead with lightning!"

"I cannot!" Angelo exclaimed, wringing his hands around his half-ruined staff. "I'm not a real wizard, regente!"

The words were out before he could stop them.

She eyed him as if she had never seen him before. Angelo felt his heart sink into his borrowed boots. Her voice dropped to a dangerously quiet tone.

"What do you mean by that, Angelo?"

He bowed his head. The truth had at last come out, as he knew one day it would.

"I am but a humble illusionist, my liege. Your father was satisfied with my skills. So far they have been adequate to my position. Unfortunately, I can't call down the lightning or cause a chasm to open in the earth, as dearly as I would love to do that for you. I would work any wonder you wished, if only I could!"

"But, all those things you do? The pixies? The grand fireworks?"

"What I do, I do very well," he admitted. "But they're not great workings of magic. I can fool the eye, the ear, even the hand. I change the seeming, not the substance."

"Oh." That small syllable cut through to his heart.

"You must hide, my lady," Angelo said. "He means to marry you tomorrow! I mean, me. Go back, now, before . . ."

"Before *what*?"

To Angelo's horror, the Solognian prince was at the door. Francour looked gleeful. Angelo longed to have the power of the lightning, if only to strike the expression from his face. The invader stalked into the room and circled the two.

"Well, two delectable treasures! I don't know which one to kiss first. Which of you is the real Zoraida?"

"Me, of course, my lord!" Angelo said, at once. Francour grabbed him by the arm. Angelo began to create a physical illusion to hide his mustachios, but Francour cast aside his staff before he could complete the illusion. He pressed his lips to Angelo's. As the wizard feared, the Solognian got a mouthful of beard. Francour shoved him away, sputtering.

"A hairy face! That is disgusting! So, this must be my promised bride!" He seized Zoraida and bent his mouth to hers. She promptly chomped down on his lower lip. He punched her in the side of the head, so she let go and fell dazed to the floor. Francour hauled her up by one arm. "Yes, that is the Zoraida I remember. We will be married *now*, and you shall return with me to my father's kingdom. As for you," he said, kicking Angelo in the side as the wizard's disguise failed, "to the dungeons with you! To the most remote cell, to await your execution! Impersonating the sacred person of the heir to the throne, humiliating me and my people and," he added, shuddering, "making me kiss you!"

"No, your grace!" Angelo begged, falling to his knees. "I am a creature of the light! Do not shut me in the darkness!"

Francour let out a bark of cruel laughter. His men seized Angelo and dragged him along the corridor. The prince led the way down the three flights of dank stone stairs to the dungeon.

"They told me there was treasure here," he said, signing to the shamefaced jailor to open the banded wooden door at the very end of the cavern. "Just like all the other lies here, there was nothing. Now, you can have all the treasure to yourself."

Francour's men threw him into the cell, then slammed the door on him before he could spring up and escape. Angelo heard the key turn in the lock. He peered through the pinhole-sized opening in the door. The prince grinned at him.

"Never let him out," the prince told the jailor. "In fact—" He snatched the key and snipped it in half with a metal pincer. "There. No more interference. No more illusions. Now, I shall claim my bride!"

Angelo turned away as the light receded. All preparations had been made for the next day, so there was no reason to delay. Zoraida would no doubt be thrust into a gown and cloak, decked with flowers and tied up by Francour's minions so she could not escape. She would be married against her will.

*Fortunately*, the court wizard mused, feeling his way toward the rear wall of the cell, *Francour is oh, so predictable*. Yes, the notch in the brick was exactly where he had made it. A little digging in the clay helped to dislodge it. *Carefully, now,* he admonished himself. Wrapped in a tiny scrap of silk was a fragment he had chipped from his whitstone, to be left here in case of need. He let it rest in his hand, letting it absorb what energy he had in him. Sitting on a hank of decaying straw scattered on the cold stone floor in the dark, he drew from his imagination, the storybooks he had read, and songs he had heard from the troubadours—the dark stories, the ones that had always frightened him as a child.

Drucella wore a pendant upon which he had once used the Law of Contagion so he could see what she saw. He reached out to that.

As he had surmised, everyone in the castle had been forced at swordpoint to the chapel. Drucella stood close to the altar. Zoraida kept turning toward her, her eyes desperate. Francour held her arm firmly. He had tied her hands behind her back.

The royal chaplains, the Priest and Priestess of Life, protested the haste.

"This is not a willing union," the priestess said. "The woman must accept the man."

Francour drew his side dagger and held it to Zoraida's throat. "She accepts me. Say it, woman, or your servants will die one by one."

"No, your serenity," Rafello said. "We will die for you."

"No," Zoraida said. She tossed her head. "I consent. I brought us to this pass."

Francour pointed the knife at the priest. "Begin. Get it over with."

The priest looked angry, but he had no choice.

"May all who wish to celebrate gather here now!" he intoned, holding his arms high.

Angelo let power flow from his eyes, his ears, and his heart, filling the room with ghostly figures, their faces drawn from the catafalques and paintings that lined the chapel.

"By the light, that is the eleventh regente, Milagra!" the priestess gasped, pointing at a small figure with long braids that brushed the ground. Her hand flew toward a towering figure with shoulders twice the width of his waist and a massive jaw. "And the thirtieth, Octavio the third, and . . ." She paled, swayed and fell to the ground. Her acolytes rushed to her aid, but half the guests fled the hall, screaming in horror.

"Spirits?" Francour demanded, lowering the point of his knife. "This castle is haunted?"

"My ancestors," Zoraida said, her eyes flashing, though she looked frightened. "They come to protect me."

"From me?" Francour's voice squeezed down to a stripling's squeak.

But that was only the beginning of Angelo's imaginings. He touched the back of Francour's neck with cold and clammy fingers that made the prince jump. The memorial plaques on the walls seemed to sway, and ghostly music rose from the choir stalls, even though no singers or musicians sat there.

"Continue!" Francour bellowed.

Then, spiders the size of dogs dropped from the ceiling on webs like silver rope, reaching for the Solognian nobles. They quailed, hunching their backs to avoid the monsters. Shapeless ghosts swooped through the room, passing through the humans and leaving behind only a cold touch. Bats flew, shrieking, to chivvy out those with any courage left.

"I'm going home, my liege!" one of the Solognian nobles shouted.

"I, too!" echoed another. They ran for the door.

"Cowards!" Francour shouted, his face as red as a beet. He snarled at the priests. "Continue!"

By then, only Drucella and Rafello remained. Still, Francour held his would-be bride at the altar. The priest and priestess fought to make themselves heard over the wailing and ghostly music.

Angelo cudgeled his brain for more and more horrifying images and sensations. *Go away, curse you!* he thought.

He felt burning in the palm of his hand as the stone gave up spark after spark. With a cautious forefinger, he prodded the tiny fragment of whitstone. It had dissolved into powdery sand. The illusions in the chapel began to fade.

*No, not yet!* he pleaded with it. He channeled all the energy in his body into the stone, feeding it. All the horrors must continue.

He hung rotting faces in every corner of the chapel. He made the stones beneath Francour's feet shake. He loved Zoraida as if she was his own child. She counted upon him. All he had he owed to her and her father. If it cost him his life, he would drive away this menace. He painted the complexion of one long dead over Zoraida's beautiful face, eyes hollow, skin dripping from her bones.

At last, Francour broke, dropping her arm. "I cannot stand this place a moment longer!" he shrieked.

*That is all I needed to hear,* Angelo thought. The blackness of the cell moved in and overwhelmed his vision.

Angelo? Grandee Wizard, wake up!" a child's voice demanded. "Master? Master!"

"Oh, for pity's sake, put this in his hand," Drucella's voice insisted.

The only sensation Angelo felt was in his right palm, a smooth—stone?—shaped like half an egg. His whitstone! Greedily, he drew from it, drinking its power, feeling the warmth flow, until he had an arm, a body, feet, another arm, and a head, all of them aching. He fed on the stone's energy, though the egg shrank in his grasp. The burst of magic flowing from it jolted him back from the very edge of death.

With a gasp, Angelo opened his eyes. He was propped on the stinking, cold stone steps of the dungeon, surrounded by his apprentices, all wide-eyed with worry. The top of the silverwood staff rested in the palm of his hand. He drew it up to look at it, puzzled as to the gap at the top. Then, his muddled brain puzzled out what he was looking at. The great whitstone that he had had for decades was reduced to a mere grain of sand. Ah, well, he would have to find another. He found his voice at last.

"Is Zoraida all right?"

Drucella nodded. Her usually perfect hair was scattered over her shoulders, and she had tears in her eyes.

"It's over," she said. "They're leaving. Can you stand?"

Angelo felt as weak as a wilted leaf, but he chuckled. "To watch them leave? I can fly!"

This whole nation is a madhouse!" Francour kicked his steed in its scaly flanks. The shrieking krilla rose into the air, and the rest of his minions' beasts with it. "I leave it to decay under its own rot!"

The castle staff cheered as the Solognians flew eastward in the overcast sky.

"They will come back," Zoraida whispered. She trembled in Angelo's arm. "I don't want to see him again. He is insane."

"I think that will be highly unlikely," Angelo said. He had looked to the north the moment he had found a window to look out of. The cone of blue light in the distance was gone. He clutched the last minute fragment of whitstone in his palm. It would hold together for one more message, and one final great illusion.

*I am no warrior,* Angelo thought, guiltily. *I have no stomach for this. But Zoraida must be safe.*

He sent his will toward the north, pointing toward the rising Solognian force. *Those, my dear friend. They threaten* my *nest. Will you take them?*

The thought came back with a hearty chuckle. *Krilla are my favorite food.*

In his hands, Angelo sculpted the semblance of a plump white dove, and threw it into the air. It rose up among the circling winged snakes and their riders.

"A dove of peace!" Francour sneered down at the people in the courtyard. "My father will make war against them until the mountains crumble!"

The Solognians laughed. One of them drew his sword, making as if to chop the bird in half in midair, as a final insult to Enth.

But, something over a trimeter from the shining dove, an obstruction in the air caused it to rebound back, almost out of the swordsman's hand. The others, all of the armed krilla cavalry of the Solognian army and Francour's minions, flew close to see what the problem was. Angelo clapped his hands, and the semblance fell away. In the place of the tiny bird flew a full-grown, silver-scaled dragon. It smiled, showing rows of sharp, white teeth. The krilla screamed in panic, scattered and streaked away over the horizon.

"Stop!" Francour bellowed, as his steed raced away, wings frantically flapping, no longer under his control. His voice receded into the distance. "It's only an illusion! Halt!"

Andoria wheeled lazily on the air, and flew after them at her leisure. She liked to play with her prey a while. Angelo was glad he did not have to watch. Francour might survive, or he might not. The wizard turned to bow to the regente.

"They will not return, your serenity," he said.

The interrupted wedding feast became a celebration for all the defenders. Musicians suddenly remembered how to tune their instruments, and everyone donned their long-neglected finery. Somehow, sweetmeats, good fruit, and cheeses sprang up from the very earth. To their astonishment and pleasure, Angelo's apprentices were praised and toasted with good wine that almost magically appeared from cellars, sheds, and haystacks.

"Don't let it go to your heads," the court wizard admonished their glowing faces. "You'll be back learning basic skills tomorrow morning, without fail."

His stern words didn't diminish his pupils' joy in the slightest. *Nor should it*, he thought, expansively. Ah, he was proud of them.

The dancing and gaiety went on until the shadow of the dragon overspread the courtyard. The merrymakers screamed and huddled together in terror. The music died away.

"She will not harm you!" Angelo called. "Do not fear!"

Andoria circled the castle until Angelo pointed down the curving pathway toward the inlaid circle at the top of the road from the valley. The dragon flew to it and backwinged the air, waiting.

"I must go to her," he told Zoraida.

"I will come with you," she said.

"Not without me, your serenity!" Rafello said, horrified. "That's a dragon!"

"She is our savior," Zoraida said, taking Angelo's arm. "I owe her the gratitude of all my realm."

Andoria dropped a glowing blue egg into Angelo's hand. The dragonstone.

"Your apprentice gave me this," she said. "He makes his way back. A faithful boy."

"I thank you, great one," Angelo said, bowing. He held the sphere up to her. "Take this back, my friend. Your debt is more than paid."

"Keep it," said the dragon, a glint in her ruby eyes. "That was fun. I must return to my eggs. The imp I left caring for them will be . . . impatient."

"That is their nature," the wizard said, gravely. He bowed deeply. "Farewell, my friend."

"We will see one another soon," Andoria said. "Bring a sheep. In fact, bring two."

"I shall!" Angelo laughed, feeling at ease for the first time in more than ten days.

"Not a real magician, eh?" the regente asked, leading them back along the winding white path to the castle. Rafello fell in behind them, his big shoulders at ease for once.

Angelo smiled.

"I . . . give the illusion of one, in any case."

# *A Bitter Thing*

*written by*

## *N. R. M. Roshak*

*illustrated by*

JAZMEN RICHARDSON

---

### ABOUT THE AUTHOR

*N. R. M. Roshak lives in Ottawa, Canada, with a spouse, a young child, an elderly cat, and a revolving menagerie that currently includes a pet slug and a cannibalistic brine shrimp. The author writes:*

*"I grew up reading my father's extensive SF/F collection, from Asimov to Zelazny. I loved science, but even more, I loved imagining myself into alien points of view: what would it be like to be human-but-not, or human-but-other? I had planned to study science at university, until I read Thomas Nagel's famous paper 'What Is It Like to Be a Bat?' which argues that we can never know what it's like to be a bat, only what it's like to be a human having bat experiences. To a longtime imaginer of self-as-other, this was like waving a red flag in front of a bull. I plunged into the argument, only realizing once I held a philosophy-and-math degree that I greatly prefer* imagining *to* arguing.

*"I'm often asked what one can do with a degree in philosophy and math, other than philosophy of math. For me, the answer was a career in IT. After many years wrangling data and databases, and a few wrangling a small child, I've returned to imagining. I may never know what it is like to be a bat, a telepath, or an alien; but there's much to be learned in the imagining, to explore what it means to be human by imagining what it is to be partly or wholly inhuman."*

### ABOUT THE ILLUSTRATOR

*Jazmen Richardson was born in 1998 in Auburn, New York. Living in the middle of nowhere most of her life, her imagination was able to roam through the fields surrounding her home.*

*Jazmen has been drawing and creating stories since she could walk and hold a pencil. Whether they made sense to the viewer or not at the time, each story's characters were as real to her as another family member.*

*Though her family is full of creative hearts, she is the first to pursue it as a career.*

*After graduating a year early from high school to pursue an artistic mentorship, Jazmen was able to attend Ringling College of Art and Design of Sarasota, Florida to study illustration and the business of art and design.*

*She has been working in digital art for two years now, and is moving toward a specialty in oil painting.*

*Jazmen concurrently works convention-like events striving to make connections with other artists and improve herself and her work. She may be quiet, but there is nothing more gratifying than meeting new faces and experiencing stories other than her own.*

# *A Bitter Thing*

"But O, how bitter a thing it is to look into happiness through another man's eyes." —Shakespeare, *As You Like It* (V.ii.20)

I should have known that something was wrong when I found Teese in the backyard, staring at the sky. It was sunset and the horizon was a particular shade of pale teal. At first I thought Teese was just admiring the sunset, but then I realized he was trembling all over. His eyes were wide, and irregular patterns swept over his skin, his chromatophores opening and closing at random, static snow sprinkling his skin.

I touched his shoulder. "Are you all right?"

Above us, the sky darkened toward night. Teese shook himself like a dog, blinked, looked at me. "That sunset," he said. "We don't . . . these colors . . . this doesn't happen on our world."

"You don't have sunsets?" As I understood it, sunsets should happen anywhere there was dust in the air.

"No, no," he said. "Of course, we have sunsets, Ami, but they tend more toward the red side of the spectrum. Your planet is so rich in blues. These colors, they're not very common on my world. I suppose I was surprised by my reaction to seeing that particular shade of blue spread across the sky." He smiled down at me. "Anyway, it's all changed now. Fleeting as a sunset, isn't that the expression?"

Teese was back to his usual smooth articulateness, so I wrote it off as his being momentarily overcome by the Earth's breathtaking beauty. In retrospect, that was pretty arrogant and anthropocentric of me. But at the time, I thought: who wouldn't be struck dumb by my amazing planet?

That night, Teese stared deep into my eyes as we made love, and trembled, just a bit. Static flared across his cheeks as he came. His heart-shaped pupils flared wide, drinking me in, and he murmured "I could stare into your eyes forever."

So, of course, I thought we were all right. We *were* all right. However unlikely, however improbable, what could it be but love?

The next warning sign came weeks later, when Teese painted the linen closet blue. He moved out all the towels and sheets, took out the shelves, painted the walls (and the ceiling, and the back of the door) greenish-blue, and perched on a stool in the middle of the closet. He called it his "meditation closet," jokingly, and said that he went in there to relax. At first it was for minutes at a time, then slowly his "meditation time" grew to hours.

"The things your people do with color are amazing to me," he said. "So many colors, and you put them everywhere."

"What, you don't have paint where you come from?"

"Of course we have paint," he said. "But we use it for art. No one would think to put gallons of blue and green in cans for people to take home and spread all over their house. It would cost . . ." He paused. Interstellar currency conversions were impossible, finding correspondences of value almost as difficult. "Many years of my salary, I think, to paint just this closet."

"Well, that makes sense. If you went to an art supply store here and got your paint in little tiny tubes, it would cost a lot more here, too."

"And the colors," he continued. "I think I have told you that most of our colors are in reds and browns and oranges. Even in paintings, we don't have so many shades of blue."

"That's weird," I said. "I mean, you can see just as many shades of blue, right?"

"Yes, but . . ." He considered. "Ami, I think that you have so much blue that you don't see how it surrounds you. You can make a painting with a blue sky and blue water, and use one hundred different shades of blue, and everyone sees it as normal and right. But think of another color that you don't have in such abundance, like purple. Imagine a painting with nothing but one hundred shades of purple."

His words triggered a memory. "I actually had a painting like that once," I admitted. "I found it in the trash in college. It had a purple sky and a purple-black sea and two really badly painted white seagulls. It was so awful that I had to keep it."

Amusement fluttered across his skin. "Tacky, right? Well, that's what most of my people would think of your sea and sky paintings. But I love it. I love to be surrounded by blue."

"Meditating?"

He waved an arm noncommittally. "Ommmm," he said, brown fractals of laughter flashing across his skin.

Then Teese bought one of those fancy multicolor LED light bulbs, tuned it to the exact shade of the walls, and didn't come out for a day.

He was in the closet when I left for work, and still there when I got home. I tapped on the door—no answer. I told myself to give him his space and went about fixing dinner, even though it was his turn to cook. Teese's diet was similar enough to ours that we could cook for each other, though there was a long list of vegetables he was better off without. I knocked on the door when dinner was ready and called his name. No answer. I ate without him.

Later, I pressed my ear against the door but heard only my own heartbeat against the wood. It was dark by then, and blue light seeped out from under the door.

Finally, I eased the door open a crack and peeked in. Teese was sprawled on the floor next to the upturned stool, eyes vacant, skin utterly blank.

I yelled his name, shook him, even slapped his face. My fingers trembled as I pressed them urgently into his skin. I remembered that Teese had two hearts, but I couldn't remember where they were, or how to find his pulse. There was no one I could call, no doctor or ambulance who could help him. I was alone with Teese, and Teese was gone, sick, maybe dying.

I dragged him out into the hallway, slowly. Teese doesn't have any bones to speak of. He's all head and muscled limbs. Normally he holds himself upright on four powerfully muscled limbs and uses the other two like arms. Passed out, he was a tangle of heavy rubber hoses filled with wet cement. I had to pull the blanket off the bed, roll him onto the blanket, and drag the blanket out of the closet with Teese on it.

I stood over him in the hallway and felt terribly alone.

I had met Teese at a party I hadn't planned to go to. At the last minute I'd let myself be swayed by the rumors that one of *them* would be there. A so-called hexie. Their ship had landed months ago, and while the VIPs on board were busy hammering out intergalactic trade deals, most of the ship's crew were just sailors who wanted to get off the ship, get drunk, and maybe get to know some locals. They'd been showing up by ones and twos at bars and clubs and parties all over town. I'd seen the hexies in the news, heard about their appearances at bars and parties, but never met one in person. And like everyone else, I was curious.

I saw him the moment I stepped in the door: big head held up above the crowd, two long and flexible arms gesticulating, one of them holding a drink. His eyes swept the room, scanned over me, and snapped back. From there, it was like a romance novel, of the kind I'd always found tedious and unrealistic. Our gazes locked. He stopped midsentence, handed his drink to someone without looking, and started pushing his way across the room to me. My heart hammered in my chest. Of course, I couldn't take my eyes off him, but why was he staring at me?

He stopped in front of me and took my hand, coiling his powerful armtip around my fingers as gently as I'd cradle a moth.

"I am Teese," he said. "Forgive me for being so direct, but I have never seen eyes as beautiful as yours before."

Hackneyed words, but they sounded fresh coming from his lipless mouth.

"I'm Ami," I stammered. "And I've never seen anything like you either."

Orange and brown checks rippled across his face. Later I would learn that this meant interest, arousal, excitement. I let him lead me to a quiet corner.

We talked. He told me about the ship, the long watches tending to the cryo boxes, the vastness of interstellar space. I told him about my job at the CITGO station and my apartment and the time my cat died.

"When I look at you," he said, "I feel things that I've never felt before."

What else could I do? I took him home, and he stayed.

Now I was alone in my hallway with Teese unconscious. I stepped around his arms and closed the linen closet, and sat down on the ground next to him. Soft blue light leaked out from under the closet door. I turned on the hall light and turned off the closet light, for lack of anything more constructive to do. Then I sat back down on the ground beside Teese and wondered what to do next. Smelling salts probably wouldn't help an alien from another planet, had I even had any on hand.

I could sprinkle water on his face, but I had no idea if that would work on him. I could pinch him.

I could sit next to him and stare at his open, blank eyes and wish I'd thought to ask him for a way to contact his ship.

I could search his things for a way to contact his ship, but I didn't want to go there if I could avoid it. Teese had been living with me for two months, which is both a long time and not long at all, and as far as I could tell, he'd never gone through my closet or papers while I was at work. I owed him the same respect.

Teese stirred sluggishly on the floor next to me.

I leaned over him. "Teese?"

His eyes focused on me. "Ohhh, Ami," he said, half moaning. And then his skin was suddenly, completely covered in violently red spots. Across his face, all up and down his arms, from the dome of his head to his armtips, he was covered with hexagonal measles that shifted and spun.

Teese's emotions showed on his skin, but I had never seen this one before, never seen such a violent and complete display.

I laid a gentle finger on his cheek, trying to pin one of the oscillating spots under my fingertip. "Teese," I said. "I don't know this one."

Teese looked at me for a long moment before replying.

"Shame, Ami," he said. "It is shame."

Teese's people feel emotions the moment they see them. If I'd been one of Teese's people, I would've been flooded with shame the moment I saw the red blotches on his skin, and a paler echo would have bloomed on my own skin. It's beyond empathy: it's instant and direct and irresistible. If I'd been a hexie, I would have said: "Why are we ashamed?" while my skin and emotions thrummed in synchrony with his.

But I wasn't, and so I could only ask, "What are you ashamed of?"

Teese sighed, a sound I had taught him to make. "I spent too long meditating," he finally said.

"Did you forget to eat?"

"Hm. I suppose I did, but I don't think that's why. . . . You shouldn't have had to drag me out of the closet."

"I think we're doing something a little beyond gay here," I quipped, then wished I hadn't as gray puzzlement dusted itself over the shame blotching his skin. "Never mind, bad joke. But if it wasn't hunger, why did you pass out, or whatever that was? Teese, are you sick?"

"No, no," he said. "You don't need to worry, Ami. I'm fine." He sighed again. "It was . . . I was . . . I just don't know how to explain it."

"Try," I urged him. Partly because I was worried and scared, and partly because, as we talked, the shame was slowly fading from his skin, supplanted by the dark-orange fractal trees Teese sported whenever he was thinking hard.

"Well," he said. "I was . . . I was looking at the walls and I got . . . too much blue."

"Too much blue?" I said.

"Yes," he said. "I thought, I am meditating, I am going deeper and deeper into the blue. And then it was too much."

That was unusually inarticulate, for Teese. He was normally better at expressing himself in English than I was. His skin was clearing and dulling to a muddy gray.

This one I knew well. "You look tired," I said. "Let's get you into bed."

"Yes," he said. He started to haul himself down the hallway toward the bedroom, not even bothering to stand.

I covered my mouth with my hand. Teese usually stood himself up on four of his six limbs. The velvety undersides of his limbs gripped together along most of their length and the tips acted like feet, scooting him along the floor. It made him about as tall as a person, a head above the average man, and left him two limbs free to act like arms. Of course, I'd known that the posture was for our benefit, that Teese's people didn't spend all their time standing like that on their own ship. But he'd always kept it up, even in our apartment, with just the two of us. And now, now he was just hauling himself along the floor, one tired limb at a time.

"I'll get you some water," I said, and fled to the kitchen.

When I came into the bedroom, Teese was in bed, head on the pillow, eyes almost closed. I fumbled for a limb-tip, pressed the damp glass into it.

"Thank you," he said. "Ami, will you stay?"

His skin was still gray with exhaustion. "Yes," I said. "Teese . . ."

He opened one eye fully, fixed its heart-shaped pupil on me. "Ami?"

I'd been about to scold him, to tell him I'd had no one to call, no way of knowing whether he was near death and no one to ask. But even in the dimness of our bedroom, I could see the gray mottling his skin. If I'd been a hexie, I would have felt exhausted just looking at him.

"I was worried," I said instead. I slid into bed with him and curled up against his arm. I think he was asleep before I'd pulled the covers up. But I lay awake a long time, watching the light from car headlights slide across the ceiling, striping it bright and dark.

Teese was my first live-in boyfriend, although that feels strange and wrong to say. Teese was a friend, more than a friend, but there was no way to think of him as a boy or a man. I can't say that he was my first love. He didn't move in because I loved him. He moved in because the sex was great and because he couldn't rent an apartment to save his life. The morning after our first night together, I learned that Teese had been couch-surfing his way up the Atlantic seaboard. Then I went to my shift at the gas station, and when I came home we had fantastic sex, then ordered pizza and ate it together messily on the couch and fell into bed, and the next day was pretty much the same, and slowly it dawned on both of us that Teese was staying.

I couldn't really afford the rent on the apartment by myself. I needed a roommate, someone willing to pay me to sleep in the living room of my one-bedroom hole-in-the-wall slice of crumbling neo-Gothic pile of crap. Instead I got Teese.

"I can pay you," Teese said. "I receive high pay and long leaves in exchange for my long watches. The trouble is that local landlords do not want a hexie, and I have not found a hotel who will take my currency."

From somewhere he produced a thin, shiny rectangle. "Here," he said. "This is rhodium. I haven't checked the price for a while, but it should be worth at least a month's rent."

I took it gingerly. It was about the size of half a Thin Mint, maybe a little thicker. There were odd markings on it, presumably spelling out "YES THIS IS REALLY RHODIUM" in Teese's language.

"Teese," I said, "I have no idea what to do with this."

"You could sell it?"

"Who could I sell it to? Do you seriously think I can go to Downtown Crossing with this and find some guy in Jewelers Exchange who'll say 'Oh yeah, this is alien rhodium, we get this all the time' and give me a stack of cash?"

Teese waved a tentacle that was freckling olive-green with exasperation. "Well, at least you believe me. All the hotels I tried just pushed it back at me and said they couldn't take it."

"All the hotels . . . wait, did you try taking it to a bank?"

The olive-green freckles spread. "Of course, I did. They told me they required a jeweler's assay. The jewelers told me they required payment in advance for the assay. And of course they cannot take payment in this possibly worthless metal."

I sighed. "Well, maybe you should try again next month. Sooner or later one of your shipmates is going to get a paycheck cashed, and then all the rich people will be buzzing about the dank alien rhodium and scheming to get it out of you as fast as they can." I pushed the rhodium tablet back into Teese's tentacle.

He made the tablet disappear again. "Maybe you're right," he said. "But in the meantime, Ami, how will you pay for the rent? Shall we get a roommate?"

"Um," I said. "I don't know if that's a good idea with you already staying here."

"It would be crowded," he said, his skin stippling with agreement.

"Right," I said. "Crowded. I'll see if I can pick up any extra shifts at work, and if I can't, I'll short my student loan payment this month." Again.

I had to take two buses and a train to get to the CITGO where I worked. Metro Boston, where none of the workers at the gas stations can actually afford to keep a car. But, unlike driving, the bus gives plenty of time to watch the scenery. A sign in a restaurant window caught my eye. "We serve octopus!!!!" Not calamari, octopus. *I didn't know octopus had a culinary following,*

I thought. And then, *Wait, are they trying to say they'd serve Teese? Hexies can eat there?* But then another sign flashed by. A dish of tiny baby octopus in thick brown gravy, with bold letters shouting "THIS IS HOW WE LIKE 'EM!" *This* was underlined six times. And another: "I LIKE MINE CHOPPED AND FRIED." And another: "OCTOPUS IS BEST DEADED AND BREADED $16.95!!!" I shifted in my seat. I was starting to feel uneasy. Were people really eating octopus to express their resentment at the hexies' presence? It was stupid, a stupid thing to wonder and an even stupider thing to do; so stupid that I could just about see people doing it.

I shifted in my seat again. How many people on the bus with me felt the same way as the sign-writers? How many were chopping up octopus at home and calling it Hexie Surprise?

And what would they do to me if they knew I was screwing one every night?

Ami," Teese asked, "what are you feeling?"

I opened my eyes. "Umm," I said. "Sleepy?"

He shifted in bed beside me, propped himself up on one limb so he could look down at me in the dimness. "Besides that. Are you happy? Are you sad? Are you annoyed? It is difficult for me to tell."

I shifted too. "Well, now I'm feeling awkward," I said. "I think everyone has trouble telling how someone else is feeling sometimes, Teese. Especially in the dark, you know?"

"For my people," Teese said—he never called them "hexies"—"it's harder to see feelings in the dark, too. But it's not that dark. You can see my skin, and I can see your body and your face."

"It's probably just harder for you than for, you know, other humans," I said. "Like, I had to learn that when you go a certain kind of pattern of olive-green, you're getting really annoyed. And it doesn't hit me in the gut the way it does when I see a person with a mad face. It's like I have a, a secret decoder ring in my head that I have to check. I turn the dial to 'olive-green squiggles' and I see *Oh, Teese is feeling frustrated or annoyed.* And then I can start to have my own emotions about that."

"Hit you in the gut," Teese said thoughtfully. "When you see someone angry, Ami, you feel their anger, too?"

"Not exactly," I said. "I might feel scared, actually, especially if they're mad at me, and they're bigger and stronger."

Teese lay back down. "That is very different," he said. "In my people, if I see someone who is angry, I feel their anger immediately. And they know I feel it because they see it reflected on my skin."

"Yeah, I know," I said. "Do you ever get a surprise that way? Like, you didn't realize you were angry until you look at the guy next to you and see that he's mad, too?"

I felt Teese shift to look at me with both eyes. "Why wouldn't I know I was angry?"

"Or sad, or whatever."

"But why wouldn't I know I was sad? Ami, all my life I have seen my feelings on myself and on everyone around me. I would have to be . . . damaged not to know my own feelings by now." He paused. "Probably there are people who are damaged like this, children who are born blind and have to be told their feelings and everyone else's. But you won't meet them on a starship's crew."

*Is that how you think of me—damaged?* I bit my tongue, held in the words. But I felt my body moving away from Teese slightly.

After a pause, Teese spoke again. "I feel blind with you, Ami," he said. "I see your face change, and I don't know what it means. Or your voice, or your body. I am like that blind child who can't read skins, when I'm with you."

"Welcome to the human race," I said.

After he moved the towels back into the closet, Teese asked if he could use my computer while I was at work. I told him I was shocked that he hadn't been using it already, and showed him how to log in and how to open a web browser and how to Google. He tapped the keyboard delicately with the very tips of two tentacles, like a two-fingered typist, while I got ready for work. When I left, he was browsing Reddit at the kitchen table.

When I got home after work, Teese was still in the kitchen. "I found a way for us to make money," he called.

I stuffed my coat in the closet and headed into the kitchen. "Really? Whatcha got?"

"Look at this," he said, pushing my laptop toward me.

"Oh, ewww," I said. A naked woman rubbed a dead octopus over her genitals. "Are you kidding me?"

"I know, I know, just look," he said, pulling up another page. A woman was having sex, improbably, with a horse. And then another: a man and a . . . pile of balloons?

I was getting a nasty feeling about Teese's idea. "What the hell?" I asked.

"I know! There are all kinds of pictures of people putting their genitals in things and on things. All kinds of things! Animals, people, food, machines! And they get money for this! Is this news to you? It was news to me."

I made a face. "Teese, I am not going to put an octopus on my twat for money. That's . . ." Words failed me.

"No, no, of course not," he said quickly. "I would not ask you to do that, Ami. But there is one thing I did not see in all my searches. I found all kinds of people having sex with every kind of thing, but never with . . ." he paused dramatically ". . . one of my people!"

His big eyes focused on me expectantly. Yes, my boyfriend was suggesting that we camwhore ourselves for rent.

"Oh, Teese," I said helplessly. "Setting aside the fact that I'd probably be lynched, that's . . . that's . . ." I sighed. How was I going to explain porn to someone from another world? "Let's get delivery. That's a long conversation."

I got home the next night to find him swiping tentacles broadly across the keyboard and staring at a text editor. "I installed Python," he said. "I hope that is all right."

I stood staring at his keyboard technique. "Sure," I said, "just ask first next time, and . . . how are you doing that?"

"Doing what?" he asked, covering the keyboard with two arms. Lines of text appeared on the screen as if by magic.

"Typing?" I said. "You are typing, right?" If I looked very closely, I could just see the top of his arms twitch.

"Oh! I found that this is the easiest way to operate your keyboard, Ami. A little focused pressure on each key works just as well as striking. It took a bit of practice, but it's not too different from the interfaces on our ship."

"It just looks like you're hugging the computer, and it's writing text for you," I said. "What're you writing, anyway?" I peered over his shoulder. It looked like free verse in English-laced gibberish.

"Python!" said Teese enthusiastically. "I told you, I installed one of your programming languages. It is not terribly different from your spoken language. I am writing a program in Python. Do you know this language, too?"

"Um," I said. My nearest approach to programming had been customizing my Facebook settings. "No, can't say I do."

Teese lifted his arms off the keyboard and started telling me about his program. I tuned out and watched his skin. Watery gray patterns rippled enchantingly across his arms as he gestured. It wasn't quite like anything I'd seen before, but it was familiar, reminiscent of his skin when we were having a particularly intense conversation.

"And then—" Teese interrupted himself abruptly. "But you are not interested in this, Ami?" He peered up at me.

"I'm not a programmer, Teese," I said. "But go on. I can tell you really had fun working on this."

Teese's skin pinked and dimpled, his way of smiling. "I did indeed. Here, look at this."

He hugged the keyboard again. The screen blanked, then broke out in cheesy red hearts. "i love you ami" scrolled over the pulsing hearts.

I burst out laughing. "Is this what you spent the day on, you nutball?" It was awful. I loved it.

Teese's skin rippled with pinkish-brown giggles. "Anything for you!"

Teese kept up with his programming hobby. After the love note came bouncing hearts that filled the screen, blanked, and repeated. Then it was fractals, lacy whorls that spiraled chromatically across the small screen. Then seascapes where the shifting lines of ocean blended into deep blue sky.

I thought Teese was programming to kill time. I had no idea he had a goal in mind. Day after day, I came home to find that he'd built another seeming frivolity. His electronic compositions were getting bluer, though, tending toward the same pale teal he'd painted the closet.

I suppose that should've been the third warning sign; or maybe it was the fourth. I've lost count.

But I ignored it, like I'd ignored all the others, because every night when we made love Teese looked deep into my eyes and told me he couldn't imagine life without me.

When I got home the next night, Teese was back at the kitchen table. "I found another way to make money!" he called to me.

I couldn't help grimacing. "I think I liked it better when you met me at the door with sex," I said.

"This is better, I promise," said Teese. "I'm going to surprise you with it. Some of my crewmates have figured out the banking system, and they are the ones who will pay me."

"In rhodium?"

His skin rippled with brown giggles. "No, Ami, no more rhodium! Cash! Wire transfers!"

I came to stand next to him. The screen really was filled with gibberish, as though someone had transliterated a foreign language into English and sprinkled it liberally with varicolored emoticons, often midword.

"This isn't a program, right?" I asked. "Just checking."

"Chat room," Teese said happily. "It is a nonsanctioned

communication between members of my ship. There is a metals exchange in California where my crewmates have been able to exchange their pay at a reasonable rate. I have known about this, but I have no desire to go to California, actually"—he peeked up at me almost shyly—"I would much rather stay in Boston."

"I'd kinda rather you stay here, too," I said. "So are they going to exchange some of your rhodium for you? Like, you have a ship bank you can transfer it to them with, and then they transfer you back the US currency?"

He waved a tentacle. "Actually, shipboard regulations would make that complicated," he said. "Private crew currency exchanges are not very encouraged. Otherwise I could already have done that. But now I have something to sell."

"You do?" I said. "What is it?"

Teese pinked with pride. "I have created a program that my crewmates desire!"

"Really? What does it do?" I was really curious. I couldn't imagine what Teese had cooked up on my old laptop that sophisticated space-faring hexies would pay cash for.

Teese stroked the keyboard. The screen went black, then slowly faded into a shifting, pale aquamarine. It was a seascape, an abstract, a fractal, all of these and none of these at once. Barely visible lines radiated from the center, branched, shifted, dissolved. Dozens of fractal forms shimmered and danced in the background, shifting and changing. It reminded me of waves rippling the ocean, of sand grains roiled by wind, of the patterns on hexie skin.

It was mesmerizing. It was beautiful, it was somehow alien, and something about it was hauntingly, naggingly familiar.

After a few minutes, the screen blanked. "It has a timeout," Teese said quietly. "So that I do not become . . . lost."

I sat back. "It's gorgeous, Teese," I said quietly. "Are you an artist? Back home, I mean."

"No, no," he said. "I never had any interest in this. But now I have inspiration, Ami."

"I can see why your people would pay for this, especially if they're all as into blue-green as you are," I said. "But wait, didn't you tell me that your people would find so much blue tacky? Like that all-purple painting I had once?"

Thoughtful orange fractals rippled Teese's skin. "Actually, it is kind of tacky," he said. "But it is more than that. Ami, you can have no idea how interesting, how appealing and stimulating this is for one of us. When I look at this, I feel . . . things I cannot feel without it. That's why I put in the timeout," he added pragmatically.

Art has always prompted strong feelings in people, so I assumed that's what Teese was talking about. I thought it was a little weird for Teese to talk about his own art like that. But Teese clearly hadn't been exaggerating, because the money started rolling in. He'd never managed to get a US bank account, so the money went into my account. Suddenly, rent was no problem. I paid the rent, made up all the student loan payments I'd shorted, and still we had more money coming in each week than I made in a month at the CITGO. I thought about quitting my job, but didn't.

Teese wanted to take me out to dinner, to shows, to operas that neither of us had the slightest interest in. I demurred. We hadn't been out together since he'd come home with me. At first there had been a steady flow of invites to parties, ostensibly for me but always appended with "Oh, and be sure to bring that hexie who's staying with you." But we'd been too wrapped up in each other to go out, and the invitations had slowly dried up. Now we had piles of money and nowhere to go. I wouldn't have minded taking Teese to a few house parties, but Teese wasn't interested. "I've met lots of humans," he told me. "Now I have met you. Meeting more humans will just be . . . disappointing, I think. But I want to take you out, Ami."

"I don't really need to be taken out," I told him. "I'm pretty low maintenance." *And I don't want to be lynched*, I added silently. Teese might have met lots of humans, but they'd mostly been liberal, East-Coast, college-educated twentysomethings at house parties. As far as I know, he'd never even seen the "we serve octopus" signs I passed on my way to the CITGO. And I wanted to keep it that way.

We compromised on a museum date in the afternoon. Boston is dripping with museums. We went to the ICA and looked at all the blue things.

"I think your computer art is better," I murmured to him, just to see him pink.

He rippled brown with laughter instead. "I did have unique inspiration," he said cryptically.

"Being inspired to pay the rent is far from unique," I shot back. He just laughed in return.

That might have been the fifth warning sign; or maybe I'm just paranoid in retrospect.

The next day, I had a double shift at the gas station. I came home to a dark, silent apartment.

"Teese?" I called out, groping for the light switch. Maybe he'd gone out?

Something moved in the darkness. Startled, I dropped my coat and hit my head on the door frame. "Ow! Shit!" My hand finally found the light, and I snapped it on.

Teese was hunched in the corner of the room, skin soot black. He'd been nearly invisible in the dark.

"Teese, what's going on? Are you okay?" As I spoke, I noticed that the little duffle bag he'd brought with him when he moved in was sitting beside him.

"Ami," he said quietly. "No. I am not okay. I have been recalled to my ship."

I came in and closed the door behind me. "Why? What's going on? Are the hex . . . are your people leaving?" I hadn't heard anything on the news.

"No," he said. "Not as far as I am aware. No, this is personal. My commander is displeased with my actions and has terminated my leave."

"Your actions . . . Teese, what did you do?"

"It's about my program," he said. "And about selling my

program to my shipmates. This has been ruled, ah, *trafficking* I believe is the word."

"Trafficking? Like your program is a drug?"

"Exactly like that," he said. "I told you that it has a strong effect on my people. It has been deemed an intoxicant."

"Your art is a drug?" I slid down to the floor, back against the door. "Are you in trouble?"

He waved a tentacle. "Yes and no," he said quietly. "If I report to the ship immediately, it will not be so bad for me. I should have left a few hours ago, I think. But I had to speak with you first."

"I had a double shift," I said inanely. "Wait. Wait. Are you coming back?"

"No," he said softly. "I will not be allowed to come back. And I have more bad news to tell you." He was still coal-black, but now his skin blotched red with shame as well. "The money has to go back. Everything my shipmates have paid for the program must be returned. Even though I made a gift of it to you. The ship's bank will take it back, right out of your account." His voice had faded to a whisper on the last.

"But we spent some of it," I said. I'd go into overdraft.

"I know," he said. "I . . . I will leave you the rhodium. Perhaps you will be able to exchange it soon."

I stared at Teese. The red hexagons spun and spun on his coal-black skin. He focused his heart-shaped pupils on the floor.

"I know the red," I said, "but what's the black?"

He murmured, so softly I could barely hear him, "I am afraid."

"You're scared of what they're going to do to you?"

"No. I'm afraid of how I will feel, not seeing you. I am afraid of how it will hurt me."

"I could come with you," I said suddenly. "It's an interstellar ship, right? And you have yearslong shifts watching over your frozen shipmates? You must have some provision for bringing your partners on there or you'd go crazy."

Violent brown lightning flashed across his black-red skin. *A bitter laugh*, I realized. "Take you with me!" he said. "Ami, don't you realize? How don't you realize? You are the problem, Ami, you are the last human they would ever allow on the ship!"

I felt as if he'd slapped me. "What? Why? How am I the problem?"

The shame-red bled away from black skin that crackled with jagged, bitter laughter. "How are you the problem!" he repeated. "You'd be a walking riot. My shipmates would fight each other to look into your eyes. They'd beat each other to death to be the one to make you come."

"Make me come," I said slowly. An awful light was dawning inside me. All the times Teese had said he loved to look into my eyes. My greenish-blue eyes. The strange familiarity of his program, as though I'd seen it somewhere before. His greenish-blue program that was, I realized now, the exact shade of my eyes. Just like the sunset that had so captivated him, and just like his "meditation closet."

"The way your eyes change," he said, "Ami, the way your eyes change when you come. The blood vessels, the tiny capillaries, they dilate."

I saw it now. "Fractal patterns moving through them, like hexie skin," I said. "And what you see, you feel."

"And what I see in your eyes, I have never seen anywhere else."

Teese's romantic-sounding words came back to me. *I have never felt before what I feel with you.* He had meant it literally. His limbic system responded to something in my changing eyes with a new emotion, one that none of Teese's people had ever felt before, while his skin struggled and failed to keep up, lapsing into static.

I sat with my back against the door and thought back over the past months. Teese had only said he loved me once, in a cheesy e-valentine. But he'd told me that he loved to stare into my eyes at least a dozen times. I'd naively thought that that meant the same thing.

"I was never your girlfriend," I realized out loud. "I was your drug."

"Please don't say that," he said. But I was pettily satisfied to see red shame-spots creeping back onto his black skin.

I stood up. "You'd better get back to your ship," I said, moving away from the door. "Just tell me one thing. What did it feel like? What did you feel when you looked into my eyes?"

He was silent for a long moment. "What is the word," he said finally, "for a color no one has ever seen? How could there be a word for it?"

"Was it a good feeling, at least?"

He closed his eyes. "It was like nothing I'll ever feel again."

He paused at the door, as if wondering whether to kiss me goodbye. I stared him down. He looked into my eyes one last time, and left.

Once Teese was gone, I pocketed his rhodium and went for a walk. I wanted to hate Teese, but I couldn't. He'd never lied to me. He'd been telling me exactly what he saw in me from the moment he'd first seen me. I just hadn't heard.

And what if I'd been the one given the chance to feel a brand-new emotion, one never felt by anyone before? I probably would've taken it. Hell, I'd let an alien move in with me mostly for the sex. And if I'd loved that alien later . . . well, that wasn't his fault either, not really.

I fingered the rhodium. Teese hadn't been able to get anyone to exchange it, but that might've had more to do with his tentacles than with the metal's value. I still couldn't see myself haggling over it at Jewelers Exchange, but I could probably pawn it for a few hundred to tide me over, and buy it back when I had the money to pay for an assay.

Because I did plan to have more money. Teese might be a terrific programmer, but he'd never learned to clear his browser history. It'd be easy to find the hexie message boards where Teese had sold his now-banned software. I didn't need the software. I'd just aim a webcam at my eyes, and the money would come flooding in.

I'd have dozens of hexies staring into my eyes, chromatophores fluttering. Maybe hundreds of hexies—who knew how many Teese had hooked on his program? Enough to worry his bosses.

JAZMEN RICHARDSON

Enough, I realized, to enforce a ban on Teese if I made it a condition of my show.

It wouldn't be porn, not in any human sense. Not as long as Teese wasn't watching.

I couldn't truly hate Teese. But I'm only human. And I couldn't help thinking of Teese, sitting alone in his quarters, skin rippling with regret, while his shipmates watched my eyes as I came. And I felt . . .

Well. If I had been a hexie, my skin would have pinked and dimpled at the thought. But I'm human, so I had to make do with a smile.

# *Miss Smokey*

*written by*

## *Diana Hart*

*illustrated by*

ANTHONY MORAVIAN

---

### ABOUT THE AUTHOR

*Diana Hart lives in Kent, Washington with her nerd-tastic husband and a panhandling peahen. She speaks fluent dog, wields an epee, and escapes into the woods whenever she can. In fact, "Miss Smokey"—her debut piece and part of a larger urban fantasy setting—is the product of several storm-sodden jaunts through the Olympic rain forest. In the rare moments Diana's not writing or dangling from a tree, she fills her time with clamming, cake decorating, and loose-leaf tea.*

*Storytelling has always been Diana's passion. Her love affair with the craft stemmed from a well-used library card, enough mythology books to crush a cat, and years immersed in the oral traditions of the Navajo. After a tumultuous migration across the United States, her work took on a more "earthly" note, melding fantasy with narratives inspired by the peoples, customs, and hardships she encountered on her journey.*

### ABOUT THE ILLUSTRATOR

*Anthony Moravian is an illustrator that uses classical techniques to create realistic fantasy themes. He specializes in charcoal drawings and oil paintings. Anthony was born and raised in Brooklyn, New York and began drawing at the age of three.*

*As a child, Anthony would draw from the collection of comics he had in his basement. He also admired the creativity in fantasy and science fiction stories, and today he works to capture some of their creativity in his paintings. He really began taking an interest in drawing fantasy art when he began playing fantasy-based video games.*

*Anthony graduated magna cum laude from the Associate program at the Fashion Institute of Technology. Upon recommendation from a professor, he worked sketch nights and events at the New York Society of Illustrators. It was there he began to take a great interest in realistic painting.*

*As a result, he began to work to capture some qualities that were often featured in classical realistic paintings while maintaining his interest in fantasy concepts. He currently lives and works in New York as a freelance illustrator.*

*Anthony had the honor of being an Illustrator Contest published finalist for* L. Ron Hubbard Presents Writers of the Future Volume 33, *and his art can also be seen in that volume.*

## *Miss Smokey*

The squeals of the horde grew closer. I pulled in a breath, thick with wood and old newsprint, and reared onto my hind legs. My knees ached as I staggered to the center of the room. Standing upright was a breeze as a woman, but I was in bear-form, and grizzlies sure as hell aren't meant to walk that way. My muzzle wrinkled as I pawed my wide-brimmed hat into place and braced for impact.

A pack of first-graders rounded the corner, flapping coloring books and screeching like howler monkeys on espresso. I snorted. They made a beeline for the menagerie of stuffed wildlife that lined the visitor center walls. Somehow the National Park Service expected coarse rope and a burned wood "Do Not Touch" sign to stem the tide. It never worked. I cleared my throat as the grade-school piranhas reached for their taxidermied victims. The horde turned toward me and eyes and mouths went wide.

A girl with mussed hair and a Last Unicorn T-shirt raised a chubby finger. "It's—"

"That's right," I said. Well, rumbled, really. Being a grizzly kind of screws your "inside voice." I jabbed a paw at them. "Remember, kids: Only you can prevent forest fires."

A collective screech hit my ears. I winced and then they were on me. Most were well behaved, content to bounce up and down and jabber at me as if I were some woodland Santa Claus, but there's always those few who mistake me for a jungle gym. By the time Kelsi and the chaperones arrived, a pair of boys clung to my shoulders and somebody dangled from my ruff. Their prim, proper, perfectly human teacher just laughed and took pictures.

I clenched my jaw and glowered at the woman. Her heavily moussed curls showed no signs of abuse and her dress was shoe print free. Oh no, her little angels wouldn't dare treat a normie like this, but shifters? A boy stuck his finger in my nose. I sneezed and wrestled him off my shoulder and plopped him on the floor. According to the president, we're just animals. And thanks to his Supernatural Registration Act, I'd been downgraded from NOAA researcher to Park Service mascot.

The remaining shoulder-percher tried to steal my hat. Cooing over his cuteness, one of the chaperones blinded me with a camera flash. My pulse rose. I slapped a paw on top of my hat and weighed mentioning they were technically photographing a topless woman. I knew from experience it'd stop the pictures. I also knew it shrank my paycheck.

Instead I bit my tongue and locked eyes with Kelsi. The humanoid, five-foot-six raccoon had a child wrapped around each leg and her Stetson hung akimbo. My brow creased. *What the heck is it with kids and hats?* She shook her head and mouthed "Get on with it."

I took a deep breath and bellowed over the din, "Do you know what the number-one cause of forest fires is, Ranger Rick?"

One of Kelsi's leg-limpets wiped his nose on her calf. Her tail puffed from irritated to "just-shoot-me-now."

"I dunno, Smokey," she said, sticking to the god-awful script.

I put a paw on my hip and frowned. It didn't take much acting. My knees were screaming. "Well, that's no good." I flashed a sharp-toothed grin at the pair still yanking my fur. Their faces paled. "Do you know?" They just slid to the floor. My muscles unknotted. *Finally.* I rolled my shoulders and turned to the horde. "Can anybody tell Ranger Rick the number-one cause of fires?"

All of the kids babbled their guesses, including a shrill cry of "dragons." My smile turned just a bit real.

The teacher finally settled her class in neat, cross-legged rows so Kelsi and I could give our presentation on fire safety, conservation, and how feeding the bears got people mauled. I'd done the routine so many times my brain just clicked to autopilot and let me watch the crowd during our show. Usually when Kelsi started juggling cans and tossing them in a recycle bin, the kids' attention would drift, but every once in a while, you'd get that one child whose gaze stayed bright, boring into us with a hungry fire. Most wanted to be Rangers or scientists. Others were happy just seeing fellow shifters flash fur after the Registry.

My shoulders slumped. Today was just window-gazers and coloring enthusiasts.

After the Hoh Visitor Center closed, I shifted back to human form. Having thumbs and an athletic build was a welcome change from "nature's tank." I traded oversized trousers for human garb, grabbed my gear from my locker, and dashed for the trail, my grizzly-brown locks whipping in the wind. I grinned as the air kissed my face. There were a few hours of daylight left, enough to take some readings of the river if I hurried.

By the time I reached my favorite spot—a fast-flowing curve of water, shielded from intrusion by a steep hike and moss-covered hemlocks—the light had faded to a pale orange blush. Looming night and the glacier-fed river chilled the summer air. Goosebumps spread over my skin as I crunched along the gravel bar. A goldfinch sang somewhere along the far bank and the scent of evergreens and wet earth flooded my senses. My muscles relaxed as nature's perfume washed away memories of pulled fur, sticky fingers, and painfully boring scripts.

I headed for a fire-downed hemlock. The charred tree was over a hundred feet long, trailing through the woods, across the bank, and into the river. I set my pack beside the dead giant and admired its blanket of ferns and spindly saplings. My breath slowed in quiet awe. *Even in death the trees give life.* Snags like this one allowed fresh growth and, when they dipped into the water, sheltered fish and other aquatic fauna. It was the latter I was really interested in.

I pulled out a flow meter and stake, then waded into the river. Liquid ice hit my calves. I gasped. Good money said it was about fifty degrees, but I'd check that last. My brain didn't need any help on the "this stuff will give you hypothermia" front. I waded midstream, teeth chattering.

"You should be watching around you, Lily," a deep voice rumbled. I clutched my chest and wheeled toward the sound. A black grizzly sat at the end of the snag, camouflaged by the tangle of branches, munching a trout as the water churned about his belly. He fixed me with moss-green eyes. "Dangerous, startling bears."

"Jesus, Michail!" I said. My heart was stuck on "seizuring rabbit." "What are you doing here?"

His brow furrowed. "I was missing you," he said, Russian accent deepening his rumble.

My chest squeezed. *It's been, what, three weeks? Four?* Long enough I couldn't remember. Guilt bowed my shoulders. I knew he couldn't come by the visitor center—dodging the Registry had ended that years ago—so on my days off I was supposed to hike up Mount Tom Creek and meet him at our arch. I buried my face in my palm. "I'm sorry. It's field trip season. . . ." The excuse tasted sour, yet I kept babbling. "They're splitting my days off and I had to get readings before—"

Michail clicked his tongue. "*Lyubov moya,* no apologies for your research." I heard the lip-curl in his voice. "You are more than carnival exhibit."

I lifted my chin. "That's Interpretive Ranger, thank you." I was aiming for offended, but, judging by the tilt of Michail's head, I'd landed somewhere between "pouty" and "pitiful." My lips tightened. *Great.* He dropped his trout and waded toward me. *Double great.* I averted my eyes and drove the flow meter's stake into the riverbed. The last thing I needed right now was distraction and Michail was delightfully good at that.

"Lily."

I attached a temperature probe to the post. "Bit busy, Michail."

Small waves lapped my waist. His muzzle slid under my jaw

in a cool caress. Eau de wet fur spiced the air. Most people would find the odor off-putting, but when you can turn into a bear—and have shared god remembers how many showers with one—it's comforting. Homey, even. I inhaled despite myself.

*"Zolotse."* His voice vibrated my bones. "I worry for you."

I pinched the bridge of my nose. This script was as familiar as my Smokey routine. He would start with "I escaped Motherland, fled Soviet persecution," then move on to "Registry is seed of American tyranny," and finish with another plea for me to join him as a nature-preserve-nudist. My chest lurched. *Would it really be that bad?* Wandering the mists, plucking fish straight from the rivers, dew settling on our fur in the mornings. . . . I huffed and skipped to the end of our verbal dance.

"Running tells the normies harassment works. Makes it harder for the next shifter." Checking my cables one last time, I slogged out of the river, shivering as wet clothes clung to my skin. Michail strode after me. "Besides." I turned around and shrugged. "Playing Smokey earns brownie points, means Park Manager Dawson publishes my data." Bitterness clung to my tongue. These days it was the only way I could get something in print.

Michail frowned. Well, as much as a grizzly can, anyway. "Appeasement only means you are on knees when knife comes out."

My mouth went dry. I put my hand on my hip, as much to banish fear as to halt protest. "Did you come to argue with me or what?"

His jaw tightened. ". . . No." Michail never liked backing down but after a few years and a couple of bear-brawls, he'd learned to let things drop. Still, it took a few seconds for his gaze to cool from pissed to smolder. He grinned. Paced closer. "There are better things to do."

I laughed as he loomed over me. *Lord, don't let a hiker see us now.* They'd think Michail was attacking and jump in to save me. "You're terrible," I said. "I have to take readings, remember?"

Hot breath brushed my neck. Water dripped on my skin in cool contrast. "As you Americans say, 'all work and no play'. . ."

"You could help, *medved*," I said and swatted his nose. "Make it go faster."

He rolled his eyes playfully. "If I must." A hearty shake sent water everywhere. I squeaked and threw my hands up.

Michail grimaced as the shift began. Soft pops of bone echoed over the river's churn. Midnight fur gave way to rosy skin, exquisitely toned muscles steaming with shift-fever. His muzzle shortened and twisted back to the square jaw and high cheekbones I'd loved to trace in the mornings. Fading scratches and a thin new scar granted him a feral look.

I didn't gape. Just . . . flushed more than I cared to admit.

Michail let out a whoosh of air and brushed back now-untamed hair. Warmth lurched through me. While I was stunned, he leaned in for a kiss. His tongue still carried the light, gamey tang of fish. Our lips parted, and he gently hooked my chin. "You were staring again, *zolotse*." Hot-faced, I sputtered some excuse, but he just laughed and headed for my backpack.

While he rummaged through my gear, I touched my lips and rolled the taste of fish in my mouth. My eyes narrowed. *Cutthroat trout?* The sneak knew it was my favorite. He was tempting me, reminding me what civilization lacked. I crossed my arms. I wasn't sure if I should beam or growl.

Michail produced my battered notebook. "I will record data for you, yes?" he said, leafing through the pages.

I let my arms drop. It was too nice a night, the company too pretty, to stay stressed. "Yeah. Sure."

He turned around and took up a wide-footed stance. A rakish grin left no doubt that the view was intentional. "So," he said, twirling a pen. "Where is it you want it?"

Dawn brought crisp air and cold rain. Soaked and breathing hard, I jogged into the dingy locker room and threw my pack on the bench. Currently human, Kelsi peeked around her locker door. Minus raccoon-gray hair and mottled eyebrows, she reminded me of an Octoberfest ad: econo-sized bosoms, ample curves, and a smile that could heatstroke a penguin.

"Decided to camp out, huh?" she said.

I mumbled an affirmative and spun my lock.

"Hold still." Kelsi plucked a leaf from my hair. "You brought a souvenir."

Heat crept up my neck. Traces of Michail's bear musk clung to my skin. Add in twiggy locks and any shifter with a decent nose would know exactly what I'd been up to. Still, Kelsi didn't cock an eyebrow or anything. Either she had the best poker face ever—unlikely, given her delighted squeals during Uno—or she had the nose of a normie.

Acting as if nothing was amiss, I opened my dented locker. "Just getting some early readings."

"You should have taken longer," she said and pulled up her sweater. Fabric muffled her voice. "Missed the first bus."

"The job's not that bad," I said. Water dripped from my nose. A quick puff blew it away. "Free park admission, free uniform . . ." I pulled out my oversized pair of trousers. "Well, part of one, anyway."

"It'd be better if the kids gave a crap," Kelsi said and traded pants for short-shorts. Ranger Rick was always drawn commando, but she'd talked Dawson into letting her keep some semblance of dignity. "If I were you, I'd take a gig at the zoo."

I paused. ". . . What?"

"Yeah, Woodland Zoo? They pay shifters to hang out in the enclosures." She plopped her Stetson on her head. "If I wasn't a hybrid-form, I'd do it. Put some glass between me and the little monsters."

I nodded to the clock over the door. "The ones here in seven minutes?"

Kelsi's eyes widened. "Crap!" She threw on her vest and the scent of raccoon filled the air. A pained gasp escaped as her tailbone popped and stretched to four feet of plume. Fur in place, she dashed into the darkened visitor center, shouting "I have to get the coloring books ready!"

I wasn't expected to lay out activities for the kids, bears lacking thumbs and all, but I still hastily peeled off my clothes.

When the kids arrived I needed to be in place with my back to a wall. Walking through the visitor center only turned the horde into piggy-back-hungry velociraptors. I waded into my pants and summoned the change.

An inferno swept through my blood, turning it to a furnace. Pain sledge hammered me into an ursine shape. Once the heat and shakiness faded, I lumbered for the door, claws clicking on the tile. A draft made me stop. *Uh oh.* I peered down. Sure enough, I'd forgotten to close my fly. I lolled my head back. Having thumbs would save my dignity but a wardrobe adjustment wasn't worth shifting to human and back.

"Kelsi?" I called. Turns out swallowing pride makes your ears droop. "I need a zip."

The next few hours continued to slide into what we called "retirement impetus": no eager learners, Q&A mostly focused on if we pooped in the woods, somebody turned our six-point buck into a five-and-a-half, and a rug-rat spilled apple juice on me.

During a lull I went to the bathroom, pawed the water on, and wasted a tree's worth of paper towels trying to get clean. All I really accomplished was soaking the front of my trousers. I grumbled and swatted the faucet shut. *No kids, Smokey just gets super excited putting out fires!*

Padding back into the visitor center, a wave of newsprint-scented air hit me. Gun-oil and fear came with it.

Ice whispered up my spine. *Appeasement only means you are on knees when knife comes out.* Pushing back Michail's warning, I snuffled the air, certain there was a less-paranoid explanation. Dawson's cologne teased my nose. I loped toward the scent, taxidermy animals staring after me with dead eyes.

Three Law Enforcement Rangers waited in the lobby. The trio projected that "everything's under control" vibe, but the tightness of their jaws told a different story. Dawson, back military straight, talked with Kelsi in a low and furtive tone. Her eyes were wide and her tail tucked.

I cleared my throat. "Everything okay?"

They turned. Worry darkened Kelsi's gaze. Dawson's was a flat, cold gray.

"There's been an attack," she squeaked.

"Hikers, near Mount Tom Creek," Dawson said. His grip tightened on a Ziploc full of rags. Even sealed, I whiffed blood and grizzly. My throat constricted. *Michail.*

"Casualties?" I asked.

"One dead, two injured."

My pulse thudded in my ears. *He had to have a reason.* "What happened?"

Dawson shook his head. "Group stepped off the trail, black bear charged them—"

"Grizzly," one of the guards interrupted. "Said it was nine feet when it reared."

"That's impossible," I said. My insides were a leaden mass. "There're no grizzlies in the Olympics."

"And Lily was here all morning," Kelsi said quickly.

Dawson sniffed. "Misjudged size in the confusion. Standard fear response." He took off his Stetson and rubbed his buzz cut. "Still. Bear that'll attack people . . ." His unspoken intent roared in my ears. *It needs to be put down.* Nausea washed over me. Dawson kept talking. "When the next class comes, escort them on and off the bus and keep them in the visitor center."

"What's your plan?" I asked, voice shaking. Hopefully they would misread my concern and think I was fretting over the visitors.

"For now we're closing the trail and escorting hikers to safer areas." He waggled the bag of rags. "In the meantime, we've asked local hunters to bring their dogs."

Bile filled my throat. *Dogs.* My legs ached, screamed with the need to run and find Michail before the law did. *They're bringing dogs.* If I could just talk to him, let him explain, we might be able to convince Dawson that the attack had been provoked, an act of self-preservation. But if the dogs found him first—

"Lily." Dawson put a hand on my shoulder. I jerked. "Until we bag this thing, no more readings, okay?" he said, trying to give me a little shake. Didn't work. I was over eight hundred pounds. "We can't lose Smokey."

I nodded. Inside I was growling. "Yeah. Sure."

Branches whipped my face as I ran. Rain pounded my Gore-Tex and roared in my ears. My pulse was louder. *He has to be there.* I kept running, lungs burning as I dodged roots and night-shrouded trees. Being a shifter let me see in the dark, but with hunters on the way I had to stay human, dulling my senses. Still, my nose was sharp enough so I could smell Michail.

His trail, sweet, musky, and male, twined along Mount Tom Creek, quickly eroding in the rain. A coppery tang knotted my gut. *Blood.* Shifters were spectacular healers, able to close most wounds in a few days, but we could still bleed to death. And in this storm there was no telling how much Michail had lost. I scrambled upstream, fear lancing my heart.

*He has to be there.*

A pair of familiar hemlocks loomed in the night. I let out a sobbing, foggy breath. The ancient trees straddled the water, undercut by the river ages ago, but instead of toppling into the currents they'd fallen against each other, their combined strength resisting the elements until time had fused them together. Branches reached as one for the sky while conjoined roots formed a slight shelter. I spied Michail inside the ancient tangle, hunkered over in human form.

"Michail!" I called, staggering closer.

His head snapped up. Pain rasped his voice. "Lily?"

I ducked under the roots, frigid water pouring into my shoes. Blood-tang filled my nose. Michail sat on a tangle of driftwood clutching a denuded, gore-coated stick. An unusual pallor haunted his skin.

His brow wrinkled. "*Lyubov moya,* why—"

"I smelled you on those hiker clothes," I said. My throat constricted. There were . . . holes in him. On his side. His back. In the dark they wept black.

"Poachers, *zolotse,*" he hissed and dug the stick into a hip wound. I yelped and darted for the branch. A flash of metal stopped me. Michail held up the deformed slug, fingers stained. "Thought I was a prize black bear." He flicked the bullet into the gurgling stream. *"Mudak."*

I swallowed bile. *Self-defense.* They'd tried to shoot him, and he'd fought back. I threw my arms around him, shaking. *It was self-defense.* "We have to get you to the Ranger's Station." From there we could summon a doctor, call the police—

"No."

The word hit like a punch. I pulled back. "What?"

"I go back, my name is in Registry as bear."

Temper warmed my blood. I grabbed him by the shoulders. "Damn it, Michail! You're not running from Stalin anymore!"

"Chernenko," Michail corrected. He shrugged. Winced. "And doesn't matter. Judge says innocent, someone always says guilty. They find me by Registry and . . ." He put his fingers to his head and mimed a gunshot.

My jaw dropped. "People aren't like that!"

Michail's eyes narrowed. "*Zolotse.* My father died for raising me Orthodox." His words were sharp as a blade. "Because friends told Special Committee." He set aside his stick and twined his bloodied fingers in mine. "Poachers will demand bear. Vengeance." He squeezed. "You must come, run to Mount Tom."

I pulled loose and pinched the bridge of my nose. "Michail, I can't—" He lolled his head back and started to rumble. It died with a wince. My retort withered on my tongue. I touched his arm and waited while he expelled the pain in short, foggy bursts.

"What's wrong?" I asked once he'd regained composure. Stupid question, really, but my brain was still rebooting.

"Shoulder," he said, resting against a gargantuan root. It was the same one he'd carved our initials into years ago. "Cannot reach."

My lips tightened. "Turn around."

Moving gingerly, Michail presented his well-muscled shoulder. I pushed back my hood and leaned in close, fighting nausea as I gently manipulated savaged flesh. *At least he's human now.* Translational injury would leave the bullet a centimeter or two below the skin, rather than inches deep in a bear's beefy shoulder.

"They will never respect you, *zolotse*."

Dawson's voice rang in my ears. *We can't lose Smokey.* "I know," I murmured. "But that's not why I stay."

Metal glistened in the wound. I fished the hunk out with the stick, Michail's fists clenched the whole time, and flicked the bullet aside. I slid off the root, bark catching my jeans, and scrubbed my hands in the frigid stream. Michail just watched with sad, tired eyes.

"Then why?" he asked.

As I sat in the dark with blood on my clothes, the answer seemed . . . weak. And so very faraway. I took a deep breath. "Not everyone can run. Some of those kids—"

A howl drifted through the woods. My breath caught. *Dogs.* I whipped around. Michail was no fool. He'd already gotten to his feet, scanning the trees with narrowed eyes. "One, maybe one-and-half kilometers," he said.

My chest squeezed. *Not his first manhunt.* I touched his cheek. Stubble pricked my fingers. "Dawson brought hunters." My voice shook. "Go. The rain . . ." Stones filled my throat, but I choked them down. "The rain'll wash out your trail."

He grabbed my arm, nails lengthening into points. "No." He nodded to my stained Gore-Tex. "Blood all over you. Dogs will come to you."

"I know." I flashed a smile I didn't feel. "But they're hunting a bear, right? Not like they'll shoot a human." *Please, please God let that be true.*

Michail's grip constricted, his nails puncturing my jacket. Fear and anger warred in his eyes. I held my breath. Another howl rang in the distance. He grimaced and squeezed his eyes shut. His fingers fell from my arm. *"Chert voz'mi,"* he whispered. He leaned in and kissed me deeply. This time I tasted only him. "Spring, if hunt is over . . ."

I rested my forehead against his. Pain raked my heart. ". . . I'll meet you here."

He breathed into my hair. Kissed the top of my head. Fur sprouted from his skin, and he stepped into the river, using the water to hide his trail. I caught a whiff of fresh grizzly and then he was gone, swallowed up by rain and night.

Tears burned down my cheeks. "Run fast, *medved.*" I sniffed and wiped an arm across my face. It just smeared mud and bark everywhere.

Shivering, I waited and listened to the dogs. Their tone grew excited. Frenetic. *Let them get right on top of you.* I'd get only one chance, and the rain would strip Michail's scent fast. I shucked my coat and picked up the gore-coated stick. *Then I'd better leave a big damn trail.*

Downstream, a flashlight winked between the trees. My pulse quickened. *They're here.*

I leaped from the shelter, dragging my bloodstained coat behind me. Rain hit like cold, hard bullets. I ran into the wind and up a ridge, jumped over roots and crashed through every fern and huckleberry, lashing the foliage with Michail's surgery-stick. By God, if those dogs couldn't follow this mess they were useless.

Bays soon turned to keening barks. Branches snapped as the hounds gained behind me. My heart lurched. *Not yet!* I veered down a steep slope. Adrenaline surged through my body and spurred me on like some sort of daredevil mountain goat. I gasped for air. Wet dog hit my nose.

A huge mutt angled into my path, teeth flashing. I yelped and changed course. In my panic I smacked into a tree. I went ass-over-tea-kettle, bouncing off rocks and plowing down saplings, until my leg caught a boulder. Something crunched and pain exploded across my senses.

I screamed. Or vomited. Not sure which, but something definitely came out.

Agony throbbed through me, kept me on the ground until the hounds came. Hot breath and warm noses snuffled over me.

ANTHONY MORAVIAN

One mutt kept barking in my ear. I just kept my eyes shut and gritted my teeth against the pain until somebody shined a flashlight in my face.

"Holy shit," Dawson said. I groaned and blocked the glare, squinting between my fingers. His jaw hung slack. "Lily?"

While Kelsi juggled and sang to the kids about recycling, I sat in my own personal hell, claws twitching as I endured the twelfth day of Itch-toberfest. Dawson wasn't able to replace Smokey and I needed to eat, so I'd agreed to heal up as a grizzly and had the cast applied in bear-form. I stifled a whimper. *Stupid move, really.* Fur took the itching from "torture" to "Circle of Hell," and my painkillers weren't doing squat. My ears flattened. The only plus to it all was that Dawson and the hunters had dragged me back to the visitor center, canceling the hunt until an ambulance showed.

I glanced out the visitor center window, slumping like a fern in the rain. *Hope you're in better shape, Michail.* It'd be another five months before I knew. A Law Enforcement Ranger, reeking of cheap cologne and gun-oil, loitered by the stuffed deer, examining Kelsi's glue-job. I sighed and held up a recycling bin, doing my best to ignore him. *And that's if I can ditch my escort.*

When Dawson had asked how I'd wound up in the woods covered in blood, I'd made something up about not having readings during heavy rainfall, slipping out, and running into the "Big Bad Bear." She'd been a mother with cubs, bloodied by her earlier run-in with the "hikers," so she'd attacked and chased me until I'd crashed down the hill and broke my leg. I stifled a huff. *Dawson smells a rat, though.* Officially Ranger Cheap Cologne or one of his buddies were here so I didn't sneak off and get hurt again, but a twenty-four-hour-shadow was less "caring" and more "surveillance." Doubly so when you added in cold glances and high-caliber side arms. The whole affair had left me with whiplash; I'd been looking over my shoulder constantly and Michail's warnings haunted me like a perpetual swan song.

Kelsi pitched her cans into my bin one by one, punctuating her act. A few kids clapped. The rest popped up despite the protest of the teacher and swarmed me to croon get-betters and sign my cast with crayons.

"Aw, thank you, kids." I wriggled in my seat, trying to relieve my aching rump. Turns out bear-butts aren't designed to sit on wood crates all day. Who knew?

A girl with orange and black hair shouldered through the crowd. A faint scent of tiger wafted from her, spicy and sharp. Her yellow eyes were bright. "Miss Smokey," she said.

The weight on my shoulders lifted. *Finally.*

"Smokey's a boy, Whiskers," one of the kids snapped.

Tiger-girl put her hands on her hips and shot them a withering glare. "Smokey's a boar. *She's* clearly a sow."

"That's right," I said, surprise creeping into my voice. *She knows her animal terms.* I smiled and cocked my head. "Did you have a question?"

She nodded. "Well, you said fires were bad, but—"

A blond boy, tall for his age, stopped signing my cast. His face pinched as he studied me. "You're a shifter?" Disgust marinated every syllable. He flicked his head toward tiger-girl. "Like *her*?"

My muzzle wrinkled. *How do you think I'm talking, kiddo?* "Yeah . . . And?"

Kelsi shook a bag of candy and shouted over the buzz. "Who can name a native fish?" Chocolate proved more exciting than talking bears. The locusts moved to Kelsi, squealing "pink-eye salmon" and other imaginary species. Only tiger-girl remained, glowering down at her sandals and clenching her coloring book, knuckles white.

My chest squeezed. God, how many times had I been in the same position? At her age I'd wanted to run away, hide from it all like Michail. Stones filled my gut. *Of course she doesn't have that choice.* Tigers weren't exactly local wildlife. "What's your name?" I asked.

She sniffed and glanced at me. ". . . Antimony."

"So, Antimony, what was this about fires?"

Dark clouds faded from her vision, letting some sparkle back in. "Well, Douglas-firs and fireweed need fire for their babies to grow . . ." That was an oversimplification, but she was in what, fourth grade? I nodded. Her posture slowly straightened. "And different animals need them for food and homes, right?"

"Correct."

Antimony's brow furrowed. "So fires are good." She frowned and chewed her lip. "Well, sometimes."

"That's true," I said, voice upbeat. "In fact, that's part of my research."

Her mouth formed a tiny little O. "Shifters can do that?"

Hearing her disbelief, the raw strength of it, made my throat constrict. "Of course!" I leaned in conspiratorially and braced my paws on my knees. Bad move, really. Fresh pain shot through my leg. I grimaced. Antimony's eyebrows rose, but thankfully she didn't change the topic. I let out a slow breath and transferred all my weight to the other knee. "Some people told me that I can't do research, or that because I'm a shifter it won't go anywhere, but you know what?"

Antimony leaned closer, voice dropping to a whisper. "What?"

"I do it anyway."

Her lips twitched with the start of a smile. She jabbed a thumb toward the rest of her class. "So when they say I can't be a scientist 'cause I'm a shifter . . . ?"

I plopped the Stetson on her head. It seemed the right thing to do. Kids were obsessed with that hat. "You can be anything, Antimony, fur or not."

She grinned so big I caught a glimpse of fangs. Pain, sweet and sharp, filled my heart and washed away the days until spring. I smiled too. *This, Michail . . . this is why I stay.*

# *All Light and Darkness*

*written by*

## *Amy Henrie Gillett*

*illustrated by*

DUNCAN HALLECK

---

### ABOUT THE AUTHOR

*Amy Henrie Gillett lives in Texas with her husband and three kids. She was raised by a book-loving father and a word-loving mother, and she received her first personal rejection at nine years of age thanks to a loving grandmother. All three ignited her lifelong need to write and her dream to publish. Amy received her BA in sociocultural anthropology and Middle East studies at Brigham Young University–Provo with an eye toward international development. Currently, she employs those studies in her writing. She hopes that by producing stories that kindle people's hearts and minds, she contributes a little light to a world that sometimes seems so dark.*

### ABOUT THE ILLUSTRATOR

*Duncan Halleck is an illustrator and concept artist working in the entertainment industry and specializing in the genres of science fiction and fantasy. He began his journey as an artist at a young age, copying cartoon characters and superheroes from books he found around the house and spending hours studying movie stills from* The Lord of the Rings. *As he grew older, he developed a deep passion for science fiction and fantasy literature and devoured the works of authors such as Ray Bradbury, Ian M. Banks, and J. R. R. Tolkien. Always an avid doodler, his love for the arts never ceased throughout his school career, his notebooks attesting to his ceaseless drive to create and explore new ideas.*

*After graduating high school, several yearlong stints in cities across the US and a close brush with architecture school, Duncan settled down in Belgium with his wife and aged English Pointer. Shortly after the birth of his first daughter and a time as a landscape painter, Duncan decided to pursue a full-time career in digital art and illustration and began in earnest to study the fundamentals of art and improve his skills as an image-maker. His passion for the fantastic carries through to this day and finds an outlet in the alien landscapes and future metropoli that populate his hard drive. Currently he freelances for small publishers and developers out of Brussels, where he can be found hiding from the rain with a cup of tea, a good book, and a photon blaster.*

# *All Light and Darkness*

I crest the hill, panting, sweat trickling through the filthy coils of my blue hair and down my dark face. The monochrome of the Dustlands pains my eyes—yellow and brown below and yellow-brown above. Dust cyclones rain down slivers of salt and sand, a fine powder that coats the throat. The blue moon, a mercury smile, waits for her red sister on the horizon. Strauch trees, short and knotted, speckle the rolling dunes, and the Traege River winds through them, a gash in the redundant landscape.

"Hell's sandbox," I murmur, remembering a description my Da favored. This is my past and our future, a wasteland. But if it means leaving the Wahren Reich behind, I'll take it.

Refugees pass me, heads and shoulders bowed against the wind and sand. They trickle south from the Kaltstein Mountains to the port of Rettung. *Rettung,* "deliverance" in Ancient Deutsch. It's the largest city in the Dustlands, and the only city on the continent unspoiled by the Wahren Reich, the grasping empire north of the mountains.

I clasp a scarf across my mouth and nose, but briny dust catches in my throat regardless, tasting like blood. Wind claws at my clothes, and sand stings my skin between the rips. I tug at my sleeves, trying to cover my wrists, but my arms are too long for the grimy sark, my legs too tall for the trousers. My wrists and ankles protrude like reptilian scutes, hornlike. I'm a starveling—a boy who grew to a man without fodder.

I feel the strike of sand through my bones as grains bombard the Titanite nodes in my arms, legs, and torso. Each node, none larger than the head of a nail, peeks from the center of a puckered scar. I hide them as best I can. Luckily, my scarf covers the Kog Port in the back of my head.

A refugee glances at me, his reptilian eyes sharp and hard like obsidian. I look away, pulling my scarf tighter.

A solitary wagon draws my attention. It sits a few kilometers off the trail and out of sight except from this vantage. Three figures outfitted in black leave the wagon. They walk a few meters into the Strauch trees. Then, with a sudden flash of white light, they disappear.

Familiarity tightens a cord of anxiety in my gut. Anzug combat suits flash like that when the user triggers the camouflage mechanism. It momentarily blinds opponents and obscures the rendering delay. Many of my former comrades in the Wahren used them.

I stagger down the slope, feet sinking ankle-high in sand, satchel slapping my side. A part of me begs to put as much distance between me and the anzug users as possible, but I know too well that I need to identify the threat. I don't want to run if I don't have to.

At the bottom of the hill, I strike out toward the wagon. I scour the trees for movement. My skin prickles with sweat and salt, dust and nerves.

Wood snaps.

I dive into a thicket of Strauch trees and slip a pocketknife from my satchel. I keep the blade low, away from the sunlight, and watch. The crack of branches and snapping twigs crescendos only a few meters away. Then silence.

I still my breathing, listening.

Suddenly, a man stands up not a meter away from me, his back turned. He's short and muscled, gray streaking his greasy black hair.

I shift for a better view, and a twig snaps under my heel.

Without a backward glance, the man charges through the trees in the opposite direction. I growl in frustration, shoving my knife in my bag and lunging after him.

A winter hiding in the mountains has whittled my physique down to matchsticks. My bones ache and my muscles burn. Dry air tears at my throat. I struggle to catch up.

We reach a fork and the man takes one ravine and I take the other. I know mine is shorter. Just as I reach the end of it, I see the man pass my exit. I launch at him, knocking us both into the sand. Thankfully, my weak muscles still know how to move. I pin him, a knee in his back and arms leveraged painfully.

"Get off me, ya browned fec," he screams. His city cant jumbles his words, over-enunciating the "t" and dropping other consonants.

I wrench his arms. "Who are you and what were you doing by that wagon?"

"Wha't wagon?" he growls.

I wrench his arms again and shove his face into the sand.

"Lights Above, lay off! I saw it out there and went t' see if they needed help," he shouts.

"How very chivalrous of you," I reply, twisting a finger.

"Gods save me, y'ill rip it off!" he says. "I went t' see wha' I could steal," he finally answers, his voice shrill. "Solitary wagons is easy pickings."

I release his finger. "And what did you find?"

"They're dead," he replies with a whimper. "They're all dead."

Fear cords the tendons of his neck like a noose, and panic rims his eyes. I release him and step back. The man grumbles, lunging to his feet and stumbling away. He rolls his shoulders as he turns to face me. A scar spans his face from hairline to jaw, turning one eye milky and twisting his lips. He spits to the side and wipes sand from his face.

"Fractured schist," he snarls at me. "Piece of work, ain't ya?"

I fake a lunge at him, and he flinches, bringing a cold smile to my face.

He snorts, makes a rude gesture, and walks away.

I head toward the wagon again. I smell it before I see it, burning flesh and blood. A middle-aged man, his skin dark and hair steely gray, lies on the ground. A woman, probably his wife, rests nearby. Blood clots the sand around them, but the blood is not all theirs. The corpse of a half-butchered draft herp contributes most. Its tail and most of its belly are gone, and swarms of bloodflies crawl over its scaled back and reptilian head. The wagon huddles behind the carnage like a frightened animal, empty and broken.

I think of the scar-faced man searching the wagon and frisking the corpses. My fists clench. He didn't kill them, but still . . . bastard.

I turn to leave since nothing here tells me what I need to know. Who were those men? What did they come for? Did they come for me? I grind my teeth in frustration.

Then the silver-haired man's hand twitches. I almost can't believe it, but his hand twitches again. Hopeful, I turn him over.

The stench of burned flesh fills my nose. My stomach heaves. Peeling white and gray skin covers his chest where an ion cannon blasted him. I see blackened bone and cauterized blood vessels. He's dead, but his body hasn't realized it yet.

"Sir, can you hear me?"

His lips move, but I can't hear him. I lean my head down, and my ear brushes his lips. "Daughter," he whispers.

Daughter? The attackers were slavers then, and they took his daughter for the brothels.

"Daughter," he whispers again, his voice grating. He says the word once more, weakly pointing to the east.

I take my water and scarf and try to cleanse the wound while I sort my thoughts. If the slavers left on foot, they would be perhaps only twenty-five kilometers away. If they had an auto, they would be much farther. Either way . . .

My hands go still. Either way, what?

Either way, I won't save his daughter. Even when I can.

I look down at my arm. A glinting node peeks from beneath my sleeve. I scowl and pull the sleeve down.

The Wahren Reich gave me a way to save her; they cut into my flesh and gave me a secret weapon. But using that secret comes at a cost, and I won't exchange my life for hers. There is a place worse than in the hands of slavers, a place worse than death: being in the hands of the Wahren Reich.

"Sorry," I murmur as I dab his flaking flesh. "I'm so sorry."

He groans and pinches his eyes shut. A tear trickles down his cheek, cutting a clean track in the dust. I rinse his face and pour a little water into his mouth. He coughs, spitting most of it out.

"Daughter," he says again, slipping into unconsciousness. He dies a few minutes later, and I walk away.

Who's the bastard now?

That night, I build my fire and warm my too-thin limbs over it. I stare at the yellow flames as they consume the salt and wood together. I prod the embers with a stick. Smoke curls into the cool night like ribbons and carries the scent of charred Strauch tree sap. The smell reminds me of children's toys and *vanillekipferl* cookies—of a canary yellow kitchen and musty couches that billow dust—the home my mother raised me in; the home I left in another land in another life.

Sometimes, I see that home in my dreams and wish I could stay there, find that place and never leave, find a place where no one ever leaves. But such a place doesn't exist. It never has.

I sigh, flicking the stick into the fire. It catches and bursts into flame. Then, just as suddenly, it turns to embers and ash.

Freude looked striking in his cap and blue uniform. The emblem of the Wahren Reich emblazoned his right sleeve and the lapels of his jacket. The blue against his auburn hair turned his hair to copper and flame.

He, Ehren, and Keim all had Mum's red hair. Not me. Mum used to tease me, saying that the Capricious Mother kissed me at birth and turned my hair the hue of her beloved blue moon. I asked Mum if the goddess kissed her too, then. She shook her head and replied with a sad smile, "No, she spat on me."

Guess she spat on my brothers too, then.

Da, tall, broad, and swarthy, grumbled about the draft. "Shattering slavery, that's what it is," he muttered. Mum shushed, but it wasn't anything we hadn't heard before. As the

Bluebloods' coup dragged on, they demanded new blood to sustain it, and they'd found ways to get it.

The military auto arrived, and Freude set down his duffel bag to say his farewells. He hugged Mum, and she handed him a bag of her *vanillekipferl* cookies. He kissed her on the cheek and put the bag in his duffel. When he straightened, Mum placed a hand on his face, tears in her eyes.

Freude smiled. Taking a few steps back, he gazed at us together. Ma fidgeted with her goddess pendant. Da put an arm around her waist, stilling her, and a hand on Keim's shoulder. I hugged the gift Freude had given me, a stuffed toy beastie called an *elephant*. Ehren stood a little distance away, as if feeling too mature to betray emotion and too upset to look up from his shoes.

Except for Mum, Ehren loved Freude best. Ehren had always done as Freude did and gone where Freude went, until now. Now, Ehren would not look up as Freude shouldered his bag and smiled. He would not look up as Freude turned and walked away from him, away from us.

He would not see Freude again. Neither would we.

A message arrived a year later. Freude had died in an "unfortunate incident." His remains were not suitable for transport or for proper burial. He had no personal effects. Condolences.

Ehren ran out of the back door with his eyes boiling over with tears. Da held Keim while I asked questions and received no answers. Mum never baked *vanillekipferl* cookies again.

In the morning, I head to the river to fill my canteen. When I hear raised voices I decide to leave, but as I turn, I glimpse a boy and girl wrestling on the bank of the river. The boy wears nothing but a ragged girding, and he tears away the girl's shawl in their scuffle, exposing her torso wrap and leaving her head and shoulders bare.

Clouds of dust churn beneath their feet. The girl grits her teeth, her lips pulled back into a snarling grin. The boy, smaller and browner than the girl, wriggles like a weasel, slipping through one grasp and then the next, using his nakedness against her.

I'm entranced. I check my scarf, tucking it more tightly around my neck, and walk to the edge of the water and pretend to wash my dishes. I watch the kids in astonishment. Are they laughing?

The girl, actually a young woman, just slight, tries to bathe the boy, but he squirms and bucks, soaking them both and kicking up dust from the shore. When he wriggles entirely out of her grasp, she gives up in despair.

*"Du klines shvine,"* she shouts in exasperation. *"Tzee kommen har."*

The words slip away before I grasp them, but the meaning is obvious: Brat, get back here.

When the woman notices me her smile fades. She busies herself with brushing mud from her clothes. She wears a common girding, baggy pants tight at the hips and ankles, and a top made from a swath of fabric that wraps her from hips to collarbones. I force myself not to stare at her bare shoulders.

The boy stands several meters away in his mud-caked girding. His chest heaves, accentuating his protruding ribs. Bare-chested, girding in tatters, hair wild—he reminds me of a beastie, like a cunning creature up to no good. His blue eyes gleam with mischief, which puts me on my guard.

"Mikael, *tzee kommen har bitte*," the woman beckons.

The beast-child shakes his head, planting his feet and placing his hands on hips.

*"Tzee kommen heehar zerook,"* the woman yells, her patience gone.

Her words trickle through my mind, familiar, but I can't quite grasp their meaning.

The boy sticks his tongue out at her and disappears into the trees. The woman throws her hands in exasperation and begins rinsing dust and mud from her clothes. She washes her dark hair with a bar of soap, working the lather through with care.

I wash my dishes a second time, stalling, watching her from the corner of my eye. I see girls and boys like her so often now—older sisters turned mothers and older brothers turned fathers. I guess with near certainty that the boy is her brother.

"Is it good in rinsing my hair now?" she asks suddenly, interrupting my thoughts. Her Northern accent lengthens the "oo" and softens her n's and d's.

"What?" I reply, startled. Her dark-blue eyes twist my stomach into knots, such a strange sensation. Not the same as when someone shoots at me, but similar.

"Is it good to you in rinsing my hair now? It will not . . ." She searches for a word. ". . . be annoying you?"

I look at her blankly. Then, finally, it clicks. I'm downstream. She doesn't want to rinse her hair until I'm done washing dishes. "Go ahead. I'm finished," I blurt.

She nods, saying "thank you" in her native tongue, *"Danke."* The word twists in my mind like a key, and the language flows out. Bleak memories, ones I prefer sunk in forgetfulness, surge into my mind. Screaming. Blood. Burning bodies. I blink rapidly, and the past resolves into the present. I see her slight figure again. Pale skin. Blue eyes. Brown hair.

She's a Blueblood. The realization feels like a knife twisting in my ribs. But, if so, what's she doing down here? Bluebloods belong up north. Is she a religious deviant? Maybe a cur?

I search for signs that she's a mixed-blood, a cur, but the woman's features betray no indigenous features. No vibrant hair or eyes. No slotted pupils or tympanic membranes. No pointed teeth, scales, tail, or claws. A pure-blooded human if I ever saw one—blue eyes, dark-brown hair, and pale skin straight from the ancestors' bloodlines.

She catches me staring and her face turns the palest shade of pink. I look away quickly, my own face burning and my heart beating like a kettledrum, but I watch in periphery. She squeezes out her hair and twists it up over her head, pinning it in place. Then she retrieves a ragged gray shawl and covers her head and shoulders.

A Blueblood from the north. Could she identify me? If she got a closer look, would she—

The clatter of dishes interrupts my thoughts. I lash out with an open hand, not looking to see what's upset my satchel. I already know.

My hand strikes the boy in the chest, and he falls over backward. He lands on his rear in the dirt, stunned. He clutches my stuffed elephant. I try to take it from him, but he recovers. I catch the wrist of one scrawny arm before he can escape. He bares his teeth like a small savage. I note their predatory points.

Blue eyes, brown hair, and an indigenous feature. This boy is a half-brother, a mixed-blood, a cur. . . .

The boy takes advantage of my surprise and kicks at me. I catch his foot and lift him into the air. He dangles sideways, shouting at me in that foreign tongue. The words avalanche through my mind. The boy is exceptionally versed in insults.

He drops my stuffed elephant and claws at my hand. It shackles his wrist like *Eisen*. Then one of his clawing hands strikes at my face. He misses but snags my headscarf and pulls it from my head.

I glance at the woman, half-expecting her to scream. She must see the silver disk in the base of my skull. She must recognize it and know what I am. She'll call for help, and I'll run because that will be my only choice. If the Wahren finds me, its creatures will drag me back, and I'd rather die than go back.

I reel in my panicked thoughts, counting my inhalations to slow my breathing and brace myself.

But, she doesn't scream. She stands quietly with her hands clasped in front of her, an expression of mild concern on her face.

I look between her and the snarling beast-child and back.

To my surprise, she begins to giggle. Then she points at her brother. *"Endlik! Tzine fett vegkreegen,"* she teases. Finally, you get what you deserve!

She doesn't recognize me. Either she doesn't see the port, or she doesn't care.

Relief floods me like a drug. Then comes an idea. I know I should leave. I should release the boy, turn my back, and walk away. Yet, I continue to stare at the boy wriggling and snapping in my hands. So much energy! And the woman . . .

I glance at her.

Her skin is as fair as the Kaltstein snow and her eyes reflect the deep blue of the frigid mountain lakes—serene, still, and clean. A lock of hair, nearly black with water, clings to her forehead, curling into her eyes. She tucks it away with long, delicate fingers.

Beautiful.

Then I note the sores on her hands and the peeling sunburn on her face. I note her hollow cheeks, cracked lips, and shadowed eyes. I look past the brilliant blue of her irises and see the haunted expression behind them.

Yet, she smiles. Despite the dirt and the heat, despite hard work and an uncertain future, despite terror and loneliness, she smiles. It makes my soul ache like icy hands exposed to warmth, and even though it hurts me, I want to be near her—I need to be near her.

I'm a fool. I know I'm a fool, but I want to pretend anyway. I want to pretend that I'm not what I am. Just for a while. Then I'll leave.

I nod to myself. Of course, I can leave whenever I need. I'll walk away as easily as anyone—as easily as my brothers—as easily as my father. Leaving is easy. Why shouldn't it be? It's all I have ever known.

She laughs, a sound like chimes in a warm breeze, and my reservations flee.

I carry the beast-child toward the stream. His eyes widen when he realizes what I'm about to do. With a light toss, I send him splashing into the river. He breaks through the surface, spouting water from his mouth and shivering. He scrambles out near his sister.

*"Du drecksau,"* he shouts, making a rude gesture at me.

His sister continues to laugh, and for the first time in a long time, I feel a smile on my face.

I rested on my stomach on the floor, my chin propped on my hands. I could smell the dust trapped between the floorboards and feel the grit on my skin. The staccato taps of Keim's pencil played counterpoint to the tinks of sand and sticks pelting the windows from the sandstorm outside. Mum and Da worked somewhere out there in that sand, trying to get the beasties into the barn.

I contemplated the plastic figurines before me, my mind absorbed in childish fantasy. Toy soldiers perched on the backs of legendary herps—dinosaurs! A tyrannosaurus rex clamped his enormous muzzle on the spine of a triceratops. A brachiosaurus crushed the life from a hapless foot soldier.

"Hey, Keim!" I shouted from my spot beneath the coffee table.

"What?" Keim replied, refusing to glance away from his homework.

"Dinosaurs are real, right?" I asked excitedly.

He shook his head in annoyance, muttering to himself, but I wouldn't be ignored. I clamored over the couch and stood directly in front of his desk.

"Dinosaurs are real, Keim! Right?" I hollered.

"Lights Above, shut up!" Keim shouted, slapping the back of my buzzed head. "I don't care about your stupid toys. Get out of my face!"

I sat on the floor in shock, the back of my head tingling from the strike of Keim's open palm. "But dinosaurs are real, Keim. . . ." I whimpered.

That night, Keim came into my room. When I heard him, I pretended to sleep, afraid he was still angry. But he didn't pour water on me or stick a herp down my back like I expected. He just stood at the end of my bed and cried.

I stayed silent.

After a few minutes, Keim set something beside my bed and left, closing the door behind him so that all the light from the hallway disappeared.

I slid out of bed and snatched my torch from off my dresser.

With a few quick twists, I wound it up. When I clicked it on, it illuminated the glossy plastic of Keim's blue brachiosaurus toy. I snatched it and tumbled back into bed, curling around my new treasure beneath the sheets.

I held it against my chest, trying to push away the ugly feelings inside me. Because the gift didn't mean Keim was sorry for smacking me. The gift meant Keim was sorry he was leaving. Not tomorrow or the next day, but soon. Ehren left his toy soldiers on my bed the day he left.

First, Freude. Then, Ehren. Now, Keim.

I hugged the plastic toy harder, missing my brothers more than I missed anything in the whole wide world.

The woman is Sara and the boy is Mikael, but I don't dare use their names; to name someone is to claim them. I don't give them my name either, but I teach the boy how to turn leaves into whistles. I gather wood for the woman, and the woman cooks food for me. But each night, I return to my camp and sleep alone. Still, it's not my fire I think of when the cold of the deep night creeps into my bones, and in the mornings, I wake, gather my things, and find the woman and boy.

Each day, we draw closer to Rettung, and the woman talks excitedly about the future. In stilted phrases, bursts of her native language, and lively gestures, she talks about her plans, her skills, a job, a home, and school for her brother.

I keep my many thoughts to myself. I speak rarely, and never about myself. If I do answer, it's never truthful, and she can tell. It's not fair, but she doesn't complain.

After a hot afternoon, we camp early because a sandstorm gathers on the horizon. The boy and I catch a dune skink in the muddy ravine that was the Traege River. The woman laughs when I clamber out caked in sludge then screams when I flick a clod at her.

I clean the arm-length beastie, plucking the short legs from the snakelike body and emptying the innards, and the woman cooks it into a stew. We sit together in the dusky light, the remnants of our meal in a pot on the ground drawing flies. The skink tasted like coprolite and chewed like boot leather, but it feels good to have a full belly for once. I relax into our routine, content. The woman talks while she mends clothes and I listen.

Silence falls between us. One stitch, two, three, four stitches, and a breath, then she speaks again. "What happened to the people of your family?"

"I'm going to meet them," I lie.

"Where?" she asks, pausing mid-stitch.

She wants me to stay, but if I stay, who will be the next to leave? The boy? The woman? No, only me. I will be the one to leave.

"Where's the boy?" I murmur, avoiding her question.

"Sleeping," she replies, nodding at a heap of ragged blankets behind her. She hems her brother's shirt. It looks like a patchwork quilt my mother once made.

"Shirt, please," she says, holding out a hand.

"What?" I blurt, startled.

"For the mending," she says, her hand hanging in the air and the hint of a smile on her face.

"Oh."

I look down at my shirt. Tan, lightweight, and simple, I wear a sark any farmer in the Dustlands might wear. The tattered laces allow the front to fall open, exposing my bony chest and my mother's goddess pendant. The hem hangs agape, a rip running parallel to the seam. I sigh and pull the shirt over my head, the necklace clinking against my chest. I drop the shirt into her waiting hand.

But her eyes are on me, not the shirt. She stares at my torso and arms.

I've been careless. Washing away the sludge this afternoon has left me cleaner than I've been in months. As the last sliver of sunlight shines across my scars, the nodes in the center of each glisten, small but distinct.

The sun sets, and she drops her eyes.

I wait for her to speak, my stomach churning.

"Where I was child, the sages say . . ." She pauses, searching for the right words. ". . . they say, *Tyfel spreken vahrhite unt angel leeghen*—demons speak truth and angels lie. They say the world is not *ghetilt*—not divided—into light or shadow. They say the world is *likt unt shaden*—light and shadow. All things are both."

She picks up her needle and thread and begins stitching the hole in the hem of my shirt. She pauses, gazing past me at nothing. "Some are not believing this. They seek the things that is perfect." Her brow furrows, and she sews with renewed vigor. "These people—they want to kill my brother. They call him 'cur.'" She spits the word, not looking up. "His father was my father. His mother was servant, but my father loved her. My father loved my brother." She chokes on the words. Her sewing slows again, and a tear steals down her cheek.

I wait, standing rigid and shirtless before her hunched figure.

Suddenly, she lifts her eyes to me. "He is *mensklik*, correct? We are all human." She points her needle at me, stabbing the air to punctuate each word. "You are human."

Why is she telling me this? I look away, staring into the distance. Her words twist around each other in my mind. My thoughts take them apart and put them together. They tell me one thing for certain: the woman knows what I am.

I stand patiently while she finishes sewing the hole and replaces the ties of my shirt. How did I allow this to happen? How could I have been so foolish? How could I have been lulled into such carelessness? Will she tell anyone? Should I kill her? How can I kill her? I can't. How can I even leave her?

But, I know the truth. I must leave her to spare her.

She hands the shirt back to me, and I slip it over the scars.

"I feel a storm coming," I say quietly. "I'll get you more wood before I sleep. I'll leave it nearby." I snatch my satchel from beside the campfire and toss it over my shoulder. The stuffed elephant muffles the clatter of dishes as it hits my back.

"You will come back tomorrow?" she asks gently as I step

out of the firelight. A hint of sadness tinges her voice, as if she already knows my answer.

"I'll be back tomorrow," I lie.

She knows I'm lying.

All of us knew he was lying.

Da stood with one hand on the back door's latch and a crumpled page in the other. He peered over his shoulder at my mother. Keim and I hid in the hallway. Mum's eyes sagged with exhaustion, her gaze distant. Since Freude, she'd struggled to keep her mind in the present. Da, his hands bandaged against urvogel scratches and his hair gray with dust, glared at her with a flinty expression.

"I just need time to think," he said in a dead voice. "I'll be back before bed." His lies swarmed around me, stinging like wasps. I flinched with each word.

*He's leaving,* something whispered to us. Our hearts told the truth even when our tongues wouldn't.

"No! Don't go," I cried. *Don't leave me.*

Da's eyes searched for me. He stepped toward the hallway with his brows pinched like *vanillekipferl* cookies and his mouth as rigid and crooked as a crowbar.

My mother stepped between us and blocked my view of him. "Just leave if you're going to leave."

Her quiet voice turned my bones to ice. She was sending Da away. She did that sometimes. She'd tell us to leave, her voice cold and sharp, stabbing us to the heart. But, didn't she see? Didn't she see that this time he would leave, and for good?

His patience cracked. He shook the crumpled, tattered page in her face. "Woman, you had more sons than just Freude. If you'd have remembered that, Ehren wouldn't have left, too."

Her eyes turned blank and cold. "Leave."

*Leave*. Always *leave*. Never *stay*.

The back door slammed against the wood frame and swung back open, creaking. Outside, the battered auto shrieked and then roared to life, like a siren in the fading light.

Mum slumped onto the couch. Freude's death notice lay on the floor at her feet.

When Ehren left, she'd watched with empty eyes. Even when the door had kept bashing its frame, she just stared through it. Finally, I'd shut it for her, understanding. Sometimes that door could be so hard to close.

This time she didn't watch. She sat with her face in her hands, but I knew she wasn't crying. She hadn't cried since Freude died. Instead, she bottled her sadness inside, and the tears she would not shed ate away her soul like a gullywasher.

I ran out of the house after Da, dashing into the road, but all that remained of Da was a trail of dust and the silence of bad things happening. I went back inside after the last slice of yellow sunlight crumbled into shadow. I shut the door tightly after me.

None of the lights were on in the house. Keim lay wide-eyed in his bed, staring at the ceiling. I didn't dare disturb him.

The living room looked and felt empty. Mum had stacked Da's abandoned belongings on the dust-bloated couch already. On impulse, I snatched Da's pocketknife from the pile. A crack had split the wood handle, and the joint ground with dust when it opened. It wasn't worth much, but Da had spent weeks excavating the midden heap on our property in search of valuables. The knife was all he'd found. When Mum asked why he kept it, he said it reminded him not to go searching for buried treasure when he had treasure enough at home. What did it mean now that he'd abandoned it?

Blue darkness enveloped the house. I crept silently to my room in the blue shadows. I crawled into bed with my clothes on and pulled the sheet over my head. I fell asleep clutching the pocketknife.

Keim wasn't in his room the next morning. He wasn't in the house. His backpack was gone; and, the back door was unlatched and blowing in the wind. Its slamming woke me.

Leaving speaks in two languages, lies and silence. I prefer silence because lies are tiring.

After the woman speaks to me, I walk into the trees. When I turn to peer back at the encampment, hundreds of refugee fires dot the hillside in front of me. Shadows lurk around and between the spots of light.

There are a few people, like the woman, who are bright lights, fires burning with compassion and wisdom, but the rest of us are only shadows of humans, shades. We shades gather around these lights for warmth and comfort, but in the end we smother them.

I won't smother her light.

I find a dead tree and begin wrenching joints of wood off its trunk. I break branches with my bare hands, feeling splinters sting my palms with a perverse pleasure. I gather more than usual. Knowing the woman, she'll share her wood with her neighbors in the morning.

A pained smile tweaks my lips.

She's too kind; I can only hope someone will be kind to her in return. I worry for them. I wish I could see them through this harshest stretch of our journey. I wish I could eat more meals with them. I wish I could listen longer to her talk. I wish. . . . But, no.

A sliver of blue moon hangs above the horizon, and the red moon lights the night dimly, little more than a muted circle in the sky. Its wan light tinges the world slightly red. Thunder groans in the distance, a sandstorm stirring.

I approach the woman's campsite cautiously, carrying the wood under one arm. But as I creep into her camp, I sense a wrongness that causes my belly to clench. My senses heighten, like a beastie that's caught the scent of a predator. The sensation feels so familiar that I inwardly cringe from it.

I step into the dull glow of ember light and realize the woman and the boy are gone. The wood drops from my hands into the dust.

Boot prints score the ground, and dust and twigs lie on their disheveled bedrolls. I follow a trail of shattered branches and find the woman's shawl shoved into a bush a few meters away.

DUNCAN HALLECK

The boot prints, mixed with the small shoe prints of the boy and woman, lead through more broken trees. I follow the path a few meters farther. Something flutters on a tree, catching my eye. I pinch it between my fingers and recognize a bit of blue fabric from the woman's torso wrap. I turn, squinting into the darkness. A few meters farther, I spot another fluttering piece of fabric tucked among shattered limbs.

I clench my eyes shut. She left me a trail. She wants me to come after her. She expects me to come after her. But I can't. I can't give myself up for her.

I rub the fabric of her shawl between my fingers. The threads snag on my rough skin. I run my fingers over my head, my hair as snarled as my thoughts. Isn't this a good thing? They'll sell her in Rettung and send her far away from the Wahren and me. This solves my dilemma, doesn't it?

An errant breeze whips past me, tossing the woman's shawl in my face. Her scent fills me. I see her hunched in the firelight stitching the holes in my ragged shirt. I see her face alight as she describes the future she dreams of.

She called me *mensklik*—human, in spite of all she suspects.

"Lights Above," I mutter, both a prayer and an oath.

I wrap her shawl around my neck like a scarf. Her smell soothes me. It eases my muscles and focuses my mind. I close my eyes and trigger the mechanism installed in my brain and fused to my nervous system.

The nodes open and waves of black nanomechs surge out, sliding beneath my clothes and webbing across my skin, threads thickening into an armored membrane. With a barely audible snip, the membrane closes over my scalp, cutting through my hair. Filthy blue locks fall to the ground. It closes over my head and face, covering my ears, eyes, nose, and mouth. Satiny armor envelops me; yet, the nanomechs allow sound, light, and air to permeate the membrane.

After months without it, I am unused to the suit. My body responds slowly, like a snake on a cold morning. Months of malnutrition-induced fatigue ebbs away. I flex my arms and shoulders. The layers of nanomechs slide over one another easily. With a burst of speed, I charge several kilometers into the darkness, my body bursting through trees and lunging over dips and ravines. Urvogels and tiny, four-winged microraptors erupt from the trees, screaming as they scramble into the sky.

I revel in the sensation of having every increment of effort magnified tenfold. I crush a boulder of granite the size of my head, dust erupting between my fingers, just because I can.

But that is the inherent danger of the suit: *Just because I can.* That thought leads men down dark paths. It leads them to consider doing what they should not, even if they can.

My hands ball into tight fists, the joints aching. I will not be that creature again.

I run until the last campfire disappears from view. Then I stop and listen, waiting for the last raptor cry to die out. I fidget nervously, breaking twigs in my palm smaller and smaller while I wait. I'm afraid, but I will do what I must.

The nanomechs give me strength, agility, and armor; they give me my demon body. The enhancer is my demon heart. But the port—the Titanite disk connected to my brainstem—that is my demon soul. It is what I know and who I am, my knowledge and memory. With it, I can manipulate the nanomechs, either manually or instinctively. With it, I can access information and download it directly into my mental archive. And, with it, the Wahren can find me.

With a deep breath, I tap into the Wahren's servers.

"Hello, Leviathan," a familiar voice, neither male nor female, says in my mind. My skin crawls with revulsion. I still despise this mechanical creature. The AI enforced all the Wahren's policies and commands, sometimes using my endocrine performance enhancer to do it.

"Hello, Kog. Could you please retrieve a detailed map of this area for my use?"

"Leviathan, you are listed as absent without leave."

"Not absent, Kog, only on a brief hiatus. The map?" I ask with false confidence. To my relief, a map forms in my mind's eye. "Kog, please cross-reference this map with known slaver movements in the area." I don't even consider that the Kog might not have the information. The Kognitive Network thrives on patterns.

Kog complies without comment, and its compliance makes me uneasy. It means it's focusing its processing power on discovering my location. At least it will divine little from my nanomechs. My surroundings are resoundingly nondescript, as I intended. No people. No campfires. Only desert and darkness.

The data emerges and, with a glance, I identify the slavers' main encampment. "Thank you, Kog. That is all. Going dark," I state hurriedly.

Kog attempts to argue, but I quickly lockdown all frequencies coming to or going out from my Kog Port. Using dark mode also removes me from the Kog's tracking apparatus, but it will have marked my general location. Not only have I confirmed that I am alive, but I have told the Wahren where to look.

I am a fool, and yet, I feel no regret; I know the location of the woman and boy. Like a hound with the scent, my body yearns for motion.

Not yet.

I touch the shawl to my lips, just briefly. "For the woman who speaks of *likt unt shaden*," I murmur. Then, I sprint into the darkness.

The slavers have arranged their equipment to look like a refugee camp, but their autos, massive rigs with powerful engines and lots of cargo space, are kept in too good of condition to belong to refugees. Besides, only men stalk about the camp, packing and growling at each other.

I observe the slavers from a copse of trees on a hill above them. My tech-fused eyes show me at least a dozen hostiles, and I think I know which truck the woman and her brother are held in. Three slavers stand guard around it. It seems they are the only captives.

My eyes readjust to six-six vision, and I tune my hearing to reach their camp, but other noises interfere. Animals scurry through the underbrush. The wind rattles branches. Thunder roars in the distance. I use my Kog Port to focus on the voices, filtering out the distractions.

"Why didn' ya watch that one, ya shattering gyp," a man snarls. He talks with the clipped inflection of Rettung's slums. "I don' care if he seemed dangerous. Ya could'a jumped him all on his lonesome as he left their camp or nabbed him in his sleep."

He stands near the center of camp. A snakelike tail, as brown and yellow as the Dustlands, trails from the man's tailbone and hangs over his shoulder. The tip curls and uncurls on his chest as he talks. His companions work around him, packing camp.

"At least we got the Blueblood," a large man with thick lips offers.

The leader sneers. "At least we got t' girlie," he mocks, before striding over to the man and knocking him to the ground. His tail slips around the man's neck, and he presses his face into the dirt with his boot. "If you'd think wit' your head instead of your pecker, ya little schist, then maybe ya'd realize a young man like that's worth more and easier for selling than a shattering Blueblood. We'd have to go all t' way to Endonia to sell t' little witch. As it is, we'll have to pawn her off to a whore shed in Rettung before we sell t' boy to t' Wahren just to keep t' Wahren from stringing us up."

Mention of my former master brings bile to my mouth, but it's their plans for the woman and boy that sicken me most. I bite my tongue to trim my anger, and I taste blood. I take deep breaths through my nose, trying to bring my emotions back under control.

"Don' know what t' Wahren's doing in the south anyway," one of the other slavers mutters.

"It don' matter what ya know," brays the leader. "This,"—the man points to his temple with a knobby finger—"this is why I'm t' boss and ya clinkers work for me. What ya think don' matter! What I think don' matter! All tha' really matters is understandin' what's really going on, and I can do that."

I narrow my eyes. As if a worm like him could understand what really turns this world. No one understands until they have nanomechs in their nerves and a voice in their head.

"Now," he continues, after releasing the thick-lipped man. "I'ma go fec, and this job better'll be done by t' time I get back."

The leader tramps away to relieve himself, and I finally make my move.

I set the woman's shawl aside. Then I picture the leader in my mind and set the nanomechs to moving. They slide across my skin. They layer themselves, altering my features, and change color to imitate the image. Hawkish face. Stringy blond hair. Narrow jaw. Lean, long, and tense, quivering like a whip ready to strike. And a tail hung over my shoulder. I'm not wearing their leader's clothes, but this will throw off his henchmen long enough.

"Goddess, save me," I murmur. Then, with a deep breath, I stride into the camp.

The slavers become frantically busy, but the subterfuge doesn't last long. I don't know what I missed. Maybe my silence gives me away, or I didn't get his nose quite right? Regardless, one of the men looks closely at me, the thick-lipped one. He has a paunch, but he's tall and heavyset. I see his hand reaching for the gun shoved haphazardly into the waistband of his pants.

He knows I'm a threat. What he doesn't know is that he's already dead.

I strike before he can say a word. My disguise falls away as I leap at him; I'm a black creature, a demon, again. As soon as I twist his neck, the suit's endocrine performance enhancer triggers my brain, and my blood swells with endorphins and dopamine. I feel incredible. I feel invincible. I feel the need for more.

The slavers scatter like insects. I convert armor into greater speed and pounce on the nearest one. He screams until I crush his trachea. A group rushes me, and I sift through my archive of information, falling back on hundreds of hand-to-hand combat lessons downloaded from the Kog before I left the Wahren. The kicks fall precisely and the punches land exactly.

As I kill the last man, I smell ozone and immediately dodge to the side. A lightning ball streaks past and strikes a tree. The tree explodes, splinters ricocheting off my suit. I spot a spindly man guised in black hefting an ion cannon. I bolster my armor as I stalk toward him. I feel the drain on my speed as my energy focuses on armoring the nanomechs.

The spindly man fires again. The lightning ball explodes against me, lightning coiling around my arms and down my legs like snakes. Some of the nanomechs spark, smoke, and die, overloaded, but the nodes replace them. The cannon is useless against my Koganzug; a crossbow could do more damage. The man fires again but with the same result. Since the fool stubbornly depends on his cannon, I reach him easily, crushing the barrel in my hand. The gun explodes, killing the slaver. I toss aside the twisted scrap metal.

"Don' move or I kill t' runt," a familiar voice bawls.

I turn and face the leader outfitted in his anzug. Black nanofabric covers him from head to toe, and he holds the beast-child hostage in front of him. His tail wraps the boy's throat. They stand twenty meters from me, but I can smell excrement on the leader's boot. His hawkish face, still prominent beneath the black fabric, looms over the boy possessively. The boy winces, his arm twisted behind his back. His blue eyes, bright with firelight, glance back at the man with—what? Fear? Panic? No, annoyance.

I hear his sister crying for him in the truck. The sound is like blood in the water.

The remaining men slink into view. Some pull anzug masks over their sneering faces and activate their suits, hoping to intimidate me. They think they've won. They can't see that I'm smiling, too.

Anzug combat suits have standard abilities—stealth, speed enhancement, auto and manual armoring, strength augmentation, combat technique assists—every suit-bearer enjoys these. But I wear no mere anzug, something to slip on and off again. No, I wear a Koganzug, a combat suit that uses nanotech to integrate with the user's nervous system, mind, and the Kog. Because of this, Koganzug users develop unique abilities—signature abilities. They called me "Leviathan" for a reason.

A single tendril of nanomechs trails from my suit to the man, weaving up his clothes like a needle and thread. A thin glint of metal flashes in the firelight as it slides across the leader's throat like a bow across a string. The nanofabric, normally resilient, might as well be silk.

The leader stares at me for a moment, his feline eyes terrified. Then blood pours from his throat. His tail falls from the boy's neck. The man collapses, hands clamped over the wound. The boy glares at the dying man, absently massaging his sore shoulder. Then he scrambles into one of the autos.

The remaining slavers stare at their fallen leader in shock. Then, before their leader even gasps his last, they flee. I watch them run for a moment, considering letting them go. Then I think of the dead refugee and his daughter, and my woman and the boy.

"No," I growl through clenched teeth.

I stretch my arms out to either side, the fingers splayed. Rigid threads of nanomechs shoot from them. The thin wires slash through the air, cutting flesh and into bone. Some slavers trigger their camouflage mechanisms, but no matter. I wave my hands like an impassioned conductor directing his masterpiece. My hands rise and fall, chopping through the air, and the threads cut down my enemies.

The enhancer floods my bloodstream with adrenaline, dopamine, and endorphins. "More, more, more," the enhancer tells me. As if on their own volition, my hands move faster. Men die, flesh in tatters.

I laugh. Shame burns through me as I laugh, but I can't help it; my body rides high on endorphins and dopamine. There is no truer form of guilty pleasure than this. I want to scream.

Finally, with no targets left, I allow my arms to rest. I reel in my tendrils, pulling the nanomechs back into the main body of the suit. The nanomechs that failed during the battle return to the nodes for repairs. My suit tells me I have no injuries, but my blood pressure and heart rate are high. It issues serotonin to calm me.

I trigger my infrared vision, noting those still alive. I approach each one and kill him quickly, a mercy. Some suit-bearers draw out the end, prolonging the enhancer's pleasure. I never have. I hated inflicting pain even before escaping the Wahren.

Then I see the last slaver. He's whimpering on the ground curled into a ball. He can't hear my footsteps, not with my suit activated, but he looks up. Perhaps he felt death coming. I squat on my haunches, studying the man.

His eyes widen in terror. One eye is milky white, a scar splitting his face.

"It was you, wasn't it?" I say, my voice quiet. "You've been watching us this whole time, scouting targets for your crew and keeping tabs until your crew was ready."

The man's larynx bobs as he swallows.

"You took them," I hiss.

The man stares at me blankly, eyes ringed with terror. He doesn't recognize me since he can't see my face. He doesn't know who I'm talking about, and he doesn't care.

I clench my fists. Gods, I want to peel his skin away with my tendrils. A part of my mind urges me to do it. "More, more, more," it whispers. I lift a hand in front of the slaver's face and open my fingers slowly. Black tendrils lengthen from my fingers. They surround the scar-faced man, prepared to trace mazes into his flesh.

He stares at them, his whole body trembling. He can't look away.

*"You are human,"* the woman's voice echoes in my mind.

I bow my shoulders, closing my eyes so I don't see when the tendrils lop off his head. It is a much kinder death than he deserves.

I leave the bodies where they lie, unwilling to touch them again.

I find the slavers' water barrels and try to wash away the blood coating my combat suit. Technically, the nanomechs return to the nodes for cleaning and repair when I disengage the suit, so I don't need to wash, but I shudder at the thought of allowing the slavers' blood to enter my body through the nodes. I scrub so hard that the joints of my fingers and wrists ache.

Serotonin trickles into my bloodstream, attempting to balance my mood, but I disengage my suit, cutting off the supply. The nanomechs skitter back into the little holes that punctuate my body. My skin tingles, and my body trembles from exertion and shock. I feel a headache blooming behind my eyes, the first sign of an enhancer hangover.

There was a time I could use the suit for weeks, but not now, not in this condition. The Wahren meant the suit to be used by someone in peak physical condition, not a half-starved clinker like me. But at least the suit didn't suck me dry. Cursed way to die.

After washing away as much blood as possible from my clothes, I surreptitiously check on the boy and his sister. The boy is searching the trucks and crates while his sister waits in the back of an auto, her hands still shackled to the floor. I pray the night hides the bloodstains on my clothes, grab the woman's shawl from where I stashed it, and jog toward the boy.

"What happened?" I ask, gasping. "I went by the camp—found boot prints and this." I wave the shawl at him. Then, I look at a body and feign alarm. "Is that guy dead?"

The boy crossly ignores me, continuing to search the stacked crates and barrels, probably for something to free his sister.

"Here, let me help." I find a crowbar in another truck and use it to pry the chain from the floor. Meanwhile, the boy finds the keys on the leader's body and jingles them in my face. He has no scruples with patting down the bodies. I snatch them from his fingers. He laughs and runs off.

I release the woman from the manacles and help her down from the auto.

"You came," she murmurs, as if to herself. She looks over the carnage and shudders, rubbing her bare shoulders briskly. I wrap her shawl around her. She doesn't seem to notice. "Where's Mikael?"

I shrug. "I'll find him."

She nods tiredly. Worry pinches her face.

The woman rinses her chafed wrists while I search for the boy. If I wasn't certain I killed every shattering slaver, I'd be worried. I find him standing over the scar-faced slaver's body. He spits on the corpse. The woman comes up behind us, sees the corpse, and tows her brother away.

I lead the woman and boy back to camp. The boy practically sleeps on his feet, so I carry him. By the time we arrive, the red moon has set, and I barely distinguish the horizon from the night sky. It's chilly despite the walking so I build a fire. The woman gasps at the bloodstains on my shirt. I pull it over my head and throw it in the fire. She makes no comment, but she watches me, not the burning shirt.

The boy sleeps in his sister's arms. I try to reassure her—coax her to sleep—by promising to watch over them. But it's a lie. They don't need me. At this point, the longer I stay, the more danger I draw to them. Best I leave by daybreak.

My lie doesn't deceive her. She watches as I move the abandoned stack of wood to her pile. A question lies beneath her expression that I don't answer, and she won't ask. I believe she understands what happened to the slavers, and I believe she understands what I must do now.

I turn away from her so I don't have to look into her eyes, but I still feel them.

I walked through the back door and into the living room, leaving a trail of boot prints on the dust-covered floor. After nearly a decade away, I returned home, somehow expecting things to be different from what they were, despite the intervening years.

I trailed my hand along the tops of the couches, sending an avalanche of dust into their seats. In my room, dust covered my bed and caked toy soldiers and plastic dinosaurs. I pulled my old school bag from my closet, shaking the dust from it, and took my Da's pocketknife from my dresser. I found my stuffed toy elephant still tangled in my bed sheets and clutched it to my chest like a frightened child.

All silence.

All emptiness.

No redemption.

No forgiveness.

I found my mother's pendant on her dresser, the overlapping moons also dust covered. I put it around my neck and stared into her blemished mirror. In the speckled image, I saw a soul as empty and ruined as my home. With an unarmored fist, I shattered it, gouging my knuckles and leaving bloody streaks on the glass.

Then, I dumped my home's guts into the yard, and I burned it all. I burned the trash, the couches, the sheets, the pillows, the books, the souvenirs and keepsakes, the gifts, the pictures, the frames, the toy soldiers, and the plastic dinosaurs. I built a bonfire of a lifetime, a pyre for my soul, and filled the wasted land with the stench of melted plastic and ashen memories.

And, when I left, I left the back door swinging.

The woman falls into a fitful sleep. The gentle rise and fall of her chest matches the rhythm of the swaying trees. It reminds me of my mother holding me in her arms and rocking me, singing a song in a voice as thin and clear as dragonbug wings. I leave the stuffed elephant near the woman's bed, a gift for her brother, just as my brothers left gifts for me, and lift my satchel onto my shoulder. I leave my full canteen near the woman's woodpile. I think I can do without it. If I can't, well, that's one less demon in the world. Then I turn toward the mountains.

"Who are you?" the woman whispers.

Her voice startles me. I spin, staring at her still form. Her eyes are closed. Sweat polishes her furrowed brow. She murmurs unintelligible words, talking in her sleep.

I sigh in relief, but her question still unsettles me. Watching her, I can't help feeling I owe her something, some part of myself.

She has given me so much, her past, her future, her dreams, her company, her trust. . . . I don't have much to give, but the truth is something.

"Leiden Talson," I tell her.

"Leiden," she whispers. Her voice carries the hint of a smile.

That smile—it's as if I face my mother's mirror again. With that single honest answer, the glass breaks, and my wall of silence ruptures. I'm bleeding words—the words I would have said during these many weeks with the woman. They're pouring from my soul. Now, when I won't have another chance. Now, when it doesn't matter what I say because she can't hear me.

I laugh softly at the irony and emerge from the shadows to sit on a fallen tree by the dying fire. I rest my satchel behind me. The sound of my name from her lips eases me into my past, like slipping into a warm bath. It soaks away my careful reserve. I try to think of the last time someone called me by my name. I rub dust between my fingers as I think. Dust, the only constant in my life.

"My mum," I say quietly. "I haven't heard my name since that time. I had kissed her cheek good night after another silent evening. After years of just the two of us, we didn't have much to say. I told her I loved her, but her mind was already somewhere else. She never said 'I love you' back. I don't hold that against her though. She didn't know slavers would drag me away that night and sell me to the Wahren. She didn't know she would wake alone." I bow my head and run my fingers over my scalp. The thin layer of hair feels like velvet. "So, that was the end of her and that was the end of Leiden."

I scrub my burning eyes with the heels of my hands, then I tilt my head back and stare at the stars. I pick out Stonehenge and the Great Wall from the constellations. The blue moon sits on the western horizon, a frown stitched into the tapestry of constellations with silver thread. In a week, it will disappear beneath the horizon. If I'm lucky, I'll see it again when it rises in a half-year, when the growing season begins. If I'm not lucky, well . . .

"I went back," I confess. "The house was still there, but empty—emptier than emptiness explains. Less than the absence of its parts. That's how I knew she'd left. For the afterlife or somewhere else, I don't know." I sigh. "The truth is she'd been gone a long time. When my brothers left, and Da, she just . . ."

I let the sentence fade, my throat tight. I turn my gaze to my clasped hands. They're shaking. "You know, every one of those schists left the back door swinging, knowing somebody else would close it. I did it. I shut and latched the door after every shattering one of them."

My hands clench and in that moment, I realize I hate my Da and brothers for leaving. I hate them as much as I love them.

"Is there longing in you for this home?" The woman's voice reaches out from the darkness and pulls my mind back to the present.

I flinch away from her, my body tense and ready to flee, but I hold back. I focus on her silhouette outlined in dull firelight and a distant dawn. She sits up, the boy still asleep beside her.

"How long have you been awake?" I ask quietly.

"Leiden is what you are called?" she asks, softly. Her voice drifts to me in the silence like a dry, brittle leaf.

"How long have you been awake?" I repeat.

"You are alone? You are meeting no one?"

"How long have you been awake?" I ask again, my voice growing stony.

"You are leaving us. You want aloneness?"

"Yes, I'm leaving," I state firmly, not sure if I am answering her question or trying to sound like I am.

"Thank you," she whispers quietly, slowly pronouncing the words.

"For what?" I ask in surprise.

"For saving us. For being part of us. For bringing happiness in my heart for a short time."

She's not stopping me, I realize. There is freedom in that, and also pain—more pain than I expect. Mum never stopped any of them from leaving either.

I can't think of what to say. When my brothers left they never had anything to say and neither do I. The ache in my chest roars in my ears. I glance at the sleeping boy, wondering if he truly sleeps or if he waits to fold into his sister's arms after I turn my back on him.

I am still, but it is the stillness of a coming storm.

The first smudges of purple light touch the horizon. Nothing stirs but lightning in the far distance as the night transitions to day. I see the contours of the woman's pale face, the glimmering whites of her eyes, and her smooth bare shoulders in the soft pale glow of dawn.

"Please, don't leave," she says.

"How can you say that?" I ask harshly. She knows, but she must not understand. I shake my head, knowing I cannot describe to her what I am. . . .

I cannot describe to her what I am, but I can show her. In silence, I trigger the mechanism. Sitting on the log with my elbows propped on my knees and my hands supporting my chin, the nanomechs close over me. I watch, expecting her expression to change from sadness to terror as I transform—as I confirm that I am responsible for the slavers' bloody corpses. I show her what I am and I know she will despise me.

She draws in a sharp breath; I hear it as clearly as if she sits beside me.

I smile acerbically. "This is what I am, a perfect killing tool in human form. A demon."

*"Tyfel spreken vahrhite unt angel leeghen,"* she recites in a whisper, like a prayer. "We are all *likt unt shaden* and we are all *mensklik*."

"Human," I scoff. "I don't think so. Look at me! You saw those corpses." My lips curl into a bitter smile. "The worst part is that I enjoyed it! Human? I'm a monster, *ein tyfel*—a demon." I disengage the Koganzug. The nanomechs skitter back into their nodes, retracting like liquid sucked down a drain. I study my hands, too ashamed to look at her.

"You are human," she states firmly, each word enunciated with precision.

"You've seen what I am," I argue.

"Yes, I see what you are," she replies fiercely. "You long for your home—for family. You work hard. You watch over us. You saved us! You are patient. You are kind. You are ashamed. And, ya, you are broken. *Likt unt shaden*. You are human and *ein gooter mann*—a good man."

My heart clings to every word. Why? "The things I've done," I whisper.

"There is things past for each of us," she says passionately. "That is all past is, that thing behind us that brings us to this place we are at. *Das ist alles*—that is all! What you choose now, *das ist vas du bist*—that is what you are."

"It's not that simple," I reply softly. "They're going to come for me."

She doesn't ask who. She simply holds my gaze, her expression intent, while she speaks. "But they do not come yet."

Her words shock me into silence.

"Please, stay," she says.

The words she speaks are the words my mother could never bring herself to say. They cut through me like blades, excising the past I felt bound by. I see the stuffed toy elephant sitting in the dirt. I see the toys my brothers gave me melting into puddles of slag. I see my father's pocketknife atop a pile of castoff possessions like the dregs of a discarded life. I see my mother's dusty pendant and her empty house—an empty house in an empty land with an open door slamming in the breeze because there is no one left to close it.

I realize, suddenly, that I've been trying to leave behind the wrong things.

"Can I stay?" I whisper. The morning breeze snatches the words from my lips.

# *The Year in the Contests*

## LAST YEAR'S ANTHOLOGY

Each year we as judges and administrators strive to bring together an anthology that is of the highest quality that we can create, mixing articles and stories from judges, fantastic new illustrations from great new artists, and of course the stories that come from the best new writers that we can glean from around the world. So we hope each year that our efforts are well received, and last year we got some great reviews.

First of all, the anthology met with critical success, eliciting praise from *Library Journal*, *Publishers Weekly*, and this nice review from *Omni Magazine*: "Outside of easily being the best gateway competition for new and upcoming genre fiction writers, WotF also puts together a fantastic anthology book every year containing high-caliber stories that longtime fans and newcomers will enjoy. . . . The artwork is top-notch."

Just as importantly, last year's anthology, *Writers of the Future Volume* 33, hit #1 on the bestseller list for science fiction on Amazon, hit #1 on Barnes and Noble, hit #6 on the UK's *Daily News*, and hit in the top ten on sixty-nine other bestseller lists.

## CONTEST GROWTH

The L. Ron Hubbard's Writers and Illustrators of the Future Contests are some of the largest and longest-running contests in the world—and they are still growing by leaps and bounds.

In 2017, we celebrated the highest number of entrants ever for both the Writers of the Future and the Illustrators of the Future Contests. For example, the fourth quarter saw a 33%

increase of entries making it our largest single quarter ever. We love seeing this level of competition. It means that each quarter, we have a better chance of discovering great new talent.

## JUDGES WHO PASSED IN 2017

This past year we were saddened to lose two of our writing judges.

Dr. Jerry Pournelle passed away in September. He, of course, was famous for his megahit novels, such as *Lucifer's Hammer* and *The Mote in God's Eye*. He had also been a judge for the Writers of the Future Contest since 1986, so he helped mentor writers in the Contest for thirty-two years, always attending the awards ceremonies and speaking personally to the new winners during the writing seminars.

We also lost Dr. Yoji Kondo, a distinguished astrophysicist working with NASA since 1965. He wrote science fiction under the name of Eric Kotani. He was also an accomplished aikido instructor. Yoji passed away in October. He attended the Writers of the Future Awards ceremony each year with his wife and took great delight in encouraging our new writers.

## PUBLICATIONS BY PAST WINNERS

Each year, we go to great lengths to try to discover what our past Writers and Illustrators of the Future winners have been up to, but given the proliferation of online books and magazines, any numbers we give out would probably not reflect everything that has been released. For example, we counted over 100 novels by our writer winners this past year, but that doesn't include the hundreds of short stories they published. The same is true for our illustrators, who continue to publish dozens of book covers, illustrated books, graphic novels, comics, and so on. And, of course, much of the artwork done by our illustrators goes into products like video games, movie and television designs, etc., and that art is only seen once the work hits the screen. Rather than attempt to list everything, we give the highlights in our awards section below.

## AWARDS WON IN 2017 BY OUR PAST WINNERS AND JUDGES

*World Fantasy Awards*: Rachael K. Jones was a finalist for a World Fantasy Award in the short fiction category for "The Fall Shall Further the Flight in Me," which was published in the anthology *Clockwork Phoenix.* Karen Joy Fowler was a finalist for best anthology, *The Best American Science Fiction and Fantasy 2016*, which she edited along with John Joseph Adams. And Ken Liu was a finalist for his collection, *The Paper Menagerie and Other Stories.*

*Washington Science Fiction Association's Small Press Award*: Brad R. Torgersen was a finalist with his "Jupiter or Bust" (*Intergalactic Medicine Show*, Mar/Apr 2016). Aliette de Bodard was also a finalist for "A Salvaging of Ghosts" (*Beneath Ceaseless Skies*, Mar 2016).

*Sunburst Award for Excellence in Canadian Literature of the Fantastic*: James Alan Gardner was a finalist for his story "The Dog and the Sleepwalker," which was published in the anthology *Strangers Among Us.*

*Aurora Awards*: Writers Contest judge Robert J. Sawyer won Canada's Aurora Award for best novel for *Quantum Night*. He also won the Aurora Award for best novel of the decade for *The Neanderthal Parallax*.

*Hugo Awards*: Ken Liu was a finalist for best novel as translator for *Death's End*, written by Cixin Liu. Also, Carolyn Ives Gilman was a finalist with her novelette "Touring with the Alien," (*Clarkesworld*, Apr 2016).

*The David Gemmell Awards for Fantasy*: The Morningstar Award for best fantasy debut went to Megan E. O'Keefe for her novel *Steal the Sky*. Writers Contest judge Brandon Sanderson was a finalist for the best fantasy novel with *The Bands of Mourning*.

Locus *Awards*: Ken Liu was a finalist for best fantasy novel for *The Wall of Storm*. David D. Levine was a finalist for best first novel for *Arabella of Mars*. Aliette de Bodard placed as a finalist for her novelette "Pearl" published in the anthology *The Starlit Wood.* In the short story category Aliette de Bodard scored another finalist for "A Salvaging of Ghosts" (*Beneath Ceaseless Skies*, Mar 2016), Ken Liu for "Seven Birthdays" from the anthology *Bridging Infinity*; and past winner and current judge Nnedi Okorafor for "Afrofuturist 419" (*Clarkesworld*, Nov 2016).

The award for best collection went to Ken Liu for *The Paper Menagerie and Other Stories*. Ken Liu was also nominated for *Invisible Planets: An Anthology of Contemporary Chinese SF in Translation*.

The *Locus* Award honored past winner and current Illustrator Contest judge Shaun Tan for his book *The Singing Bones*.

Shaun Tan and Illustrators of the Future judge Bob Eggleton were finalists for best artist.

*Theodore Sturgeon Memorial Award*: Carolyn Ives Gilman won second place for her story "Touring with the Alien" (*Clarkesworld*, Apr 2016).

*Ditmar Awards*: Jason Fischer was a finalist for his novelette "By the Laws of Crab and Woman" (*Review of Australian Fiction* Volume 17, Issue 6). Also, Cat Sparks won for best short story with "No Fat Chicks" published in the anthology *In Your Face.* Tim Napper was a finalist in the short story category with "Flame Trees," which he wrote while in our writing workshop (*Asimov's Science Fiction*, Apr/May 2016). Tim was also a finalist for best new writer. For the best art Ditmar Award, WotF contest winner, Shauna O'Meara won for her illustrations in *Lackington's Issue #12.*

*James Tiptree Jr. Literary Award*: Rachael K. Jones was on the honor list for "The Night Bazaar for Women Becoming Reptiles" (*Beneath Ceaseless Skies*, Jul 2016).

*Compton Crook Award*: David D. Levine was a finalist for his novel *Arabella of Mars*.

*Nebula Awards*: William Ledbetter won the Nebula Award for Best Novelette with "The Long Fall Up" (*The Magazine of Fantasy & Science Fiction*, May/Jun 2016).

*Andre Norton Award for Young Adult Novel in Science Fiction and Fantasy*: David D. Levine won for *Arabella of Mars*.

Analog *Award*: C. Stuart Hardwick was a finalist for his novelette "Dreams of the Rocket Men." The award for best short story went to Frank Wu for "In the Absence of Instructions to the Contrary" (Nov 2016). The best cover award went to Illustrator Contest judge Vincent Di Fate (Dec 2016). Other finalists included Eldar Zakirov (Mar 2016), and judge Bob Eggleton (Jun and Apr).

*Asimov's Readers' Awards*: James Alan Gardner won in the short story category with "The Mutants Men Don't See" (Aug 2016).

*Aurealis Awards*: Nick T. Chan won for best science fiction novella with "Salto Mortal" (*Lightspeed*, Jun 2016). The winner for best science fiction short story was Samantha Murray for "Of Sight, of Mind, of Heart," (*Clarkesworld*, Nov 2016), and a finalist for best science fiction short story went to Ian McHugh for "The Baby Eaters" (*Asimov's Science Fiction*, Jan 2016).

In the category of best fantasy novella, Jason Fischer was a finalist for "By the Laws of Crab and Woman."

T. R. Napper won best horror short story with "Flame Trees" while another finalist was R. P. L. Johnson for "Non-Zero Sum" published in *SNAFU: Hunters*. Shauna O'Meara was a finalist for best young adult short story with "No One Here Is Going to Save You" from the anthology *In Your Face*.

And in the category of best children's fiction, Lee Battersby was a finalist with *Magrit*.

*Colorado Independent Publishers Association Book Awards*: Gabriel F. W. Koch won third place for his novel *Paradox Effect*.

*Gaughan Award*: Illustrator winner Kirbi Fagan is the 2017 recipient.

*The Robert A. Heinlein Memorial Award* went to our writing judge Robert J. Sawyer.

*Science Fiction Hall of Fame*: Past Illustrator judge Jack Kirby was inducted into the Science Fiction Hall of Fame.

This is the news from 2017, and we are looking forward to another stellar year!

## FOR CONTEST YEAR 34, THE WINNERS ARE:

### Writers of the Future Contest Winners

#### First Quarter

1. *Jeremy TeGrotenhuis*
   The Minarets of An-Zabat
2. *Diana Hart*
   Miss Smokey
3. *Janey Bell*
   The Face in the Box

#### Second Quarter

1. *Vida Cruz*
   Odd and Ugly
2. *Amy Henrie Gillett*
   All Light and Darkness
3. *Eneasz Brodski*
   Flee, My Pretty One

#### Third Quarter

1. *Darci Stone*
   Mara's Shadow
2. *Erik Bundy*
   Turnabout
3. *N. R. M. Roshak*
   A Bitter Thing

#### Fourth Quarter

1. *Erin Cairns*
   A Smokeless and Scorching Fire
2. *Cole Hehr*
   What Lies Beneath
3. *Jonathan Ficke*
   The Howler on the Sales Floor

## Illustrators of the Future Contest Winners

### First Quarter

*Bruce Brenneise*
*Duncan Halleck*
*Anthony Moravian*

### Second Quarter

*Adar Darnov*
*Reyna Rochin*
*Brenda Rodriguez*

### Third Quarter

*Alana Fletcher*
*Maksym Polishchuk*
*Jazmen Richardson*

### Fourth Quarter

*Quintin Gleim*
*Sidney Lugo*
*Kyna Tek*

# WRITERS' CONTEST RULES

1. No entry fee is required, and all rights in the story remain the property of the author. All types of science fiction, fantasy and dark fantasy are welcome.

2. By submitting to the Contest, the entrant agrees to abide by all Contest rules.

3. All entries must be original works by the entrant, in English. Plagiarism, which includes the use of third-party poetry, song lyrics, characters or another person's universe, without written permission, will result in disqualification. Excessive violence or sex, determined by the judges, will result in disqualification. Entries may not have been previously published in professional media.

4. To be eligible, entries must be works of prose, up to 17,000 words in length. We regret we cannot consider poetry, or works intended for children.

5. The Contest is open only to those who have not professionally published a novel or short novel, or more than one novelette, or more than three short stories, in any medium. Professional publication is deemed to be payment of at least six cents per word, and at least 5,000 copies, or 5,000 hits.

6. Entries submitted in hard copy must be typewritten or a computer printout in black ink on white paper, printed only on the front of the paper, double-spaced, with numbered pages. All other formats will be disqualified. Each entry must have a cover page with the title of the work, the author's legal name, a pen name if applicable, address, telephone number, e-mail address and an approximate word count. Every subsequent page must carry the title and a page number, but the author's name must be deleted to facilitate fair, anonymous judging.

   Entries submitted electronically must be double-spaced and must include the title and page number on each page, but not the author's name. Electronic submissions will separately include the author's legal name, pen name if applicable, address, telephone number, e-mail address and approximate word count.

7. Manuscripts will be returned after judging only if the author has provided return postage on a self-addressed envelope.

8. We accept only entries that do not require a delivery signature for us to receive them.

9. There shall be three cash prizes in each quarter: a First Prize of $1,000, a Second Prize of $750, and a Third Prize of $500, in US dollars. In addition, at the end of the year the First Place winners will have their entries judged by a panel of judges, and a Grand Prize winner shall be determined and receive an additional $5,000. All winners will also receive trophies.

10. The Contest has four quarters, beginning on October 1, January 1, April 1 and July 1. The year will end on September 30. To be eligible for judging in its quarter, an entry must be postmarked or received electronically no later than midnight on the last day of the quarter. Late entries will be included in the following quarter and the Contest Administration will so notify the entrant.

11. Each entrant may submit only one manuscript per quarter. Winners are ineligible to make further entries in the Contest.

12. All entries for each quarter are final. No revisions are accepted.

13. Entries will be judged by professional authors. The decisions of the judges are entirely their own, and are final and binding.

14. Winners in each quarter will be individually notified of the results by phone, mail or e-mail.

15. This Contest is void where prohibited by law.

16. To send your entry electronically, go to:
    www.writersofthefuture.com/enter-writer-contest
    and follow the instructions.
    To send your entry in hard copy, mail it to:
    L. Ron Hubbard's Writers of the Future Contest
    7051 Hollywood Blvd., Hollywood, California 90028

17. Visit the website for any Contest rules updates at
    www.writersofthefuture.com

1. The Contest is open to entrants from all nations. (However, entrants should provide themselves with some means for written communication in English.) All themes of science fiction and fantasy illustrations are welcome: every entry is judged on its own merits only. No entry fee is required and all rights to the entry remain the property of the artist.

2. By submitting to the Contest, the entrant agrees to abide by all Contest rules.

3. The Contest is open to new and amateur artists who have not been professionally published and paid for more than three black-and-white story illustrations, or more than one process-color painting, in media distributed broadly to the general public. The ultimate eligibility criterion, however, is defined by the word "amateur"—in other words, the artist has not been paid for his artwork. If you are not sure of your eligibility, please write a letter to the Contest Administration with details regarding your publication history. Include a self-addressed and stamped envelope for the reply. You may also send your questions to the Contest Administration via e-mail.

4. Each entrant may submit only one set of illustrations in each Contest quarter. The entry must be original to the entrant and previously unpublished. Plagiarism, infringement of the rights of others, or other violations of the Contest rules will result in disqualification. Winners in previous quarters are not eligible to make further entries.

5. The entry shall consist of three illustrations done by the entrant in a color or black-and-white medium created from the artist's imagination. Use of gray scale in illustrations and mixed media, computer generated art, and the use of photography in the illustrations are accepted. Each illustration must represent a subject different from the other two.

6. ENTRIES SHOULD NOT BE THE ORIGINAL DRAWINGS, but should be color or black-and-white reproductions of the originals of a

quality satisfactory to the entrant. Entries must be submitted unfolded and flat, in an envelope no larger than 9 inches by 12 inches.

7. All hard copy entries must be accompanied by a self-addressed return envelope of the appropriate size, with the correct US postage affixed. (Non-US entrants should enclose international postage reply coupons.) If the entrant does not want the reproductions returned, the entry should be clearly marked DISPOSABLE COPIES: DO NOT RETURN. A business-size self-addressed envelope with correct postage (or valid e-mail address) should be included so that the judging results may be returned to the entrant. We only accept entries that do not require a delivery signature for us to receive them.

8. To facilitate anonymous judging, each of the three photocopies must be accompanied by a removable cover sheet bearing the artist's name, address, telephone number, e-mail address and an identifying title for that work. The reproduction of the work should carry the same identifying title on the front of the illustration and the artist's signature should be deleted. The Contest Administration will remove and file the cover sheets, and forward only the anonymous entry to the judges.

9. There will be three co-winners in each quarter. Each winner will receive a cash prize of US $500. Winners will also receive eligibility to compete for the annual Grand Prize of $5,000 together with the annual Grand Prize trophy.

10. For the annual Grand Prize Contest, the quarterly winners will be furnished with a specification sheet and a winning story from the Writers of the Future Contest to illustrate. In order to retain eligibility for the Grand Prize, each winner shall send to the Contest address his/her illustration of the assigned story within thirty (30) days of receipt of the story assignment.

    The yearly Grand Prize winner shall be determined by a panel of judges on the following basis only: Each Grand Prize judge's personal opinion on the extent to which it makes the judge want to read the story it illustrates. The Grand Prize winner shall be announced at the L. Ron Hubbard Awards ceremony held in the following year.

11. The Contest has four quarters, beginning on October 1, January 1, April 1 and July 1. The year will end on September 30. To be eligible for judging in its quarter, an entry must be postmarked no later than midnight on the last day of the quarter. Late entries will be included in the following quarter and the Contest Administration will so notify the entrant.

12. Entries will be judged by professional artists only. Each quarterly judging and the Grand Prize judging may have different panels of judges. The decisions of the judges are entirely their own and are final and binding.

13. Winners in each quarter will be individually notified of the results by mail or e-mail.

14. This Contest is void where prohibited by law.

15. To send your entry electronically, go to:
    www.writersofthefuture.com/enter-the-illustrator-contest
    and follow the instructions.
    To send your entry via mail send it to:
    L. Ron Hubbard's Illustrators of the Future Contest
    7051 Hollywood Blvd., Hollywood, California 90028

16. Visit the website for any Contest rules updates at
    www.illustratorsofthefuture.com